The Cowboy Who Came Home
Second Chance Romance & Small Town Saga

Second Generation in Three Rivers Romance
Book 1

Liz Isaacson

The Small Town of Three Rivers

Welcome to Three Rivers! There have been three complete series here already - Three Rivers Ranch, Seven Sons Ranch (Walker Brothers), and Shiloh Ridge Ranch (Glover Family).

That's 37 books. Loads of characters. I'm going to list them here, but you don't need to know them all comprehensively for this book. I just know some of you like seeing these amazing small towns and who lives here!

THREE RIVERS RANCH:

Frank and Heidi Ackerman - patriarch and

matriarch. Frank died 20 years ago; Heidi is re-married to Malcolm Rust.

SQUIRE AND KELLY ACKERMAN

Son: Finn - 30, almost 31
Daughter: Libby - 25
Son: Michael - 22
Son: Samuel - 18

PETE AND CHELSEA MARSHALL (CHELSEA IS Squire's sister, and they own Courage Reins, which is housed at Three Rivers Ranch)

4 sons:
Paul - 25
Henry - 23
John - 20
Rich - 17

REESE AND CARLY SANDERS: THEY'RE THE admins for Courage Reins, Pete and Chelsea's equine therapy unit at Three Rivers Ranch. They have no children.

. . .

GARTH AND JULIETTE AHLSTROM (FORMER foreman; vet technician)
Son: Jake - 22
Son: Carson - 20

CAL AND TRINA HODGKINS (HE'S THE FULL-time vet at Three Rivers Ranch)
Daughter: Sabrina - 33
Daughter: Abby - 25
Daughter: Olive - 20

ETHAN AND BRYNN GREENE (THEY OWN Bowman's Breeds, which is housed at Three Rivers Ranch)
Daughter: Carolina - 22
Son: Tyson - 20
Son: Bryan - 18

BEAU PETERSON (FOREMAN AT THREE RIVERS Ranch), single

. . .

BENNETT AND ELLIE PETERSON (HE'S A cowboy, she works on the finances on the ranch with Kelly)
Daughter: Joy - 8
Son: Jaxon - 5

TAD AND SANDY JORGENSEN (HE'S A COWBOY, she owns the pancake house in town)
Son: Nathaniel (Nate) - 20
Daughter: Helen - 17

KENNY AND TARYN STOCKTON (HE'S A cowboy, she works for a local online newspaper in town)
Daughter: Joelle (Jo) - 19

JON AND GRACE CARVER (HE'S A COWBOY, SHE helps Heidi run the bakery in town)

. . .

ANDY AND LAWRENCE COLLINS (HE'S A cowboy, she owns a clothing boutique in town)

SUMMER AND TANNER WOLFE (HE'S A cowboy, she's a nurse at the hospital in town)

GAVIN AND NAVY REDD - THEY OWN THEIR own single-family ranch on the northeast side of Three Rivers

BOONE AND NICOLE CARVER (SQUIRE'S cousin) - they own and operate the full time veterinary clinic in town

CAMILA AND DYLAN WALKER (HE'S A COWBOY and an electrician, she owns a plumbing shop in town)

.   .   .

Seven Sons Ranch:
Momma & Daddy: Penny and Gideon Walker

1. Rhett & Evelyn Walker
Son: Conrad - 21
Triplets: Austin, Elaine, and Easton - 17

2. Jeremiah & Whitney Walker
Son: Jonah Jeremiah (JJ) - 19
Daughter: Clara Jean - 17
Son: Jason - 15
Daughter: Emily - 13
Daughter: Hattie - 10

3. Liam & Callie Walker
Daughter: Denise - 25
Daughter: Ginger - 21

4. Tripp & Ivory Walker
Son: Oliver - 33 (and married to Aurora Glover)
Son: Isaac - 21

· · ·

5. Wyatt & Marcy Walker
   Son: Warren - 18
   Son: Cole - 16
   Son: Harrison - 15
   Daughter: Rachel - 12

6. Skyler & Mallery Walker
   Daughter: Camila - 18
   Son: Sawyer - 16
   Son: Gideon - 13

7. Micah & Simone Walker
   Son: Travis (Trap) - 17
   Daughter: Daisy - 15
   Son: Jensen - 12
   Daughter: Laurel - 9

Shiloh Ridge Ranch:
   Lois & Stone (deceased) Glover, 7 children, in age-order: (Lois is now married to Donald Parker)
   1. Bear — Sammy, wife

- Lincoln (25), adopted son
- Stetson (Smiles, 16), son
- Russell (Rock, 14), son
- Heather (12), daughter
- Sunnie (10), daughter

2. Cactus — Allison, ex-wife / Bryce, son (deceased) // — Willa, wife

- Mitch (26), adopted son
- Cameron (21), adopted son
- Kyle (19), adopted son
- Charlie (Chaz, 17), son
- Lynn (16), adopted daughter
- Melissa (13), daughter

3. Judge — June, wife

- Lucy Mae (31), step-daughter
- Birch (14), son
- Willow (11), daughter
- Linden (8), son

4. Preacher — Charlie, wife

- Betty (15), daughter

- Hank (12), son
- Daisy (9), daughter

5. Arizona — Duke Rhinehart, husband, living at the Rhinehart Ranch, just south of Shiloh Ridge

- Shiloh (15), daughter
- April (12), daughter
- Dwayne (10), son
- Dallas (7), son

6. Mister — Libby, wife

- Belle (12), son
- Marley (10), daughter
- Hazel (7), daughter
- Brantley (5), son

7. Bishop — Montana, wife

- Aurora (33), step-daughter and married to Oliver Osburn
- Robbie (19), son
- Georgia (13), daughter

Aurora and Oliver have 3 children, who are Bishop and Montana's grandchildren:

- Jewel (6), daughter
- Laramie (Lara, 3), daughter
- Mason (8 mo), son

DAWNA & BULL (DECEASED) GLOVER, 5 children, in age-order:

1. Ranger — Oakley, wife

- Wilder (16), son
- Fawn (15), daughter

2. Ward — Dot, wife

- Glory Rose (16), daughter
- Silver (13), son
- Flint (11), son

3. Ace — Holly Ann, wife

- Gunnison (15), son
- Pearl Jo (13), daughter
- Ashton (10), son

4. Etta — August Winters, husband

- Hailey (22), adopted daughter
- Joey (13), son
- Nash and Nellie (twins - 10), son and daughter

5. Ida — Brady Burton, husband

- Johnny and Judy (twins - 16), son and daughter
- Riggs (11), son
- Sonora (8), daughter

BULL AND STONE GLOVER WERE BROTHERS, so their children are cousins. Ranger and Bear, for example, are cousins, and each the oldest sibling in their families.

1

Edith Baxter nudged her horse forward while keeping her voice silent. She'd been working with Cocoa since the day Courage Reins had brought the beautiful bay to their stables. In fact, Peter Marshall, who owned this therapeutic riding facility, had called her and asked her to come help him train the horse for other clients.

She'd said yes immediately. She didn't get to work with as many horses as she'd like on her brother's farm, where she lived and wrote her children's books, where she took care of the house and all the smaller animals—and her brother.

He'd had a terrible time since the death of

their cousin, and while Edith felt that loss too, she hadn't been as close to Carson as Alex had been.

She'd suffered a massive loss in her life too, and she'd been frequenting Courage Reins as a client since her return to Three Rivers three years ago.

Now, she shelved her thoughts, because being present with a horse was a big part of riding. She couldn't forget for a single second that the beast upon whose back she sat could spook and spark at any moment. And Edith could end up with a broken back—or worse.

Cocoa had come a long way in the past couple of years, but she was still a horse. And horses had fickle personalities at the best of times, and this horse could *feel* what Edith felt.

So she couldn't think about Alex's troubles, or her own, while riding and guiding her. That was part of the therapy—the blessed release of thought. The fact that she didn't have to worry about the dirty dishes piling up in the sink, or the dozens of errands she needed to get done before businesses closed in town, or the fact that she lived mostly alone, on a ranch with her younger brother in a state she thought she'd never return to.

But for right now, she breathed in. She centered herself on Cocoa's back, right here on this tiny speck of land in a huge country, world, and universe.

Her fingers tingled, and she released her too-tight grip on the reins. Cocoa moved how she should've then, and Edith relaxed and smiled softly to herself. She could use this horse in a book now, and words and pictures flowed through her head as she moved Cocoa around the cone.

Getting the equines used to brightly colored objects was absolutely necessary, and Cocoa did great with the rest of the course. As Edith slid from the saddle so she could walk alongside Cocoa for her cooldown, the door to the observation room opened.

A cowboy stepped onto the dirt of the arena, his black cowboy hat wide and smiling up on the edges. "You're both lookin' good," Peter Marshall said.

Edith trained her smile on him. "I know what you're going to say."

"Do you?" He grinned at her, because he was a tall, good-looking, happy-go-lucky, sensitive, perceptive man.

"You think Cocoa doesn't need me anymore."

"She doesn't."

"What if I need her?"

"You can choose any horse you want when you come for personal sessions."

Edith nodded and kept walking as Pete fell into step beside her. "You got a new horse?"

"Sure did."

"What's his name?'

"Reagan."

"He needs me?"

"He does."

Edith sighed, though it sure felt nice to be needed. Didn't everyone want to feel that way? Important? Special? Necessary? The last few years of Edith's life had put her in the top spot of "necessary" for so many people, and sometimes she craved a time where no one needed her. Or someone on whom *she* could rely on for everything, so *she* could have a weak hour, or day, or even a whole week.

"You don't see Margot when you come work with Cocoa," Pete said gently.

"Here we go," Edith said, cutting him a look out of the corner of her eye. "I don't pay for these sessions. I'm not going to take Margot's time for free."

"Hm." That was Pete-speak for *You need it.*

And maybe she did. Edith wasn't opposed to counseling and therapy. With all she'd gone through in the past few years, talking to someone without any skin in her game had helped immensely. But so did training horses—and Pete paid her for that.

"I need this job," she said quietly. "And if you add on the counseling, then I feel like I have to pay, and then I'll ask you not to pay me." She looked over to him. "Alex's ranch does fine. It really does. But it's not like this place. We watch every dime."

Pete nodded like he understood. Maybe he did. Three Rivers Ranch spanned hundreds of acres and raised thousands of head of cattle. Pete's best friend, Squire Ackerman, owned and ran the ranch, but Pete had built and expanded his equine therapy unit here on the same property.

Bowman's Breeds, a rodeo horse training facility, also existed out on this ranch about forty-five minutes north of Three Rivers. They employed dozens of people, and everyone at Three Rivers went around and helped at other ranches during harvest, round-up, and branding. That was how Edith knew most of them; they'd come to help on her brother's ranch at crucial times of the year.

Edith had no idea what their financial situation was, but she'd been honest. Pete could do what he needed or wanted to do now.

"We have grant money to cover the full experience for you," he said just as quietly as she'd spoken. "In fact, I *want* you to go through these sessions the same as a client would, so we can see how working with a specific horse and a specific counselor go together. Sometimes different counselors do better with different horses."

Edith thought about that for a beat. "I don't get that, but I believe you."

He chuckled, but he didn't go on to explain what he meant. Edith *had* been avoiding her counseling sessions when she came out to Courage Reins, so she couldn't argue with him there.

"All right," she drawled out. "I'll start seeing Margot."

"Well, actually." Pete darted his eyes to her now. "When you start working with Reagan, I'd like to pair him—and you—with...."

"Do not say Bull."

"Bull," Pete said almost on top of her last word. They looked at one another fully then, and with Cocoa plodding along beside them, they both laughed.

Edith let it cleanse her from the inside out, and as she quieted, a keen sense of peace and goodness filled her. She felt God watching over her and guiding her expertly in that moment, and she nodded.

"All right," she said in a firm, agreeable voice. "I'll work with Reagan and Bull."

"Your pay won't change."

"I can schedule extra sessions with Cocoa?" She reached over and ran her hand along the bay's side. "Would I have to see Margot if I do that?"

The cowboy sighed, which meant *yes*, but he said, "I'll leave that up to you."

She nodded, and the exit that led back to Cocoa's stable, where Edith would unsaddle her and brush her down and put her away for the day loomed only several paces ahead. Pete slowed to a stop. "Thank you, Edith. I sure appreciate you and all you do here."

"Thank you, Mister Marshall," she said diplomatically. "I love coming out here." She led Cocoa through the wide doorway and out of the arena. Fences stood guard on either side of the wide road, but they didn't obstruct her view of the homestead on this property.

She couldn't stop herself from glancing over to it and thinking about the boy she'd gone with in high school, albeit briefly.

Finley Ackerman. He'd been handsome and funny in high school, but their young love had been cut short when her family had moved to Florida. She'd seen him briefly over the summer after his first year of college too, but then he'd entered the Army, and Edith hadn't seen or spoken to him in almost a decade now.

She'd gone off to live her own life as a nanny back East. She'd started writing books there, after taking an internship with a publisher in New York City. All of that felt like a different life, that had happened to a different person.

Because there was Edith Before Levi and Edith After Levi.

She looked up into the sky, imagining she could see all the way to heaven. "I miss you so much sometimes," she whispered. "And other times, it's like we never met."

Edith didn't understand the human mind and heart as well as she'd like. She wished a clear blue sky, without a single cloud in sight, didn't make memories—good and bad—stream so readily through her mind.

She sometimes wished she didn't see whole stories in her head. That she wasn't so visual. That she didn't romanticize everything. But all of those things made her a very good author, and the publication of her children's books paid a lot of bills around the ranch.

She put Cocoa away properly, and in the shadows cast by the stable this afternoon, she leaned against the wood and checked her phone. She still had to fill out her paperwork for what she and Cocoa had done during their session, and she had a chapter to write in her current work-in-progress, but she just wanted a minute to catch up on the outside world.

She always put her phone in a locker when she trained, and all clients had to do the same. Cell phones and horses didn't go together at Courage Reins, something that allowed Edith the escape she craved when she came here. But she liked catching up too.

Alex had texted a couple of times, reminding her of the prescription she'd promised to pick up for him. She had a couple of emails that needed answering, one about the chicken feed she'd been trying to secure, and one about a library event in Amarillo.

She smiled as she read the invite to be one of the signing and speaking authors at this library's Summer Reading introduction event for patrons.

She'd love to do that, but she'd craft a professional acceptance email when she got home and got on her computer to handle her authoring business.

Everything else didn't matter, and Edith closed her phone and stowed it in her jeans pocket. She looked up and over to the row of cabins that lined an immaculately kept gravel path. Stables and barns lined this side, with the administration building for the ranch down to her right, and the homestead to her left. She didn't have any business with Three Rivers Ranch, but Courage Reins shared their stable facilities, so she came over here to get her horses.

A couple of cowboys came out of a cabin a couple down, and she lifted her hand in greeting as they saw her.

"Howdy, Edith," one said to her. "You comin' down to the homestead for dinner?"

She shook her head. "Nope, I've got a ton going on tonight." Plus, she had no idea why she'd ever go to the homestead here at Three Rivers Ranch for dinner. She hadn't been invited tonight either, and she didn't know what the occasion was. "But you guys enjoy."

Manny and Falcon continued on, and Edith figured she better finish up her work here and get going on the rest of her to-do list. So she returned to the big, glass-front Courage Reins building and filled out her paperwork.

"There you go," she said to Reese Sanders, who ran the office here at the facility.

"Thank you, Edith," he said without looking at the paper. "She do okay today?'

"She's amazing," Edith said, her voice brightening as she spoke of Cocoa. She did love that horse, and she was going to miss her.

As she left the building, she took another moment to breathe in the mid-May air and look over to the homestead. It didn't look any different than she'd seen it before. A couple of unfamiliar trucks sat in the driveway, but so many people came out here to the ranch, and Edith certainly wouldn't know every vehicle that came here.

The grass shone green around the homestead, and she watched Beau Peterson, the current foreman at the ranch appear and climb the steps to the deep deck that spanned the width of the side of the house. He slid open the glass door and went right inside, and Edith wondered what that would be like. To have people coming and going from her private, personal residence all the time.

She'd asked Finn about it once, but he'd said he hadn't thought about it. That such a thing was just part of his life. He'd grown up with it, so it felt normal to him.

Edith reached up and removed the ponytail holder from her hair, and she ran her hands through it to get it to lay right. Now she felt ready to re-enter the normal world, the town and atmosphere away from Three Rivers Ranch, and she turned toward her SUV.

This place did have a vibe Edith had only ever felt here. Troubles and worries couldn't touch her here, but the moment she drove from dirt road to highway, the weight of her life would descend on her shoulders again.

"It's okay," she told herself as she started the car and adjusted the air conditioning. "It's okay to have a real life and an escape. You can't live in la-la land forever."

A couple of hours helped her get through the

week, and then she'd come back to Courage Reins and get away from everything all over again.

She pulled her phone from her pocket, where it didn't quite fit now that she'd sat down, and she put it in the middle console with her soda pop. That would be warm and flat by now, so Edith didn't reach for it. She liked her soda pop ice cold, fizzy, and flavored with grapefruit, lime, and orange.

Before she could twist to get her seatbelt on, someone knocked on the glass of her driver's side window. Edith spun that way as she both yelped and leaned away from the would-be attacker.

Her pulse sped through her bloodstream, and her adrenaline told her to find something she could use to ward off whoever had dared get so close to her, with only a simple pane of glass separating them.

But Edith kept her car neat, and all she had at her disposal was her phone. She forgot all about trying to grab it as she took in the terribly familiar features of the man on the other side of the glass.

Understanding and recognition kicked in, and Edith sat up straight and reached to roll down the window.

True, Finn now wore a beard, which he hadn't

in high school or afterward. But his blue eyes sparkled with the smile on his face, and as the glass lowered, she heard his low chuckle.

That struck a familiar chord inside Edith too, and her own smile formed. She pressed one hand to her still-flailing heartbeat. "Finn Ackerman. You scared me."

2

inley Ackerman couldn't believe who he was looking at. The gorgeous Edith Baxter. "I'm sorry," he said. "I didn't mean to. I just saw you, and I couldn't believe it, and...." He trailed off. "It's you." His back pinched because he had to lean down only slightly to see inside the SUV, and it wasn't a natural position. But he would not move. Oh, no, he would not.

Edith hadn't buckled in yet, and she opened the door. Finn got out of the way to allow her to stand, the moment between them tense and awkward. What did he do here? The last time he and Edith had been together, he'd kissed her. He hadn't known when he'd see her again, but he'd known he would.

The door closed, and Finn decided to do what was natural. He had no idea if she was married or seeing someone, but he moved into her personal space and took her into his arms. "Oh, wow. it's so good to see you."

She murmured, "It sure is," as she wrapped him up in her arms too. "What are you doing here?"

"I just got home," he said. "This morning. My momma is planning a big welcome home party tonight." He stepped back, ideas firing through his mind like machine gun shots. "You should come."

Edith's blue eyes widened, and she shook her head. "No, I don't think so."

"Why not?"

"I—" She looked over to the homestead, but Finn only had eyes for her. He couldn't look away, because he couldn't quite believe *Edith Baxter* stood in front of him. He'd seen her from the window that overlooked the ranch, and he'd left the cowboys his daddy had bribed into coming to help set up for the party mid-conversation. He'd have to answer for that, but for now, he simply basked in Edith's presence. Her beauty.

Her eyes came back to his. "I wasn't invited."

"I'm inviting you."

She shook her head again, that lovely blonde hair swaying with the motion. "I have a lot to do tonight." She scanned him down to his boots. "I can't believe you're here."

"I'm the one who lives here," he said. "I mean, sort of. For the next little while."

"Are you out of the Army then?"

"Yep." Finn rocked back onto his heels and shoved his hands in his jeans pockets. "I retired at my ten-year mark, and now...I'm here."

If that didn't scream, *I still don't know what my life should be*, Finn didn't know what would. He might as well have broadcast it from the speaker system and into the peace and serenity that still existed here at his family ranch.

"Well, welcome home." Edith smiled at him and tucked her hair behind her ear. "I'm glad you're here, safe and sound."

Finn was glad for that too, and he could talk for years and still not tell his friends and family everything he'd done in the past decade. Some of it he *couldn't* talk about.

"You seein' anyone?" He figured he might as well go straight for the bullseye. No sense beating

29

around the bush, not when his attraction to this woman buzzed and fizzed through him. It popped and soared, and Finn needed to know if he could take her to dinner and when.

"No," she said.

"Married?"

"No." She shook her head again, those eyes shining like sapphires in a dark night. How could he have forgotten about her eyes?

"When can I take you out?" he asked.

Edith blinked at him, but Finn had learned in the Army to be direct. Maybe he was coming off a *little* strong. "I mean, I just got home, and I'll need to settle in, but I'd love to get your number, so when I'm sitting in front of my schedule, we can set something up."

Finn told himself to stop talking. He'd put a lot of words out there, and he just needed to *stop*. Edith looked like he'd hit her with a wet eel, and the cold water had just now started to spark with the electricity.

She blinked a couple of times, then opened her mouth only to promptly close it again. She once again looked back to the homestead, but Finn refused to do that. He could practically feel the eyes of this place on him. His momma's. Daddy's too, though he tended to leave Finn be until he had his lectures all planned out. The other cowboys. Heck, the building they stood in front of was filled with people who knew him and his parents, would be at the party tonight, and could see through each and every window—as the whole front was made of glass.

His skin itched to be somewhere no one could see him, but he couldn't walk away from Edith without getting her phone number. He wouldn't.

It had been a long time since Finn had been face-to-face with a woman who made his feet shift and his throat go dry. He cleared that as he tried to find solid ground beneath his boots, and he knew Edith saw and heard it all.

She gestured half-heartedly toward her car. "My phone's in there."

"You don't have your number memorized?" Finn teased, adding a smile to his face as he pulled his phone out so he could type her number into it. He focused on the screen for a moment, just long enough to put in his PIN and get the phone open. Then he looked at Edith again. "We can just... text. Talk. If you decide you don't want to go out with me, okay."

"It's been ten years," she said. "I just...don't even know where to start."

"How about with giving me your phone number?" He felt sparky and electric himself, and he hadn't had this much energy running through him in a long time. If ever. "Or I can give you mine, but you know, your phone is in there." He nodded toward her blue SUV.

"Good to see the Army didn't beat your humor out of you," she said dryly, placing one hand on her hip. That only accentuated her curves and caused Finn's smile to widen.

He tried to beat it back down. "Seriously," he said. "We don't have to go out. No pressure. But I'd love to catch up with you. Find out what these past ten years have been for you."

Something shuttered right over those eyes, and Finn wasn't sure what. He also didn't want to find out from his momma, though surely she knew. Ranch wives had a special network in Three Rivers, whether it was official or not, and his momma had been hovering around the gossip mill here in town for two and a half decades.

She'd know.

In fact, his phone chimed as a text from her

popped up on his screen. Dread weighed down his chest on his next breath, because she'd asked, *Where did you go? We need you here to go over some things.*

He needed to get back before she sent out a search party. He looked up. "Where are you living? Maybe I'll just come by once all the hoopla of my coming home has died down."

Edith had folded her arms around herself, almost like she was trying to ward off a chill. *Or something bad*, he thought. Could that be him? Could she not feel this energy between them? How could that be one-sided?

It has been with other women, he reminded himself, and some of the bubbling attraction inside him grew cold too.

"I'm living with Alex," she said. "On a small ranch not far from here, actually. It's called Coyote Pass. Not sure if you remember—"

"Oh, sure," Finn said as his Three Rivers memory fired at him. "Coyote Pass. We rode the horses down there one day, remember?" He burst out laughing, the sound of it going with this near-perfect almost-summer day. "Boy, was my daddy *mad*."

He was glad to be home, as everything felt so

much lighter here. "Old Man Tompkins owned Coyote Pass. Wonder what happened to him."

"He passed," Edith said quietly, without all of the gusto and joviality Finn had laughed and spoken with. He wasn't sure why she seemed so melancholy about an old man passing away—especially one she surely couldn't have known or been close to. "His family went through everything, but no one wanted the ranch. They listed it for sale, and Alex...well, you know Alex. He has a gypsy soul, and he's wanted to return to Three Rivers since we left."

"I knew Alex once," Finn corrected gently. "Just like I knew you once." He exhaled as another text from his momma came in. He dared look toward the homestead, and sure enough, she stood on the deck now, one hand up to her forehead to shade her eyes as she scanned for him. Part of him wanted to duck down behind the cars here in the Courage Reins lot so she wouldn't see him. But the other part knew that wouldn't be enough. She'd find him, and fast.

"Ten years is a long time," he said, looking at Edith again. "I have to go. My momma wants me back at the homestead."

Edith looked that way too, and when her attention came back to his, she nodded. "Okay, here's my number." She rattled it off quickly, but Finn had fast, fast, fast fingers from his time behind keyboards. He recited it back to her; she nodded again; he tucked his phone away.

"It's so great to see you," he said again. "I mean, really, *really* great. You have no idea." Finn told himself not to get too carried away. He didn't need to confess all of his female failures in the first fifteen minutes of his reunion with Edith. He wasn't even sure it would become a reunion, his own attraction to her notwithstanding.

He couldn't just walk away either, so he lunged at her and took her into his arms again. "We'll talk soon, okay?" He swept his lips along her cheek and told himself to get out of there.

"Okay," ghosted behind him as he walked away, his eyes locked onto his mother's now. And oh, she'd have seen the beautiful blonde behind him and have multitudes of questions once Finn's boots ate up the distance between then.

Sure enough, he'd only just started up the steps to the deck when Momma asked, "Who was that?"

He'd be thirty-one years old in a couple of months, and he didn't have to hide an innocent kiss from his mother. He did wait until he'd reached the deck to say, "Edith Baxter, and I'm not talking about her."

His mother didn't frown the way she would've in high school. He was certainly old enough to date and fall in love now, and Edith had always been out of his league. That hadn't changed one whit, so Momma had no reason to be upset. Still, she looked back toward Courage Reins, which sat across the lawn and across the street to the west, something contemplative on her face.

"Are you going out with her?"

"Nope." Finn moved toward the door, because while it wasn't technically summer yet, the temperatures in Texas always hovered too high.

"Did you ask her out?" Momma asked.

"Yes." Finn opened the door and stepped into the blessed air conditioning. Several cowboys had been working, setting up tables and chairs, and most of them looked over to him. He wasn't sure what rode in their expressions, but he didn't like it. Pity, maybe? Reverence? Maybe simple wariness? He wasn't sure, and Finn just wanted to escape.

"She told you no?" Momma asked, her voice shocked.

"It was a short conversation, Momma," he said. "Because you kept texting me." He surveyed the tables and chairs. "You don't need me here."

"I do too," she said. "Daddy's going to be home with the bus any moment, and your brother will want to see you." She held her head high. "Plus, he picked up Grandma and Grandpa, and they're simply dying to hug you again." She gave him one of her piercing looks, and Finn really didn't want to disappoint his mother. "You just ran off mid-sentence, the boys said."

"Thanks, guys," Finn said dryly. That got the other cowboys to smile a little. "I just saw a pretty girl, and well, I knew her." He turned and looked out the window, but he didn't see Edith standing on the sidewalk, running her hands through her hair to get it to lay flat. He'd seen her do that so often in the past.

Yeah, high school, he told himself. And he was way past high school.

"At least I used to know her," he murmured to the trail of dust still hanging in the air, probably from Edith's car as she'd left the ranch. "Does she work at Courage Reins, Momma?"

"She does a little training for Uncle Pete, yes," Momma said, her voice wary.

"Who is it?" Beau asked as he came to stand next to Finn.

He looked at the foreman. "Edith Baxter."

"Oh, sure," Beau said easily. "She's real good with horses. Writes books about 'em and everything."

"Edith writes books?" Finn really had no idea who she was anymore, but a stinging, fizzing need to learn and re-learn everything about her started in his gut.

"Bus is here," Beau called next, and Finn blinked as the big yellow school bus filled his vision. His daddy drove it today, and the only reason Finn hadn't gone with him was because he hadn't wanted to put on a show. He didn't need all the kids fawning over him, or Sammy bursting into tears at the sight of him.

Of course, Momma had said Sammy had grown right up while Finn had been gone. He was almost eighteen now, and he'd graduate from high school in another couple of weeks. Oh, and he didn't go by *Sammy* anymore, but *Sam*.

As he stood there and watched the bus come to a stop and the kids who lived here at Three Rivers start to spill out of it, Finn wondered if there'd been another reason he hadn't gone with his daddy for the school bus pick-up. A reason he'd stayed here, that he'd *needed* to be here.

And that was to see and meet and talk to Edith again. Get her number. He slid his hand into his pocket and felt his device there, all while a feeling of goodness and rightness came over him.

It sure was good to be home.

And you won't make a fuss over your parents making a fuss over you.

The stern voice in his head reminded him of the General he'd worked under in Germany. There were no jokes while on duty in the intelligence department, and Finn had learned that quickly. The work they did there mattered, as it did in every department of the Armed Forces, but General Hutch did not allow for joviality. That could happen outside of the tactical room.

Finn watched the kids, ages five to eighteen, scatter toward the various houses and cabins out here on the ranch. Uncle Pete and Aunt Chelsea lived across the street, in the two-story house with the blue door, but Finn didn't see their youngest head that way.

Instead, Rich and Sam walked in through the garage door, both of them bellowing, "Where you at, Finny?" They laughed as Sam came through the doorway and into the kitchen first, and wow, Finn did not recognize him at all.

His hair had grown a little long, and it waved and curled in all directions. He had broad shoulders and stood as tall as Daddy now, with Momma's blue eyes shining at him as they crinkled with his smile.

"Sammy," he said, unable to censor himself. And then it didn't matter. It didn't matter that Sam was only his half-brother. That they only shared the same genes as their mother. That Finn had missed the last ten years of life here in Three Rivers, on this ranch, with his family.

He opened his arms and saw Sam's face fall, the crinkles for a whole new reason, a brand new emotion.

All Finn could feel was love. Love and acceptance and forgiveness. He'd relive Sam's life through the stories they'd tell each other over the next few days, weeks, months, and years.

"I missed you, brother," Finn whispered in Sam's ear as he held him tight, right against his chest. "I love you so much." His voice broke on the last word, and he couldn't even imagine the reunion he'd have with Mike and Libby.

They wouldn't be home in time for tonight's

party, which meant Momma would simply have another one when they arrived. He wished he could've told her when he'd be arriving sooner, but the Army didn't exactly play by a Texas momma's timeline.

He'd found out yesterday that his flight would be that evening, and he'd land on the ranch this morning. And that was what had happened.

Libby had graduated from Faithview, a Christian college in Amarillo, and she now held a degree in ranch and business management. She hadn't come back to Three Rivers yet, because she wanted "outside experience." Those had been Momma's words, and Finn had only read them in an email. He could hear her voice as she said them, though, and Momma just wanted all of her chicks to come home.

Daddy had assured Finn multiple, multiple times that he'd always have a place at Three Rivers Ranch. Whenever he wanted it. In whatever capacity he wanted it. The problem was, Finn had no idea what he wanted.

Libby worked at another ranch as their general controller, and she claimed to really like Oklahoma. She couldn't just up and leave her job with only twelve hours' notice, and she'd said she'd talk to her boss about coming home for the weekend to see Finn.

Mike had just finished his junior year at Baylor, and he was off living the life Finn was pretty sure his momma had anticipated he'd live. He'd gone to Baylor for a year, but the environment simply hadn't suited him. He wondered if it would now, and he prayed that God would simply illuminate the path Finn should be on.

He hadn't yet, and Finn was starting to wonder if He ever would.

Then he thought of Edith standing on that sidewalk, in plain view, and Finn knew God loved him, cared about him, and had possibly shone a light on the first step Finn should take. Maybe.

Edith hadn't seemed all that keen to rush out to dinner with him that night. She'd even turned down his invitation for tonight's party.

In truth, Finn didn't want her to come to any of his welcome home shindigs, and relief filled him as he stepped back from Sam.

His younger brother wiped his eyes. "When's Mike coming home?"

"The weekend," Momma said, and Finn let her hug her youngest as he moved over to Rich.

"Look at you all grown up." He grinned at his

cousin and hugged him too. "What's it like being the only kid at home?"

"It's not so bad," Rich said. "I mean, Daddy's not yelling at Henry all the time, so it's good." He grinned as he stepped out of Finn's arms. "You've got a beard."

Finn's hand went to it, and he grinned. "Yeah, I think it's nice."

"It looks great," Rich said.

"Your neck needs to be trimmed up," Momma said, her eyes appraising every little thing.

Finn simply grinned at her. "I'll do it for the family party this weekend. It'll just be a family thing, right?"

Momma didn't answer, which meant the weekend welcome home party could be as big as the one tonight. She'd invited everyone who lived or worked here on the ranch, and with the number of chairs they'd set up, Finn expected a big crowd.

"Finn, let's take a look at that closet door," Daddy said. He motioned to Finn from the mouth of the hallway, and Finn saw his escape.

"Sure thing." He headed that way, his eyes hooked on his father's. "Thanks," he murmured as he went past him into the darker, cooler, calmer hallway. He continued around the corner and down the steps to the basement, where he'd be living. Again.

He tried not to feel like he was moving backward. He wasn't. He'd taken control of his career in the Army, and he'd retired. He'd be thirty-one in a couple months, he had a decent amount of money saved, and the doors to his life were wide open.

If only he knew which one to walk through.

"Okay." Dad sighed as he walked into the basement bedroom where Finn had put his two duffle bags on the made and ready-to-sleep-in queen-sized bed. "Let's see if we can get this door to close all the way. It might just need a new knob."

Finn sat on the bed, then laid back between his bags. "What time is dinner tonight?"

"Your momma told everyone six."

"Six," Finn repeated.

"I told her not to expect more than an hour out of you."

"I can do it," Finn said, his voice quiet. His dad didn't respond, and only the sound of clicking came from the faulty doorknob. Finn closed his eyes, and he felt the serenity and peace that had always existed on this ranch, in this house.

"Dad, I'm really happy to be home." Finn's voice broke again, but he didn't care if his daddy heard it. He wanted them to know how glad he was to be there, how appreciative he was for their sacrifice, for having this bedroom ready for him at a moment's notice, for taking him in so completely.

Squire Ackerman had done that for Finn every day of his life since he'd met him when he was four years old. "I'm so glad you're my dad."

"I love you, son," Daddy said, and Finn's tears ran down from the corners of his eyes toward his ears. "It's so good to have you home."

Finn took a big breath and steeled his nerves. "Now, it would be great if I could figure out what to do with my life."

3

Edith groaned as she lifted several bags of groceries up onto the counter in the kitchen. "Alex," she called, for his truck had been parked beside the garage. He could go past it and out onto the ranch, and sometimes he parked going the other direction too.

"I'm on the back deck," he called. "Bandit got into the burrs again." He sounded cross and disgruntled, and Edith wiped her bangs off her forehead before going to see how she could help.

She went by Gumbo, her gray fat cat she'd brought from Long Island, hoping he'd become a barn cat. He hadn't, and he meowed at her as she went by. "Come on, then," she said. Alex refused to have a litter box in the house, so Gumbo had to go outside with the dogs to take care of his business.

Edith wasn't surprised to find her two dachshunds—Frankie and Otto—laying on one of the loungers on the deck, in the full sun. Gumbo meowed his way over to them, a yowl for every step, and hopped up with the dogs before lying down.

Alex, in all his tow-headed glory, looked up from where he had one of his border collies pinned to the ground. "He won't stay out of the burrs. I've got to get them cleared out from the raspberries, because Bandit loves them as much as he loves chasing cows." He bent down and picked out another burr.

"Where's Olive?" she asked, because she didn't see Alex's other collie. Edith looked over the backyard, where she and Alex had already planted their vegetable garden. Past the shed in the corner of the yard, and out to the barn. A stable stood beyond that, and then the fields opened up. Pasture upon pasture, where Alex raised his beef cattle.

Edith fed the two dozen chickens they had, took care of the cats and dogs since the majority of them were hers, and took care of the four horses that lived on the ranch with them. She helped Alex with anything she was strong enough to do, which admittedly wasn't much, and she loved taking walks on the ranch out to the bridge that crossed over the middle of the three rivers that flowed through town and gave it its name.

This far north and east, and the water petered out to a stream that they used to water their animals and not much more. The left-hand branch extended north, all the way to Three Rivers Ranch, something Edith knew from her horseback explorations with Finn as a teenager.

She could lift a hay bale one at a time, and she could paint houses, barns, and stables. The work on a ranch never seemed to end, and Edith had to set limits for herself to avoid becoming overwhelmed, a skill she'd become quite adept at since her fiancé had been diagnosed with an aggressive and advanced form of brain cancer.

So much had overwhelmed her then, and she and Levi had planned and executed a cross-country move, mostly due to her ability to compartmentalize, work until she felt like dropping, and her utmost faith in God.

But Edith was tired. She was tired of managing so many pieces, from picking up the prescriptions to making sure all the living things at Coyote Pass got fed, stayed healthy and accounted for, or keeping the floors swept.

Her eyes caught on movement near her she-shed, her one condition for living at Coyote Pass. She'd needed help with Levi, and Alex had needed help, period. She'd requested a twelve-foot by twenty-four-foot shed, and Alex had delivered.

She'd decorated it with posters of her book covers, a large couch where she could lie down or relax, her favorite throw pillows and blankets and scented candles, and of course, her writing desk.

She tapped out her novels in her she-shed, usually in the evening hours, after dinner. She'd put in a doggy door, so any of the animals—besides the cattle—could come and go while she wrote about ranches, farms, horses, and families with tween children. She wanted to create an escape for kids who lived the not-so-idyllic life, and she gained a lot of comfort from her own novels as well, which always had good overcoming evil, and all wrongs being made right by the last page.

Edith prayed for her own happily-ever-after, where the Lord would provide the goodness she yearned for, the wrongs becoming right, even if it wasn't perfect or easy.

"Olive's coming out of my she-shed," she said.

"She found a bone," Alex said. "She probably took it in there to hide it from Bandit." He straightened, and his cheeks held a bit of a flush, probably from bending over in the late afternoon heat. "I think I've got most of them."

"I'll finish up with him," she said. "You go put the groceries away and get a cold drink."

Alex trained his own blue eyes on her, and Edith could see so much of their father in him. He kept his blond hair cut short so it didn't rub wrong under his cowboy hat, and his glare turned into a grin. "Thanks, Edee." He gave her a quick side-hug. "Did they have the peach soda?"

"Yep," she said. "I got it for you, but it might still be in my car." She hadn't even finished bringing in the groceries. It wasn't like Edith to only do half the job, but she reasoned it was simply bringing in groceries from the garage, and Alex had been frustrated when she'd arrived.

Olive's claws clicked as she came up onto the deck, and Edith put one hand on her hip, the same way she had while standing in front of Finn Ackerman, only a few hours ago. "Where have you been, huh?" she asked the border collie.

The dog simply looked up at her as if she'd

done nothing wrong, but Olive was known to bring vermin into the she-shed and leave them, as if they were gifts for Edith. As if she needed to clean up feathers before she could start writing her chapter.

Bandit edged over to Edith, and she dropped to her knees and began using both hands to feel along his sides for burrs. "And you," she said to him, wondering what Finn would think of her talking to the dogs. She'd done it her whole life, but she'd curbed her tongue whenever he'd come to her house as a teen.

"Getting into the burrs again. You're going to give your daddy an aneurism, and then what will we do? I can't run this ranch without him, and those raspberries aren't even ripe enough yet."

She found a burr, and her thinner fingers with longer fingernails plucked it out of the dog's hair. "Besides, if you keep eating the berries, there won't be enough for jam later this summer."

Edith didn't particularly love canning and jamming, but Levi had enjoyed everything about the country life with a boyish charm that had helped Edith see the simple joys of life with new eyes. Childlike eyes.

He'd never seen or made raspberry jam, and

Levi had claimed that seeing it done was so much better than just taking a jar from the grocery store shelf. He'd only made cakes from boxed mixes, and Edith could hear him chuckling in her ear, feel the weight of his hand on her waist, as she opened her family recipe binder and showed him a cake recipe.

They'd made it together, and while it hadn't been as light and airy as her mother's homemade cakes had been, it had done a great job of celebrating his last birthday here on earth. Tears filled her eyes, but Edith kept them from falling as she kept rubbing Bandit's body to find more burrs.

She picked them out one by one while Olive lay against her legs, panting. She sniffled, and heard the ridiculousness of it in her own ears. "I'm okay," she told the dogs, and Bandit lifted his head and licked her arm. "Really, I am."

She rocked back on her heels and wiped her face, though she hadn't shed a tear. "No more burrs, Bandit."

He licked her again, and Olive looked over her shoulder at Edith. "If you left me a bird in the shed...."

Olive closed her eyes halfway and turned to face the ranch again. Surely the work out there wasn't done, but Edith would go out to do the evening feeding after dinner.

Edith got to her feet with a groan, because she didn't spend time working out. The work around the ranch and with the horses kept her busy, but it wasn't the same as doing actual exercising. She huffed a couple of times once she stood, and she said, "Come on, everyone. Let's go get supper ready."

All the dogs knew the word "supper," and she wasn't surprised that her black and brown dachshunds started wiggling as they got to their feet. Frankie, the browner of the two dogs, looked at her with such hope, as if he'd been starved all day long.

Edith got such joy from him, and she grinned at her animals. "Come on, you lot. Let's get inside." Her phone rang as she stepped toward the back door, and she freed it from her back pocket to see Aggie's name on the screen.

Her heart leapt against the roof of her mouth. Had she forgotten girl's night? No, it was only Wednesday, but she swiped on the call with, "Howdy, Ags. What's up?"

"Two things," she said, and she'd always

spoken at the speed of light. "I'm on a break, and I can't talk for long."

"Okay, go," Edith said with a smile.

"You're still good for Friday night? At my house?"

"Yes," Edith said.

"Okay, the theme is going to be...babies!"

Edith's mother heart squeezed, and it squeezed hard. She'd always loved children, and she wanted nothing more than to be a mom. "Babies?" she asked, the word choking out. "Why's that?"

"JoJo's pregnant again!" Aggie laughed, and a tight wad of two warring emotions swirled through Edith. Joy and relief for one of her good friends fought against a deep well of worry. She'd reunited with Aggie when she'd moved back to Three Rivers, because she was the same age as her —and as Finn.

They'd been forever friends in high school, and that bond had been there again, after seven years apart. Aggie's sister had passed away in a terrible car accident, and after Levi had gone, Aggie had invited her to the grief meetings in town.

She'd met Christie Hedger and Joanna Finch,

and the four of them had become fast friends. They got together a couple of Fridays every month, and Edith really looked forward to her time with her friends. They provided her a similar type of relief from the cares and weight of the world that working with the horses at Courage Reins did.

JoJo had lost an infant at full-term, and she'd been hesitant to try for another baby. Christie had lost her mother, and the four of them had formed a bond through their tragedy. But Edith liked how they didn't dwell on the bad. They tried to help each other see the good that still existed in the world, in the blue sky above them, in the scent of raspberries on the air that kept attracting a naughty dog to tromp through burrs to get to them.

"She told you?"

"She told Christie, and swore her to secrecy, so of course, she texted me immediately." Aggie laughed again, and Edith waited for Gumbo to streak inside before she entered the farmhouse and sealed out the afternoon heat.

"Of course," Edith teased. Everyone knew not to trust Aggie with secrets. Of her own admission, she couldn't keep anything to herself for longer than sixteen seconds.

"So I want to do a little celebration. Nothing crazy, because JoJo will hate that."

"Most likely." Edith exchanged a glance with her brother before he bent down and started loving on his border collies, both of them right in front of him, begging for his attention.

"So I'm wondering if you can make those cupcakes shaped like booties. It's way too early for her to know if it's a boy or a girl, but you can do green or yellow or whatever you want."

"Okay," Edith said, though it added to her to-do list. "I can do that."

"Grams is coming over with dinner," Alex said, and that felt like the biggest miracle of Edith's life. She nodded to Alex and let Aggie chitchat with her for a few more minutes, one ear on that conversation and one listening to the radio Alex had on. The announcer there talked about the heavy rainfall this spring and warned everyone that the rivers flowing through town were still closed to the public due to dangerously high water levels. When the call ended, she put down her phone and picked up the boxes of cereal Alex hadn't put away yet. The radio announcer had moved away from the possible flooding and now played a country music ballad, and she moved over to the pantry with their breakfast items.

Alex had done all the fridge and freezer food, and she asked, "What's Grams bringing for dinner?"

"Gramps has been smoking chicken," he said. "And she made mashed potatoes and pea salad to go with it."

Edith's stomach grumbled for some of her gram's sweet pea salad, because she liked nothing better. They didn't have it back East, and while she'd enjoyed other delicacies that the Texas Panhandle didn't offer, she'd missed pea salad the most.

"I don't feel any more burrs," Alex said.

"I think I got them all," Edith said as she pulled out a barstool and sat down. Her legs and back thanked her instantly, and she sighed.

"Busy day with Cocoa?" Alex asked, watching her. They did take good care of each other, because she kept an eye on him to make sure he wasn't working too hard and didn't slump into a depression, and he made sure of the same for her.

"Yeah," she said, reaching up to run her hand through her hair. "And Pete has a new horse for me, and—" She cut off, the words about meeting

Finn surging forward. She decided she didn't have anything to hide, least of all from Alex. "And I met Finn Ackerman again after ten years apart. He's back from his military service."

Alex straightened, his eyes locking onto Edith's easily. "Finn Ackerman, huh?" His eyes danced, and Edith wished they wouldn't.

She smiled and ducked her head. "Don't look at me like that."

"Like what?" Alex teased. "You should see yourself. You're glowing."

Edith didn't deny it, because she couldn't see herself. "He asked for my number."

"Oh, yeah? Just like that?"

"Just like that." She watched her brother for his reaction, because Alex hadn't dated much this year, since his last girlfriend had decided she didn't want to marry a rancher and be a cowboy's wife.

"And I suppose you gave it to him."

"I did," she said. "I made him work for it a little. I mean, we haven't seen each other in a decade."

"Has he texted you?"

"Yeah." Edith looked down at her phone on the countertop. "Just once though."

Alex came around the island and sat down beside her. "What did he say?" He'd been friends with Finn too, because Finn was fun-loving and kind, and he'd always been nice to Alex, despite their five-year age difference.

She nudged her phone toward him, now a little embarrassed she'd brought up Finn when there didn't seem to be anything to tell. Alex looked at her, then the phone, and then he picked it up and swiped it on. She didn't have a code on hers the way Finn did, and Alex got to the messages pretty easily.

"This is Finn Ackerman." He looked up, pure question in his eyes.

"Yeah," she said with a sigh. "That's all he said."

"Maybe he got interrupted." He set down her phone. "When did he get home?"

"This morning."

"This morning?" Alex half-chuckled. "He's probably swamped out on that ranch. His parents, his aunts and uncles. Cousins everywhere. Siblings." He got up and picked up a couple of boxes of Rice-a-Roni and headed for the pantry. "He'll call you later, I'm sure."

"They were having a big party tonight."

"So tomorrow," Alex said. "He's always liked you so much, Edee." He put the rice away and returned to the counter for the last item that needed to go into the pantry: a couple of sleeves of instant yeast. He jabbed them toward her. "You know, you could text him back. Maybe he's waiting for that."

Edith picked up her phone, trying to think of what she could say to Finn. "It's just—it's been so long since I've texted a man."

"You text me all the time," Alex said.

"You know what I mean." She looked at the words on her phone—*This is Finn Ackerman*—her mind blank. She had no idea what to say back. She hadn't flirted with anyone in years. She didn't know how to be with anyone but Levi. "I loved him so much, you know? When you fall in love with someone like that, you think you'll never be able to do it again. That no one will ever be able to take his place."

She looked up, feeling lost and untethered and hating it.

"Do you feel disloyal?" Alex asked. "Because you shouldn't. I was here with Levi, Edee. He wanted you to move past him. Find someone else. I know he did."

"Yes, well." Edith remembered the slow mornings when she'd go into Levi's bedroom and crawl into bed with him. They'd lay there in the soft morning light, nothing said between them. He'd simply hold her, and she'd listen to his heartbeat, and then, after a while, he'd say something like, *You'll meet someone else, Edee.*

You'll fall in love with him, and maybe he'll be able to do what I can't. Marry you. Love you for your whole life. Give you babies and as many cats as you want.

She'd smile then, but such a gesture with words like that always came with tears. Near the end of his life, he'd started to change what he said to, *Promise me you'll try to meet someone else, Edee.*

I know God doesn't want you to be alone forever.

Promise me you won't be too sad after I'm gone.

Promise me you'll write me into books and always love me, but don't box up your heart.

Promise me.

Promise me.

Promise me.

Edith had promised him too, because it had

meant so much to Levi. She'd have done anything to make him happy, make him more comfortable, make him smile in those last days and hours of his life.

"I miss him a lot today," she murmured.

Alex sat down beside her again. "I know you do, Edee. I can see that on your face too." He put his arm around her and pulled her into his side. Edith collapsed against the strength of her brother, her eyes burning yet again with unshed tears.

"What would I even text back?"

Alex took a moment, and then he said, "How about something like—It was great to see you today, Finn. I hope your party is fun."

"That sounds so fifth-grade," Edith said.

"But it says a lot," he said. "I know I'd like it if a certain redhead from the feed store would send me those simple words—*it was great to see you today, Alex.*"

Edith laughed then, because Alex did have a pretty massive crush on Nicki Johnston at the feed store. He went even when he didn't need to, and that was one errand Edith never had to do.

"Why don't you just ask her for her number?" Edith asked.

"Maybe I'll ask Finn how he does it," Alex said dryly. "But seriously, Edee, don't torture the man for any longer than you already have." He got to his feet when both collies perked up and looked toward the front door.

The dachshunds started barking and even Gumbo went into meow-mode, which meant someone had come to Coyote Pass. "Gramps and Grams are here," he said. "Better text fast." He left to go welcome their grandparents to the ranch, and Edith stared at her phone.

Then she thumbed out a quick text and sent it, praying with all she had that she knew what in the world she was doing.

4

Finn re-read Edith's text a half-breath before Momma said, "It's time to start. Squire, it's time to start! Let's pray."

He'd answered her a couple of days ago, and they'd exchanged a few texts. Several. Fine, a lot of texts. But he always went back to that first one for some reason, trying to find that thing that made him feel so good about her.

This is Edith. It sure was good to see you today. I hope you have fun at your party.

She'd texted during his first welcome home party on Wednesday. Tonight was the sibling and family party, but while it should've been a much smaller group, the house felt just as full. Maybe because they'd gathered across the street at Aunt Chelsea's. Didn't matter. There were too many eyes on Finn again.

This party would be way more fun if she were here with him, and her message burned on the back of his eyelids as he bent his head and closed his eyes to pray. *It sure was good to see you today.*

He hadn't seen Edith since, though they had messaged back and forth. He'd been bold and Army-like in asking for her number, but he wasn't sure how to bring up going out with her again. She hadn't brought it up either, and he didn't hear a word of the prayer as he contemplated his current situation with Edith.

"Amen," chorused through the house, and Finn figured his grandfather had given a fine prayer worth emulating. So he repeated the "Amen," and glanced around as conversations broke out.

"The boys got another five feet of sandbags on that curve today," Daddy said to Uncle Pete. "Even if we get more rain this weekend, I think she'll hold."

"I hope so," Pete said. "I'm downhill from that, and I'll be wiped out first."

"If the river floods," Grandpa Armstrong said.

"We'll all be wiped out. We haven't seen this much water in decades. No sirree." He shook his head like having rain in a usually drought-ridden area was bad.

And perhaps it was. The soil didn't know how to absorb all that water. The three rivers that ran through town had been closed for weeks, apparently, due to a heavier snowfall this winter, and then massive rainfall in the past month. Finn hadn't been around for that, and it hadn't rained since he'd returned to town, but the forecast definitely called for rain tonight and into tomorrow.

Everyone around town was on-edge, his daddy included. Finn had pitched in and helped fill sandbags in the past couple of days since his return, and that had only served to show him that he wasn't so sure about life on this ranch. God threw them curveballs, and everyone here seemed used to it. They stepped right up to the plate and batted, while Finn felt like someone had put him on a merry-go-round and kept spinning it faster and faster and faster.

At the same time, he'd been spinning in Army intelligence for the past ten years. He'd hit fast balls, curve balls, sliders, all of them. Yes, Finn had been very, very good at his job in the Army, and maybe his hyperfocus on every little detail there was why he needed a break now.

He moved over to the line to get food, automatically grouping up with his siblings and Pete's kids. He had four sons, and they'd all made it home in time for this party. Poor Libby was the only girl, and who Finn found himself behind in line.

An idea sprang into his mind. "Hey, Libs," he said as she turned toward him. "I have, uh, a thing I want you to look at."

Her eyebrows went up, because Libby didn't miss much. She was too much like Momma in that regard, though the skill of seeing and knowing everything surely came in handy for them. "A thing? What kind of thing?"

Finn glanced over to where Momma stood with Aunt Chelsea. They'd been best friends in high school, and while their paths afterward had diverged, they'd still ended up here at the ranch together. He saw a parallel between him and Edith in that moment, and buoyed by that, he met his sister's eyes again.

They were seven years apart, so he hadn't been terribly close to Libby growing up. He'd finished high school and left for the Army before she'd even moved into junior high. He'd kept in touch with her the most over the years of his military service, mostly because she wrote to him constantly.

"I ran into Edith Baxter the day I got home," he said under his breath.

Libby leaned forward though the line moved away from her. "What?"

Finn sighed and rolled his eyes. Grandpa Armstrong had moved to keep up with the line, but it snaked around the countertop, which meant he now stood almost right next to Finn. With Daddy and Uncle Pete.

He glanced back to Libby, then over to Mike and Henry. Libby and Henry were the exact same age, and she exchanged a look with him too. Finn honestly didn't know them as adults all that well—none of them. He barely knew himself as an adult.

And Edith?

He didn't know her at all, no matter if they'd sent a few dozen flirty texts in the past few days.

He shored up his courage and looked at them all. "I ran into Edith Baxter the day I came home." He held up his phone and refused to look away. "We've been texting, and I would appreciate some help in asking her out." He hit the T hard on the word "out," Henry's face already lit up.

The boy had been super girl-crazy as a teenager, and Momma claimed he hadn't calmed much. That he dated someone new every other week. Whether that was true or not, Finn didn't know. He knew Henry wasn't married, had never been married, and his current relationship status was single.

He also took the phone first. "Edith Baxter, wow."

"Shh." Finn glanced over to his father, but the rain and river still dominated his—and everyone's attention. In that moment, Finn realized how worried all the adults looked. His momma. His grandparents. His grandma on his dad's side and her new husband, whom Finn had only met a handful of times. Malcolm couldn't even be considered "new," as he and Grandma had been married for eight years now.

He was simply new to Finn. So many things were.

"You're flirting hard-core with her," Henry said, his eyes glued to the phone and his voice nowhere near shh-level.

"Henry," Libby said delicately, and she

slipped the phone out of his hand. "I don't think Finn wants the world to know about Edith quite yet." She pocketed his phone, gave him a wide-eyed look, and turned to pick up a paper plate.

Relief coated Finn's nerve endings, and he met Henry's eye, then Mike's, Paul's, and Rich's. John and Sammy chatted in the line behind them, and Finn figured they'd get drawn into the drama soon enough. They all would.

Paul grinned at him. "Edith was always really nice."

"Yeah," Finn said, as that was one adjective he'd use to describe her.

"Her brother bought a small place east of here," Rich said. He and Paul were about eight years apart, and maybe Paul hadn't known that. "Oh, I don't know. Four or five years ago. Edith's only been back for—I don't know. Less than that."

Finn hadn't gotten to the part where he asked where she'd been living for the past decade. For some reason, he'd assumed she'd only just returned to town, same as him. "How long?" he asked. "Like, a couple of months?"

"No," Rich said. "A couple of years, at least. She did a big event at the junior high when one of her books came out, and I was still there. She'd moved here then."

So a couple of years. Maybe longer. *Between two and five years*, he told himself, his mind ever-working. He moved through the line while the conversation went on to something else. He still didn't have his phone, and as he settled at a table with a full plate of food he didn't remember getting and all seven of his siblings and cousins, he knew the topic of Edith would not be forgotten or dropped.

Libby had his phone discreetly beside her plate as she ate, and when she finished, she passed it to Paul. He started reading the texts while Libby asked John how his classes were going at TCU.

College talk bored Finn, and he kept his eyes on his device as it went round the table and back to him. By then, everyone had finished eating, and all their casual conversation had come to a close.

"Okay." Libby leaned her elbows up on the table and clasped her hands together. "This isn't too hard. You're already talking to her. You simply find something going on in town that she'll like, and you ask her to go with you." She nodded like such a thing was so easy to do, and Finn reminded himself that he'd been out with other women before. In foreign countries. Who didn't even speak his language.

Somehow, Edith felt as exotic as them, and he had no idea how to talk to her.

"There's always a ton going on in the summer here," Paul said. "Summer dances?"

Finn shook his head immediately. "We're not in high school."

"Some of the cowboys on the ranch go every week," Henry said.

Finn gave him a glare that said, *Yeah, those who still think they're in high school.* Henry laughed and held up one hand. "Fine, not the summer dances."

"There are museums," Libby said. "Tours. Historical sites. There's plenty to do besides the summer dances." She looked around the table at all the boys. "And you know what? It's just oc-curred to me that none of y'all have a girlfriend, so maybe Finn shouldn't be taking advice from any of you."

"You're not dating anyone either," Paul said swiftly, and Libby's fierce blue eyes jutted over to him.

"I am taking a break," she said. "After that last

disaster I called a boyfriend." She folded her arms, her ire all up now.

Finn grinned at her, because he'd gotten the story of her Disaster Boyfriend via email. "What do you think Edith would like?"

No one said anything, which was why Finn couldn't ask her out either. "I guess I'll have to text with her some more to learn what she'd like," he said.

"Or you could just ask her," Henry said. "Why beat around the bush when you can go right through it?"

"Through what?" Uncle Pete asked, suddenly looming above them.

"Nothing, Dad," Henry said. "Just a figure of speech."

"You know what I don't miss hearing now that you don't live here?" Pete grinned at his son, who grinned right on back. "Nothing, Dad." He mimicked Henry as he said it, and they both laughed.

Finn tucked his phone away, shot another look at his sister—who'd only be here for the weekend —and right then and there, they communicated that they could talk about this again later, without the rest of the boys around. And especially without Uncle Pete, Daddy, Momma, and Aunt Chelsea to overhear them.

You could just ask her, he thought. *Ask her what she'd like to do around town, and then take her to do that.*

Finn needed to get online and do some investigating as to what the town of Three Rivers had coming up on their community schedule, that was for sure. Good thing his specialty was finding the important, meaningful things that other people missed.

LATER THAT NIGHT, HE WOKE WHEN HE HEARD footsteps overhead. He hadn't been sleeping deeply anyway, and now, he got out of bed and went upstairs. He expected to find his father in the kitchen, and he did.

Fully dressed, Daddy had just finished pulling on his cowboy boots, and he stood from the kitchen table in jeans and a long-sleeved shirt. He reached for his cowboy hat and said, "I'm heading over to Uncle Pete's."

"It's the middle of the night."

"It's rained six inches in the past hour," he said.

"Have you even been to bed?"

"Mother Nature don't care if it's day or night." He gave Finn a somber-eyed look.

"What are you going to do over there?"

"Turn on the flood lights and watch for water." He sighed and shrugged into his heavy jacket, though it couldn't be that cold outside.

"What can I do to help?"

"Turn the floods on here, then get on over to Brynn's place and do the same. I told her she didn't need to come do it when I'm right here."

"Got it," Finn said. He knew where the flood light switches were here at the homestead, and with several flips, the whole ranch would be lit up all the way from here to the admin building, in all directions.

Over at Bowman's Breeds, he had no idea where the switches were, but they couldn't be that hard to find.

"Then I want you back here with the other kids," he said. "Can you stay up on your phone? The moment I see water, I'll call you, and you can sound the siren and I'll text out to everyone."

Finn suddenly realized how serious this was. "Do you think it's going to flood?"

"Yes, son, I do." Daddy pulled him into a hug. "Bear called from Shiloh Ridge, and he said there's so much debris in the water, it'll take out everything in its path." Dad stepped back and cleared his throat. "It's okay. We plan for emergencies like this."

Maybe he did, but Finn didn't. "The river forks into three in town," he said. "Maybe it won't be as bad as it is at Shiloh Ridge." He'd been south to the ranch up in the foothills to help plenty of times, and they sent their cowboys here too. Plus, a lot of the Glovers came to ride here at Three Rivers Ranch, at Courage Reins. Finn would recognize any of them, even after ten years away.

"He said the river at Shiloh Ridge is twice as wide as usual and already overflowing. It'll only be worse once it forks, because the arms get smaller." Finn swallowed as Dad put on a plastic poncho over his clothes. "Stay alert and by your phone. Can you do that?" He looked at Finn with urgency in his eyes, and Finn would not let him down.

"I can do it," he said, because he'd done missions like this many times over the years. He could stay awake, fight off sleep, as he listened to recordings of active missions and heard things no one else heard. As he heard things that saved lives and preserved secrecy.

"Flood lights. Set up by the siren. I'll call you when we see the water."

"Yes, sir." Finn cleared his throat. "Will we have to evacuate?"

"Might could," Dad said.

"Where do we even go?" Finn thought of the row of cabins. They all sat eight or ten steps up off the ground. Uncle Pete had two stories to his house, as did the homestead. Would the water rise that high?

"Didn't you read my emergency text this morning?" Dad grinned at him. "We evacuate to the third floor of Courage Reins." He nodded out the window, where rain lashed the glass. "Momma and Chelsea are already over there, getting out blankets and moving chairs and couches. My guess is I'll see you over there in a bit."

With that, Dad flipped up the hood on his poncho and stepped out into the torrential rainstorm like he was simply going out for another day of work. At three-thirty in the morning.

Finn watched the darkness swallow him, as

the deck lights didn't reach very far. Then he spun toward the corner of the dining room where the flood light switches waited. He strode over to them and flipped them all up, using the butts of both palms.

Light filled the homestead as if it were daytime, and as Finn moved over to the window now, he could see out onto the ranch in every direction. Rain poured down, causing strange, watery shadows among the light.

He hurried downstairs to get properly dressed, and he grabbed his phone from his nightstand and turned the volume all the way up on all notifications. Back upstairs, he grabbed a poncho from the table and pulled it over his clothes.

He left through the garage, which would get him the closest to Bowman Breeds. It wasn't cold at all, but the ground at his feet had puddled with rain and he couldn't take a step in any direction without landing in a shallow pool of water.

"So it's already flooding," he said. "Whether the river breaks the bank or not." Hurrying through the mud and muck to the facility down the lane a bit, Finn began to pray. Not only for his parents and himself, who were all out in the storm, but for everyone who lived here at Three Rivers Ranch.

For the horses at Bowman's Breeds and Courage Reins. For their chickens, the barn cats, the dogs, the bulls, their cattle.

"Dear Lord." He sucked in a breath. "What is this going to do to our cattle?"

Raising and selling cattle was how the ranch made money. Would they be wiped away in floodwaters? What about their crops? Would they survive under feet of debris-riddled water?

Finn reached Bowman Breeds and as he reached for the door handle, a locking mechanism whirred. Brynn Greene said, "Thank you, Squire. The switches are to your left, up high, almost to the top of the doorframe."

He wasn't his father, but he didn't correct her. Finn slipped inside and turned left. Sure enough, up high on the wall sat several switches. He flipped them all on, and more light joined the rainstorm.

The intercom beeped again, and Brynn said, "Back in my office, there's a single button that will open all the stalls for the horses. Would you activate that? If the waters come through swiftly, I want them to be able to swim or run."

Finn's throat closed. "Sure," he said. "Will you guide me? Oh, and this is Finn, by the way."

"Oh, Finn." Brynn's voice pitched up. "Thank you for going over."

"Dad thinks it's gonna flood. I'd get out now if you're worried."

"Ethan's getting the kids up." She sighed and said, "Down the hall to your right is my office. It's got a big red door. The button is on the wall about as high as the switches you just flipped."

"And I don't need to check them?" Finn looked down the hallway, where some of the light pouring in from outside reached. "The horses, I mean."

"Their stalls will open, and they'll be able to go out into the paddocks and pastures. If the flood comes in fast, they should be able to swim or run. In their stalls...they'll be trapped."

He swallowed. "What about the horses at Courage Reins?"

"Beau's on it." Ethan Greene's voice came through the intercom this time. "Work fast, Finny. Get your siblings and get over to Courage Reins."

"I have to sound the sirens," Finn said. "But I'll get everyone up once I'm back to the homestead."

"God bless you," Brynn whispered, and those three words alerted Finn once again to the seriousness of this situation.

He strode down the hall and into the office on the right. He found the button and pushed it. He had no idea if it worked or not, but he had to trust Brynn. He had to trust God.

Outside, the standing water on the dirt and gravel seemed to have risen in the five minutes he'd been inside Bowman's Breeds, and Finn ran back to the homestead this time. He closed the garage and sprinted up the steps and into the house. Dripping, dripping, dripping, he started calling for Libby, Mike, and Sam to get up.

"You've got to get dressed and get over to Courage Reins," he said. "It's flooding. Everything's flooding." He heard the desperation and worry in his own voice, and thankfully, none of his siblings argued with him.

"Do they need food?" Libby asked. "Clothes? Blankets?" She peered out the window and then over to Finn. "Where's Momma and Daddy?"

"Whoa," Sam said as he pulled a T-shirt over his head and entered the main living area of the house. "It's *pouring*."

"They're out there," Finn said, nodding to the

rain and chaos in front of him. "Momma's at Courage Reins, prepping for everyone to arrive. Daddy's at Uncle Pete's, watching for a river surge." He faced his younger siblings, a fierce need to protect them coming over him. "Mike, you make sure Libs and Sammy get across the street. I'm staying here until Daddy calls, so I can sound the siren."

He moved into the living room and flipped open the shallow cupboard where their emergency system sat. He flipped a switch, and the red light came on. Now, all he had to do to send the wailing, warning siren across the world was press a button.

Finn looked over to his siblings, and they'd frozen. "Mike," he barked. "Libby. Sam. Get moving." They all flinched, and Finn marched over to them. He gathered each one into his arms, spanning them as wide as he could. "Third floor, guys. Momma's there. Get goin'."

Libby sniffled, then nodded. With her head high, she led the way toward the exit. "Come on, boys."

"Love you guys," Finn called out.

"Love you too," came back to him three-fold, and then Finn watched them all step into the rain.

It rained and rained and rained, and Finn marveled at it.

He took up his post by the siren, and he looked at his phone. Only twenty-four minutes had passed since he'd come upstairs to talk to his father. How much could change in such a short time.

His mind whirred, and before he knew it, he'd tapped to call Edith. "Come on," he said. "Please, Lord, wake her."

"Finn." She breathed out the word, and pure joy filled him at the sound of her voice.

"You've got to get to high ground," he said. "The river is flooding."

"I know," she clipped out. "We've been up all night sandbagging."

"Edith," he said calmly. "I don't think the sandbags are going to hold."

Pure, horrible, chilling silence came through the line.

"Edith?"

"We live in a one-story farmhouse, Finn," she said. "Where are we supposed to go?"

"A barn?" he guessed. "Get in your truck and get here. We've got three levels at Courage Reins."

"I can't—" she sobbed into the phone, and she

said more, but Finn couldn't make it out. His heart tore for her, and he wished he could get in his truck and go collect her and her brother.

"Edith," he said again. "Calm down, sweetheart. It's going to be okay. Can you and Alex come here or is that impossible?"

"It's impossible," she whispered.

"I'll be there the first chance I have," he promised.

Someone shouted on her end of the line, and she said, "We're going up into the loft of the barn. I have to go."

"Go," he said. "Edith, stay safe."

"You too."

The call ended, and Finn sighed as he bowed his head. "Lord, bless that woman and her brother, please." He lifted his eyes toward the ceiling, toward heaven. "Please protect them. Put a barrier around them somehow. And their land and animals and loved ones. Please. And please do the same for us here at Three Rivers Ranch."

His phone rang, and his heart leapt. It wasn't Edith's name on the screen, calling him back. But his Daddy's.

Finn reached up and pressed the button to sound the siren. The shrieking wail of warning started out low and rose in pitch and volume as it revved up, and just when he thought he'd go deaf, it started to wane again.

His daddy's text filled his screen, in all caps. *EVACUATION MANDATORY ASAP. MAKE YOUR WAY TO THE THIRD FLOOR OF COURAGE REINS. TEXT UP YOUR CHANNEL IF YOU NEED HELP.*

Finn had no idea who was in his channel, but he grabbed his phone as the wail started to gain strength for the second time. He intended to leave it on, but Daddy texted, *Stay for another five minutes, if possible, Finny. Then turn off the siren and get across the street. I love you.*

"Five minutes." That felt like an eternity in that moment, and Finn reached down deep for his military training. Five minutes was three hundred seconds. He could do anything for that long, and he took a long, deep breath to steady himself.

If it's not possible to stay, turn it off and go, Dad texted next. Finn moved over to the window, trying to judge how much water he'd have to wade through to get across the street. Because of the powerful lights, he could see cowboys with backpacks moving steadily toward Courage Reins. He saw families, with men, women, and children. Dogs and cats too.

The siren wailed and wailed.

The sky sobbed.

When he reached three hundred, he shut down the alarm system, flipped up his hood, and stepped out into the flood, his prayers streaming out loud from his mouth.

5

"We've got to go, Edee!"

Edith spun from the window in her bedroom and took in the three animals on her bed. There was no way she could carry both dachshunds and her grumpy, fifteen-pound cat. The electricity hadn't gone out yet, and all six pairs of eyes locked on her.

"Come on," she told them. "Frankie, Otto, you stay right by me." She grabbed Gumbo, who meowed at her, and ran out of her bedroom. "Frankie! Otto! Come on!" Down the hall and in the kitchen, she found Alex wearing two jackets, with leashes in his hands.

"Come on, guys," he called, and the dachshunds ran toward him. He leashed them up, looked at Edith, and said, "We're not letting go of one another, no matter what. You got that?"

"Yes," she croaked out as she got closer to him.

"I've got a coat for you," he said. "Just in case."

"What about Olive and Bandit?" They weren't leashed, and Edith looked at them helplessly.

"They'll stay with me." He reached for her hand with one of his and the back doorknob with the other. "We need to go now. I swear I can hear the water rushing right now." He didn't sound scared, but his words held fear inside them, in the curved letters where the emotion couldn't just slide off slants and straight lines.

Outside, on the deck, Edith could hear it too. "Isn't the river pretty far from here?"

"Apparently not." He led them to the edge of the deck, where the roof no longer covered, and one more step and he'd be in the torrential rain. He didn't hesitate as he led her down the steps, and Edith squinted against the enormous raindrops now pummeling her.

She'd never thought the barn sat too far from the house, but this journey felt like it took a really long time. Finally, Alex pulled open the door and ducked inside, pulling her and the dachshunds with her. "Bandit! Olive! In here!"

Both border collies ran inside, and Alex flipped on the lights. "Electricity is still on." He handed her the leashes and moved away from her, his long legs moving fast. He flipped more switches, and more light filled the barn and now flowed in from outside.

Edith turned and looked back into the storm. It flowed down in near sheets, and she'd only seen water like this when she'd lived through a hurricane that had hit Long Island. The ground had stopped absorbing the water, and it ran away from the concrete foundation of the barn.

"Close the door, Edith," Alex said, his voice less barky and filled with far less urgency. "And let's get on the second level." He moved toward the aisle that separated a tack room and a feed room from this larger main room. "I'll get the ladder down. Can you get all the animals over here?"

"What about the horses?" she asked. "What if the stables flood?"

"I'm going to get you all upstairs, and then I'm going to let them loose." His voice echoed back to her, and for some reason, that only helped keep her feet frozen right where they were.

"You're going back out there? Alone?"

"It's not flooded yet. The horses will get to higher ground and stay there. We'll round them up once the danger passes." He made a holy loud racket getting down the ladder that led up to the loft. "You go up first, and I'll hand up Frankie and Otto."

Alex came toward her, still moving with plenty of urgency. "You turned on the lights. I'll be able to see over to the stables, and I'll be back in five minutes."

"Alex." Edith trembled with fear, not cold, and she hated feeling this wild and out of control. What if he didn't come back? She had her phone in her pocket and the clothes and shoes on her body.

"You go up first," he said. "Take Gumbo with you." He steered her to the ladder, and Edith accomplished something she'd never done before: she climbed a wooden ladder to a loft while carrying a constantly meowing cat.

When she could, she set him on his feet and said, "Shush." Gumbo would continue to talk, because he was one of the most vocal felines she'd ever encountered. She turned back and bent down, her legs trembling with the requirement she put on them, and reached for Otto. She then straightened and twisted to drop the black and brown dachshund into the loft. She repeated that for Frankie, and with the mostly brown dog up in the loft, Alex said, "You go up. Bandit and Olive can climb the ladder."

"They can?"

"They'll bowl you over if you don't get out of the way." He certainly wouldn't kid about this in such a situation, so Edith climbed the rest of the way into the loft and looked around. Olive came up first, followed by Bandit, and then Alex appeared from the waist up. He took off both coats and handed them to her.

"Five minutes," he said. "I've got a first aid kit downstairs I'm going to hand up when I get back. And we have our emergency binders out here too. They list all of our horses and have emergency tools to fix fences."

"Okay," Edith said, because they certainly couldn't do any of that until the sun rose. If it ever did again.

Of course the sun is going to rise again, she told herself. The rain would stop. The sun would come out. The land would dry up again. Edith knew this rationally, but at four o'clock in the morning with the rain pounding the roof of the barn only inches from her head, it was hard to conceptualize.

"Five minutes," Alex said again, and then he disappeared down the ladder. She moved over to the big cut-out window where they'd throw down hay bales or load them up using a conveyor belt. She didn't open it, though she really wanted to. The need to do it gnawed at her, because she wanted to see what was going on beyond these walls.

But she didn't want to let the rain inside, so she kept it closed, and she paced back and forth a couple of times, wondering how long it really took to run over to the stables and let out four horses.

Her phone beeped, and she tugged it free from her pocket. Finn's name sat there, but it got sucked back up into the top of her phone before she could read his message. She tapped to open her phone, and she navigated to his text.

Let me know if you're safe. We're all on the third floor of the Courage Reins building, and believe it or not, my momma is passing out cookies.

"Oh, I believe that," Edith said, actually

smiling to herself as she typed out the message and sent it. *We made it into the loft of the barn. Alex went to put the horses out to pasture, in the hopes that they'll get to higher ground if we flood.*

This is great news, he said. *Thanks for letting me know, Edith.*

She sank onto a hay bale and sighed. She hated the blaring, unnatural light when the rest of the world sat in darkness, and the beginnings of a headache started behind her eyes. This was going to be a very long day.

Surely Alex had been gone for five minutes by now, but Edith distracted herself from a full-blown panic attack by looking up the weather report. It came as no surprise to see the bright red banner across the top of the screen, urging people to get to higher ground and then stay indoors.

Scrolling messages went by for all the counties and affected areas, but Edith didn't need to know that. She wanted to know when this would end. "Mid-morning," she murmured to herself. "By ten-thirty, there's only a ten percent chance of rain."

She wasn't sure she believed that, because weather seemed to do whatever it wanted, and meteorologists were simply paid estimators. But they could see storm systems from space now, and track how fast they moved, and as her eyes flicked up to the top of her screen to see the time, she told herself, "Okay, six more hours."

Alex still wasn't back, and Edith pressed the power button on her phone and left it on the bale of hay. "Alex!" she yelled. She wasn't going to sit here for another second. Getting down the ladder was considerably harder than going up it, but she managed without falling. She did have a couple of splinters she'd have to deal with when she had a moment, and she figured she'd have plenty—once she found Alex and made sure he was here, in this dry barn with her.

She moved over to the door and opened it. "Alex!" she shouted into the storm. "Alex, where are you?"

He didn't answer, and Edith hesitated as she took in the wall of rain. She told herself she'd done much harder things than walk in the rain, and that got her to take the first step. Water soaked her in the first moment, and she pressed on toward the corner of the barn so she could go around it.

About halfway to the stable, she heard Alex hollering. Edith broke into a run, and she burst into the stable, not caring that the door slammed into the wall behind it. She scanned the stalls in front of her, her pulse bouncing through her veins like a night club beat.

She found Alex almost at the end, the last horse in the place rearing up in front of him. "Whoa, whoa, whoa," she said, rushing forward. "Frodo, down. Calm down. Down." Without hesitation, she took the rope from Alex and added, "Go on. Back up."

He knew to be gentler with Frodo, but the horse really only responded well to Edith when under stress. He huffed and nickered as he settled onto his front hooves. "Come on, now," she said. "You don't want to be trapped in here if this place starts to fill with water. It's a few steps. Come on."

None of the horses here loved to swim or anything, but they could handle rain. "It's just like a little bath," she told Frodo as she led him down the aisle to the open gate. "It's not even that cold."

Edith went out into the rain first, getting soaked all over again, and she reached up and unlooped the rope from around Frodo's neck. "Go on. I'm sure everyone else is out there waiting for you."

Frodo kept his big horsey head by hers, then lifted it and looked out toward the ranch.

"Go on," she said again, starting to feel more like the fourteen-year-old version of herself. The one who'd deliberately leave the house in a massive thunderstorm, spread her arms wide, and laugh as she spun in a circle. She'd once looked up into the heavens during a rainstorm like this one, and she'd seen every individual drop as it fell to the earth.

That rain moment had cleansed her, and as Frodo trotted away from the stables, Edith found a smile on her face. She took a breath and looked up into the dark sky. The lights from the ranch could only reach so high, and she saw every drop as it emerged out of the darkness and got illuminated.

She laughed, feeling freer than she had in a while, and she wasn't even sure why. It was springtime in Texas, her favorite season, and as they moved into summer, Edith should be riding a high.

But she knew what came at the end of the summer, and that made it hard to enjoy the long, sunshine-filled days, even if she got to ride horses and write about horses most days.

"What in the world are you doin'?" Alex reached out and gripped her arm, and Edith realized she'd lifted them up, the same way she had as a girl.

"Spinning," she said.

"Let's get back to the barn." Alex kept a good grip on her hand on the way back, but Edith felt calmer than ever. All four dogs waited for them right at the top of the ladder, while Gumbo meowed from the highest hay bale.

"Back up, you hounds," she told them, but they barely made any room for her. She managed to get up, and she pulled Bandit back so Alex had room to put his feet in the loft. With both of them finally at the goal, Edith paused.

"Can we say a prayer?" she whispered, the rain on the roof the perfect background music.

"I wish you would." Alex sighed and gave her a weary smile. He wasn't wearing his cowboy hat, something he almost always did. He bowed his head and closed his eyes, and Edith did the same.

As she dripped in the hay loft, with Alex's hand in hers, she took several long moments to simply listen to the rain. The pitter-patter of it, along with the earthy scent of hay and wet dog, reminded her of the good place she had to live. Her family, who loved her and whom she loved.

And somehow, Finn Ackerman entered her mind.

"Lord," she whispered. "We thank Thee for this amazing place to live. Both Alex and I love Texas, and we have worked real hard to try to take care of this ranch, these animals You've blessed us with, and each other. We know there are a lot of people who are probably going to be affected by the rain here in the Texas Panhandle, and we're not asking for a miracle. We're simply asking that whatever damage does happen, that it won't be more than we can handle."

"Amen," Alex whispered, because they'd always done that in their family when one of them prayed for something the other agreed with mightily.

Edith found she didn't have anything else to say—at least not out loud. She wanted to plead for Finn and his family ranch too, but she believed God heard the unuttered prayers inside a person's heart, so she kept the words there, opened her eyes, and said, "Amen," too.

Alex stepped away from her and wiped his hands down his face. "Could you hear me calling?"

"No," she said. "But you didn't come back in

five minutes, and I just felt like…something was up."

He nodded and sat down on the same hay bale she'd been on earlier. She joined him and leaned her head against his bicep. "Daddy used to pray for that," he said quietly. "That we wouldn't be given any challenges we couldn't handle."

"It was the mantra of our childhood." Edith smiled to herself. "And I gotta say, I've felt like God has given me some really heavy things that I can't possibly carry."

"Not without Him, at least," Alex murmured.

"Yeah." They fell into silence then, with only Gumbo meowing every so often around them. The dogs gathered at their feet, circling until they all found a space to be, with the littler dachshunds up on top of the collies. Edith found such comfort with them, and she knew by their calm demeanor that she had nothing to fear.

If something truly horrific was about to happen, the canines wouldn't be nearly so docile. They'd be pacing, especially the collies, so despite Gumbo's refusal to be quiet, Edith relaxed a little bit.

"You want to lay down?" Alex asked, and she jolted back awake. "Sleep a little until the sun comes up?" He helped her move over to the corner of the barn, and he covered her with one of his jackets.

Edith dozed, not sure what she'd find when the morning came. But no matter what, she knew another morning would come, because they always did. Even after the worst day of her life, the one where Levi had taken his last breath and passed from this world to the next, morning had come.

The day got lighter and lighter, and eventually Edith opened her eyes for good again when Alex unlatched the lock on the window and opened the two halves outward. "Still raining," he said as he pressed his palms into the wide windowsill and looked out. "Not as hard, though."

Edith groaned as she got up. She shook the hay from his jacket and laid it on the bale before joining him. "The weather report said it should be gone by ten-thirty."

"There's a *loooot* of water down there."

She took in the enormity of the ranch, and yes, the ground straight down was nothing but a giant puddle the drops continued to plink into. Water ran past the stable in a rivulet that shouldn't be there, and she wished this side of the barn faced the farmhouse and her she-shed.

All she could hear was water. Water falling. Water landing. Water rushing. "The river is loud," she said.

"It's got to have taken out a ton of fences," Alex said.

"But not our barn or stables."

He nodded to their left. "The chicken coop is gone."

Edith's heart plummeted to her sneakers. "The chicken coop is gone," she repeated, her voice much more haunted. "What about the hens?"

"They'll have gotten somewhere safe," he said.

"But how do we get them back?"

He didn't answer her then, and Edith went back to taking in the ranch. She couldn't see the horses, nor any of their cattle. No chickens at all, anywhere. They didn't have much more than that —no goats, or sheep, or donkeys. Just horses, cattle, chickens, and their dogs. Oh, and Gumbo, who was almost hoarse from all the meowing.

She turned and picked up the feline, stroking him to try to calm him. Miraculously, Gumbo did quiet, and Alex turned from the window. "I think it's tapering even more." Sure enough, the raindrops didn't even register on the roof anymore. Edith had grown so used to the noise, that the absence of it left behind a void she hadn't experienced before.

"I think we should head out to the river and see where it is," he said.

A vibration of fear strummed against her heart, but Edith wasn't going to let Alex go alone. As he went down the ladder first, she put Gumbo in the middle of the dachshunds and said, "Let's go down and go potty. Everyone. Alex?"

"I heard you."

It took several minutes to get the animals down the ladder and outside, and thankfully, Frankie, Otto, and Gumbo only went a few feet, took care of their business, and came rushing back into the safety of the barn.

Edith half-climbed the ladder and took the wet pets from Alex again, setting them all safely in the loft once more. As she dropped Gumbo in the middle of Frankie and Otto, she said, "You guys take care of each other, okay?"

Bandit and Olive waited with Alex, and together, the four of them faced the nearly-gone rain. "There's so much water," she murmured.

Alex's phone started to *bing!* and *bing!* and *bing!* some more. Distracted now, he looked at it, and while Edith waited for him to read and then fill her in on who was messaging, she took out her phone and texted Finn.

The rain's stopping, and we're headed out to check on things.

My daddy's texting faster than anyone his age has a right to, Finn said. *You should see him! It's incredible.*

She smiled, because she'd always liked Finn's daddy. *My brother is too.*

Probably on the same thread, Finn said. *He's talking to all the ranch owners around town, because they'll do the rounds and come help anyone who needs it.*

"Are you talking to the other ranch owners?" she asked, a bit of surprise running through her.

"Yep."

A measure of pride filled her, because Alex had always wanted to own a ranch, and here he was, doing it. Talking to ranch owners twice his age like equals. She was so glad he was living his dream, and she thanked God for her small role in helping him do that.

"Will they come help us?"

"If we need it." Alex lifted his head and faced the dripping wet ranch. "Let's go see if we need it." His phone continued to chime, but he tucked it away and led the way out of the barn. "Stay behind me, Edee. Be careful."

"Yes, sir," she said, and she wasn't mocking him. She stepped where he stepped, and it didn't take long for them to pick their way through debris. Logs. Fence poles. Chicken wire. Pieces of metal roofing. More wood, this the chopped kind that someone would keep near their house to take in to build a cozy fire.

The noise of the river got louder and louder, and though Edith generally had a terrible sense of direction, she knew the river had never been this close to the barn before.

All at once, Alex came to a complete stop, and he threw out his hand in case Edith tried to go by him. She didn't, but came to his side and stopped too.

"Dear Lord in Heaven," she whispered. In front of her, a brown river raged, and it looked as if it were the thickness and viscosity of chocolate milk. Chocolate milk with tree branches and trunks in it, as well as other various items that obviously came from homes and farms.

Edith looked up, her eyes traveling across the width of the river. She'd come out to the footbridge many times, and it took her maybe five strides to cross it. If there had been a bridge here, it would've taken her fifty strides to cross it. Maybe one hundred.

"I think we're gonna need some help," she managed to say.

"Yep," Alex said, his voice grim. "And we don't need to be standin' here." He turned back to the front of the ranch, and as Edith did, she saw with perfect clarity how much clearance they'd been given.

They'd only walked about fifty yards from the stable. Beyond that sat the barn, and within a football field's length sat the she-shed and the farmhouse. Behind her, floodwaters raged. In front of her, she saw the hand of God.

As Alex started to walk away, Edith pulled out her phone and took pictures in all directions. Then she could send them to Finn and show him how close they'd come to being washed off the face of the earth.

6

Finn's fingers flew as fast as his father's over his phone. "Edith's sent pictures, Momma. Look at this." He couldn't believe what he was seeing. Of course, he had no experience with Coyote Pass or what it should look like, but Edith said she usually had to walk twenty or twenty-five minutes to get to the river.

Now it's less than a hundred yards from our back deck, she told him.

His momma looked over his shoulder at his phone, and Finn swiped through the few photos Edith had sent. "My goodness." She turned and called, "Squire, the Baxters at Coyote Pass will need help."

She moved away from Finn, who was already typing out another message to Edith. *Has your brother asked for help? My daddy is coordinating a lot of it. He and Britt Bellamore. I can give you their numbers.*

He was texting them, Edith said. *But he put his phone away so we could check things out. We're getting the pets and heading back to the house.*

Do you have power? Finn asked, because theirs had gone out a couple of hours ago. They had blankets and bean bags and plenty of places to sit and lounge. Food and water both packed a six-foot-long folding table, and as Finn looked around, he saw so much abundance.

He'd been six years old when his momma had married Squire Ackerman, and they'd moved to College Station for Daddy to go to veterinary school. They'd lived there for four years, and Finn had done most of his elementary school there, so he had memories away from this ranch. He had memories of when they didn't have the abundance he saw surrounding him.

Times when Momma made pancakes and spaghetti for every meal, and packages came from both sets of grandparents in Three Rivers that kept him clothed and with new shoes on his feet. His parents hadn't bought anything like that for Finn until they'd returned to Three Rivers Ranch and Daddy started working as the lead vet for the ranch. He also ran the ranch as a whole, as his parents had retired and moved to town by then.

"Daddy's talking to Alex now," Momma told him. "Can you come help Uncle Pete and Beau with the chore sheet, please?"

"Sure thing." Finn didn't want to put his phone away, but he'd been using it for hours, and it could use some time plugged in. He took a moment to text Edith one more time—*I'm going to be there later today, okay? I'll call you before I come.*

He hoped he hadn't just overpromised something he couldn't deliver, but the quick way that Edith responded with, *I'd like that, Finn. Thank you*, told him he better do whatever it took to get out to Coyote Pass today.

"Can I plug in my phone somewhere?" he asked his father, and his daddy gestured in the general direction of the chest-high counter.

"Uncle Pete has a mini-generator there for devices."

Finn headed that way, and once he'd secured a cord for his phone and it had chimed at him that it was indeed charging, he turned and faced the room where about forty or fifty people had spent the last several hours together.

He really wanted to get out of this room, but he took a deep breath and headed over to the table where Reese Sanders, Uncle Pete, and Beau Peterson bent over several sheets of paper. They filled the whole table, and as Finn arrived, so did Cal Hodgkins, the other vet here at the ranch.

"What we got?" Cal asked.

Uncle Pete nodded to the iPad. "Sent the drones out over the cabins. They don't look bad."

"Standing water everywhere," Reese said.

"Yeah, but it's what? A foot or so deep?" Pete tapped and the screen on his tablet moved. The drone flew steady and straight, and it showed the homestead with standing water in the driveway, on the lawn, and down in the patio area that led to the basement.

"Might be water in the basement at the homestead," Pete said, and Reese made a note on a sheet of paper. Finn saw that a couple of other sheets had already been filled with might be's. Nothing had been said about the cabins, but the barns and stables had a couple of pages each. They sat right on the ground, so that made sense.

"Have you found the herd?" Cal asked.

"Not yet." Pete moved the drone over to Brynn's place, and Reese made a few notes. Finn saw his truck sitting there, and since it hadn't been washed away, his thoughts of leaving the ranch and going to check on Edith grew tiny wings that fluttered behind his pulse.

"My house has a couple of broken windows," Pete said, nodding to Finn. He reached for a blank page and a pen and wrote it down, noting the locations for Pete. "And my whole backyard is now a river."

Finn looked at the tablet then, a feeling of wonder pulling through him. No, he didn't want to see the majesty of God in a destructive way, but there was something powerful and silence-inducing in seeing a raging river where it shouldn't be. Where he'd never seen it before.

"Pastures," Pete said, and Finn pulled himself out of the mini-stare-fest he'd fallen into. "Fences around all the pastures. Those are gone."

"This is the west side," Cal said. "The lower end of the ranch. The herd'll be east."

"Do you think the road to town's been washed out?" Finn asked. "Are we going to go check on grandparents today?"

"Your daddy says tomorrow," Uncle Pete murmured, his concentration on working the drone. "Here's the wash. Or what was the wash."

"Trees down," Reese said, pulling forward another piece of paper. "Fences gone. The path for free ride from Courage Reins is obliterated."

The list went on and on, and the small tributary that broke off from the west arm of the river just north of town—the one river of the three that ran right through ranch property—was now a gushing waterwork of its own.

It got listed, as did the outlying cabin that had the front door standing wide open and water inside it—five steps up.

"But that water is all coming back in toward the ranch," Cal said. "To that tributary and the pond here." He pointed to the top left corner of the tablet. "The herd has to be up here."

"Let's see." Pete navigated the drone, and since Three Rivers Ranch was such a big place by square miles, it flew over nothing but fields for a minute. Then two. "The water's not standing here."

"Doesn't look like it." Reese watched the screen, as did Cal.

"Horses there," Cal said, pointing to the

bottom left. Pete adjusted the movement of the drone, and sure enough, a sizable herd of horses came into view. "Looks like most of 'em."

Uncle Pete kept the drone above the equines for several long seconds. "I don't see Rebel," he murmured. "Or Queen Elizabeth."

Finn's patience started to wane, but he kept his attention on the task at hand, and they found the herd taking up the northeast corner of the ranch, where all the fence lines were still intact. That butted right up against the highway that led back to town, and it didn't have standing water on it either.

The drone came back down the half-mile lane and around the corner, and it was wet, but not washed away. Finn's hope lived on, and once this task completed, he got the task of finding his father so assignments could start being made.

In Finn's honest opinion, the men in the room seemed ready to fling themselves from the windows just to get out, and he found Dad just out in the hallway, talking on the phone. "...think that should work. Pete's doin' our assessment right now, and I'll know more then." He caught Finn's eye and turned toward him. "I'm being summoned, Bear. We'll stay in touch...yep...sure thing. 'Bye."

He lowered his phone and met Finn's eye. "How's it look?"

"There are pages and pages of things," he said. "And some of it we can't do until the water is gone."

"Of course." Dad turned to go back into the room, but Finn took a half-step in that direction. His father's eyebrows went up.

"Could I...go into town and check on Grandma Heidi and momma's parents?"

"I'm sure they're fine," he said. "We've got a ton going on here."

Finn scuffed his boots along the floor. "Could you spare me for a couple of hours? I want—I told Edith I'd come out to Coyote Pass to see what they need help with."

Daddy, who'd seemed so frazzled since the first rays of light had started to appear, who'd had his attention exclusively on his phone, slowed and focused solely on Finn. "Coyote Pass, huh?"

"Can we not make this a big deal? You know I'm texting her."

"How'd they fare? Alex says the river came almost up to their stable."

"Edith sent some pictures. It definitely looks worse than here—about like Pete's backyard."

"Wow." He rolled his neck and then his shoulders. "Uh, yeah, you should go, but can we get through team and section assignments? And you'll have to sign out with your team lead." He thumped Finn in the chest. "And your mother." He grinned, turned, and re-entered the room.

"Daddy," Finn whined after him, but his father kept moving with the energy of someone who hadn't been up all night. Finn leaned into the doorway of the room and watched as his father called everyone together.

"If he thinks having to clear it with Momma will stop me from going, he's got another thing coming," he muttered to himself. Then he caught sight of his mother, and she'd found Henry and Mike lounging on the bean bag and was currently getting them to their feet so they could go join the others.

Fine. Maybe his father was right.

"Finn," Momma said, appearing in front of him somehow when he'd just been watching her. "Get in here. Your father is making teams and handing out assignments."

"I know, Momma," he said. "I just talked to

him, and you know what? I can hear just fine from here." He wasn't anyone special here on the ranch, and he wouldn't be a team leader. He'd be assigned to a crew, and he'd do whatever was required of him—and after spending an hour at the table with the drone, Finn knew how much work needed to be done.

But Edith had just as much, and as Finn looked at the twenty other cowboys in the room, he had the distinct impression that Three Rivers Ranch could spare him. And Edith, Alex, and Coyote Pass needed him.

Surely Momma wouldn't be able to argue with that.

"Thanks, Beau," Finn said a couple of excruciating hours later. "I'm going to be gone for a couple of hours, and I'll check back in with you when I get back."

Beau looked up from underneath his cowboy hat. He wore a long-sleeved shirt and a look of annoyance on his face. It melted away a moment later, and he said, "Sure. Let me know. I'm sure we'll still be here, trying to get these ridiculous fences back up."

"I'm sorry," Finn said. "Two hours, tops. I just want to really see how things are at Coyote Pass. I don't think they have a drone to see things the way we have here."

"Pete's letting you take it?"

Finn grinned as he pulled off his gloves. "I had to sign my life away, but yeah." They both chuckled, and Finn took another look at the few men on his crew with Beau. Finn wasn't stupid, and he knew his father had put him with the foreman purposely. He wanted Finn to feel ownership of the ranch, to want to run it one day.

Probably tomorrow.

He'd promised all of his kids that they had a place here on the ranch if they wanted it, and Libby would certainly come back here and run things out of the administration building, from the desk just inside the door. But Daddy had an office in the corner down the hall, and Momma ran all the finances.

Finn didn't have an accounting degree, and while he could do math, he didn't love it. He wasn't sure how he'd feel in the corner office, as he'd spent the last ten years in the military in an office role, and he'd thrived there. He'd enjoyed it, even. But it wasn't ranching, and he wasn't even sure how his father filled his day.

He knew what cowboys like Beau and Cal did, and that definitely seemed more like something he could spend his life doing.

Here?

The thought came unbidden to his mind, and Finn didn't have an answer for it. He took his gloves with him, and he stopped by the Courage Reins building to collect the drone before he got behind the wheel of his truck and headed toward Coyote Pass.

He had to drive almost all the way back to town before the road out to the ranch appeared, and then he had to go back north again. Definitely more east too, and about forty minutes after he'd left Three Rivers, he pulled up to a quaint farmhouse at Coyote Pass. The front porch spanned both sides of the house, with the front door right in the middle and a peaked roof above that.

"Big house," he said to himself, wanting to know what had brought Edith here. He hadn't seen her since they'd met again on Wednesday, and the anticipation of being in the same space as her had Finn's heart pumping hard as he got out of his truck.

Edith opened the front door before he could round the hood, and she called, "Finn," as she crossed the porch and came down the steps.

He couldn't help laughing, despite the very non-laugh-like situation they found themselves in. "Ah, aren't you a sight for sore eyes?" He had a second to drink in her jeans, the navy puffy vest over the pink and white plaid shirt. Then she arrived in his arms, and Finn's eyes drifted closed as he brought her close and held her against his chest.

Fire burned in his stomach and up into his brain, but he also sensed something amiss with Edith. "Hey, you okay?"

"It's just so much," she whispered, and she made no move to leave his embrace.

"Did you get your horses back?"

"Yeah." She drew in a sharp breath through her nose as she stepped away. "All four of 'em. The chickens are still out there somewhere. Well." She rolled her shoulders forward and then back. "We got three of them back, and then Bandit chased one of those off, so we're still down about fifteen."

Edith offered him a smile, and Finn wanted to take it and tuck it into his pocket for when he next needed a ray of sunshine. "Come see Alex. He's jazzed to meet you again."

"Jazzed?" Finn chuckled as Edith slid her hand into his. "Who says that?"

"I say that, Chatterbox," she said. She led him up the steps while he chuckled over her funny name for him. She used all different ones, at different times. "He said I can give you a tour, and then he wants to get to work with the drone."

"Yeah, for sure," Finn said.

"So this is the porch," Edith said needlessly.

"It's a ten out of ten for you, Edith," he said. "You've always wanted a wraparound porch."

"Then it's not a ten out of ten," she said. "This one clearly goes from corner to corner. No wrapping around anything."

"It's huge," Finn argued back. "You seriously can't be upset about this porch."

"No." She sighed. "You're right. I'm not." She moved to enter the house, but Finn tugged on her fingers.

"Hey, answer something for me, would you?"

A hint of trepidation slid through her expression, and then she reached to tuck her hair back.

Finn had done that for her in the past too, and he wanted to again. "All right," she said. "Maybe."

Finn wanted to challenge her on that, but she rushed ahead of him. "I mean, there might be some things I'm not ready to tell you."

That gave him pause for a moment, and he searched her face. "I think I have things I *can't* tell you." He gave her a half-smile. "So how about we say the things we're comfortable with, and as we get more comfortable with each other, then we'll tell each other more."

"Okay," she said, reaching to tuck her hair again.

"You do that when you're nervous." Finn leaned closer, his grin growing. "It's cute."

To his delight, Edith smiled too. "Cute is what you call a dog or someone's shirt."

Finn burst out laughing, the old conversation from their past suddenly there between them. "Fine," he said among his laughter. "You're beautiful. Pretty." He reached out and tucked her hair, the moment turning absolutely still and sober. "Gorgeous."

Edith cleared her throat, and Finn realized he'd started leaning forward as if he'd kiss her right now. That clearly made her uncomfortable, and she turned and opened the front door. "Living room and kitchen," she said.

As he followed her, he also knew she'd avoided his question. His gaze scanned past the couches, the TV, the dining table and chairs, and landed on the sandy-haired man in the kitchen. Finn's laughter bubbled back to the surface, and he dropped Edith's hand like he shouldn't be holding it.

"Alex." He strode toward the young man and embraced him too. "Look at you." He moved away and actually scanned Alex down to his boots and back. "Owning your own ranch in Three Rivers? Is this insane?"

"It's normal most days." Alex grinned and grinned, his eyes sparking with that same blue energy that Edith's did. "Today? Not so normal. Right, Edee?"

She moved to his side, and they smiled at one another before facing Finn. He'd forgotten that her family called her Edee; he never had, though. She'd always been Edith for him. "Not so normal today, no."

Claws clicked on the tile, and she gasped as she looked down. "Oh, the dogs. You're going to love the dogs."

A cat meowed, and it sounded like it was made of metal but had been put through a washing machine. Rusty and overused, another "Meow," filled the air.

"You got the drone?" Alex asked.

"In the truck," he said.

"You said I could give him a tour first," Edith protested. "You boys can wait to play with the toys." She glared at Alex, who nodded.

"Fine," he said. "Give him a tour of what's still standing, and then let's see what mess we're dealing with outside."

Finn grinned at him and then moved back to Edith's side for the farmhouse tour. He wanted to be in whatever space she was in, and though she spoke with enthusiasm about the house, he got the distinct impression that she had plenty of questions to answer about her own life.

As they moved down the hall and into a guest bedroom, Finn noticed some pictures with another man. Clearly not a Baxter, as his hair was dark and his nose far too thin and sloped. There were three sitting on an eye-high shelf—one with him and Edith, one with him, Edith, and Alex, and one of just him.

"Who's this?" Finn asked as he picked up the

photo of the man solo. He had a happy smile, with plenty of life streaming from his face. Finn wanted to grin just seeing him grin. "One of Alex's roommates?"

Edith had gone completely still, and Finn didn't notice it for another few moments. When he did, he raised his eyebrows, and feeling very much like Momma, he asked, "Well?"

"Edee," Alex said as he came jogging down the hall. "Come see. The chickens are back."

Edith took the framed photograph from Finn and replaced it on the shelf. She took his hand as she brushed by him. "The chickens are back. I'm so glad you're here to help us round them up."

Finn chuckled, but he once again had the very real feeling that Edith had just dodged something he wanted answered. *You came here to work*, he told himself. And then, he also reminded himself that he had plenty of time to get to know Edith as she was now.

For she certainly wasn't the same nineteen-year-old young woman he'd kissed on the curb outside the Amarillo airport almost eleven years ago now. She'd changed. She'd lived a life he knew nothing about, and he wanted to know every intricate detail.

Then he could stitch together a reality for the two of them, where she'd never get hurt again, and he'd always be her soft place to fall.

And today, that was helping her gather the chickens that had lost their coop during a nighttime flood. Finn could only imagine what tomorrow would bring, and he hoped and then started planning that it would be more time with Edith.

You'll get your questions answered then, he vowed, and Finn very rarely broke a promise to himself or others.

7

Bear Glover heard the whispers around him, but he kept his head bowed and his thoughts focused. His children could wait. Heaven knew Bear had spent plenty of his life waiting on them, so he took his time finishing his prayer, and then he opened his eyes to the bright blue sky around him.

Joy filled his soul, because this view at the Glover family cemetery couldn't be beat. "It's a good place, Mother," he whispered. The burden Bear carried as the oldest male in the Glover Family had only tripled when they'd lost Mother last year. At least she'd gotten to see one more Angel Tree, but that meant she hadn't even been gone for a full year yet, and sometimes Bear's pain tugged until it pulled until it ached.

"Ready, Daddy?" Lincoln, his oldest boy, appeared at his side. Bear had only dropped to one knee, but he still used the help and support of Link to stand.

"Ready," he told the young man. He dusted his hands and flashed a quick smile at his son, reminding himself that he didn't have to be the big, bad grump just because he felt like it. Just because he hurt. Just because it was his default, and easier than being kind to those around him.

They were likely hurting too.

Physically, mentally, emotionally, Bear *hurt*. And this blasted flood hadn't helped any of his sixty-year-old muscles and joints, that was for dang sure.

He turned to face the rest of his brood. "What are y'all giggling about?"

Smiles was always giggling, even as a sixteen-year-old. He faced Bear first, with the brightest smile, of course. He carried so much of his mother's light, and Bear loved him fiercely. Technically, Smiles was his oldest child, as Link had come to him through his wife. He'd legally adopted Lincoln about seven years ago now, right before the boy had graduated from high school. He'd changed his last name to Glover, because it meant something to be a Glover.

"Nothin', Daddy," Smiles drawled. "How's Grandmother?"

"She's irritated that you lot couldn't be quiet during the prayer." He took a couple of steps toward his teens and tweens, and then opened up his arms for all of them to step into. They did, each of them used to his quips and jabs—and also his great big marshmallow heart.

Sammy always reminded him of that "heart of gold," she called it, and she could send him a look from across the kitchen to remind him to use it. Rock, his fourteen-year-old had definitely inherited some of Bear's more grizzly genes, as had his first daughter, Heather.

Sunnie, who sat behind all the other children at nearly eleven had never given neither him nor Sammy much trouble at all.

"Uncle Ranger is comin' out," Link said, and Bear pulled away from his kids.

"We've got a lot of work to do today," he said.

"You say that every day," Heather griped. "It's not like today is any different than yesterday, Daddy."

"Of course it is." He threw her a look out of the side of his eye. "For one, it's Friday, and that means Momma will let us go to town and get dinner." He grinned at her as she rolled her eyes.

"Can we get the fish fry?" Sunnie asked.

"Ew, I hate fish," Rock argued with her. "Why can't we ever just do something normal, like burgers and fries?"

"We had burgers and fries at the beginning of the month," Smiles said.

"I'm sure you could give us the exact date." Rock sounded like his name—gravely and hard—but Bear smiled as he reached the gate that led into the family cemetery that overlooked part of Shiloh Ridge Ranch.

"And secondly," he said, glancing past Link, who'd said nothing, to Sunnie. "All the other cowboys from all the other ranches are comin' to help us here today. We have to show them a good time —and that we know how to work."

"We obviously do," Heather said. "We spent all day yesterday at Aunt Libby's place."

And the day before that, they'd been out at another ranch. A smaller, one-man unit run by Ace's wife's sister, Bethany Ann and her husband Kevin.

Today, Shiloh Ridge Ranch had the honor of hosting everyone from the surrounding ranches, and he wasn't surprised at all to see Ranger and Oakley piling their teens into the truck. Bear didn't turn toward the homestead where Ranger lived with his family, but instead, he steered his children toward True Blue, the bright blue family barn where they held almost all of the large gatherings on the ranch.

Yes, the Angel Tree still got decorated in the homestead, and some meals eaten there too. Birthdays, anniversaries, things like that. But big family parties for Easter or feeding all the cowboys on Market Day or after the round-up—those happened in True Blue.

Today's festivities—if they could be called that —would stem out from True Blue. He'd left Sammy there twenty minutes ago to take the children to the cemetery, which was one of the first sites they'd cleaned up after the flooding.

It hadn't been damaged much, as the river which flowed through the ranch sat much further back than the cliffs that led down to the second homebase of their property. Preacher and Mister lived down there, closer to the highway, and they'd built a horseshoe of cowboy cabins, a couple of barns, and a storage facility too.

As Bear let his children bicker about who got to do what that day, and who would pair up with the teens from Seven Sons Ranch, he let his feelings of gratitude flow through him. Not only that, but he could feel an inkling of heaven in his old bones. A light from above telling him that he'd done a good job with this ranch. That his father and grandfather were proud of him, and that it would be okay if he receded further into retirement.

He certainly had enough brothers and cousins —and now another rising generation—to help him. Bear had resisted fading further than he had in the past decade or so. Ward and Preacher were both foremen of the ranch, and they ran the day-to-day operations. Things Bear had used to do, so he could focus on his family.

But they had families too, and all the Glovers still stepped up and in to help each other whenever possible. Bear couldn't even imagine what he'd fill his days with if it wasn't getting up, getting his chores done, helping Sammy get the kids off to school, and then spending his days with fields, feed, animals, and the glory of the sun and sky. His horses. His dogs. His family. His land.

No, Bear wasn't the *sit-in-a-rocking-chair-and-sip-coffee* type of cowboy, but as he watched Link reach the door to True Blue first and hold it open while everyone else went by him, Bear wondered if that sitting, rocking, and sipping lifestyle couldn't also be part of what he did every day.

"Link," he said just as the twenty-five-year-old turned to follow his siblings.

The young man turned back to him, and though they shared no genes, Bear could see so much of himself in Link. "Yeah?"

"You're a good man, son." Bear wasn't sure how to articulate everything he felt. He'd been working on it with Sammy for a decade and a half, but it was easier with her. "Do you want to welcome everyone to the ranch?"

Link's eyes grew wide. "I—me?"

"Yeah, you." Bear smiled. "You know what to say. Lord knows you've heard me or Ranger say it a thousand times." He stepped into his step-son who felt like his own flesh and blood and pulled him close, his hand curling up behind Link's cowboy hat. "I'm getting old, and I want you to have whatever you want here on the ranch."

He'd moved out while earning a two-year degree in agricultural management from City College in Amarillo, and when he'd come back to the ranch a few years ago, he'd not moved back into the two-story house where Bear lived with his wife and family.

Rather, Link had moved into a cowboy cabin with three other men, most of whom were at least ten years older than him. He was an agreeable man who didn't say much, put his head down, and worked hard.

"I like working with Uncle Ward on the rotational ranching," Link said, his voice quiet. He pulled back, and Bear let him go. Link looked past him, to those approaching True Blue. Their time was running out, and Bear didn't need to practice a welcome speech. He certainly had given one plenty of times in the past.

"I'm not sure I'm meant to do what you or Ranger do," Link said quietly. "But I sure do like working on the ranch. I like planning crops and moving the turkeys and sheep from place to place." His eyes, which had been flitting all over tarnation, came back to Bear's. "I could just do that?"

"And live in a cowboy cabin forever?"

"It's not like I'm dating anyone." Link gave him a smile. "So yeah, I'm okay there."

"For now," Bear said with plenty of emphasis. "You never know when you'll meet someone and fall in love. Do you want to live on the ranch?"

Link took a big breath and blew it out. "Yeah," he said. "I love it here."

"Morning, boys," Ranger said, and that ended their conversation. *For now*, Bear told himself again as he turned toward his cousin and the man who'd been at his side, running Shiloh Ridge, for decades.

"Morning, Range." Bear drew him into a back-clapping hug too, and then he looked over to Ranger's kids and wife. "Oak. Wild. Fawny." The thirteen-year-old gave him a bright smile.

"Uncle Bear, did you know Momma got another cat?"

Bear grinned and grinned, his gaze traveling to Oakley in time to see her roll her eyes. "I heard."

"We have a whole ranch to clean up," Oakley said. She'd dressed the part too, because she'd never shied away from a ranch task. Before she'd come up here to be Ranger's wife and raise her kids, she'd owned a massive motor sports complex, and before that, she'd been a winning Formula One racecar driver.

So if she wanted another cat, Bear wasn't going to tease her about it.

"And if you're going to tell everyone about that kitten." Oakley nudged her daughter toward the door. "Remember, you're helping Aurora with her kids today."

"Momma, I don't want to babysit all day," Fawn complained as they walked in and the door to True Blue closed behind them.

Wilder would turn sixteen this year, and he looked so much like his name. His hair grew long and curled—a little wild. He had both Ranger's and Oakley's dark, dark, deep eyes, and he could look like he might go postal in one moment and then those eyes sparkled with life and laughter in another.

"Daddy, can I work with Link and Smiles today?"

"I don't even know if Link and Smiles will be together," Ranger said. "But go on in with him. Stand by 'em, and you'll probably get your way."

The two boys went inside, leaving Bear with his cousin. Behind them, gravel crunched under tires and engines growled as cowboys from other ranches started arriving in their trucks. Bear sighed and looked at Ranger. "We've been here before. We can do this."

"Tornadoes," he said. "Blizzards. What's a flood?" Ranger grinned, and together, they turned to start greeting the other ranchers and cowboys from around Three Rivers.

Hours later, Bear's back ached as he helped Finn Ackerman lift a fence post that had once been the cornerstone of a pasture. "Got it?" He grunted out the words as the man half his age bore the weight of the post.

"Yep." Finn too spoke in a clipped tone, and his face scrunched for a moment while he got the heavy post up and over the lip of the trailer. Relief sang through Bear's muscles then, and he hadn't even been doing most of the work.

"Lunch time," he said, and Finn clapped his gloved hands together.

"You guys have way less water up here," Finn said, something Bear had heard multiple times from the cowboys at Three Rivers. "Have you been to town?"

"Several times," Bear said, glancing over to Aaron, one of his cowboys from here at Shiloh Ridge. He had Rock, Wilder, and Robbie with him too, and Finn came with a cowboy named Thomas from Three Rivers, and Alex and Edith Baxter from a small ranch northeast of town.

"Seems like all the water flowed out of the hills," Edith said as she came to Finn's side. She had a smudge of mud on her face, and as she looked at Finn, Bear definitely saw fireworks between them. "We've still got quite the raging river at Coyote Pass."

"Same," Finn said.

"That's why we haven't been up north yet," Bear said. Everyone would be working at Shiloh Ridge today and tomorrow, and then they'd all take a much-needed break for the Sabbath. Monday, the cowboys had agreed to work in town, where water still ran down some streets as it continued to drain out of the foothills.

Rhett and Tripp Walker lived on the same road—Quail Creek—at the bottom of the hills here at Shiloh Ridge—and they'd been flooded the entire week. Thankfully, they could relocate to Seven Sons Ranch across the highway and further south, but Bear wouldn't want to have his whole family living in someone else's house for very long.

"Seven Sons on Tuesday," Aaron said. "Won't we start heading up north next week?"

"Three Rivers is on Thursday and Friday," Finn said. "I know that." He slid his hand into Edith's. "When are we going to your place?" He glanced over to Alex, who'd pulled out his phone.

"Saturday," Alex said without looking up. "We're hoping the river recedes before then."

"Another week," Bear said. "And it's not supposed to rain. Should get back to normal."

"Well, water has to have somewhere to go," Aaron said. "Our lakes and ponds are overfull, so."

Bear's stomach growled, and he turned away from the conversation. "Come on, boys. It's lunchtime, and then Ward or Preach will have more work for us."

"Can I drive, Uncle Bear?" Robbie asked.

"I'm older than you," Wilder said. "If anyone gets to drive, it's me."

"I'm his son," Rock said. "I should get to drive."

Bear rolled his eyes toward the heavens and prayed, "Lord, help me survive these boys."

Behind him, several people laughed as they loaded up into the big dump truck they'd brought out here to pick up their large fallen items.

"I'm driving," he said over the teenage boy bickering. "It's Aunt Dot's truck, and it's not your normal fare. Just get in." All three boys could fit in the space for two, as they all seemed to be made of skin, bones, and muscles, and Bear got behind the wheel.

He waited for the other cowboys to load up in Aaron's ranch truck, and he didn't miss for a moment the way Finn and Edith stuck super close to one another, all smiles despite the soggy mess here at the ranch.

"Wonder how Squire feels about this," Bear mused to himself as he started the growly dump truck. After all, Finn had only been home for a week now, and he was already dating someone? That felt fast to Bear, but he hadn't started dating seriously until his forties, so he didn't really know how young people operated these days, especially in the realm of romance.

Back at True Blue, several tables held platter after platter of food, and Bear had never been so happy to see it.

"Wow, you're a mess," Sammy said, and Bear

growled as he swung his arm around his lovely wife's waist and pulled her into him.

"Some of us have been out working," he murmured just before he touched his lips to hers.

"Yeah, and some of us have been *in* working," she whispered back.

Bear had no idea what it took to feed a hundred people, but Sammy did, and he kneaded her closer. "Thank you, my love."

"How's it look out there?"

"About like I do."

Sammy grinned up at him and stroked her hand down the side of his beard. "I'm sure it'll be immaculate again before too long." She looked away, her eyes tracking those who'd just come in behind Bear. "Look at Finn and Edith."

"I've seen 'em," Bear murmured.

"They're cute. They dated a little in high school."

"Mm."

"Oh, and something a little closer to home...." Sammy's head swiveled and then she nodded toward the far side of the hall, which had hosted weddings, anniversary dinners, birthday parties, and Thanksgiving dinners. "There. See him?"

"Who am I looking at?" Bear asked, because

between where he stood closer to the kitchen and behind the tables of food, and the front entrance of True Blue, there had to be sixty people.

"Mitch."

Bear found the young man, who was slightly older than Link, and he currently stood with Ollie, Aurora, and a woman Bear didn't know. "Who's that?"

"Sarah Hedger."

"Who the devil is Sarah Hedger?" Bear frowned. "You say things like I should know them."

"You shouldn't," Sammy said, taking his attitude in stride. "She's not a cowgirl. Doesn't work at a ranch."

"Then what's she doing here?" He watched as she signed something as she said it, and Mitch's face glowed like Judge's house at Christmastime— with lights and music and rays from heaven. He laughed next, and when he looked at Sarah, it was with all the stars in the sky. "Oh, boy."

"She came to help," Sammy said, hitting the P hard. "And she has, but I think she's trying to help herself to some of Mitch Glover." She grinned, and then someone called her name, and she slipped away from Bear.

As he stood on the cusp of everything and everyone at Shiloh Ridge Ranch that day, he had the very real feeling that things were about to shift again. He'd started the tilting and restructuring of the Glover family years ago, when he'd finally broken the bachelor mold and started dating Sammy.

She'd brought the perfect feminine touch to the ranch, and all of his siblings and cousins had gotten married after him. They all had families, and the majority of them lived and worked right here on the ranch.

And now, some of them were old enough to date, get married, and start building a family of their own too. Bear relaxed at the thought, because that was what they were meant to do. This ranch wouldn't be his forever, but he'd taught his kids the legacy of it. All of the Glovers had.

Their next generation would do just fine, and as Bear watched another young woman—this one actually wearing jeans and boots and a cowgirl hat —join the conversation near the entrance, he smiled.

She was talking to Link. And he spoke back.

"Yeah, we'll be okay," he murmured to himself. Things would change, as they always did, but with a little luck and a lot of faith and hard work, Shiloh Ridge Ranch would live on.

"Bear," his sister called. "Stop staring and come eat."

He found Zona sitting down with her husband and Bishop, and Bear grinned at them. Then he stopped staring and went to eat.

8

Edith hung her leg over the side of the hammock and pushed herself back and forth, most of her attention on her phone. Frankie, Otto, and Gumbo had jumped up into the hammock with her, and her feet and shins would probably overheat in another few minutes.

But she didn't mind so much. She didn't really feel the muggy heat of today, because she and Finn had been texting back and forth like wildfire. Sometimes their conversations stopped abruptly at night, because he'd fallen asleep.

Edith liked to tease him about that, and he didn't deny it. He'd been coming by Coyote Pass every day, even if he only stayed for an hour and helped them get their animals fed.

The water receded a ton today, she tapped out to him. He'd been getting closer and closer to more personal things, and Edith wasn't sure she wanted to tell him about certain things via text.

"They feel like in-person conversations," she muttered to herself. But when Finn came over, they'd been catching up on other things. What she'd been doing the past several years. What he'd been doing. He'd told her he'd lived in Washington D.C. for a while, then Germany. She'd told him about her time in Long Island, her internship, the creative writing classes at NYU, all while skirting around Levi and why she'd come back to Three Rivers when seemingly everything back East had been going so well for her.

Finn wasn't a stupid man, and his next text came in only a breath behind hers. *I was wondering what brought you back to town.*

Edith needed some time with him to talk about that. She wanted to be in his physical presence, so she could see his face, watch his reaction, hold his hand. She hadn't had the warming contact of another human being she wasn't related to in so long, and while Finn had only held her hand a couple of times—it was kind of hard to cuddle and snuggle and intertwine fingers when they were shoveling out stalls, changing bandages on a horse, and fixing fences.

Edith sighed out her frustration, because it was only with herself. She tapped to call Finn, something she'd not done before. But the cowboys from his ranch would be at Coyote Pass tomorrow, and she needed things to accelerate a little if she wanted to take a step forward with him.

He'd been a little too laid back, and Edith hadn't realized it until this moment.

"You're calling me," he said.

"You don't say," she teased.

"I'm just—what's up?" His voice pitched up happily, and Edith smiled too.

She closed her eyes and felt the movement of the hammock beneath her. "I want to tell you why I decided to come back to Three Rivers," she said. "But Finn, it...it...it's something I want to do in person, so." She took a breath, trying to find the forward version of herself.

She'd never really asked out a man before. They usually asked her, the way Finn had that day in the parking lot at Courage Reins over two weeks ago now.

"So I'm wondering when you're going to ask me out," she said, lifting her chin as she did. Her eyes popped open, and she took in the bright blue sky above. "I mean, I know we're both running at both ends of the candle, so maybe—I don't know. Maybe you'd like to—"

"Stop talking," he yelled, and Edith snapped her mouth closed, her dinner invite at the farmhouse tomorrow night dying in her throat. Finn sighed heavily over the line. "I'm sorry, Edith. I just—didn't want *you* to ask *me* out."

"Okay," she said, that warmth starting to glow inside her chest.

"We *have* been busy with all the flooding and all the work at all the ranches," he said. "I've been looking at the community calendar, trying to find something I think you'd like to do, but they've canceled so much."

"You know what I like to do?" she asked.

"I have some idea," he said, his voice somewhat defensive. "I've been getting to know you with the texts too. But since you're so anxious to see me, what about dinner tomorrow night? We can go out, or I can bring something to the ranch and just...stay after everyone else leaves."

Edith had been about to offer to cook for him

but going out or having him bring something sounded better. She and Alex would feed lunch to everyone who came to help. It wouldn't be anything like the women from Shiloh Ridge Ranch, but Edith had ordered sandwich boxes from The Bread Company. She had to get up extra-early to go pick them up.

"So if you've been gathering ideas," she said. "Where would you take me for dinner in town?"

"That's a trick question," he said. "Not everywhere is open."

Edith grinned and even allowed a light laugh to come out. "I was going to suggest you stay here for dinner."

"At the farmhouse?"

"Yes," Edith said, the word only scratching slightly in her throat. "Here. I can arrange for Alex to be somewhere else."

"Somewhere else? Where would he be?"

"Well, he's been retreating to his bedroom the moment he can," she said. "He's exhausted, and he's got that little cold, so if I feed him and give him some meds, I'm fairly sure we'd have the farmhouse to ourselves for a couple of hours."

"You're going to drug your brother?" Finn

started to laugh, and the sound of it filled her from head to toe with joy.

"You should know I'm not a great cook."

"I doubt that," Finn said among his chuckles. "You told me about your baking habit just the other day."

"Baking and cooking are two different things."

"So what will you make?" he asked. "You're going to be busy tomorrow, Edith. People at your place. You're already feeding them. I don't think me making you then cook for me is a great idea for a first date. I'm trying to impress you, not drive you away."

"You're trying to impress me?"

"Of course I am," he said.

She couldn't erase her smile if she tried. "Okay, well, if you've been looking at the community calendar and know what restaurants are closed, what's the best option for what's open?"

"My grandma Armstrong's," he said.

Edith paused, her mind running now. "Your grandma's...?"

"She's got a great backyard," he said. "It was one of my favorite places to visit when I was a kid. And she's a great cook, and I bet if I call her, she'd make us something awesome. And she won't bother us."

Edith liked it when Finn talked a lot. He didn't always, but when he did, Edith learned a lot. "You lived with your grandparents for a bit, didn't you?"

"Yeah," Finn said. "You remember that?"

"Yeah," she said. "So dinner tomorrow?"

"Edee," Alex called, and she lifted her head. "Do we have any more of that cold medicine you gave me last night?"

"Go drug your brother," Finn teased. "I'll arrange dinner for tomorrow. Just the two of us."

"Just the two of us," Edith whispered. "Sounds nice."

Finn cleared his throat. "It does, doesn't it?"

"See you tomorrow, Finny." His old nickname came out before she'd even thought about it, but Finn didn't correct her. He simply said, "See you tomorrow, sweetheart," and ended the call.

"Edee," Alex called again. "Are you in the hammock? Did you fall asleep?"

Her sigh could've blown up a hot air balloon, and she struggled to get out of the hammock while she called, "I'm not asleep."

Frankie yipped as she tipped the hammock,

and then Otto jumped out before she could dump him out. Gumbo meowed as Edith walked away, and she went around the corner of the house. "It's in that skinny cupboard beside the stove. Second shelf, above the salt and pepper shakers."

"I looked there. It wasn't there."

"Maybe we're out."

"We can't be out." Alex looked miserable. "My head feels like someone pumped it up with air."

"I'll go get more," she said as she came up the steps. "Finn's going to stay for dinner tomorrow night. Can you be scarce?"

Alex managed a small smile, about the best he could do when he didn't feel well. "I'll take a bunch of meds and watch TV in my room."

"Thank you." Edith met him and cradled his face in one palm. "I'm going to have to tell him about Levi."

"Yeah, you are."

Edith moved past him, her mind whirring. "I don't know how to do that."

"You just open your mouth and start talking."

"Sounds so easy," Edith muttered to herself. Inside, she couldn't find more medicine, though she also didn't remember giving him the last of it yesterday. "I'll head into town. What else do we need for tomorrow or the weekend?"

"You'd know better than me." He opened the freezer and stuck his face inside. "I'm so hot."

Edith rolled her eyes, because she'd seen her father act this same way when he got the slightest sniffle. "I'll get you some fever reducers. Lay down and sleep until I get back."

"I haven't eaten either."

"I'll get us something in town." Edith didn't have much energy left, but she suddenly did want to be away from this place, in a car by herself, where she could think through how to talk to Finn tomorrow night.

By evening the following day, Edith suspected she'd started to come down with her brother's cold. They'd had thirty men and women at Coyote Pass that day, and everything that could be set right had been.

All their fences had been rebuilt, checked, or strengthened. Their chicken coop rebuilt. A temporary irrigation system put in place to move the water out of their fields and back to the river downstream.

It continued to get smaller and smaller as the hot Texas sun shone on the land, and Alex had met with Ward Glover and Paul Marshall, both trained in agriculture, to get their fields replanted or beefed up after the loss from the flood.

Debris had been raked into a couple of piles, one for smaller twigs and branches, and one for the bigger logs from their fences that couldn't be reused. Alex would do a planned burn once things had dried even more, and one of the cowboys from Seven Sons had even mowed their grass.

Finn had said he'd run home to shower, and Edith had done the same. She took a couple of pain killers and one nasal decongestant and finished clipping her hair back on the sides. She put on her favorite lipstick, a shade called Pretty Peony that made her mouth have any color at all.

She lined her eyes with black and put on mascara only to make her fair features stand out. And with that done, she pulled on a pair of white shorts she'd bleached clean last night, and then pulled a blue flowered blouse over her shoulders and did up the buttons. The blue would bring out her eyes and make her blonde hair shine, and Edith did know how to make herself look good.

She didn't always do it, but this was her first date with Finn Ackerman, and she had some hard things to tell him. Hard for her, at least.

The doorbell rang, and Edith froze. She'd told Alex that they didn't need the house after all, and he'd said he wanted to answer the door when Finn came over. Edith had rolled her eyes, but she'd let her brother have his fun.

She moved to the edge of the doorway, the guest bedroom right across the hall. The pictures of Levi sat on the shelf just inside the door, and Edith glanced down the hall as she heard male voices.

They didn't come closer, and Edith darted across the hall. She picked up the picture of her and Levi, noting the pure happiness in both of their faces. Levi, with his dark hair and those shining London fog eyes. He was so handsome, and he'd been so charming. So smart. So perfect for her.

"Can there be another man for me, Lord?" she asked. "Or does every person just get that one glove that fits so well, and no one else will do?"

Levi had been her glove. Everything about

him had agreed with her, and Edith felt like she'd already had the fairy tale love story. Too bad her tale hadn't turned out with a happily-ever-after.

"Edee?" Alex called. "You ready?"

She kept her eyes on Levi's face for another moment, and then she said, "I'm going out with someone else, Levi. It might be a nightmare, but I'm even more worried that it won't be...." She trailed off, because she had no idea what the next two hours looked like or felt like.

Go on, she heard in her mind, but it wasn't Levi's voice. He'd been gone too long for her to hear him anymore. But she felt prompted to put down the picture and go see if this date with Finn would be the start of something amazing or the end of her dating experiences for good.

"I'm coming," she said as she replaced the picture on the shelf. She went down the hall and past her brother. She could only see Finn in all his cowboy glory.

He wore jeans and cowboy boots, but they were a step up—probably four or five—from the working ones he'd worn an hour ago. His shirt was orange, navy, and white in a sexy plaid pattern, and as she neared, he reached up and tipped his dark, deep, rich brown cowboy hat.

"Ma'am," he said. "Don't you look like a million bucks?"

"You look incredible," she said.

"He wore that hat earlier," Alex said in a deadpan.

"It's actually a different one," Finn said. "I borrowed it from my uncle. He said it's what he wears on date night every week. He says it never fails."

Edith smiled at him and laced all ten of her fingers through his. That touch felt so intimate and so perfect, and they hadn't even left the farmhouse yet. She twisted and looked over her shoulder. "You're okay here, Alex?"

"I know where the pills are," he said. "And we have extra sandwiches from lunch."

"Okay." She faced Finn again, a sudden bout of shyness pulling through her. She fought against ducking her head and tucking her hair, because she always did that, and it told Finn how she felt.

Seeing as how Edith couldn't really categorize her feelings as more than sheer desire and attraction, she didn't want him to know that.

"Should we go?" she asked.

After slipping one hand out of hers, he offered

her his arm, and said, "I'd go anywhere with you, princess."

Edith felt like a princess on his arm, and she didn't look back though Alex said something under his breath. She couldn't wait until he started seeing someone, and then she could tease him.

But for tonight, she wanted to enjoy her alone-time with Finn—and she had to find the right words to tell him about Levi.

9

Finn had learned to take life one day at a time. When he'd decided to retire from the Army, he'd deliberately made no plans other than returning to Three Rivers. For a couple of weeks there, he'd even debated doing that.

"But in the end," he said as he shook out the last of his potato chips. "I had to come home. I don't think my momma would've forgiven me if I hadn't." He smiled at Edith, who hadn't seemed nervous on the way over to his grandma's house.

He hadn't even taken her inside to introduce them. Grandma Armstrong had set everything out on the picnic table in the backyard, where they currently sat in the shade, a nice breeze keeping them comfortable.

There had been no flooding here, as Grandma and Grandpa Armstrong lived in a suburb on a little swell of land, and all the water had stayed at the lower elevations. Even a foot or two made such a huge difference.

"So." He ground his voice through his throat, because he'd done most of the talking already tonight. "You said you'd tell me why you came back to Three Rivers after I told you why I did."

"So you came so your parents wouldn't be upset."

"Yeah," he said.

"Are you going to stay?"

He gave her a smile that felt a little false on his face. "Right now, I'm exploring options." If that didn't tell her he had no idea what next week or next month or next year would bring, Finn didn't know what would. He also hated not having at least a skeleton plan for what he was doing in his life.

"You sure seemed to like living back East," he said. "You had a good job. Your publisher was there. Why would you come back to the barren Texas Panhandle to work a ranch with Alex?"

"We've always gotten along really well," Edith said, her back straightening. It shot a hint of lightning through Finn, and not in a good way.

"You're dodging this," he said. "Why can't you just tell me why you came back?"

She blinked at him, and he realized he'd used his military intelligence voice. "I'm right," he said, looking away. "It can't be that bad, can it?"

"I just don't know how you're going to take it."

"Then you better give it to me, so I can take it." He glanced at her and quickly looked away when he found her eyes down on her hands as she picked at her nails. That wasn't a good sign, as he'd seen her do that when she was nervous. Still, he liked knowing that some of her tells were the same.

Edith Baxter was still in there, even if she'd had a decade of experiences he needed to catch up on.

"I was living in Long Island," she said. "Then the city, as I took some classes, worked at Glory Publications, and wrote my books."

"Mm."

"I—I—Finn, can you let me just say everything, and then we can talk about it?"

He looked at her again, and he could tell this ask was very important to Edith. "Okay," he said.

"I might cry," she said, and she sniffled and wiped at her eyes already. "It's fine. I'm fine, okay? It's just—sometimes I cry when I talk about this."

"Can I come sit by you and hold your hand?"

"Would you, please?"

Finn got up and rounded the picnic table. They both faced away from the house now, and he used to be able to see out into the wilds of Texas from this vantage point in his grandma's backyard. But new houses had gone up, and now he saw fences and other yards in the distance. Still, it was a quiet neighborhood, with nothing to distract them and no one to overhear what they said.

He took her hand in both of his, effectively quieting her nervous nail-picking habit as he hoped to infuse her with some semblance of comfort. "Whatever it is, it'll be fine," he said. "I can't promise to react well, but once I know, then I can —at least I'll know."

"Right," she said. She drew in a long breath, held it, and started her story as the air left her lungs. "I met someone at work. His name was Levi Kingsley."

Finn said nothing, as she'd requested, though the pause made him feel like he should at least hum or say, "Okay." But he refrained, because she was talking about another man. And she didn't have to say more—he knew she'd been in love with him.

"We—were—engaged," she said, her voice laboring over every word. "I loved him so much, Finn," and in that moment, Finn realized how past-tense everything she said was. His heart pounded, because he wasn't sure what had happened or how this had led Edith here.

If she'd gone through a painful break-up, wouldn't she want to be with her mother in Florida? Why Three Rivers, with Alex?

He squeezed her hand and murmured, "I'm sorry, Edith."

She shook her head, her lovely blonde hair swinging. Her eyes and voice held tears, but none trailed down her face. "He got diagnosed with a rare form of brain cancer one benign day in March, after he hadn't been feeling well for a few months. He'd been acting really weird, and not at all like himself, and well, the brain tumor explained a lot, actually."

Finn wasn't sure what he'd been expecting her

to say, but it wasn't that her fiancé had been diagnosed with brain cancer.

"So we decided to move here," she said. "Alex had just bought Coyote Pass, and they gave Levi thirty days to live." She sniffled then, and she started to weep. Finn wanted to take the pain right from her and put it on himself. He put his arm around her and brought her close to his chest, where the heat from her breath and tears touched his skin through his shirt.

"We started making plans to move, expecting that I would do it after he passed away in the city. But he didn't."

Finn stroked her hair, wondering how he'd feel if someone he loved enough to marry had been suddenly diagnosed with something terrible enough to take them from the earth in only thirty days.

"We moved here in May, and he was able to see this town where I grew up. He loved the wide open fields and the fresh air. He'd never been to Texas before, and he lived with Alex and I in that farmhouse, in the guest bedroom where you saw those photos."

Ah, of course, Finn thought. "Did you marry him?"

Edith sat up straight and shook her head. "No, because the move took up so much energy, and then we were focused on providing him with the best experiences possible. I started to plan a wedding, especially because Levi made it to thirty days, and then sixty, and then ninety. He survived a cross-country move."

Finn sensed a "but," but he didn't say it. Edith cried softly and quietly for several long moments, and Finn wanted to console her. Tell her everything was okay. But how could he? What words would make this okay?

She'd asked him to let her tell the story before he said anything, and he now knew that was one of the hardest things he'd ever agreed to do. He fought against the words in his throat, and he prayed for the right reaction. He didn't know what it would be for Edith, and he didn't want to hurt her more than she'd already been hurt.

"He died in September," she whispered. "Coming up on three years at the end of this summer."

"I'm so sorry," Finn said. Why had God given the human race those words when they weren't anywhere near adequate enough?

"He's buried here in town," she said. "His parents came, but he was an only-child, and they said he should be near me."

Finn's stomach hollowed, and he had no idea how to respond to that. She didn't say anything else, and Finn's questions piled on top of one another. Did she go visit Levi every day? Did she confide in him still, the way his Daddy sometimes went to the cemetery to talk to his father?

Could she ever fall in love with someone else? Had she dated since Levi's death? Did she regret coming to Three Rivers, especially now that it had some negative memories attached to it? Would she ever leave with Levi buried here?

His throat felt like he'd stuffed a sock down it, and none of his questions came out.

"I do love it here," Edith said next. "It's so peaceful. So quaint. There's nowhere like Three Rivers."

"So I guess you'll be staying."

"I have nowhere else to go."

Finn nodded, though she wasn't looking at him. She cuddled into his side, and he kept a good grip on her body to keep her close. "Have you dated anyone since...since he—?" Finn couldn't even say the words.

"No," Edith said quietly. "You're the first."

He wasn't sure if he liked that or not. She'd had time to grieve somewhat, but Finn knew from the experience of losing his grandfather that loss was loss, and it could sneak up on a person at any time. Time didn't always dull it, and the human brain could hold so many memories.

After several minutes of the two of them sitting quietly together, Edith had calmed and Finn took a breath. "Well, the good news is that my break-up stories aren't anything compared to this."

Edith managed a laugh, and that got Finn to smile. She looked at him, and even with her smudged eyeliner, she was the most beautiful woman he'd ever laid eyes on. She laughed harder, and then harder, and Finn was sure what he'd said wasn't so funny.

"Edith," he said.

A horrified look crossed her face, and her demeanor started to fall. "I'm sorry," she said just before she started weeping again. This wasn't exactly how Finn had hoped tonight's first date would go, but he'd known she had something to tell him.

"Let's go," hc said, though it was barely eight o'clock, and they still had plenty of daylight left.

"Go where?"

He stood up and started cleaning up the dinner his grandma had made for them. Sloppy Joes with cole slaw, potato chips, and fruit salad. A lot of his favorites, which he hadn't requested but had hoped for.

"I'll take you home," he said as he stacked their paper plates and put them in a garbage bag his grandma had left on the table.

"I don't want to go home," Edith said.

Finn paused in his work and looked over to Edith. She blinked at him, and Finn hadn't planned anything but this romantic outdoor meal. He figured they'd eat and talk and laugh and talk, and it would be amazing.

He had not anticipated a fiancé, and least of all, one who'd passed away.

"Let's go walk Main Street," he said. "We can get dessert."

Edith brightened. "Yeah, dessert. I like dessert."

Finn put a smile on his face too. "I'll find you the richest brownie I can, I promise."

"Someone's been paying attention to my texts."

He wasn't going to deny that. "Trying to impress you, remember?"

"I think you're miles ahead of me," she said. "You haven't sobbed and ruined our first date."

Finn took her trash and put it in the bag. "You haven't ruined anything. We can go up to the house, and you can...freshen up, and then we'll go."

"I want to tell your grandmother thank you, too."

"Yeah, me too," he said, though he hadn't planned on introducing her to his grandparents that evening. Of course they'd know her, as the Baxter's had lived in Three Rivers for years before they'd moved.

With the table cleaned up, Finn went over to her and took both of her hands in his. "Thank you, Edith. For telling me." His pulse rioted in the vein in his neck, but he couldn't just move on with the night, move on to some other conversation, and get brownies.

"I can't even imagine what you've been through. I...don't know what else to say." Something popped into his head, and he let it flow right out of his mouth. "I don't need to go fast. If you're not ready to go out with me, it's fine. Or, if you want to, we can just take things day by day, thing by thing."

She nodded and relaxed visibly in front of him. "Day by day sounds good."

"Would this be a bad time to ask you on a second date?" Finn grinned at her, glad when she smiled too.

She giggled, and it was such a cute sound. "You've survived me sobbing my eyes out, so I think you've earned a second date."

"Great," he said easily. "But maybe you'll want to wait to make sure I can get you the perfect brownie."

"I believe in your abilities, Finn," she teased. "Now, take me inside so I can fix my face and tell your grandmother thank you for dinner."

"Sure thing, sweetheart," he said, and while she did that, he'd call Fresh Baked and make sure they had the double chocolate dark brownies Edith had referenced in a text last week. Then, maybe this date would be salvageable. Then, maybe he wouldn't feel like he'd never be able to measure up to the man Edith had once loved.

And probably still loved.

As he led her inside, he told himself he could only be himself. Only Finn Ackerman. And that had to be enough. And if it wasn't...well, they'd take things day by day, like she'd said.

And to give himself something extra, Finn prayed while Edith exclaimed over dinner, then went to fix her makeup.

Just tell me what to do, he begged the Lord. *And I'll do it.*

He didn't get an answer right that moment, but Finn never had. He could be patient, and as he stood in his grandparent's kitchen, he remembered that within a few hours of returning to Three Rivers, he'd seen Edith from a window, a hundred yards away.

His heart took courage, and when Edith came out of the bathroom and asked, "Ready, Finn?" he smiled at her and felt stronger than ever.

"Ready."

10

Edith suddenly didn't know how to exist inside her own skin. She couldn't make her thoughts settle as Finn found a parking spot next to the park on Main Street. They hadn't spoken much since leaving his grandparent's house, because honestly, Edith had no idea what to say.

It felt like letting Levi's name out of her mouth had brought him back to life somehow. All she could think about was the things they'd done together. Walks through parks much bigger than the one she currently looked at. Finding all the dessert shops in the city. Laughing and learning about one another. Holding hands and kissing and falling in love.

Oh, how she'd loved falling in love with Levi.

She glanced over to Finn, who looked straight out the windshield. He turned toward her and gave her a handsome smile. "What's in your head right now?"

She smiled, because she'd forgotten that he used to ask her this. And she had to tell him the truth.

"You're hesitating," he said.

"I'm embarrassed," she said. "I feel like I've thrown ice water all over our spark."

He leaned his head back against the rest behind him. "We have a spark?"

Edith rolled her eyes. "If we don't, why'd you ask me out?"

"Probably because you're so pretty," he said. "And all those sparks I felt when I saw you standing on the sidewalk."

"Mm, right." She turned toward the park to get out of the truck. "Should we go get some ice cream to cool off?"

"Yep." He met her at the corner of the truck. "I'd have gotten your door."

She met his eyes, all the vulnerability inside her doubling and then tripling.

"Edith," he said softly. "You don't have anything to be embarrassed about." He took her hand and squeezed, and Edith sank into the touch of his skin against hers.

"I love holding hands," she whispered as he turned and fell to her side. "It's so simple, and yet it makes me feel so warm. It makes me feel like I belong somewhere, to someone." She shook her head, her emotions once again teetering on the edge of tears. "It's silly, I'm sure."

"It's not silly," he said. "I haven't held someone's hand in a long time." They walked along slowly, as if they didn't have a care in the world. "It feels really nice."

Edith smiled to herself as some of her humiliation started to bleed away. "You'll tell me what you think about...all of it, won't you?"

"I'm not sure what I'm supposed to think," he said. "I mean, I dated people too over the years. Nothing as serious as an engagement, but I don't— I don't know what I'm supposed to think."

Edith wasn't sure what she wanted him to say either. They walked to the corner to the light so they could cross the street, and she finally landed on a thought and found enough courage to look at him. "Finn, you're such a handsome man." She smiled at him, liking the bright fire of life in his eyes. "You're so sweet, and so good, and I guess I just want to know that I haven't ruined us before we even know if we can be us."

He reached up and covered her hand against the side of his face. "You haven't ruined anything."

She wanted to hug him, because she sought comfort through physical touch, so she eased into his arms. A thrill moved through her, and then she simply sank into his strength. "Thank you, Finn."

"I never get enough hugs," he whispered. "This might surprise you, but the Army isn't known for being touchy-feely."

Edith giggled, the sound releasing more of her tension and embarrassment, and she pulled back and looked up at him. "Are you touch-starved too?"

"Is that a thing?"

"It's absolutely a real thing," she said. "They mostly study it in infants who've been abandoned, but it can happen to anyone." She leaned back into his chest, wrapping her arms around him tightly again. "As you can imagine, Alex isn't the super huggy type."

He said nothing, but he held her just as tightly as she held him. "Please don't worry about what you said tonight. It's not like you could've kept him a secret from me forever, and my job in the Army was literally to think of and ask all the hard questions."

Edith's heart felt like a block of ice for a single beat, and then she melted to his side. "I'm sure that's true."

"What does that mean?"

"It means you're really smart, and you're right. You're going to make me tell you everything, even things I don't want to tell you."

"Day by day," he said. "And tonight, all I want to do is find something sweet and eat a lot of it." He led her across the street, where shops all connected together in old buildings lined the sidewalk. "Now, you said ice cream, but I know you want a brownie."

"I'd take both," Edith said. "Would you buy me both, Finny?"

"I'll get you whatever you want, sweetheart." He pressed a kiss to Edith's forehead, and her pulse boomed for the moment when she might be able to actually kiss him. But for tonight, she'd take that brownie and maybe some cherry chocolate ice cream and holding Finn Ackerman's hand.

THE FOLLOWING MORNING, EDITH PULLED ON her knee-high waders and headed out of the kitchen. The sun had come up, because June would arrive in only a couple more days, and it was hard to rise before the Texas sun in the summer.

Edith paused at the bottom of the steps beyond the deck and took a deep breath. She needed a moment to feel the sun on her bare shoulders. She needed to smell the grass that had come back with a vengeance after all the rain, and the dirt on the paths that led further onto the ranch, and the simple goodness of the air here.

"I miss you, Levi," she said, barely loud enough for her own ears to hear. "But not as much as before, so I'm okay." She squinted up into the sky. "Okay, baby? I'm okay."

Feeling better than ever, she headed into the stables to get the horses taken care of for the day. She put them out to pasture and mucked out the stalls, her dachshunds with her every step of the way. The collies went with Alex, and he hadn't been in the kitchen that morning.

The coffee had been made, so he was obviously up, and Edith would catch up with him later. She let her imagination run wild while she worked, because she hadn't worked on her book in several days, and she could feel the scenes piling up on top of one another.

After they'd gotten brownies, cookies, and ice cream in waffle cones, the conversation had been easy and light. He'd told her stories about Washington D.C., which wasn't that far from New York City, where she'd been living.

She'd learned that he'd dated—"seriously dated" in his own words—four women in the past several years. He'd never been in love, and he'd told her that his last girlfriend in Germany was a story for another date.

And they did have another date, something that still made Edith giddy and shocked at the same time. He hadn't kissed her when he'd dropped her off last night, but neither of them seemed to be able to stop touching the other.

Edith knew she was touch starved, which was why she had two small dogs and a meowing cat to stroke whenever she needed to. But dogs and cats didn't compare to the delicious touch of a kind, generous, good-looking man.

Her phone chimed with Alex's notification, and Edith wiped her brow, feeling dirty and sweaty and like God had put her exactly where she needed to be. She picked up her phone from the shelf where she'd set it and saw his *HELP* easily.

She turned quickly from the bags of feed she'd been cataloguing, swiped her phone into her hand, and left the barn. "Alex," she called.

He spent more time dealing with the herd, checking fences, and making sure their fields didn't have pests and kept growing. All of that meant they stayed in business, could pay their bills, and had food on the table.

But he could be anywhere on the ranch, and he hadn't exactly dropped her a pin. "Alex!" She half-jogged toward the equipment shed where Alex kept a small office among all their machinery. The door stood open, but that wasn't that unusual.

The sound of her own breath and the hammering of her heart clouded her hearing, but she heard something that made her blood turn into icy shards.

Her brother cursing. Alex never did that.

"Alex?"

"We've got sinkholes," he called, and Edith rounded the corner to head out past the equipment shed.

"Sinkholes?" She found him out in the middle of a field, taking pictures on his phone. As she neared, she could definitely see that they didn't stand on the same level, that he stood down several feet. "Well—what—wh—what are we going to do about sinkholes?"

Edith had no idea what to do—she wasn't even sure what a sinkhole *was*—and by the look on Alex's face when he looked up at her said he didn't either. "I'm going to call Finn."

"Good idea," he said when she'd expected him to argue with her.

Edith pressed against the desperation building beneath her ribs, and she tapped aggressively on her phone. "Dear Lord," she said. "Sinkholes? Really?"

Finn's line rang, but she had no idea where he was or what he might be doing. Three Rivers Ranch spanned at least ten times as large as Coyote Pass, which was why they had ten times the personnel working it.

"Edith, my beauty," he said in the middle of the fourth ring. "What can I do for you?"

Edith exhaled, mostly to try to find the right thing to say. "Sinkholes," came blurting out of her mouth. "We have sinkholes on our ranch. What in the world do you do with a sinkhole? Just mow around it? Hope the land shifts and comes back up?" She threw her free hand up in to the air. "Why do sinkholes even exist? What *purpose* could they possibly have?"

"Edith," Finn said.

"Like, why did God create sinkholes? To torture those of us who've already had massive flooding on our ranches?" She shook her head, the sunshine hot and bright overhead.

"Are you done?" Finn asked, and how he had a teasing lilt in his voice, Edith wasn't sure.

"Yes," she said.

"So you've got sinkholes?"

She turned to face the one in front of her again. "Looks like it."

"How deep?"

"I don't know. At least six or seven feet. Alex is down there taking pictures."

"You've just got the one?"

"I have no idea."

"Do you need me to bring out the drone?"

"Let me ask Alex." She lowered her phone and called out to her brother. "Finn says he can bring the drone, so we can see if there's more than one."

"Yes, please." Alex faced her and started back toward her. "This says we have to excavate down to rock to fix this." He held up his phone as he marched toward her. "We need special equipment for this."

And that wasn't a bad thing for Alex. He loved vehicles of all kinds, including farm machinery. Tractors, balers, ATVs, and oh, boy, an excavator.

"He says he'd love to use the drone to see if we have more sinkholes."

"I'll talk to my uncle and be there as soon as I can."

"Thank you, Finn."

"What about lunch?"

"What...about lunch?"

"Have you eaten lunch?" he asked. "Either of you?"

"No," Edith said. "Is it lunchtime?"

Finn laughed, and he said, "I'll be there as soon as I can."

"As soon as he could" for Finn meant another ninety minutes, by which time Edith's stomach clawed at itself for something to eat. He'd texted several times since she'd called, keeping her updated with his progress, so she knew he was bringing Chinese food with him and the drone.

She sat on the front steps of the farmhouse when he rolled up, and Edith stayed right where she was, her phone on the plank beside her. Finn took several seconds to get out of the truck, because when he did, he had the bags of Chinese food looped over one wrist and the drone in the other hand.

"Need some help?"

"I can see I'm not gonna get it from you." He grinned at her as he neared. "Stay there. I've got it." He came up the steps and set the drone on the porch table where she sometimes sipped her coffee before church on Sundays.

Finn groaned as he sat down beside her. "We eatin' out here? Alex isn't hungry?"

"You try prying him away from the computer," she said dryly. "He's been researching how to fill sinkholes for an hour."

"My daddy's done it loads of times," Finn

said. "I mentioned it to him, and he said it's do-able."

"Yeah, well, maybe he should come do-able it." Edith leaned her shoulder into his. "It's good to see you."

He put his arm around her, and she settled further into him. "I looked up that touch starvation thing," he said. "You were right. I pretty much think I've been starving for a while now."

"I'm starving physically too," Edith said, though she didn't want to move away from his side. "Did you get that cashew chicken?"

"You told me to four times." The plastic bag rustled as he started rifling through it. "I figured I'd be dead if I showed up without it."

"I didn't tell you four times."

"You so did," he said. "I got that same text four times."

"That was a glitch then."

"Sure," he said with plenty of sarcasm. He handed her a white Chinese container and a pair of chopsticks. "Cashew chicken. I'll take Alex his, and we can drone after we eat."

"Is *drone* a verb?" she teased him as he got to his feet.

"You're the author," he said. "You should

know that." He flashed her a sexy, playful smile as he turned and took Alex's food into the house. She heard them talking behind her, but she flipped open her cashew chicken and took a bite.

Sure is nice to have someone to call for help, she thought. And Finn had come, bringing all the things she and Alex needed. The drone. Lunch.

And as he settled next to her on the steps again and said, "I got the orange chicken, and I'd be willing to share if you let me have your fortune cookie," Edith thought the best thing he'd brought was himself.

"I don't even like fortune cookies," she said with a smile. "So that's a done deal."

"You don't like fortune cookies?" He scoffed and used his chopsticks to move a chunk of orange chicken from his container to hers. "How is that possible?"

"It's possible, Chopstick."

He coughed and then burst out laughing. Edith grinned from ear to ear too, then she started giggling as she said, "Sorry, I don't know where that came from."

"You've always done that, Edith," he said.

"Done what?"

"Call me funny nicknames," he said. "Or whatever they are. Terms of endearment."

"*Chopstick* is a term of endearment?"

Finn stopped laughing, but his smile remained. His gorgeous blue eyes sparkled at her seriously as he said, "Coming from you, it is."

"All right, Butterscotch," she said next, and they laughed together, his hip and leg pressing against hers. Yes, Edith had been starving in so many ways before Finn, but with him at her side, she might finally be able to feel whole again. To heal completely when she hadn't been able to for years. To fall in love again.

11

Finn walked beside his father as they left the church with the other people who'd come to church that morning. They didn't speak, but Finn knew Daddy needed a moment with his daddy, and Finn didn't mind the slower, calmer atmosphere in the graveyard behind the church.

Momma had gone home with Aunt Chelsea and Uncle Pete, and Finn assumed a huge meal would be served at either the homestead or his uncle's when he and Daddy finally made it back to the ranch.

He stood in front of his grandfather's grave, his thoughts still circling Coyote Pass, Alex Baxter, and of course, Edith. He'd spent the afternoon there yesterday, and he wanted to head there again right now. He hadn't seen the Baxters in church, but he knew Edith and Alex attended.

Glancing over his shoulder, he caught his father swipe his cowboy hat from his head as his eyes drifted closed. Another couple had entered the cemetery, but they went left, away from where Finn stood with his praying daddy.

He looked back to the grave, the feeling inside him growing and growing and growing. "I'll be right back," he murmured, and Daddy grunted his acknowledgement.

Finn turned away from the familiar headstone, the one that brought comfort and peace to his soul, and wandered down the row. The breeze wafted through the leafy trees here, adding more coolness to the shade.

He tucked his hands in his pockets and drank in the Texas stillness. The bright blue sky. He reached the paved path that ran down the middle of the cemetery, and he walked to the end of it, where a gloriously golden field of wheat grew on the other side of the fence.

"I love it here," he whispered to himself. His heartbeat skidded through his veins as he realized

God had just given him a step to take. Or rather, a piece in the puzzle of his life—and that was to stay right here.

"But where?" he asked. "I can't live in my mother's basement forever."

Daddy would give him anything he wanted. An acre of the ranch to build a house. Or a cowboy cabin to himself. The whole ranch. The entire world.

But Finn had siblings, and he wasn't sure he wanted to run a cattle ranch. He'd enjoyed his time in the Army, and he'd been trained in some computer science for his job in intelligence. There were new companies in Three Rivers now, and Finn wondered about getting a job there. A small hobby farm. A wife, kids, someone to plant the garden with the way he had with his momma, daddy, and grandparents.

Finn knew farm and ranch work too, as he'd grown up at Three Rivers, and no one there simply lived without pulling their weight in some way. "I don't mind farm work," he whispered next, and that rang true in his heart too.

Turning back, he saw his daddy still holding his cowboy hat in front of his belt, and Finn went down the row to his right. He'd only taken four steps when he saw the name Levi Kingsley. Finn sucked in a breath and stopped.

"Levi Kingsley." He crouched down and wiped his hand across the letters of the man's name. "Beloved son, uncle, fiancé, and friend."

This was Edith's fiancé, and pure wonder streamed through Finn. He'd been twenty-eight years old when he'd passed, and that was simply far too young. Sadness that Finn didn't understand flowed through him, and then a sense of complete protectiveness. For Levi or someone else, Finn wasn't sure.

Edith, maybe?

He couldn't even imagine what it must've been like for her to stand here and mourn the loss of the man she'd loved. He straightened, the breath in his lungs streaming out. "Life's not very fair, is it, Lord?"

He stood there for another minute, and then the breath he took cleared his mind and his fears. "Help her to have an easier life now, okay?" With that, he smiled at Levi's headstone and turned to rejoin his father.

Daddy met him on the paved path, and Finn said, "Daddy?" in a voice quiet enough so as to not disturb the peace here. Daddy put his arm around

Finn and cocked his head in his direction, his cue to say, *I'm listening, son. Go on.*

Finn's nerves trembled, but he said, "Could the ranch spare me?"

"Spare you?"

"I've been thinking and praying a lot since yesterday," he said. "And I want to offer my help to Coyote Pass. They have nine sinkholes, Daddy. It'll consume Alex for a month, and that means the ranch won't be looked after. I could—" He swallowed. "I want to do it."

Daddy said nothing, but he dropped his hand from Finn's shoulder. They left the graveyard before his father said, "The ranch can spare you, son."

"It's not all about Edith," Finn said.

Daddy smiled with only half his mouth. "Of course it is," Daddy said. "And that's okay. I think you should be prepared to tell Momma more details than you have if you want to get up every morning, eat breakfast at the homestead, and then drive to Coyote Pass. But otherwise, it's fine if it's about Edith."

Finn got in his father's truck and buckled his seatbelt, his thoughts circling again. "I sure do like her, Daddy. She works all day on the ranch, and she writes at night. It hasn't been easy to see her."

"Working with her all day sure will make it easier, then, right?" His dad pulled out of the church parking lot and aimed the truck north.

"How should I talk to Edith about it?"

Daddy scoffed and half-laughed. He looked at Finn, who wasn't kidding. "Uh, I don't know?" He focused back on the road in front of him, but it was straight and boring. Finn had driven it many times, and it certainly didn't distract from any hard conversations. In fact, his father had often taken him to town for something completely un-needed simply so he could talk to him on the drive.

"She won't want me there," Finn said. "I'll have to have a really good reason."

"Nine sinkholes isn't a good reason?" Daddy asked.

Finn watched the fields go by. "She'll say they're fine. Maybe I should talk to Alex first." But that idea rang like a discordant gong in his head. No, he had to be a man, and bring it up with Edith first. She'd feel betrayed if he talked to her brother first and they doubled up on her.

His hand wandered to his phone, but he didn't

want to text her about this. "Daddy, will Momma be upset if you drop me at Edith's now and I skip lunch?"

He flipped on his blinker and slowed the truck to take the turn to Coyote Pass, the only answer Finn needed.

Fifteen minutes later, Daddy eased his truck to a stop in front of the farmhouse where Edith lived. Finn looked at the peaked roof, the spanning front porch, and the cheery wreath of yellow daffodils someone had put on the front door since the last time he'd been here. Which was yesterday.

It screamed Edith, as she'd always loved yellow flowers. Tulips, roses, daffodils, daisies, all of them. Finn couldn't believe he'd just now remembered that, and he wished he carried a bouquet of them right now for her. It might make this proposition of his easier for her to accept.

"Go on," Daddy said. "Surely you don't like her more than she likes you, right?"

"I think I might, actually," Finn admitted.

"I doubt it," Daddy said. "Go on, Finny. Just speak from your heart."

"Speak from my heart," Finn repeated. Then he flashed a smile at his father Daddy reached for the door handle. He climbed the steps. Rang the doorbell. Took a breath as he realized the daffodils were real and smelled like pollen.

The door opened just as he went into a sneezing fit, and as he achoo'ed once, twice, three times, Edith asked, "Finn? What are you doing here?"

He felt way too much spittle leaving his mouth, and he ducked his head and turned away from the gorgeous blonde he wanted to see every single day. "Sorry," he said after his mini-sneezing fit. "Something's—" He cut off as he started sneezing again. He had these rapid-fire fits some-times, usually around black pepper, and that was when he smelled it.

"Alex is making hash for dinner," Edith said. "He always puts in too much black pepper." She grinned as she stepped out onto the porch and closed the door behind her. "Your daddy is driving away."

Finn twisted and watched the big white truck disappear around the corner. "Yeah, uh." He faced Edith again and found both of her eyebrows cocked up in a silent challenge. "I want to talk to you and Alex about something."

"Edee," Alex called from inside the house, and Edith turned as her eyebrows went down.

"Sounds intriguing," Edith said. "You wanna come in?"

"Yeah." Finn wiped his hands on his slacks as he followed Edith into the farmhouse. She hadn't changed out of her dress yet, and it flowed around her in pale blue fabric with silver stripes down the length of the skirt. The upper half fit her like a glove, and wide straps went over her shoulders, leaving her arms bare and tan and muscled.

"How did the writing go last night?" he asked

"Good." Edith turned back to him and walked backward for a couple of steps. "I finished the scene with the fireworks, and I've got the horse where I need him now."

Finn grinned at her enthusiasm for her fiction writing. "That's great, Edith."

She smiled too. "Alex, Finn's coming for lunch."

"Fine," Alex said over the sizzling of bacon and more on the stove. "Howdy, Finn."

"Alex," he said, and he kept working in the kitchen by pulling down plates and setting them on the counter.

"Can I help?" Finn asked when Edith sat at the big oval table in the kitchen.

"Oh, no," Edith said. "Alex gets spiny if I get in his way."

"Spiny." Finn chuckled and sat next to her. "So you don't cook?"

"I do," she said. "From time to time. Lunch, especially. But Alex thinks cooking is a release from the other type of work he has to do, so when he gets in his chefy moods, I just let him go for it." She brushed her hair off her face and smiled at her brother in the kitchen.

She turned back to him. "What about you, Pork Chop? Do you cook?"

"I can," he said, grinning at her nickname. "Enough, at least." He leaned forward to brush his lips along her cheek. "You're gorgeous, Edith."

"That's why you had your daddy drive you out here?" she asked.

"No." Finn shook his head. "No, but it's still true."

She didn't look away from him, and Finn swallowed as he shifted in his seat. "Edith, there are nine sinkholes here on the ranch."

Her smile fell. She blinked a couple of times. "Yes," she said. "There are."

"I wanted—" Finn looked over to Alex, now stirring something in a big pan on the stove. "I wanted to talk to you and Alex about—well— about—uh—"

Edith leaned closer, her smile reappearing. "You're cute when you're nervous."

Finn exhaled in a puff of air, his laugh following. "I want to come work for you guys."

"You want...." She trailed off, her smile disappearing and her eyes widening as she blinked. Blink-blinked.

"We're ready to eat," Alex said as he put a plate piled high with bacon and sausage on the table between Edith and Finn. "Edee, you wanna grab the juice?"

"Yes, sir." She got up, her eyes flitting away from Finn. They both returned to the kitchen, and Edith brought over a carton of orange juice and the stack of plates while Alex tossed a potholder down and put the big pan of hash on it. The crispy potatoes, onions, and cheese made Finn's mouth water, but he wasn't sure he'd ever get a bite down before he got the go-ahead to come work with Alex and Edith.

They both sat down, and everyone looked around at one another. The tension in the air felt too high to Finn. This was an easy Sunday afternoon lunch, after a Sabbath-day sermon.

"I'll say grace," Alex said. He cleared his throat, folded his arms, and squished his eyes shut. Finn could barely get his cowboy hat off before Alex said, "Lord, we're grateful for the many blessings Thou has bestowed upon us. We're glad for the blue sky today, and clear weather. We're grateful we had a good sermon today about service, and bless us to serve those around us."

He continued on, but Finn could only hear the rushing of blood in his own ears. The preacher *had* talked about service today. Surely Edith and Alex wouldn't turn away his offer of service.

"Amen."

Finn lifted his head, and he looked at both Alex and Edith. Alex didn't seem to notice the charge in the air, because he reached for a plate and the spatula for the hash. Edith didn't move a muscle.

Finn reached out and picked up a plate and handed it to Edith. "Alex, I just told Edith I'd like to come work on your ranch until you get the sinkholes fixed and your fields back in order."

"That is not what you said," Edith said.

"That is so what I said." Finn used the tongs to pick up a few pieces of bacon, and he went back for some sausage as Edith scoffed.

"No, you said you wanted to come work for us."

"I do," Finn said, glancing at her. "There are nine sinkholes here. They'll take a while to get patched up and reseeded, and meanwhile, someone has to look after the ranch."

"I can look after the ranch." Edith snatched the tongs from Finn, and he pulled his hand back while she angrily got her own breakfast meats.

Alex had said nothing, and Finn looked over to him. "I don't need pay," Finn said. "Or room and board. I'll just come in the morning and do whatever you need me to do. Then I'll go home at night."

Alex chewed and swallowed his food. "I'm sure we'll get by." He met Edith's eye, and Finn didn't like the silent conversation they had.

Frustration built inside Finn, but he managed to spoon some hash onto his plate. "So Pastor Scott said today to serve those around you," he said, not sure where the words had come from. "But that requires that there's people who need serving, and that those people are humble enough to accept the help when it's offered to them."

His words got spoken into pure silence in the farmhouse, and that meant something with how many animals Alex and Edith had surrounding the table. Their dogs and cat went with them into the house or outside of it.

And right now, they'd all fallen silent. Finn forked up a bite of hash, his stomach cursing him for being hungry and attempting to eat in a moment like this. He put the perfectly seasoned potatoes in his mouth, waiting for Alex or Edith to say something.

He managed to swallow, and he finally dared to look over to Edith. She ducked her head instantly, her cheeks a lovely shade of pink that indicated her embarrassment. Finn didn't want that, and he reached over and covered her hand with his.

"I want to come work here at Coyote Pass with you two," he said with as much force as he dared. "I think you could use the help, and I'm not doing anything at Three Rivers." He looked over to Alex, who had gone back to eating. "I've been prayin' about it, and it feels right, and that's why I had my daddy drive me out here to crash your Sabbath Day lunch."

He finished his strip of bacon and asked, "So, what do you think?"

12

"All right," Alex said, and Edith flinched with the words.

"All right?" Edith asked.

Her brother ignored her. "Have you fixed a sinkhole before?"

"Sure have," Finn said, and Edith felt like the world was completely out of control. Hurtling through space too fast, on a collision course with an asteroid or a moon. Something.

"Then I'd love your help," Alex said. "Because I haven't." He flicked a glance over to Edith, who stared back at him. "Neither has Edee."

"You love big machines," she said.

Alex grinned at her. "Sure do."

"Alex." She wasn't sure why she was whining. She'd get to see Finn every day if he came to work at Coyote Pass. Her face felt like someone had implanted hand warmers into her cheeks.

She didn't want Finn to come work at Coyote Pass, because it was embarrassing for her. She didn't want to admit they needed help, but that didn't seem to matter. Everyone with even one working eyeball could see they needed help. God knew it, and He'd whispered as much to Finn.

And blast him, the cowboy had listened.

"Excuse me," she said as she pushed her chair away from the table.

"Edee," Alex said.

"I just—I'll be right back."

"Edith." Finn's voice made her heart sing and her cheeks flame even more, but she couldn't look at him.

"Just one minute." She nodded and left the kitchen, not sure where she was going or why. She went down the hall and instead of turning right to go into her bedroom, she went left and into the spare bedroom where Levi had lived until she'd had to take him to the hospital because he'd become paralyzed along the entire right side of his body.

He'd died there, thankfully, and Edith didn't have to think of him here, in that way. She did pick up the picture of him from where it sat on the shelf by the door. She smiled back at him, and then, without thinking, she replaced the photo face-down on the shelf.

She took a breath and looked out the window. *You need the help, and he's offering the help. Take it.*

Edith didn't like accepting help, she knew that. And yet, she stood there in the sunlight streaming in through the front of the house, and she felt the Lord gently chastising her. Humbling her. Whispering to her that it would all be okay. Accepting help from Finn didn't mean she was weak.

"How many times will I have to do hard things?" she whispered.

God didn't answer her, and Edith knew she'd already gotten the answers He had for her. Now, she had to act on that.

She wiped her face, embarrassed all over again that she'd been found crying. Finn would think she was such a crybaby, and Edith didn't want that. After a steeling breath, Edith held her shoulders back as she walked back into the kitchen.

Both Alex and Finn looked at her, her brother without much emotion in his expression but Finn's held nothing but hope. He got to his feet and came toward her. "Hey, I'm sorry," he whispered. "It's fine. I don't have to come help." He folded her into his arms, and oh, how Edith just wanted someone to hold her and protect her from the outside world.

From sinkholes, and photographs that reminded her of hard times, and floods, and everything else that could—and did—go wrong.

"I just thought of it yesterday when we found those sinkholes, and I haven't been able to let go of it." He pressed his lips to her temple, then further down, closer to her ear. "I don't want to upset you."

"I'm not upset," she whispered.

"Alex said you've never left the lunch table when there's bacon in the vicinity."

Edith burst out laughing, and that somehow made all of the tension and frustration and sadness inside her flee. She leaned back and looked at Finn, her gaze dropping to his mouth and rebounding back to his eyes.

He smiled softly at her, and he was the most handsome man on the planet. He knew how to hold her; he knew exactly what to say and when; he simply knew.

Edith smiled back at him and said, "We sure could use your help at Coyote Pass with the sinkholes."

"I don't want you to be too tired to write at night," he whispered. "I promise, you won't see me any more than you want to."

"I want to see you, Finn."

"Great," he said without missing a beat. "Because I want to see you too."

"Please wait until I'm done eating to start making out," Alex called, and Finn turned back to him. He shielded Edith from her brother in another protective move, and Edith appreciated that too.

She took a moment to wipe her face, and then she slid to Finn's side. "Alex, we can have Finn come help with the sinkholes, right?"

"I already said yes, Edee."

She smiled as she slipped her hand into Finn's. She squeezed, and they went back to the kitchen table. "Great. Then maybe I can make out with him later."

Finn coughed and choked, his whole face turning a ruddy shade of red. Alex laughed too, and Edith calmly picked up her fork so she could finally eat breakfast-for-lunch.

LATER THAT EVENING, EDITH LEFT THE STABLE after the nightly feeding of the horses. This time, Finn followed her, and he took her hand the moment he came to her side. He didn't say anything, and Edith didn't know how to tell him that she sure had enjoyed spending the afternoon and evening with him.

Maybe the golden silence around them could convey it for her, and she simply basked in the warmth and light of Finn's hand in hers.

"What time do you guys get going in the morning?" he asked as they rounded the barn and the farmhouse and backyard came into view.

"I get up when I want," Edith said. "I do the morning feeding, but it's not until eight."

"So I'll come around eight," he said.

Edith glanced over to her she-shed, wondering if she should get on the computer tonight. She always had something to do, that was for certain, but her mind took her in a different direction tonight. "Do you want to tour my she-shed, Hot Shot?"

"Do I ever," Finn said, grinning as wide as the sky.

She laughed and said, "Really? Why?"

"It's like...where the magic happens," he said. "Your very own space, where you create whole worlds, with magnificent horses and the boys and girls who love them."

"Magnificent horses?" Edith giggled through the words.

"Yes," Finn said, holding his head high. "Magnificent horses."

Edith loved walking with him, talking with him, laughing with him. "Let me show you where the magic happens then." She led him across the lawn to her she-shed, which didn't even have a proper sidewalk leading up to it.

She paused just outside the door and thought about what he'd see inside her shed. "Okay, this is my personal space."

"I know." Finn didn't look at her, but he leaned closer to the window in the door.

"It might be messy. Writing is a process."

He looked at her then, and Edith had no idea what he saw. "Sweetheart, I'm not going to laugh at you or judge you."

Butterfly wings fluttered in her pulse. "Okay."

She took in a slow breath as she reached to open the door. She stepped inside first, the familiar and soothing scent of citrus greeting her like an old friend.

The room opened up before her, and Finn said, "Sweetheart, you're blocking the door."

She stepped to the left where the large, plush couch sat. Her favorite fuzzy blanket had been folded and laid over the armrest closest to the small table where she had a lamp.

A window let in light there, and Edith admired her brightly flowered rug before she took in the posters of her book covers, the table which held her scented candles, incense, and her air diffuser—the source of the orange hanging in the air.

"It smells great in here," he said as he moved further inside.

Edith tucked her hands in her pockets as he took a few steps to her desk. Her laptop sat there, as did several piles of papers and books, and the end of it covered a mini-fridge, which she kept stocked with her favorite soda pop and ice cream.

She had a short, two-drawer filing cabinet next to the mini-fridge, but it too had been piled with things. Journals, a sweatshirt, another candle, pens, note cards, and her travel keyboard.

And an empty bowl of ice cream. The desk also held various bags of candy in various degrees of fullness, two water bottles that were probably empty or close to it, and a dirty nacho plate from last night's snack. Edith tucked her hair behind her ear and watched as Finn turned away from her desk.

"This is so perfectly you, Edith."

"Yeah?" she asked. "Why?"

"The desk." He glanced at her. "It has your personality. So put together. Every piece you need, right where you need it. But it's used. It's got charm." He smiled. "I love your posters. Are these all your books?"

Edith took in the three posters she had on the walls. "Just the ones from a library event I did in New Orleans," she said. "They had these big posters blown up for the signing, and I got to keep them afterward."

"How many books have you written?"

"Six," she said. "I'm working on my seventh right now."

"Amazing," he said. "And look at this couch. The pillows." He grinned at her and indicated the couch again. "Can I sit?"

"Go right ahead."

He sighed mightily as he did, and Edith couldn't help grinning at him. "Do you take naps here? Sit and read?"

"Both," she said. "Sometimes I write by hand in a journal. Sometimes I watch videos on my phone about horses. It's just a nice place to relax."

"I'll say." He stretched his arms out wide and groaned. "Come sit by me, sweetheart."

Edith did, choosing to sit immediately next to him, in the space created by his outstretched arm. She fit there perfectly, and he settled his arm around her as if he'd done it plenty of times before.

"I spy a fridge over there. What you got in that?"

"Take a guess, Cupcake," she said, clearly flirting with him.

Finn took a moment, his head cocked slightly, that sexy smile on his mouth. "I'd say Diet Dr. Pepper in the fridge, and that freezer is absolutely stocked with orange sherbet."

She laughed, because he wasn't wrong. "I have sherbet," she said through her giggles. "And chocolate chip ice cream."

"How very plain," he said.

"I don't like marshmallows in ice cream," she

said, continuing an old argument from high school about Rocky Road.

He chuckled too. "Tell me how you came to be a writer," he said as he quieted. "I don't remember you writing in high school."

Edith leaned back and looked up to the ceiling of her she-shed. "I was nannying on Long Island, and I learned about an internship at a publisher in the city. It wasn't paid, and it was remote, though I had to go into the city sometimes. Once every couple of weeks." She shook her head, because she was getting sidetracked.

"I fell in love with the publishing process. This concept of taking something from someone's brain, and they type it out, and we print it on paper. It intrigued me."

"What did you do?"

"I read slush," she said. "I've always loved reading, and I could do it from my suite on Long Island."

"What's slush?"

"Oh." She smiled again. "It's what we call the submissions that come in. The slush pile. I worked with an editor who had very specific tastes for what they were looking for. When I read something that fit the bill, I gave it to them. Then they'd read it. They don't read every submission. That was my job."

"Fascinating," he said.

"I learned really quickly what editors liked and didn't like, though everything is beyond sub-jective."

"Is that how you started writing?"

"Yeah, this editor friend of the editor I worked with, she publishes children's books, and we went to lunch once. The three of us. She kept saying she wanted something that would remind people of a slower time. Something that would 'remind us that we were human once.' That we all knew each other and took care of each other."

"Sounds like Three Rivers."

"That's exactly what I thought," Edith said. "I suggested something with a farm or a ranch, and horses, and this editor loved that idea. Then we all lamented over the fact that there weren't any man-uscripts like that in the slush pile."

"So you wrote one."

"That I did. And I gave it to that editor, and she loved it. So, now I write books sometimes."

"Do you love it?"

"Yeah," she said quietly. "I really do."

"So," he said. "Let's do Could Be Better, Could Be Worse."

Edith pulled in a breath. "We haven't done that in years. I'd completely forgotten about it."

"You want to?"

"Yeah," Edith said, settling further into his side. "But you go first."

"Okay." He took a long moment, and then he said, "Things could be better than having nine sinkholes."

She laughed. "They sure could be." She bumped him slightly. "That one is cheating a little."

"You told me to go first."

"Yeah, I should've gone first." She looked across the small shed to her writing desk. "You did better, so I have to do worse...." She exhaled. "Things could be worse than moving back to Three Rivers."

He chuckled and said, "Fair enough. Uh... things could be worse than sitting on this amazingly comfortable couch with an amazingly beautiful woman."

"I'm just a woman?" Edith asked without thinking. Finn ducked his head and looked at her, but she didn't tilt her head back. "I think that sentence should've ended with the word *girlfriend*."

"Is that what you think?" he teased.

"Yeah," she whispered. "That's what I think."

"Well, then, I think a *boyfriend* would kiss his *girlfriend* before he asked her for a ride back to his ranch, where he lives with his momma and daddy, who are gonna have a lot of questions for him."

Edith laughed, glad when Finn joined her. Their voices together made a perfect harmony, and the way Edith fell for him made her stomach swoop. "You probably should get back, I guess."

"Yeah," he said.

She sat up and ran her hands through her hair. Then she looked over her shoulder to Finn. "I can drive you back to the ranch." She started to get up, but he tutted and touched her elbow.

Edith turned back to him, and he slid that hand up her arm and across her shoulder, sending fireworks popping in every single cell he touched. "About that kiss...."

She didn't hesitate as she leaned toward him, and he knew exactly where to put his hands. The second one joined the first as he cradled her face in both hands, making her feel cherished and worth holding.

Edith drew in a shaky breath a mere moment before Finn's lips touched hers, and then everything in the world stood on solid rock. She'd kissed Finn before, but as a much younger woman. He'd been a much younger man.

He'd said he'd only dated a few people in the past several years, but wow, the man could kiss. He moved at exactly the right speed, and his passion bled through in every stroke. Edith hadn't been kissed in a long time, and she'd missed it so much.

More than hand-holding and more than cuddling. Kissing Finn was so much better than both of those, and Edith wanted to keep doing it, and doing it, and doing it.

13

Finn pushed aside his nerves, his pounding heart, and the screaming warning in his head not to mess this up. Thankfully, kissing Edith felt like second nature to him, and he managed to relax into the movement, the feeling of her fingers as they swiped through his hair, the silky quality of the skin along her neck.

"I have missed kissing you," he whispered as he broke away from her. He matched his mouth to hers again, this second kiss as amazing as the first.

Not that this was the first time he'd kissed Edith, but he had forgotten how amazing this kind of touch was. How much it made him feel. How full his heart grew as she kissed him back, as if she liked kissing him too.

He ducked his head to break the kiss when he felt himself getting out of control. His nerves told him to talk, but his military training told him to stay silent until he had something important and necessary to say.

Edith moved forward and touched her cheek to his. "That was nice."

"Yeah." Finn wanted to stay longer, especially out here in Edith's she-shed stocked with soda and ice cream, but he knew he needed to get back home. His mother had texted him twice now, and while she'd told him to take his time, he knew she had something she wanted from him. She wouldn't have messaged otherwise.

They breathed in together, and that broke the moment enough for them to separate. "I'll get my keys," she said.

"Yep." Finn got to his feet and reached back to help Edith stand. "This was an amazing day." He swallowed his gratitude for her letting him come work for them. He didn't mention what time he'd be there in the morning. He'd simply show up ready, with coffee, and he'd put his head down and get the job done. He wouldn't follow Edith around with puppy-dog eyes, and he'd pack a lunch so he didn't impose on the Baxter's for food.

In the house, Alex stood at the counter, several sheets of paper in front of him. "We need to get to IFA tomorrow," he said. "With everything else, I forgot they have our fertilizer."

"Okay," Edith said, dropping his hand to get her keys. "We can go tomorrow."

"Okay," Alex said absently. "That bill for the rock is due."

"I can move money," Edith said.

That caused Alex to look up and blink. Finn looked between the two of them. "You don't need to do that," he said. "There's money in the ranch account."

"Okay," Edith said. "I'm driving Finn home."

"Sounds good."

He met her eyes, and they left the farmhouse together. Gold and silver accompanied the drive to Three Rivers, as the sun had settled in the west and the moon had risen already.

"Do you love your ranch?" Edith asked.

"I sure do," Finn said as he nodded. "I'm not sure if I want to run it. I think Libby will actually come home and do that. But just today, standing in the cemetery while my daddy talked to my grandfather, I had the distinct impression that I'm...home."

Finn looked over to her. "I've come home to Three Rivers." He smiled and exhaled heavily. "Now, where that is in Three Rivers, I don't know. But I'm going to stay in town and figure out the next step."

"What do you think that'll be?"

Finn didn't want to answer, but he told himself he could trust Edith. "I honestly don't know, but I'm sure I'll figure it out." She nodded, and he asked, "What about you? What's your next step?"

She glanced over to him. "This is my next step. I'm living it."

"Working Coyote Pass and writing books." He grinned at her. "Sounds like an amazing life."

"Does it?" She held his gaze for a long moment, no smile in sight. "Really?"

Finn wasn't sure how to answer. Edith had challenged him on things in the past, and they'd teased over some things too. But she seemed super serious about her question. He blinked, trying to come up with the right answer. Then he told himself that he didn't have to answer the way she wanted him to. He just needed to answer truthfully.

"I think so," he said. "You love being outside. You love writing. Your she-shed is amazing. You've got your dogs and cats." He wasn't sure what else she wanted or needed. "To me." Finn cleared his throat, wishing he had a bottle of water. "The only thing you're missing, based on what I know about you, which could be totally wrong." He waited for her to interrupt or say something.

When she didn't, he went all-in. "Is children. A family. Levi."

The last word barely hovered out of his mouth, but it still sounded loud enough for them both to hear.

Instead of correcting him, Edith only nodded. "I'd agree with you." A mile went by, and then she added, "Except for the Levi part. I'm not missing Levi."

"You're not?"

"I mean, I miss him from time to time, but he wouldn't make my life complete."

"No?"

"Finn." She carried plenty of frustration in his name.

"What? You love kids, and you've always wanted a big family. That requires a man like Levi. I'm sure—absolutely *sure*—that you were counting on that when you thought you'd marry him."

She swallowed, her jaw tight as she gripped the wheel the same way. "You're not wrong."

"So, in your ideal life, you're missing a family, and that includes a man like Levi."

"Exactly," she said, the word biting out of her mouth. "A man *like* Levi. Not specifically Levi."

"All right," Finn said. His voice pitched up as he agreed with her. "Maybe I could be a man like Levi."

Edith grinned, those blue eyes sparkling with that tease he was more used to. "Maybe."

"Oh, maybe, huh?" He chuckled as she turned onto the dirt road that led down and around to the homestead. Finn started praying no one would be outside, and he could kiss Edith one more time before he had to go inside and face the Inquisitor.

They laughed together, and as she went around the bend, Finn started looking for observers. He didn't see anyone, but that didn't mean much. With all the windows....

"Thank you, Edith," he said as she pulled into the driveway.

"Listen," she said. She put her SUV in park. "Thank you for coming out to Coyote Pass to help us. It's—It'll be hard for me at first, but it's not because I don't want you there. It's because I—"

Finn could fill in the blank for her, but he waited. *I like being in control.*

I don't like feeling weak.

I'm a little bit of an independent spirit.

"I know, Edith," he said. "You don't have to explain it to me."

She nodded and swallowed again. "Okay, then."

"Kiss me good-night?"

She turned toward him, everything on her face softening. "I'd like that."

Finn certainly would too, and he leaned across the console and let her slide her hand along his jawline. He kissed her sweetly, though he'd like to take things a little deeper.

"See you tomorrow," he whispered, and then he told himself to get out of the car and go inside.

He did, and he lifted his hand back to Edith in a good-night wave as he ducked into the garage. He heard the laughter inside the house before he opened the door, so he entered to a raucous round of laughter that sounded like his parents were hosting every cowboy on the ranch for supper.

But supper would've ended an hour ago. He

kicked off his boots in the mudroom and put his military defenses in place to be able to enter the large living room, dining room, and kitchen.

Then he stepped around the corner and found Daddy standing at the sliding glass door as Uncle Pete, Ethan, and Beau moved out onto the deck. Momma worked in the kitchen, putting away leftovers, and she looked toward Finn the moment he appeared.

"There you are," she said, wiping her hands on her apron. "Did you get dinner?"

He shook his head, his stomach growling. "I can make a sandwich."

To his surprise, Momma said, "Okay," and she rounded the island and sat at the bar while he took her place in the kitchen.

He braced himself against the open refrigerator door while he peered inside, because the questions were sure to start at any moment. Momma waited until he pulled out the sundried tomato turkey, and then she said, "There's muenster in the skinny drawer."

Finn tossed the turkey on the island and turned back to the fridge. "Did Daddy tell you I'm going to be working at Coyote Pass for the next little bit?"

"He sure did," Momma said, and that caused relief to sing through Finn. So he didn't have to break the ice with that.

He grabbed the cheese, mayo, and mustard and faced his momma. "And?"

"And what?"

"Oh, come on," he said and he bent to get the bread out of the drawer. "You surely have fifteen hundred questions."

She scoffed, and Finn kept his eyes down as he started pulling out bread and slathering on mayo and then mustard.

"I like her, Momma," he said. "We're not in high school anymore." He layered on turkey and cheese about the time Daddy finished saying good-bye to his men and joined them.

"I'm going to stay in Three Rivers," Finn said. "Edith is happy here."

"You're going to stay?" Momma looked over to Daddy, and Finn pretended not to notice the look they exchanged.

"I feel like I'm repeating the conversation my momma had with me twenty-five years ago." Daddy chuckled as he put his arm around Momma. "When I told her I liked *you*."

She smiled warmly and snuggled into his side,

and Finn put on double cheese while he envisioned a life with Edith in a house like this, on a ranch much smaller than this, with her she-shed out back.

"Yes, I heard him say he likes her," Momma said. "And that *she* likes Three Rivers."

"I'm not staying here for Edith." Finn put the halves of his first sandwich together, and reached to do it again for the second. "I'm staying here, because I'm supposed to be in Three Rivers." He met his daddy's eyes and held the gaze. "I felt it in the cemetery today. It just so happens that I mentioned it to Edith, and she likes Three Rivers too and has no plans to leave."

Daddy started nodding early in Finn's statement. "That's great," he said. "So what are you thinking?"

"I don't know." Finn planted his palms on the counter and looked at his parents. "Libby is going to come back here and run this place." He looked back to Momma. Then Daddy. "Right?"

"She hasn't said that out loud," Momma said quickly.

"I think she will," Daddy said. "Yes." He glanced at Momma too. "It would make sense for her to live here, darlin'." He looked at Finn with plenty of nerves and worry in his expression.

"That doesn't mean you can't be here too, Finny," Momma said.

"I know that." Finn picked up his sandwiches and joined his parents at the bar. "But I don't know. God's slow to reveal what I should do. I'm trying to listen to Him. I'm trying to make moves on my own to see if He stops me." He shook his head, his thoughts tangled and in the wrong order. "So I just don't know yet."

"Maybe something around here of your own," Daddy said.

"That's a great idea," Momma said. "There's got to be something like Coyote Pass for you. Something smaller. Something you and Edith can run together."

"Momma." Finn smiled at her, but it was in the *please, stop* kind of way.

"What?" she asked, swiveling her attention between him and Daddy. "I'm just saying."

"I barely kissed her tonight," Finn said, quickly filling his mouth with a big bite of turkey and cheese.

"That's his way of saying you're thinking too far down the road, sweetheart," Daddy said. He chuckled and met Finn's grateful gaze. "But I don't think it's unreasonable to start looking at real estate around here. Ranches. Smaller farms. The market is high right now, and it might take a while for you to find something you can afford."

Finn nodded, finished chewing, and swallowed. "This is a me-move, not a thing I'm doing for me and Edith." He gave his mother a pointed look. "*I'd* like a place here. A place of my own. And if Edith and I break-up, I'd still want a place."

"And if it does work out—"

"Momma," Finn said, and Daddy said, "Kelly, darlin', let's go get that paperwork for Beau."

"I'm not going out to the admin trailer again tonight," Momma griped back at him.

"Then let's put something on TV and let Finn alone." Daddy got to his feet, and Finn smiled at him as he went by.

Momma glared at his back and then switched her gaze to Finn. She softened instantly and said, "You kissed her tonight?"

Finn ducked his head, that kiss already streaming through his mind. "Yes, ma'am," he muttered. "She kissed me back. It was...nice."

Momma slid over onto the stool next to him. She put her arm around him. "I love you, baby. I just want you to be happy." She stroked his hair off his forehead. "You seem happy with her."

"I am," Finn whispered. "I mean, so far. Momma, it's been what? A couple of weeks?" He hadn't been home longer than a month yet. "So you don't need to start planning a wedding or anything, okay?"

"Okay," she said in that falsely high-pitched voice that said she was going to start planning a wedding. Finn could only smile at her, and he leaned into her embrace before she stood and went to join Daddy in the living room.

Finn finished his sandwiches, and he pulled out his phone to set an alarm for the next morning that would give him enough time to shower, pack a lunch, and make the drive to Coyote Pass.

As he did that and said, "I'm gonna go downstairs," a text came in from Edith.

Can't wait to see you tomorrow, Finn.

He wasn't sure if either of his parents said anything as he went down the hall and then down the steps. Because he was floating on clouds and already texting Edith back. He couldn't help imagining a small farm or ranch of his own, with Edith there with him, and when she finished writing that night, she'd come in to bed, and he wouldn't be alone.

That felt like coming home too, and Finn let himself daydream a little while he texted with the most beautiful woman in the world.

14

Lincoln Glover left the bedroom he shared with his best friend and cousin—though not through blood—and walked down the short hall in the cowboy cabin where he lived on Shiloh Ridge Ranch.

He'd tucked his shirt in precisely right, and his belt buckle could've been worn by Uncle Mister as a rodeo champion. His jeans had just been washed, and he'd even hung them up last night so they'd be straight and even today.

"Wow," Cutter said from where he sat on the couch. He hadn't showered yet, and he looked like he'd rolled in the fields where he'd been tending to cattle all day. "Who are you goin' out with?"

Link smiled at him and shook his head as he moved behind the shorter couch that ran perpendicular to the front door. He plucked his hat from the rack there and said, "No one. Mitch and I are going down to the summer dance." He put his hat on his head and adjusted it until he felt like himself in it. "You sure you don't want to come?"

Cutter chuckled and shook his head. "No, thanks, cowboys. Those dances are for young bucks like you two."

Link turned as Mitch came out of the bathroom. He too wore a dark-wash pair of jeans, perfectly clean and shined brown cowboy boots, a matching belt, and a plaid shirt in red, white, and blue that spoke of the Fourth of July a month too soon.

How do I look? Mitch's hands flew as he signed, and then he spread his arms wide and turned in a circle.

Link grinned at him, and since he'd grown up with Mitch since the age of ten or eleven, he'd learned sign language too. "Great," Link said with his hands and his voice. "I don't think I should go with you. If I stand next to you, no one will look at me."

Mitch laughed, the sound hearty and loud,

because he couldn't hear it and didn't know to tone things down. He was a couple of years older than Link, but he'd just returned to Shiloh Ridge a month or so ago from his accessibility dog training academy in Virginia.

He'd talked with Link until late into the night about opening a training facility somewhere, but he hadn't talked to his daddy or anyone else about it. He had a guide dog with him—his third since he'd been part of Link's life and the Glover family.

They shared no blood whatsoever, though they both bore the Glover last name, as Bear had adopted Link a few years back, and Cactus had done the same for Mitch long before that.

I'm all arms and legs, Mitch said, and even Cutter laughed. *And too skinny. The ladies seem to like cowboys with shoulders like yours.* He approached Link as he signed, and he grabbed onto Link's shoulders when he arrived, his smile enormous.

"Yeah, sure," Link said, not bothering to use his hands now. Mitch could read lips. "Let's go." He moved away from his cousin and took his keys from the peg on the wall beside the fridge. He almost always drove when he went with Mitch. Of course the other man knew how to drive, but his lack of hearing did make some things harder—driving being one of them.

Mitch led the way out of the cowboy cabin, and he had to duck his head to get through the doorway. So even if he was a little on the skinny side, he had plenty of height and plenty of good-looks and plenty of charm. Link always felt a little overshadowed when in Mitch's presence, but it had never mattered all that much.

He drove them down the hill and off Shiloh Ridge Ranch, and then it was just thirty minutes to the downtown park, which would be transformed into a dance floor tonight. Every Friday and Saturday in the summertime, the town covered the grass with squares of wood, set up lights and refreshment stations, and hired a local band or DJ.

"Local" could include as far away as Amarillo, and Link had started going to the dances last summer. Sort of. He'd gone to two or three—alone—before he decided he'd drunk enough horrible red punch, danced—alone—to enough mediocre music, and simply embarrassed himself enough.

He'd met a woman or two at the dances or church, and he'd gone out with girls and friends that were girls in high school, but otherwise, Link didn't have much experience with the opposite gender.

But now that Mitch was back in town, and he wanted to go to the dance, Link could play the part of his wingman and enjoy a few hours away from the ranch, the family, the never-ending texts. All of it. He just wanted an escape, and he thought about asking his daddy if he could go on vacation.

Maybe somewhere cooler than Texas in the summer, like the Pacific Northwest or the Canadian Rocky Mountains. "That would require a passport," he murmured to himself. And he didn't currently have one of those.

"And what? You'll go alone?" He shook his head, wondering when he'd started talking to himself the way his daddy did. He put the idea of a vacation out of his mind and got himself and Mitch to the downtown park.

Dusk had started to cover the land, and Link actually thought they'd still arrived too early. He turned toward Mitch when he tapped his arm, and then he said, *I hope Sarah is here tonight*, with a grin.

"Did you text her?" Link asked.

Mitch nodded. *Yeah, but she said she might have to work.*

Sarah Hedger had come up to the ranch to help after the flooding, but she'd really just followed Mitch around and flirted with him. At least until lunchtime, when Uncle Cactus had growled at her about helping pull a couple of turkeys out of a mud pit. Then she'd suddenly had something to do in town.

Link smiled just thinking about it. Sarah was a pretty woman, but she talked too much for Link. His daddy had said a lot of girls tended to talk too much, and Link just had to find one that suited him.

Preferably before you're fifty years old, Daddy had said with a wry smile.

Link was half that age, and he wasn't sure how he managed to keep himself alive every day. He didn't feel qualified to do much more than what Uncle Ward told him to do, so trying to find a date certainly hadn't been at the top of his list.

Mitch had definitely dated more than Link, and he led the way into the park, where the yellow tea lights made the mid-June dusk more golden than it would be otherwise. The towering trees stood watch over the dance floor, where a band in the center of the floor had already started to play.

Tonight, four guys with guitars stood on the stage, and a couple dozen people stood out on the floor. Only a few danced, and everyone else stood in clumps, talking.

Link hated clumps of people. How could he just walk up to them and join one? He couldn't, which was why he loitered on the edge of the dance floor while Mitch strode right out onto it.

He couldn't even call to his friends, but he did have an inch or two on most people, and he did have long limbs. He raised one hand, and one of the clumps broke apart and made room for him.

Cowboys and girls, and Link told himself to get out there too. He did, Mitch's little shadow, but the group welcomed him easily too.

"Howdy, Link," a man named Seth Mayer said. He shook the man's hand and put his smile on full display.

"Howdy," he said. "How's the online classes going?"

"Great," Seth said, his smile fixed in place too. "Good enough." He glanced over at someone as they joined them too. Link backed up a step as another cowboy arrived.

"Link," he said with a laugh.

"Oh, hey, Will." He shook that cowboy's hand too, marveling at how well Mitch could communicate with people who didn't know a lot of sign language. He caught him looking at Link, and he shifted over to stand next to Mitch.

"Oh, the Jessup sisters are here," Will said. "Bridget! Izzy! Over here!"

Link's heartbeat picked up, because if they had women standing with them, perhaps more would come over too. He wasn't sure who he was looking for, but he did know Bridget and Izzy Jessup, and he said hello along with everyone else.

"Link, how's your horse?" Izzy asked, putting her hand on his elbow. He looked at her perfectly manicured fingernails before sliding his gaze to her face. She'd taken time and put in effort to pretty up before coming, and he smiled at her.

"He's okay. He still favors that right leg, and I can't get him in the trailer."

"I could come work with him a little," she offered. She worked at a boarding stable over in Pampa, but she lived on the southern edge of town. "If you want." She ducked her head and tucked her hair, and Link recognized shy flirting when he saw it, even if he hadn't dated a lot.

Because right now, Izzy wanted him to flirt back. Ask her out. Tell her to come up to the ranch and help him with Royce. He liked Izzy well enough, sure. But he didn't feel a spark with her skin against his. Only heat.

And Link wanted fireworks.

The band on the stage finished a song and started another one, this one slow. A ballad. A dancing song. The lead singer even leaned right into his mic and said, "All right, gentlemen. Find yourself a lady and take her for a twirl around the dance floor!"

Link looked at Izzy, who wore such hope on her face. "Do you want to dance?" he asked.

"Sure." She giggled and took his hand in hers. Link knew how to dance, and he knew how to play a part. He hated it, because he just wanted to be himself.

But he held Izzy in his arms, and they moved around the floor. He quickly lost sight of Mitch, who'd also asked someone to dance with him.

"Got any new horses at the stable?" he asked.

"Seemingly every day," Izzy said. "If you guys have extra people at Shiloh Ridge, my boss is hiring."

Link nodded. "I'll tell my daddy."

"Did you see the theater is playing *Ghost-busters?*" she asked. "Not the new one. The old one. The classic."

"I hadn't seen that," Link admitted. "It's great the Miners bought it and cleaned it up."

"Right?" Izzy laughed again, and Link could admit that tonight's dance was better than any he'd been to in the past.

A pause came between them, and Link felt like he should ask her to go to the movies with him. But he didn't want to be her boyfriend, and he didn't want to lead her on. The conversation stalled for a minute, and then he said, "Would you believe me if I told you my uncle got another couple of dogs?"

Izzy looked up at him, her face aglow. "If it's Cactus, absolutely."

They laughed together, and then the singer yelled, "Twirl her away from you, boys!" and Link went out on a limb and grabbed Izzy's hand and twirled her away from him.

As he stepped back, his foot landed on someone else's instead of the dance floor. Izzy started coming back toward him, but his ankle buckled. She realized it too late, and they started to fall together.

The person behind them did too, and someone else somehow got all tangled up in the three of them too.

Link landed hard on his backside, his hand flailing up. Izzy hit the ground in front of him, but someone else landed right on top of him. Another woman, this one wearing a bright purple sweater with short sleeves. He knew, because her arm hit him right across the nose.

He grunted and groaned, and then people rushed at them, asking things like, "Link, are you okay?"

"Mitch, what happened?"

"Can you get up, Izzy?"

"Back up," someone said. "Let her get up."

Hands helped the woman on Link's lap to her feet, and then he took Will's hand and got to his feet. He dusted his hands down the front of his shirt, which wasn't as festive as Mitch's. Still the black, red, and white plaid did a good job of telling people how Texas-cowboy-country he was.

He looked up and into the stunning green eyes of a strawberry blonde in a short-sleeved purple sweater. The whole world fell away, and all Link could see and feel were fireworks.

More sparks than he'd ever experienced be-

fore, even at the town Independence Day celebration.

"Sorry," he blurted out.

"Oh, it was my fault," she said, her mouth
pinching on the sides like she was fighting off a
smile. "I got a little twirl-happy." She grinned over
to Mitch, who signed to her.

I love that sweater.

To Link's shock and dismay, she signed back
to him. "Thanks. My sister actually made it
for me."

"You know sign language?" Link asked with
his voice at the same time Mitch did with his
hands.

"A little," she said, and her signs were clumsy.
"I, uh." She glanced over to Mitch again. "Sorry, I
forgot to look at you. I learned some ASL in high
school."

Of course she had. And of course Mitch looked
like he'd been bedazzled by this woman, with gem-
stones glittering in his eyes, from every pore of skin.

What's your name? he asked. *I haven't seen
you around Three Rivers before.*

All the things Link wanted to say, Mitch did.
Of course. He was full of charisma while Link

only seemed to have nerves made of hissing snakes.

"I'm Misty," she said, finger-spelling her name. "I've been in town for a couple of weeks." She glanced over to Link, who smiled at her. Everyone else had gone back to dancing, and the four of them stood there. "I'm here working on the restoration of City Hall."

To his horror, Izzy linked her hand through his elbow. He even looked at her like she'd grown another head and then all her skin had turned bright red.

Misty ducked her head when she saw that. "What's your name?"

Mitch, Mitch said, and he extended his hand toward her. *Do you want to dance?*

Misty looked at him again. He said, "I'm Link. We're cousins."

"Sure, okay," she said, and Misty nodded to Link and then put her hand in Mitch's.

Of course, he thought. The one woman he'd felt anything for would be interested in Mitch.

Link wouldn't say a word to Mitch or anyone else about his internal fireworks display either, because he loved his cousin. He wouldn't take anything good from Mitch, even if his own jealousy roared through him like a pride of lions.

"Should we dance, Link?" Izzy asked.

He blinked and leaned closer to her. "You okay? Did you get hurt when you fell?"

She eased herself into his arms, and while there was heat, there wasn't anything like Link had felt while he'd barely been looking at Misty. "I'm fine, Link. Dance with me."

And since Link could see Mitch holding Misty in his arms as they swayed back and forth, he decided he didn't really have another option. "Yeah," he said, trying to swallow down his irritation and jealousy. "Let's dance."

15

Misty Granger had only come to the dance in the park tonight because her co-worker had dared her to come see if she could charm one of the country cowboys. Guilt drove through her as she danced with Mitch, because he'd clearly been charmed by her.

She glanced over to Link, who danced with a brunette who sure seemed to be enjoying it more than he was. They didn't talk, and she had her eyes closed and that small smile that said she'd finally gotten the cowboy's attention—and she intended to keep it.

Misty would be in Three Rivers for at least

the next couple of years, but she'd promised herself she wouldn't fall in love with anyone who dared to enjoy living in a town of less than twenty thousand people.

She came from the Dallas Fort-Worth area, and she saw more people on the way to work than the population of this town.

The dance ended, and she stepped back from Mitch so she could talk to him. "So you live here?" she asked.

He nodded and said, *For most of my life.* He took her hand and led her toward the edge of the dance floor. He picked up a cup of punch and offered it to her.

"Sure," she said and took it.

He turned back to get another one for himself, and then he grinned at her with those straight, white teeth. He was good-looking in that cowboy hat and that bright shirt that seemed to match his personality.

Misty smiled back at him and took a sip of her punch. She didn't want to ask if he'd been born deaf or had lost his hearing over time, so she kept her hands still as she looked out onto the dance floor again.

The music had picked up, and it seemed more groups of people danced together than couples. The vibe in this town had been totally different than she'd expected, that was for sure.

Yeah, because you judged them as Podunk cowboys before meeting a single one.

Regret pulled through Misty, and she glanced over to Mitch. "Do you come to the dances a lot?"

If I can, he said. *I work a bit south of town, and it's a big ranch.*

"Plus," another man said, and Misty looked over to see Link stepping off the floor. "He just got back to town." He smiled at her. "We work at the same ranch."

"Being cousins and all," she said.

"Right." Link made the third side of their triangle, and Mitch started signing.

Where did Izzy go?

Link cleared his throat. "She got asked to dance by someone else." Even in the yellow lights, Misty saw the ruddy quality of his face. "It's fine." He waved off the beginning of Mitch's condolences. "She wants me to take her out, and I'm just not feeling it."

Part of Misty rejoiced that he and Izzy weren't

an item, but she had no idea why. She was only here for a limited time, and she had a job to do. Several of them. Finding a cowboy boyfriend in the first few weeks wasn't on her agenda.

"Well." She remembered to sign as she spoke. "I have to get back to my—my—" Her hands stalled as her mind went on the fritz. She couldn't believe she was going to tell a little white lie to these two fine cowboys. "Boyfriend," she finished quickly, and she flubbed the sign. Maybe they'd think she hadn't known it—which she really hadn't—and that was why she'd paused before saying it.

"He's around here somewhere."

Link didn't say anything, but Mitch said, *You've got a boyfriend?* He glanced over to Link. *Too bad.*

Link said nothing, and in fact, some pretty hefty shutters had gone right over his expression, making it impossible for Misty to know what he was thinking or feeling. She didn't possess that ability, so she turned her face away from him lest he could see her little white lie showing plainly on her face.

Now, if Ralf would emerge from the gyrating bodies on the dance floor to give validity to her words, that would be great. She'd be working with him for the next couple of years, as he was the project manager for the restoration here in Three Rivers.

Lord, she prayed. But everything felt false about praying mere moments after lying to two men. Two good-looking, kind cowboys.

She huffed out a sigh and turned back to them, but Mitch had his hand in that of another woman's as they got swallowed by the crowd.

"He's pretty easy-going," Link said, and Misty jolted toward him. "He said you sure were pretty." He smiled, his chin down so the brim of his cowboy hat obscured his eyes. "I don't think you saw him sign that."

She reached out as if she'd lift his face higher. He did it naturally, and she let her hand drop back to her side. "Listen, I lied. I don't have a boyfriend. Would you tell him?"

Link blinked those dark blue eyes at her, and oh, the tea lights glimmering in them made him seem soft and strong and sexy all at the same time. Misty's stomach swooped, but she told it emphatically that she was not in town to date.

"And to you," she said. "I'm sorry I said that. I don't know why I did."

"You don't?"

Misty didn't know how to answer him, so she raised her plastic cup to her lips and took a sip of punch.

"Do you like things like this?" Link asked next, and she turned to stand beside him, both of them facing the dance floor.

"They're okay," she said.

"Where are you living while you're here?"

"The state got me a cute little rental," she said.

"The state?"

Misty turned toward him, noticing he hadn't picked up anything to drink. "Yes," she said. "I work for the State of Texas. I'm a conservationist."

Link gave her half a smile, and dang if that didn't make her heartbeat do a jig. "A conservationist," he repeated. "I'll have to look that up."

"I work specifically with buildings older than a hundred years," she said. "To make sure when they get restored, we preserve the history that needs to be preserved."

"I gotta be honest," he said. "This sounds like a made-up job."

"Stop it." She grinned wider and bumped him with her elbow. "It's a real job. I've done several buildings in the Hill Country."

"Is that where you're from?"

"No, sir." She finished her punch and took a couple of steps away from him to throw the cup in the trashcan. "I grew up and went to school in Dallas."

"Ah. A big-city girl."

"I mean, I like the country too," she said.

Link laughed then. Actually laughed right out loud.

"What?" she asked.

"You're not a great liar, Miss Misty."

The song ended, and more people flooded off the dance floor. Link grabbed her arm and tugged her away from the refreshment table.

"You're right," she said as she stumbled after him. "I'm not a great liar."

"My momma says that if you tell the truth, you have no reason to be nervous."

"Sounds like something my mother would say." She flashed him a smile, and she wasn't surprised at all to find Mitch coming their way. He had far darker hair than Link, and she couldn't really see a resemblance between them.

They were both handsome, and both had clearly gotten themselves ready for tonight. Mitch definitely had a more happy-go-luck personality, while Link almost had the dark, mysterious cowboy act down pat. At the same time, she got the feeling he wasn't pretending.

It's hot tonight, Mitch said, and Misty wasn't sure if he meant the temperature or how many people had come to the dance.

"Sure is," Link said. "There's a lot of people here tonight."

"I heard it was the first one," Misty said. Mitch frowned, and she quickly signed it for him, as she'd forgotten.

It's not the first one, he said. *There were dances last weekend too.*

"Did you boys come to those?"

"No," Link said as Mitch shook his head.

Misty didn't know what to do now, flanked by these two gorgeous cowboys. Then she chastised herself for thinking they were gorgeous. *But they are.*

"There you are," Ralf said, and Misty looked past Mitch to the man she worked with. "And who are these fine gentlemen?" He gave her a knowing look while smiling at Link and Mitch.

"This is Link," she said. "And his cousin, Mitch." She glanced at both of them. "Sorry, I didn't get your last names."

"Glover," Link said. "We're both Glovers."

"Misty." Ralf gabbed onto her arm. "We've got to go."

"Go?"

"Yep, there's a…thing in a few minutes." He started towing her away from the Glover cousins, and Misty went with him. She'd known him and worked with him long enough to know he'd have a reason.

"Nice to meet you both," she called over her shoulder, and Link signed quickly to Mitch, and then they both lifted their hands and touched the brims of their cowboy hats, as if they'd practiced that move before coming to the park tonight.

A sigh moved through her body, because they really were cowboy gentlemen. Handsome cowboy gentlemen.

Then the crowd separated them, and Misty pulled her hand away from Ralf. "What was that?" she asked.

"They're Glovers," he said.

"So?"

"So, the Glovers own the biggest and richest ranch in the state," he said. "And they have a couple of men in their family who are vocal about the growth in town. They don't like it."

"But we're not causing any growth," Misty said. "We're restoring their historic City Hall. They should be glad we're here to preserve the history of their building."

"That's why we came early," he said. "To make sure the message gets across. I still don't think it's wise for you to be buddying up to Glovers."

"Well, I wasn't *buddying up* to anyone. I twirled away from that first cowboy." Misty couldn't even remember his name now. "And into Link. I fell on him, and Mitch stumbled over us too. It was nothing."

"Sure." Ralf looked at her, that eyebrow quirked. They'd worked together on too many projects, because he could read her like an open book. "Which one do you like?"

Misty sighed in an overdramatic way, hoping Ralf would get the hint that he was being ridiculous. "I chatted with them for a few minutes," she said. "I don't like either of them."

Ralf rolled his eyes. "You're such a bad liar."

"Fine, I liked them both," she said. "But not romantically."

"Because you don't do romances."

"Right," she said, solidifying herself in her previous mantras. Not only that, but she didn't want to admit that she'd liked both Link and Mitch, and if one or the other of them did happen to ask her out, she didn't know which one she'd like to get to know better.

16

Mitchell Glover spent so much of his life in silence that the vibrant energy of a town dance filled his soul with life. So much so that he still felt the reverberations of the dance in his bones when he woke the next morning.

The Sabbath Day, and Mitch would be expected to get up, clean up, and show up at church. He didn't live with his momma and daddy anymore, but a quick fifteen-minute walk put him at the Edge Cabin, where they lived.

He could show up there for lunch, and there'd be food enough to feed him. If he wanted to crash on the couch and watch a movie, they wouldn't turn him away. When he just needed to be by himself—something that seemed impossible but that sometimes happened—he'd take the walk and then go further, to the western fence of Shiloh Ridge Ranch, where he could see seemingly forever, as it sat at one of the highest parts of the property.

A light flashed behind his closed eyelids, and Mitch opened his eyes and reached for his phone. His hearing dog, a pretty golden retriever named Honor, lifted her head too, and then she moved up from the end of the bed to put her head on his chest.

She was supposed to do that when his alarm went off, even if he was awake, and Mitch gave her a soft smile and ran his hand over her head and ears. *Good morning*, he thought as Honor squinted her eyes at him. She loved a good body rub, and Mitch loved feeling connected to another living thing.

I don't want to go to church today, he thought. And he didn't. Perhaps he could text Uncle Ward and find out if there was something to do on the ranch that would keep him home. Lord knew there had to be, as this place was huge, with countless moving parts, even more animals, and plenty that needed doing.

Then he wouldn't have to explain anything to his parents, his family, or Link.

He sighed as he rolled away from Honor and swung his legs over the side of the bed. Link was his best friend, and though they'd parted ways and taken different paths in life, they'd come back together at the ranch again.

He'd seen the way Link had looked at Misty last night. He'd said nothing, because Link wasn't the most loquacious of cowboys, and it had been dark on the way home. They couldn't talk with voices, and he looked over to the other bed in the room. The one where his cousin and best friend slept.

It was empty, the blankets already pulled up and tucked neatly. Mitch looked at his half of the room, and it held an array of bags and boxes that still weren't all the way unpacked. He never made his bed, and while he'd never realized it before, it definitely struck him now at how different he and Link were.

Movement caught his attention, because Mitch had gotten really good at using his other senses to keep track of what went on around him.

He found Link entering the room, and he signed to him. "You want breakfast? Cutter's making omelets."

Mitch nodded, and Link smiled as he left the room. He'd showered already, and he wore his church clothes, so he'd definitely be making the drive to town for services. Mitch flipped his phone over and over, and then he texted Uncle Ward.

Anything you need from me this morning?

He got to his feet and padded out of the bedroom and down the hall, where the scent of ham, cheese, and butter filled the air. Honor's nose went nuts, but her focus stayed on the back door, which Mitch opened for her. She trotted down the steps to the grass that surrounded this grouping of cowboy cabins.

Nine men lived and worked here at Shiloh Ridge full time, and during the busier times—branding, calving, breeding, and the round-up—they brought in temporary men and women too.

He turned back to the kitchen to find Link and Cutter laughing about something, and all he could do was imagine what they might sound like. Funnily enough, he had voices for everyone in his life, male and female, and he smiled at Link for a moment before his phone went off.

Uncle Ward had said, *Yeah, we need an extra man on rotations this morning. You've got it?*

I've got it, Mitch texted. He loved saddling a horse and riding with others as they moved their livestock from pasture to pasture. He hadn't gotten in the swing of their rotations yet, but Mitch wouldn't be doing it alone.

He never got to do much of anything alone.

And yet, he felt more isolated from people than ever. Why, he wasn't sure. He hadn't ever wanted for a dance partner last night. He'd been surrounded by people, music, noise, life.

At Shiloh Ridge, it was nigh to impossible to find anywhere that didn't have another person within rock-throwing distance, and Mitch should be glad of that. But he wasn't.

He wanted to hide, and that meant less eyes on him. Less people checking to make sure he understood. Less of everything.

"Omelets," Cutter said without signing it. But Mitch could read lips extremely well, and he turned back to the door to look for Honor. He didn't see her, and it was early enough that he simply opened the door a crack. She'd nose her way back in when she returned, and Mitch went to join his cabinmates for breakfast.

Cutter wasn't dressed for church either, but he'd at least put on jeans and a shirt. Mitch wore basketball shorts and nothing else, but no one said anything about his attire.

"You're not going to church?" Link asked, and he signed as he spoke.

Mitch shook his head, and reminded himself to sign slower than he normally would. He'd just returned from a dog training facility in Virginia where half of the people who worked there spoke solely in sign language, like him. They could sign faster to one another, but here, if he did that, no one could understand what he'd said.

Well, Momma and Daddy could, but no one else.

Uncle Ward needed someone last-minute, he told Link and Cutter. He picked up his fork and smiled at Cutter. He touched his chin and pulled his hand back, the sign for *thank you.*

Cutter grinned, as he'd already tucked into his breakfast, and Link hesitated. He likely wanted to pray before they ate, but in the end, he said nothing before diving into his omelet.

An hour later, Mitch had been on horseback for thirty minutes, and he'd been assigned the caboose role in the movement of their animals that morning. It was his job to make sure every last cow got pushed out of the pasture they were in and moved over to the one where Ward wanted them.

He rode behind everyone at a slow pace, his eyes roaming the trees and down into the gulch to make sure not a single head was missed. This part of the ranch had fared decently well during the flooding, and if anything, it was far easier to find stray cattle now that so many branches had been cut back and cleaned up.

They'd come across a pile of them every so often, and Mitch had no idea what the plans were for the debris. They sometimes did a controlled burn, but he suspected Uncle Ward, Uncle Ace, and Uncle Bishop would eventually go around and pick it all up. They'd take it to the family firewood pile, especially now that summer had arrived.

He had fond memories of his teen years spent here on the ranch. They had bonfires in the evenings all throughout the summer, and plenty of food and cake for every birthday. Aunt Sammy never let an opportunity go by where she could make someone feel special, and Mitch loved how she brought him a cupcake every year on his birthday.

The day had heated already, but Mitch didn't mind so much. He wore long sleeves to protect his skin from the sun, and his cowboy hat kept the UV rays off his face, neck, and ears too. He looked up into the bright blue sky, wondering if a more perfect day existed.

A sigh pulled through his body, and his thoughts roamed through possible conversations with his father. Daddy had left Shiloh Ridge to get a veterinary degree. Surely not every Glover male had to be a cowboy here on the ranch.

He twisted to reach for his water bottle, and a flash of red crossed his field of vision. He blinked, and it disappeared. Mitch instantly pulled on the reins to get his horse to stop. Honor did too, and she looked up at him with her tongue hanging out of her mouth.

Mitch looked to his left again, sweeping, sweeping, sweeping to find that crop of crimson. He'd seen it. He knew he'd seen it.

It fluttered again, and Mitch's heartbeat did the same. He could use his voice, and he yelled, hopefully to get the attention of the man up ahead of him. Mitch couldn't see Jed anywhere, but that flash of red filled his peripheral vision again.

There was something there that shouldn't be,

and Mitch pulled his horse to the right to go find out what. Honor trotted along with him, and then she went ahead.

What looked like a hand lifted into the air, and Mitch's pulse went wild. He pulled out his phone and released the reins. His horse slowed to a stop as Mitch tapped out a text. Since he spent so much time texting, he had fast fingers, and he had a text fired off to everyone who lived and worked on the ranch in under five seconds.

I just found someone by the fence line in field twenty-four.

He looked up, and sure enough, a woman had lifted her head. Her mouth moved, but Mitch was either too far away or too stunned to read her lips. Her head fell down again, and that flutter of crimson—a scarf or handkerchief or something— moved in the slight breeze.

Mitch's phone brightened, but he ignored it as he slid from the saddle and jogged toward her. How could he tell her she was okay? Her eyes fluttered closed, and her chest rose and fell in short, breaths.

We need an ambulance, he sent next. *It's a woman. She's breathing.*

He looked back to her and reached out to

brush her hair off her forehead. She felt clammy and cold, and that certainly shouldn't be the case for this summer day in June.

The ground vibrated, and Mitch looked over his shoulder to find his riding partners galloping toward him. He didn't need to wave them down; his horse stood there in plain sight.

Instead, he slid his fingers between that of the woman's and wished he could will his thoughts into her head. *It's okay*, he told her. *It's going to be okay. Help is on the way.*

He squeezed, and thankfully, she squeezed back.

Jed arrived first, skidding on his knees next to them. He spoke, but Mitch only caught "going on?"

The woman didn't answer, but her eyes did flutter open.

"Who are you?" Jed asked next, and Mitch's eyes flew to the woman. She wore shorts and a T-shirt, but she had no shoes, and as he let his gaze slide down her body and back up, he realized she was dirty, with dried blood on her knee, then her forearm, and across her cheekbone.

His stomach lurched, because he'd never been good with blood, and he tried to pull his hand away. She gripped it tighter and opened her eyes all the way.

"I'm Lily, and I crashed my bicycle somewhere."

Jed had his phone out now, and he spoke into it. "She's awake. Her name is Lily, and I gotta say, she's not breathing real well...."

Mitch couldn't hear the other side of the conversation, so he just stroked his hand across her forehead to keep her hair back.

"Did you see the red?" she asked.

He nodded, and she did too, though hers were faster and tighter.

"I tried yelling," she said. "I waved my sock, but no—one...saw."

He shook his head and touched his ear, trying to tell her he couldn't hear her. Even if she had yelled loud enough for someone else to hear, he wouldn't have.

"He's deaf," Jed said. "But he saw you, and he texted, and they're coming."

"Thank you," she said, her lips almost white. "Thank you." Her eyes drifted closed again, and Jed didn't like that. He tried to wake her, but Lily just said, "Thank you," again as she passed out.

<h1 style="text-align:center">17</h1>

"She was passed out at Shiloh Ridge?" Edith looked over to Aggie with nothing but alarm running through her body. "What happened?"

Aggie swung her car around and headed down the dirt road that led back to the highway. They'd pick up Christie and JoJo, and then they'd find somewhere for lunch. Summertime was crazy for everyone, and JoJo would be traveling over their normally scheduled Girls Night.

Aggie's dark hair had been pulled up into a tight, high ponytail, and she'd painted on the perfect cat's eyeliner around her dark eyes. "I guess Lily had gone for a bike ride the previous night—"

"Do not tell me she was out there alone all night." Horror ran through Edith. "There are wild animals here."

"She was out there alone all night." Aggie nodded with wide eyes. "A truck went by and showered gravel at her, and as she tried to get away from it, she lost control of her bike, flipped it, and crashed."

Edith crossed her arms over her stomach. "I don't like this story."

"She woke up in the ditch, and she did her best to get somewhere people could find her."

"What about her phone?"

"Busted," Aggie said. She looked left and right, then turned to head toward town. It only took about five minutes, and then the houses and condos and town of Three Rivers spread before them. "Get this—Mitchell Glover found her."

"Mitch did?"

"He can't hear, and he found her because she'd been wearing red socks, and she'd taken one off and waved it as much as she could, hoping to get someone's attention."

"Wow." Edith would add Lily Tyders to her prayers.

"She's in the hospital with a couple broken

ribs and a couple broken toes. Apparently everything else is superficial. Well, besides the concussion."

"Was she wearing a helmet?"

"Yeah, but they found it cracked practically in half."

"My goodness." Edith didn't want to talk about this anymore. "Christie will know more, I'm sure." Their friend worked as a nurse in the hospital in Three Rivers, and that was an even smaller network than the town at large.

"Yeah, I heard all about it from my neighbor. Good old Mrs. Pridders, right?" Aggie grinned and glanced over to Edith. "Anything to tell me before we get the others?"

Edith shrugged one shoulder and looked away from her friend's gaze. "Finn's been coming for a couple of weeks." She smiled, because she couldn't help it when it came to Finn. "He brings this huge thermos of coffee, and he lets Alex boss him around all day long."

"I'll bet he does," Aggie said suggestively. "He knows how to impress you, Edee."

"He knows how to fix sinkholes too," she said. "They've got two done, and they're replanting those today."

"Handsome and handy," Aggie teased.

She didn't want to talk about Finn anymore, though she was sure she'd have to say more when they got Christie and JoJo. "What about that guy you were messaging on Two Cents?"

"Chuck?" Aggie pursed her lips, her grip suddenly tighter on the steering wheel too. "He started ignoring me."

"Oh, so he's one of those mature types."

Aggie scoffed, and a moment later, she started giggling. "Yeah, he's one of those." She pulled up to Christie's house, and both her and JoJo came outside. They both wore capri jeans and tank tops, and Edith smiled at the predictability of them.

"Look at Christie's bag." She swung her attention to Aggie. "She got it?" Edith pulled the door handle with one hand and unbuckled her seatbelt with the other. She rose from the car and said, "You got the purse."

Christie shone like a star as she looked down at her black and white spotted bag. "I got the purse." She pulled it off her shoulder and held it out for all of them to see. "Isn't it fantastic?"

"It really is," Edith said as she stepped into her friend and hugged her. Christie loved purses and bags, and she had an entire closet in her house filled with them. Edith didn't even use a purse, choosing to put a few cards in her thread wallet and tuck that in her pocket whenever she left the house.

"Hey, you," JoJo said, and Edith moved over to hug her. "I got your email last night. Can't wait to read the new book."

Nerves ran through Edith, but she nodded as she moved back. "There's something not quite right with it, but I'm not going to tell you where. I just want to know what you think."

"Of course." JoJo had about six or seven years on Edith, and she currently worked at the pharmacy at Wilde & Organic as a lab technician. She loved to read in her spare time, the way Edith did, and she'd read the last couple of Edith's books before anyone else.

"You got your hair done," Aggie said as the three of them got back in the car.

"I did," JoJo said. "And let me tell you, all the gossip at the salon was about two things. Well, three."

"Do tell," Aggie said. "I never get the salon gossip."

"You should go get your hair trimmed at least," Christie said.

"I do it myself." Aggie backed out of the driveway and said, "Wait on the hot-goss. Where are we going to lunch?"

Edith kept her mouth shut, because she didn't care where they ate. Finn had run to town a few times in the past couple of weeks, and he'd brought back food from a Hawaiian place where Edith loved their macaroni salad, burgers and fries one day—Alex's favorite—and fried chicken another.

Edith didn't normally eat out too much, but she'd had plenty of opportunities lately. So she didn't need to pick or have a vote.

"I want Thai," Christie said.

"The baby is craving Pad Thai," JoJo said.

Edith grinned at Aggie. "Sounds like Thai."

"Fine, but we're driving to that place by the county courthouse."

"It's forty minutes," Christie complained at the same time Edith said, "It's too far, Ags."

"The baby will die," JoJo added, but Aggie shook her head, her jaw set.

"If I'm eating Thai, it's only from RanVan. Don't test me on this, girls. Christie, I will make you go to Subway." She glared into the rearview mirror as she turned to go west.

Christie sucked in a breath. "You wouldn't dare."

"I'm starving," Edith said. "You said 'a quick lunch in town,' not a drive to some town we don't know the name of that somehow houses our county courthouse."

"It's Stinnett," Aggie said, throwing her a glare. "You know that. We went to senior prom there."

"Wrong," Edie said as the others in the back continued to gripe about driving to Stinnett for Thai food. "I moved to Florida for my senior year of high school."

"Edith kissed Finn," Aggie yelled into the car, and that got the arguing to stop.

"Tell us about Lily Tyders," Edith bit out between her teeth. "Christie, what other news is there?"

"Or Ags could tell us about her new guy—Justin," Christie said.

"There's no new guy." Aggie glanced over to Edith as an ice-cold arrow shot through Edith's heart.

"New guy?" Aggie always told her about her texts and chats and swipe-rights. Always.

"There's no new guy." Aggie turned around

and glared at the other two in the back seat. "It's at least twenty minutes across town to the totally subpar Thai place. Or a nice drive north to a far superior one. Can we not make each other talk about things we don't want to talk about?"

"Why wouldn't you want to talk about a new guy?" Edith asked.

"Why don't you want to talk about kissing Finn?"

"Because it's intimate," Edith said. "Private."

"Right to amazing food or left to cardboard noodles?" Aggie asked. "Someone tell me where to go so I don't get in trouble with the pregnant lady."

"So you kissed Finn, huh?" JoJo asked instead of telling Aggie which way to go.

"A couple of weeks ago," Edith murmured as she turned back to the passenger window. "It was...really nice. I miss kissing."

Aggie snorted. "Truer words have never been spoken." She made a right turn to which no one protested.

They rode in silence for a few minutes, and then JoJo said, "I could tell you about the baby names Chris and I have been talking about."

"Yes," Edith said instantly. "Let's talk about that."

A couple of days later, Edith propped open the door to her she-shed and went back inside to get a box of books. Twenty-two could fit inside a case, and she carried it with heavy steps around the house to her SUV.

"What's happening here?" Finn asked as he pulled up in his truck. He rested one elbow out the window, and she didn't see his thermos yet.

"Loading up for tomorrow." She dusted her hands. "Sure would be nice to have some cowboy muscles to help with the other boxes." She planted her hands on her hips and cocked one out.

Finn laughed, parked his truck, and got out, thermos and all. He neared, and she caught the familiar whiff of peppermint on his breath. "Good morning, beautiful."

"Morning yourself, Chuckles."

He did chuckle, and then he touched his lips to hers. He'd clearly been chewing that spicy-hot peppermint gum, because she tasted it on him.

"You're burning me," she whispered before kissing him again.

"Doesn't seem to be bothering you." He grinned as he pulled away.

"I don't know how you chew that stuff. It's so spicy."

"I like it," he said. "Makes my mouth feel clean."

"Mm." She nodded back toward the house. "So...the boxes?"

"Who's gonna haul these into the library for you tomorrow?"

"I'm sure they'll have a cart or something," she said. Besides, it wasn't like she couldn't do it, but why should she with Finn here?

"Maybe I could come," he said as he started for the corner of the house.

She watched him disappear around it. "Come?" Edith's heart beat at her to follow him and find out what that meant, so she broke into a jog. In the side-shadow of the house, she found him already at the back corner. "You want to come?"

"I could help with the boxes," he said. "Go grab breakfast so I'm not bothering you during your talk. And we can stop and look at a little farm on the way back."

Edith's eyebrows shot up. "A little farm on the way back?" She stopped running to catch him, but Finn kept on moving. He went through the propped-open door and came back out a few seconds later with one of her boxes.

As he approached, he grinned at her. "A place just went up for sale only a few miles outside of town. West. Looks pretty good online, and they said I could come by tomorrow. Any time."

Edith blinked at him. "You want me to go with you?"

"I can't make a decision like this myself," he said. "And I don't trust anyone more than you."

"Okay, then, Hacky Sack," she said, a smile playing with her mouth.

That delicious grin graced his face for only a moment before he tipped his head back and poured laughter into the sky.

"Yeah, you liked that one, didn't you?" she teased, pleased she could make him laugh like that. She hadn't known this much joy in a long time, and it sure felt good as Finn shook his head and went by her with her box.

She went into the she-shed and picked up the case with her signage, as well as the small box with her signing kit, her stickers, and her horse figurines. These lighter items got carried out while Finn loaded her boxes, and then they sat on the porch, his mega-thermos between them.

"Uh, I'm just gonna spit this out," he said.

Edith looked over to him and slid her hand into his. "Okay. Sounds bad."

"It's not bad," he said. "It's just...a lot." He reached across his body and picked up his thermos. "First, maybe you should try this." He handed her his thermos, but Edith just looked from it to him.

"I've got coffee inside," she said. "Plus, it gives me heartburn, and it's way too hot to drink it in the summer."

"You'll like this," he said in this totally not-nonchalant voice.

Edith grinned at him. "I'll like this?" She twisted the top of it. "What have you been hiding in this all these weeks?"

He laughed again and said, "It's only been three weeks."

"It's still plural."

Edith sniffed the thermos, and it definitely smelled like coffee. She expected steam to rise from the thermos, but it didn't. She got a hint of vanilla, and she looked at Finn. He wore delight in his expression, his light eyes dancing with it.

"Go on," he said. "It's not poison."

Tentatively, she lifted the thermos to her lips and took a sip. The delight obviously running through Finn now coated her mouth. She moaned, because she couldn't speak, and then she swallowed.

"That's fantastic."

"I've been bringing iced coffee," he said. "But this has a couple of scoops of vanilla ice cream in it."

"Vanilla ice cream?" She shook her head in appreciation. "Genius." She passed him the thermos. "You drink this all day long. You must be buzzed constantly."

He took a big swallow. "I need it," he said.

"Why? Not sleeping?" Edith knew that burden, as she hadn't slept well in the days, weeks, and months following Levi's diagnosis and death.

"Would you believe me if I said I lie awake all night, thinking of you?"

Edith was the one who tipped her head back and filled the porch with laughter this time, but Finn nudged her with his shoulder. "Come on," he said. "It's not that funny." But he chuckled too.

She once again liked how their voices sounded intertwined together, and when they settled into silence, Edith tucked her arm around his and leaned her head against his bicep. "I'd love to go look at your place with you tomorrow."

"Great, then I'll come," he said. "Would you be game to come to the Fourth celebration at the ranch in a couple of weeks? Momma makes a red, white, and blue feast, and we have our own fireworks show, and it's a big deal." He tilted his head down to look at her, and Edith looked up at him.

She could tell from the expression on his face that it was a big deal that he'd asked. "Like a big deal with capital letters?"

He smiled softly. "I forgot we used to say that in high school."

"It's a big game," she said, letting her mind flow back to the things she and Finn had experienced in years gone by. "With capital letters."

"It's a nasty final," he said, playing along. "In *all* capital letters."

Edith grinned too, so comfortable with him.

"But yeah, sweetheart, this Fourth thing is a big deal with capital letters."

Edith's pulse played a symphony through her body. "And you want me to come?"

"Yeah." Finn said, just like that. "I'd like you to come. All the cowboys come. All the kids. We've got a couple of the Walker boys who just graduated from high school working for us this summer, so Daddy invited their family."

"All seven of them?"

"Well, Wyatt's already up in Wyoming with his family," Finn said. "But otherwise, yeah. I think they're coming too. But we have a big lawn, and we can sneak away and find somewhere more private for the fireworks show."

While Edith enjoyed teasing with him and making him say all the things she wanted to hear, she also wanted to be real with him. Because she was falling for him in a very real way, and she didn't need to play games with anyone, least of all Finn.

So she snuggled into him further and said, "I'd love to come out to the ranch with y'all on the Fourth of July."

18

Finn schlepped in the last box—the library in Amarillo did not have a cart for Edith's books—and slid it onto the last half of the second table. Edith had been busy while he'd been going back and forth, and she'd gotten one banner set up that showed the front half of a horse while she bent over, wrestling with the second one.

"Can I do it?" he asked, moving around the table to help her.

Edith looked up, and Finn stopped completely. For his beautiful, blonde Edith had dark hair now. "What...is happening?" He blinked at her, trying to put all the familiar pieces in the right place. They didn't seem to want to line up.

"My author photo is me with black hair," she said, pure nerves running through her expression. "It was this—this—this phase I went through in New York." She reached up and combed her fingers through the short locks. She could probably gather it into a low ponytail that might be three or four inches, and Finn told himself that her regular hair wasn't much longer.

"It's just a wig," she said. "Do I look ridiculous?"

"No," he said quickly. "You just don't look like you—to me. You don't look like you to me."

She huffed out her breath, clearly frustrated. "I can't get that one to unlatch."

"I'll do it," he said. "The books are all in."

"I'll start on those." Edith in her dark-haired glory turned to the boxes in front of her, and by the time Finn got the banner unlatched and extended, she'd set up the table with her books, stickers, and miniature horse figurines.

"Can you put these under the table, baby?" she asked, glancing toward the door. "I always get so nervous doing these."

"You're a natural," he said. He put the boxes where she wanted them, and he'd no sooner done that than another author arrived with her boxes and bits and baubles.

Edith gushed over her—a woman named Pauline March—and before he knew it, the library director arrived and took both authors with her. "I'll see you after," she said, and Finn lifted his hand in a good-bye and good luck wave.

He moved out from behind the table and ducked out of the children's hall where the Summer Reading intro meeting was set to start in another fifteen minutes. He visited the restroom and returned to the room to find it filling, and fast.

He took a seat in the last row in the corner and watched Edith for a moment. She chatted with the library director and her fellow author, her eyes darting out nervously to the crowd as it continued to gather.

Adults sat in the chairs behind the wide, arcing carpeted area in front of the stage, and when the clock struck ten, the library director picked up a mic and said, "Welcome, everyone, to our Summer Reading Kickoff!"

Applause filled the hall, with plenty of children's voices. The library director waved people forward. "Kids can come up onto the carpet. Children up here."

After several seconds of movement and shifting, the library director said, "We have two amazing authors with us this morning." She grinned at the two women to her side. "From Three Rivers, Edith Baxter."

His lovely Edith lifted her hand in greeting, her gorgeous smile lighting up her eyes. She seemed perfectly at ease while the director introduced the other author, and when she picked up the mic to start answering questions, there wasn't a brighter person in the room.

Finn basked in her light and warmth, and he felt himself falling, falling, falling in love with her. He knew it was fast, and he told himself to slow down. But he loved working with her at Coyote Pass, and he loved talking to her, and he loved that she got to do events like these because of her writing.

He'd also never seen anyone as good with kids as she was. She could somehow see the ones who got overlooked, and she came out from behind the table almost instantly so she could be closer to them.

"Did you draw your covers?" one little boy asked, and Edith grinned at him like he'd been turned to gold by speaking.

"No, sir," she drawled out. "A really talented illustrator drew them. He got to read the book, and then he drew several scenes from it. I got to go through them and pick one I thought would work for cover."

"What was his name?"

Edith didn't hesitate at all. "A really wonderful man named Levi."

Finn's heartbeat stopped. Just absolutely stopped, right there in his chest. Somehow, his mouth still said, "Levi was her illustrator."

Edith had not told him that. He hadn't asked how they'd met, and she hadn't said. They hadn't talked much more about Levi since she'd told him about their move here, his diagnosis, and his passing.

She continued to talk but Finn focused on how she was lit from within while she spoke about her former fiancé. While she talked about his art, and how she had all the drawings that she hadn't chosen for the covers at home, and how much she'd loved working with him.

For anyone who didn't know anything about Levi—like all the children and parents here in Amarillo—it was just a nice story. To Finn, Edith loved working with Levi because she'd been completely in love with Levi.

And the worst part was, she still was.

Finn found his throat was far too narrow to swallow through. His heart felt giant in his chest, and it crowded painfully against his other organs until he felt like he couldn't breathe. He got to his feet and turned away from the children and parents and the other author and Edith.

He had to get out, and he had to get out right now. He strode with purpose toward the exit, hoping he wouldn't cause a scene. He was maybe just a dad who needed to run to the bathroom for the second time in under an hour.

He'd originally told Edith he wouldn't stay, that he didn't want to make her nervous. She'd said he didn't have to leave, but now he wished he'd have looked up the best place to get breakfast in Amarillo and gone there instead.

Maybe then he wouldn't have had to listen to Edith talk about Levi like she still loved him. He burst outside and fast-footed it down the steps to the sidewalk. His chest heaved as he breathed, and he had no idea where he was going.

He only knew he had to go.

~

AN HOUR LATER, FINN HAD MANAGED TO swallow his pride and return to the library to help Edith with her boxes and signing supplies. She'd sold almost all of her books, and Finn stood to the side while she took a picture with a girl who looked to be ten or eleven years old. They both shone like stars, and Finn's blood felt like ice in his veins.

The event ended, and Edith's energy and demeanor fell noticeably. She started cleaning up, and when she met his eyes, she said, "Sorry that went longer than they said."

"It's fine. These go back in boxes?" He picked up the four books still on the table and put them in one of the empty boxes. Then he turned to take down her banners. They didn't speak, and Finn realized it was because Edith was simply worn out. Speaking and being on at that high level for that long had likely sapped her.

She worked in a methodical way, and it only took one trip with both of them carrying things to get back to his truck.

Finn had planned to take her to lunch and

then stop by the ranch he wanted to look at on the way home, but now he simply wanted to head straight back to Coyote Pass, drop off Edith, and go home.

His chest hurt. His head hurt. His heart hurt.

"Finn?" she asked.

He glanced over to her. "Hmm?"

"Are we not going to lunch?"

"You seem tired," he said, not sure what else to say. He also heard himself, and he was clearly upset.

It took an extra moment, but Edith asked, "Are you okay?"

He shook his head. "I don't feel well." It wasn't exactly a lie, but Finn didn't know how to tell her what hurt.

"Finn."

He turned right to get on the highway that led back to Three Rivers, his mind rushing over prayer after prayer.

"Something's wrong," she said.

"Yes," clipped from his mouth. "Something's wrong."

"What is it?"

"The fact that you're still in love with Levi," he said. "And I'll never be Levi."

"Wh—What?"

"I heard you talking about him, and I saw you." He glanced over to her. "It's obvious."

Edith didn't say anything. Didn't deny it. She sniffled, and that only made pure regret yank through him. Hard. He didn't want to make her feel bad, but at the same time, *he* felt bad.

"You're not denying it."

"I don't know how to tell you that I don't love him," she said. "I loved him, Finn. That doesn't stop just because I want it to, or you want it to, or that he's gone."

"So where does that leave me?"

"I have room for someone else," she said. "You, Finn. I have room for you too."

Room for you too.

He didn't exactly like the sound of that. "I don't know where we are," he said.

"We're on the highway back to Three Rivers."

Finn turned and glared at her. Edith wiped her eyes and said, "Finn, I got rid of the pictures in the spare bedroom."

"I just—" He glanced at the road to make sure he wouldn't drive them into a ditch. "You did?"

"I'm– yes. The human heart has room to love an unnumbered amount of people," she said. "I haven't worked very hard to clear space for anyone before now. Before you."

Finn wished he'd taken his military approach to this situation. He could've thought through things better. He could've waited to speak with her until he'd examined things from every angle. "I'm sorry."

"You don't need to apologize. I do. I didn't tell you about Levi being my cover illustrator."

"I never asked."

"But I should've told you."

Finn kept driving, hoping his silence would prompt her to tell him what she needed to tell him. He thought of the posters of her book covers —Levi's art, a constant reminder of Levi—in her she-shed.

"I met him at the publishing house where I was working. He worked with a lot of houses, doing a lot of book covers. It was like...like...remember when we first met?"

"Me tapping on the glass of your car and scaring you?"

"No, silly." She sniffled and shook her head. She'd swiped the wig off her head the moment they'd gotten in the truck, and now she ran her fingers through her hair. "When we first-first met. Ages ago."

He glanced over to her again. "I wish I could go back to the beginning of this day," he said. "Because no, I don't remember meeting you for the first time. We had to be what? Twelve?"

"Eleven," she said. "Sixth grade, when we finally went to the same middle school. Remember, I went to South Elementary and you went to North?" She sighed, but it didn't exactly sound happy.

"I thought you were the cutest boy in the whole world." She half-laughed, but it didn't hold the same wattage as usual. "Remember how we sat at the same table in history? With Mister Stuntaker?"

Finn nodded, though he wished he remembered meeting Edith for the first time in middle school.

"We sat at the same table, because your last name is A and mine is B, and I was thrilled." She gave a light laugh, though she definitely still had tears present. "Mister Stuntaker didn't care where we sat as long as it was at the same table, and I tried to get there early and save you a seat."

"You did?"

She nodded. "I thought I was being so obvious." She scoffed. "But looking back, I don't think you noticed."

"I liked you," he said. "We were friends." He remembered that much. Did he even remember when he'd started having feelings for her? Romantic feelings? He wasn't sure he did.

"Yeah," she said. "We were friends." She took in a long breath. "One day, you caught me coming out of the home ec classroom, and you said, 'Is that your class before history?' I told you yes, and you had PE, and you started waiting across the hall for me to come out of class. Then we'd walk to history together. It was...incredible. *That* was incredible to me."

"I don't know what to say," he murmured.

"I wrote your last name after my first name on every notebook I got that year. I named all our kids, and I even wrote about you in one of our assignments for Mrs. Workman. Remember her?"

Of course Finn remembered her. She was the English teacher that caused him to hate reading and writing. "Yeah," he said miserably.

"Then, one day, you asked me for help with

your history paper. I thought I'd died and gone to heaven. We got along great, and you were a fast learner, and we were practically inseparable after that."

Finn dared to peek over to her, and Edith did shine again the way she had at the library. Only this time, she had tears streaming down her face.

"Meeting Levi was like that," she whispered. "It was like meeting *you* all over again. There was just so much between us, as if we'd known each other before. He was handsome, and kind, and so talented. Everything with him was easy." She sniffled and reached up to wipe her face. "The way it's always been with you."

"Sweetheart."

She shook her head as her face crumbled again, and Finn didn't know what to do now. "I feel like a complete jerk."

"Don't," she said. "It's not your fault."

"I made assumptions."

"No, you didn't." She reached over and took his hand in hers. "I do love Levi, Finn. I don't know how to *stop* loving Levi. But that doesn't mean I can't love you too."

He met her gaze and squeezed her hand. His

throat closed again, but he managed to say, "We're too far from Amarillo to go back for lunch."

She gave him a teary-eyed smile. "I know a great Thai place in Stinnett."

He nodded and said, "Okay."

"Will you still take me to the farm you want to see?" Her voice turned tinny then. "I'm so sorry, Finn. I've been trying to take steps to get myself down the road to be where you are. I promise. You're just so much faster than me. You've always been faster than me."

Finn couldn't stand this level of hurt in her voice. He eased up on the accelerator and pulled to the side of the road. "Sweetheart." He leaned toward her, but he hated the console between them. He slid from the truck and rounded it, opening her door in the blazing summer heat.

"Hey, come on." He gathered her into his arms. "I'm sorry. I didn't mean to make you cry." Or force her to tell him all this stuff about them as kids or relive how she'd met and fallen in love with Levi

She clung to him and sobbed, and Finn's own emotions reared and swarmed and flooded through him. "I'm sorry," he whispered again.

"Me too," she said. "I'm so sorry, Finn."

He held her until she quieted, saying nothing more. The military side of him had returned, and he'd catalogued everything she'd said, and he'd analyze it later. That was what he'd been trained to do, and he could do it here, with this.

They breathed in together, and then he said, "It could be worse. You could've been that other author at today's event, totally outshined by this amazing woman from Three Rivers who writes about horses."

Edith met his eye, and it took a couple of beats until she smiled. "It could be better," she said. "Than me sobbing into your shoulder because of Levi yet again."

"Nah." He shook his head and wiped her tears away. "You're not crying because of Levi, sweetheart. You're crying because of *me*, and I promise you, it'll be the last time."

She shook her head, her eyes dropping to her lap. "It could be worse," she whispered. "You could've not been standing at the window when I left Courage Reins that day."

A smile slipped through the regret and pure humiliation inside Finn. "It could be better," he whispered back. "If you'd forgive me and kiss me to let me know we're okay."

Edith looked up, and Finn's eyes filled with tears. "I know you loved him," he said. "I'm sorry for acting like a fool and jumping to this conclusion that loving him meant you could never love me."

"Come here, cowboy." Out of all the nicknames Edith used for him, Finn liked that one the best. She slid her hands along his jaw and pulled him close. "I'll only forgive you if you forgive me."

"Okay," he said, leaning in.

"And." She pulled back. "Take me to lunch like we planned. *And*."

Finn started to smile, because he knew she wouldn't kiss him until she'd said all she needed to say.

"Take me to that farm you wanted to see."

"Okay," he said again.

Her eyes searched his, a new vibrancy in them he hadn't seen until now. "Okay." She kissed him, and oh, Finn liked that. He liked the way Edith felt things deeply, and he liked that that included her feelings for him.

Now, he had to figure out a way not to snuff her out. He had to find a place for her star to shine, because it wasn't in his daddy's basement. It might not be at the farm they'd stop by and see after lunch.

But it might be.

She could be his shining star if he didn't mess up too badly again.

"We're okay?" he whispered.

"Yes." She nodded slightly, her forehead pressed to his. "We're okay."

"Okay." He took a big breath and stepped out of the passenger doorway. "Then let's get to lunch and then Thompson Wash."

"That's the name of the place?" Edith shook her hair out and looked out the windshield. "I don't like the name of it, but I'll withhold judgment until I see it."

Finn chuckled, his emotions up and down and all around in the past couple of hours. *Withhold judgment* rang in his ears as he closed the door. Perhaps that was what he should've done when he'd heard Edith talking so reverently and lovingly about Levi. Still, as he got behind the wheel and looked over to Edith, he felt closer to her than ever.

"Did you know you're incredible at events like that?" he asked.

"I'm okay," she said.

"Mm, nope. You're *incredible*." He reached over and took her hand. "So...do I get to know the names of our children?"

Edith blinked at him for a moment and then she started to laugh. That was so much better than crying, and the last of Finn's embarrassment for causing a scene faded with the sound of her voice.

19

Edith said nothing as Finn turned left off the highway and rumbled down a dirt road, the sign for Thompson Wash on her side of the truck. She really didn't understand the name. Did the owner know what a wash was?

Because it wasn't the gently rolling landscape with lush fields growing on both sides of the lane. The alfalfa waved in the breeze, and she bet they harvested four or five cycles of it here.

"Not many trees," he said.

"It's the Texas Panhandle," she said back. "And you can plant trees."

"They take generations to grow." He shot her a look that half teased and half didn't. He sighed and added, "I suppose I'm not going to find something perfect, am I?"

"Depends on your definition of perfect."

"My momma and daddy said it doesn't exist. That I might love the house, but the land will need a lot of work. Or the barn will be falling down. Or the land will be amazing, but the house will be a shack. Or everything will be about half of what I want."

"That's what they said?"

"My momma hates her master closet," he said with a smile. "Daddy thinks the kitchen is drafty. They both want a bigger garage." He looked over to her. "You know, that kind of stuff."

"But they live there," Edith said, really thinking about how there was no one perfect place to live. "They work there. They've made it home."

"Right," Finn said quietly, and Edith wondered what lived in his head. "They made it their home. That's what I want. A place and a chance to make something my home."

Edith squeezed his hand, because she wanted that for him too. "Do you think a man can do that by himself?"

"Make a ranch his home?"

"Yeah," she said.

Finn kept his eye out the windshield as a copse of trees came into view. "I think so," he said. "But it's easier if he has a dream. Something to work for."

Edith nodded, his words in her mind. "Some*one* to work for," she said. "When I'm writing, I think of the little girls who will read my books. I think of the escape they need, and their love for dogs and horses, and match the work to them. Then it's not such hard work."

Finn pulled up to the farmhouse, which stood two stories tall and had a stone first level with cement-colored stucco above it. The trees did shade it, and Edith smiled at the porch. "It wraps around," she said.

Finn faced her. "You work on Alex's ranch because you love him."

"Yes," Edith whispered, tearing her eyes from the lovely porch, where she'd just spotted a rocking chair beside a small table. "It's not such hard work when I'm doing it for someone I love."

He nodded and said, "I need something like that. Something outside myself. I think that's why I did so well in the Army. I was part of something bigger than myself."

"You have your family."

Finn almost scoffed as he turned away. "In my family, Edith, I'm the least of them all." He slid from the truck and went to the front bumper as he took in the house. Edith got out of the truck to join him, her heart beating in a strange rhythm.

"Finn, you are not the least of anything." She took his hand. "The door is green. I don't like that."

"Doors can be painted, sweetheart." He led her toward the porch and up the steps. "They said no one would be home today, and we could just wander around as we saw fit."

Something chirped on the porch, and then a male voice said, "Finn, hey!" from a speaker somewhere.

Edith looked around for it, as did Finn. "Hey," he said, waving to the doorbell, which Edith realized had a camera on it. "We're just going to look around for a bit. That's still okay?"

"Let me unlock the front door for you," the man said. "I just ask that if you open a door or gate out on the ranch that you close it behind you."

"Of course," Finn said. "That's the first law of being a cowboy."

The man laughed and said, "The door's open, son. I'll see you when you leave."

That felt a little creepy to Edith, but Finn grinned and said, "Thanks, Mister Jenkins." He reached for the doorknob, and sure enough, the door was open. Finn looked up as he entered, and Edith followed him, ready to see this place for what it currently was—and what it could be.

"Wow," she said as she joined Finn in the foyer. A legit farmhouse foyer.

"Look at that staircase," he said, his feet rooted to the ground.

In front of her, a staircase stood right in the middle of the room, paving the way to the second floor. A gorgeous hardwood covered the floor and led into a room off the left-hand side and the right.

"This feels like a palace," she said. "Not a farmhouse." She liked it, but she didn't at the same time. It didn't feel like a place to make a home, to raise children, and to live off the land in the Texas Panhandle.

It felt fancy, when Finn wasn't very fancy.

The room on the left held plenty of built-in bookcases which held binders and books of all shapes and sizes, as well as a grand piano. Comfy couches lined the far wall, and a couple of guitars stood in stands.

The living room veered to the right, and it led

back into the second half of the farmhouse, which held the kitchen, a big dining room, and a full bath. The master suite sat behind the library-slash-music-room, and Finn whistled as he saw the closet. "Momma would love this." He grinned, but he had a glazed look in his eye.

Edith felt the same glazy-ness inside herself. The back porch made her go, "Whoa. I love this," because it faced north and showed a nice view of the hills. It would be completely private here, with the town to the south and no neighbors. She could walk out her back door and never see another living soul.

Her she-shed would fit here, just to the left there, and a bright green barn sat at the edge of the lawn. "What is with the green here?" she asked, recoiling from the barn. "A barn should never be that color, Finn." She shook her head. "Never."

"Again, a paint color is something easy to fix."

"It's work," Edith said.

"That it is." He continued to tour the rest of the property, and back in his truck, he showed her the real estate listing that showed the borders of the land and where the river ran through it for only five hundred yards before it forked back east again. "So that's it." He looked back up to the farmhouse here at Thompson Wash.

Edith took his phone from him and set it in the cupholder. "What do you think?"

Finn shook his head and started the truck. "I don't know." He backed out and turned to head to the highway.

Edith said nothing, because he hadn't asked what she thought, and she suspected that he already knew this place wasn't for him. She let him be quiet as he drove back to her house, and when he parked there, Edith turned toward him fully.

"Thank you for today, Finn." She smiled at him, her nerves vibrating strangely at her. "For helping at the library. For lunch. For including me at Thompson Wash." She reached over and slid her hand along the side of his face. "What's wrong?"

He turned to look at her, his hand covering hers. "Nothing." He blinked and seemed to come back to himself. "Nothing. Sorry. So many thoughts."

"Is one of them about kissing me?" she asked.

Finn's smile slowly crept across his face, and it held so much light and joy and happiness. "Well, one is now." He leaned forward and kissed her, and Edith sure did love the touch of this man. "I'll see you tomorrow?" he asked. "Want me to come pick you up for church?"

"Oh, you want to stir the church gossip circles into a frenzy?"

"Yeah," he whispered against her lips. "That's what I want to do."

Edith kissed him again, enjoying the slow, steady way she felt in love with him with every stroke of his mouth against hers. He finally pulled away, and she opened her eyes to look at him. He looked back, but neither of them said anything.

Finn gave her half a smile and ducked his head, the brim of his cowboy hat touching her eyebrow. "I'll help you with the boxes." He twisted away and got out of the truck, and Edith turned to do the same.

She collected her things from the backseat while he stacked her two remaining boxes and took them around the house to the she-shed. She followed him and put her bag on her desk. He straightened, and the moment intensified between them.

"I thought of my she-shed there," she blurted out. "At Thompson Wash, in the backyard. There was room for it."

"Yes," he said. "There was."

Edith took the few steps toward him and ran her hands up his chest. "Did you picture it there?"

"I did," he whispered.

"So you'll take me to see all the places you're considering?" she asked. "Because it seems like maybe we're picturing a future together somewhere around here, and I want to be able to comment on the location of my shed."

"Edith, sweetheart, I am *only* considering the location of your shed when I look at ranches." He took her into his arms, the best words in the world now out between them. Love touched her heart when it hadn't in such a long, long time, and instead of crying about it, this time, Edith smiled and leaned into the strength of Finn's embrace.

She'd been living since Levi's death, but she hadn't been dreaming. She hadn't been improving. She hadn't been growing.

Now, she saw the world in color for what it was—and what it could be.

She saw an escape from the colorless life she'd been living, and it wouldn't happen without Finn Ackerman at her side. He'd returned, and suddenly, she had a new life to live.

"Come on, now," she said to Reagan, who didn't seem too keen to leave his stable. At least not with her. Edith hadn't been back to Courage Reins since the day she'd run into Finn again, about a month ago. The flooding, the sinkholes, the library event, they'd all stolen more time from her than she'd like.

Not to mention Finn himself. The man took so much of her time and attention, but he gave her so much in return. She smiled as she stood in the stables, thinking about him. He'd come with her here, but he'd gone into the homestead to talk to his momma while Edith worked with her new horse.

But, it seemed Reagan did not want to work with her. Pete had said he'd taken the horse out a few times, but their lives at Three Rivers had been interrupted by the flooding too, and Reagan had not been worked with as much as he probably should've been.

"Your mane is so pretty," she said, deciding she didn't have to get him to leave his stall for work to be done. "I've never seen a horse with so much hair."

Edith glanced to the right and then the left, didn't see anyone else, and she entered the stall. "A horse with hair like this should have all the bells and whistles." She smiled softly at Reagan as she neared and held out her hand. He huffed, his nostrils flaring as he smelled her.

Then he settled and pressed his nose into her palm. "That's right," she whispered. "You and I are going to be great friends. But let's get your hair done up right, okay?"

She brushed her fingers through the horse's dark black mane, and she started sectioning it so she could braid it. "Who comes to feed you, huh?" she asked. "Is it Kenny? Or Beau?" Probably not the ranch foreman, but Edith didn't care. Reagan obviously couldn't answer.

"There's so much that I'm going to braid it backward, okay?" She ran her hands down both sides of his neck. "That means I'm going to need to be in the saddle. Can you take the saddle?"

She knew he could, and she left his stall to go get the tack. She wouldn't need every piece in the exact position it would need to be if she were going to ride him. But she wasn't. She left the stall door open, and she wasn't at all surprised to hear Reagan clopping out of his stall behind her.

She hid her smile as she pulled down a blanket and a saddle. She got him saddled out in the larger room of the stable and led him outside. "All right. Let's find a shady spot, with plenty of a breeze. Okay?"

Reagan walked alongside her, trying to crowd into her shoulder. "No," she said firmly but gently. "You stay back." She shouldered him, and Reagan slowed his pace to do as she asked. "Thank you, Reagan."

Doing what was required of her wasn't always what she wanted, but Edith knew it would always make her happy. Just like Reagan thought he wanted to crowd her shoulder, but he didn't. He'd be happier if he let her be in charge, because she'd never lead him astray.

Edith looked up in the Texas sky, where today, big puffy clouds sat in residence. "I will let You lead me, Lord," she whispered. "I won't crowd You, and I won't beg You to give me something that might not be good for me. Okay?"

The peaceful feeling that overtook her made tears prick her eyes, but they were out of happiness this time. Maybe she did need to slow down a little. Maybe she had been crowding God a little too closely, trying to impose her will onto His.

So she'd fall back a step. She'd do whatever she needed to do in order to keep this feeling with her.

"This is a good spot," she said as she made it to the wide open pasture that sat on Courage Reins land. A tall tree with wide, reaching branches provided plenty of shade, and Edith put her foot in the stirrup and landed in the saddle on Reagan's back.

"Now, you snack a bit," she whispered to the horse. "And I'll braid." Her fingers pulled the horse's hair back and down between his ears, and she started with three large pieces that would bubble out into a thick, beautiful braid by the time she finished.

She murmured to the horse about Courage Reins and how much he'd like it. She asked him if he'd met the other therapy horses yet. And she'd just started telling him about Finn when the man himself showed up.

"Look at you two," he said with plenty of appreciation in his voice. "Reagan, you have the most beautiful braid in the whole world." Finn ran his hand down the horse's side as Reagan lifted his head from the grass.

Edith smiled as Finn arrived near Reagan's

flank, where she was almost finished with his tail. "Isn't he great?"

"This is what you do to train them?"

"He was having some trouble trusting me," Edith said. "So we decided to go slow in the beginning." She secured the braid, which still left a good eight inches of his hair loose. She moved out from behind the horse and took Finn's hand in hers. "We'll do more and more with every session."

"You normally come every week?"

"Yeah," she said, her throat a bit dry. "And uh, Pete says I have to see the counselor afterward. So I'm not done yet today."

"Who are you seeing?" he asked.

"Bull," she said, her stomach a little nervous. There was no way she could talk to Bull the way she'd just spoken to Reagan. She supposed that was why Pete wanted her to do both halves of the equine therapy.

"I think you'll like him," Finn said.

"You know him?"

"Sure," Finn said. "I like Doctor Presley better, but Bull's good."

"He's not really my style," Edith said, glancing toward the big building where she'd have to go meet with the counselor who matched his name. "He's just a little…flippant. I like my therapists not to throw what I've said back in my face."

Finn waggled his head back and forth as if considering it. "I guess I see that too."

She nudged him with her shoulder. "You see a counselor?"

"The Army requires counseling upon discharge," he said. "I got them to approve the ones here, so…yeah."

She nodded, a new piece of knowledge in her pocket. "Help me put this horse away?"

"Sure." He reached for the lead rope, and Finn actually led Reagan back to the stable. "My momma made cookies, and I'll go help her pack them up for you while you talk to Bull."

"Thank you, baby." She pulled him closer and kissed him. "Thank you."

20

On the Fourth of July, Finn made the drive to Coyote Pass, the same as he had for the past four weeks. Today, Alex and Edith had said they'd be doing a holiday schedule of chores, which meant the essentials and nothing else.

So by the time he arrived, he found them both in the house, working in the kitchen while the scent of maple syrup and sausage filled the air. "I missed the chores, didn't I?"

"It's almost breakfast," Alex said with a smile.

"Waffles," Edith said, and she looked so joyful as she stood in front of the steaming double Belgian waffle maker. "These are the first ones, and they're usually not the greatest, so I'll make you some crispy ones after."

"I'm down for whatever," Finn said as he sat at the bar. It held orange juice already, along with butter and maple syrup, strawberries and whipped cream, and as he watched, Alex tipped a pan full of browned and sizzling sausages onto a plate covered with a paper towel.

"Ready," he said.

"These are too," Edith said. "But see, this one is a bit anemic." She forked a waffle out of the first half of the iron and slid it onto a plate. She quickly refilled it with more batter, turned it, removed that waffle, and said, "This one's better. I know what to do now."

She refilled that iron and closed the lid. "Let's pray, okay? Then these will be ready." Her cheeks held a flush of pink, and Finn grinned at her before he took off his cowboy hat and bowed his head.

"Lord," Alex said. "We're sure grateful for this beautiful summer day. Bless us to remember our ancestors who fought for our liberties, and bless us to be the best citizens we can be. We're glad to have this farm to work, and we're right grateful for Finn and all he's done for us this past month. Bless us to be safe this holiday, and that fireworks won't spark a fire anywhere around. Bless the food. Amen."

Alex wasn't one to give long speeches, and Finn appreciated that. Reminded him of his daddy. "Amen," he said, and he settled his cowboy hat back on his head.

The waffle maker beeped, and Edith hurried to check it. "Oh, yes," she said. "These are nice. Alex?"

"You come eat with Finn." Alex got to his feet and went around the counter to take over at the waffle maker. "Go on, now. I can make waffles."

She didn't argue with him, and she brought him a plate with a crispy, steaming Belgian waffle on it. "What are you going to do? Butter and syrup? Or strawberries and cream?"

"You know what?" Finn reached for the butter knife. "I'm going to have both."

"Both on one waffle?"

"That's right, Flower Pot." Edith trilled out a laugh and that sent a thrill through Finn. "You're not the only one who can use nicknames, right?"

She wore delight on her face as she shook her head. "No, but I like 'darlin' or 'sweetheart' better."

"Is that right, sweetheart?" Finn nudged her with his knee. She nodded, and he said, "All right. I'll leave the funny nicknames to you, then."

"Flower Pot is good, though," she said. "I think I'm going to name a horse that in one of my books."

"So I'm doubly useful." He indeed spread butter over his waffle, then put strawberries on it, then dolloped cream over that. He drizzled syrup over all of it, and he added his sausage to the rim of the plate too.

After breakfast, they planned to head downtown to the Independence Day Boutique, which was booth after booth from local shops, craftsmen, and restaurants.

"Two Cents has put out their top ten booths to visit at the Boutique," Edith said, nudging her phone closer. "Look at the top one."

Finn put a bite of his doctored up waffle in his mouth and peered at her phone. "Doggone Delicious?" He scoffed as disbelief tore through him. Edith had told him about the dog bakery and specialty store a week or so ago. She, apparently, bought special treats for her dogs there. "My word. It's not even for humans."

Edith giggled and kept eating.

"I suppose you voted for that one?"

"Of course I did," she said.

"And I suppose we're going to have to stop there." He wasn't asking this time.

"Of course we are," she said. "I need some of that paw balm for Olive. It's been so hot and dry since the flooding."

"We can't ever win, can we?"

"We can with the paw balm." She beamed at him, and Finn simply smiled and shook his head.

Alex joined them with his own waffle. "Did you two see the list for lunch?"

"On Two Cents?" Edith scooped up her phone. "Lord, let there be something that isn't fried twice."

Finn laughed, and even Alex chuckled. That said a lot, because he didn't do that very often. She tapped on her phone, her waffle sitting there untouched. "Barbecue Haven, of course. They do have a good food truck."

"They do," Finn said, spearing a sausage.

"Your favorite," she said. "Ice cream."

"Honey, that's *your* favorite."

"I do want to get ice cream," she said. "Will you buy me ice cream today, Finny?"

"Whatever you want, sweetheart." He pressed

his lips to her forehead as she leaned against his side.

"Those are dangerous words," Alex said.

"Are you coming with us?" Edith asked. "I wish you would. You can go to that booth with hand-carved furniture and start dreaming of what you can do with that reclaimed wood I know you're hoarding. And hiding."

Finn suddenly felt in the middle of a sibling spat, and he leaned back as Alex glared at her. "I'm not hiding it. Clearly. You know about it, don't you?"

"He'll have the sign-ups for his classes," Edith said. "And if you don't sign up for the next one, I'll...I'll...do something really bad."

Alex grinned and forked another sausage in his mouth. "I love that threat, Edee."

Finn couldn't stop himself from smiling either, and he flinched when Edith swatted his chest. "Are you agreeing with him?"

"It's not a great threat," he said with a laugh. "But Alex, you should sign up for a furniture-making class. I didn't know you wanted to do that."

"He does," Edith said loudly.

"Maybe," Alex said just as loudly.

"It would be a good side-hobby," she said. "For when I'm gone and can't give this ranch my book money."

Alex's jaw popped, and Finn decided to finish his waffle instead of adding his voice to the conversation. It didn't belong there anyway.

"I'll sign up for a furniture class if you find the Boutique director and ask how to get a booth there next year."

"Alexander," she bit out.

Finn studied her, though. "That's a great idea, Edith," he said slowly. "Why don't you sell your books to the townspeople?"

"They don't even know she writes books," Alex said.

"Of course they do." Edith threw him a poisoned look. "My name is on the front of every single one." She flicked a dangerous and sharp look at Finn. "And I'm not going to stand there for ten hours, trying to get parents to buy a book for their kids. Everyone around here knows about horses. My books do better in more populated areas, where little girls dream of being horse-riders and seeing a pasture. The very pastures we have steps from our backyard." She waved her hand toward the windows. "It's not—I'm not doing it."

"Then I'm not signing up for a class." Alex stared at her, and Edith stared right back.

Finn cleared his throat. "Anyone got any ideas for what I should be doing with my life?" That brought the silence to another level, and then he started to laugh. Thankfully, Edith did too, and Finn threw his arm around her on the left and Alex on the right.

"Now, are we going to get along today or not? Because I'm not wandering around in this heat while you two bicker."

"We'll get along," Edith said, and Finn dropped his arms.

"I'll sign up for the furniture class," Alex grumbled. "I want to do it anyway."

"Edith?" Finn asked.

"Can you imagine me in a booth?" She shook her head. "It's akin to torture. I can't do it."

"Maybe you could talk to the bookstore owner about doing a one-hour signing," he said. "In her booth. Remember how incredible you are when you turn on?"

"I like that idea too," Alex said from down the counter.

From the puckered eyebrows and blazing hot

expression in her eyes, Edith didn't like that idea, but she said nothing.

"Okay," Finn said. "You can tell me why later."

"Janice doesn't like me," Edith mumbled. "And she doesn't know how to plan an author event. You should've seen this little shop in Coral Canyon. This woman named Georgia Young owns it, and she does the *best* events in the whole world."

"Coral Canyon...like where Wyatt Walker goes in the summer?"

"Yeah." Edith smiled. "She loves my books, and I did this class there. It was really fun."

"I said you were incredible in person."

"Janice can't do that."

"I'll admit Janice isn't great," Alex said.

Edith gestured to him and finally picked up her fork to eat her waffle. Finn just enjoyed being with her so much, and he pulled out his phone and started swiping, his smile growing across his face and throughout his soul.

"I wanted to go to this booth," he said, finally landing on the Boutique page that listed all the booths. "Number thirty-seven."

"Yeah? What is it?" Edith leaned over and

looked at his phone while he tilted it toward her. "Bozeman Real Estate?" She looked up, concern firing in her eyes. "Like Bozeman, Montana?"

"No, the guy's name is Gary Bozeman," Finn said.

"Oh, I was gonna say, I thought you were going to stay in Three Rivers."

"He's got a few places listed right now." Finn set his phone down and pierced a strawberry with his fork. "I mean, I can't afford any of them, but I thought I might meet him. Talk to him about what I'm looking for, and just yeah." He took a breath to try to find what he meant to say. "So he knows me, and maybe if something comes along that's a fit for me, he'll call me first."

"Are farms and ranches moving quick these days?" Alex asked.

"No," Finn said. "But interest rates are high and so are prices. So." He swiped a sausage through his syrup and put it in his mouth, so he didn't have to say anything else.

"We'll stop by and see him," Edith promised, and the three of them finished breakfast. As Finn helped Alex rinse the dishes and put them in the dishwasher, Edith put festive red, white, and blue bandanas on the dachshunds.

"So we're bringin' 'em?" Alex asked with his eyebrows up.

"They're easy," Edith said. "They want to come." She sat back on her haunches and smiled at Frankie and Otto. She looked up at Alex. "We can't bring them? They love walking in the park."

"Could be busy," Alex said. "That's all."

"Oh, it'll be busy," Finn said. "But I can take one of 'em." He did like the bright white stars on Frankie's bandana, and he especially liked the joy pouring from Edith. "I'm just gonna use the restroom before we go."

"Hand me that sausage, Edee," Alex said.

Finn left them to finish cleaning up, and he went down the hall to the bathroom. Just across from it sat that extra room, and Finn glanced over his shoulder to see if Edith had followed him. She hadn't, and he ducked into it. The shelves hung right beside the door, and it only took a single second for him to look to his right.

Edith had spoken true. The pictures he'd seen there before had been cleared away. In fact, as Finn took in the bedroom in front of him, the whole thing had been cleaned out and turned over. A ncw bedspread covered the bed. The blinds sat open, not closed. The scent of oranges hung in the air, and Finn had smelled it before—in Edith's she-shed.

His heart filled with love, and he wasn't even sure why. Edith had said she was trying to get to where he was, but he was too fast for her. He didn't mean to be, and he didn't want to pressure her to go somewhere she didn't want to go.

But seeing this room, it really felt like she'd cleared away some of the cobwebs in her past to make room for the future.

Their future together.

He ducked back across the hall, gratitude streaming through him for a loving, benevolent God who helped people heal from even the most tragic of things. Now, if He could help Finn find somewhere to start his life.... Finn would be holding the world in his hand, and he might actually feel like he could provide a good life for Edith.

A FEW HOURS LATER, THEY FINALLY MADE IT to the booth where Bozeman Real Estate had set up shop for the day. They'd lost Alex to Mitch and Link Glover, as the three of them were very nearly the same age. Alex and Link had graduated the same year, though in different states, with Mitch being only a year ahead of them.

Alex had said he'd catch up to them later, and Finn had enjoyed holding Edith's hand, looking at jewelry, t-shirts, artwork, and more. He'd gotten Edith her ice cream, though he was sure they'd have a second one before they left this Boutique, and his stomach growled for lunch. They hadn't decided where they'd eat, though, and Finn just wanted someone else to make that decision.

"Howdy," a man wearing a big white cowboy hat said. "You two lookin' for a realtor?"

"I am," Finn said quickly, because while Edith definitely factored into his decisions these days, he didn't want her to feel any pressure to be part of this excursion. "I've seen some of your listings, and I just wanted to talk to someone."

"We've got a few things up right now, yes," the man said.

"Are you Gary?" Finn looked up from the binder of real estate properties.

"He's my dad." The man smiled. "We work together though." He glanced over to Edith, who'd moved further into the booth to look at the floor plans on a table there. "You're looking for something?"

"I am," Finn said. "But everything you've got up right now is out of my price range." He cleared his throat and reminded himself he was a first-time home-buyer. He didn't have to have millions in the bank, and he didn't have to be embarrassed he couldn't afford the one-point-three-million-dollar ranch on the east side of town.

"Sure, sure," the man said. "I'm Jerry, and do you have a couple of minutes to tell me what you're looking for?"

Edith twisted and looked over her shoulder. Finn met her eye, and they had a quick conversation. "Yeah," he said.

"Come sit in my tent." Jerry grinned and gestured Finn on back to the table at the back of the tent. Edith sat down with him, her hand in his so comforting. The dachshunds laid down, and Finn sure was glad they had a fan running in this tent.

Jerry pulled out a tablet and started tapping. "Okay, tell me your name and phone number."

Finn gave him that information, and Jerry looked up. "You're out at Three Rivers Ranch, right?"

"It's my daddy's ranch, yes," Finn said.

"You're not going to take it over?" Jerry

seemed genuinely surprised by this, and Finn shifted in his seat.

"The plan right now is to find my own place," he said. "Not anything big. Nothing like Three Rivers. A one-family operation. No full-time paid cowboys." He glanced over to Edith, well-aware that he'd said the word "family."

She said nothing as Jerry typed, and he looked up. "Housing? How many bedrooms?" He too glanced at Edith, and she looked at Finn.

"Three?" he guessed.

"Minimum," Edith murmured. "Two bathrooms, and he wants a master suite. A lot of older places don't have a master suite."

"Does Coyote Pass?"

"It does," she said. "But Alex put it in himself."

Finn nodded, swallowed, and looked at Jerry. This—meeting with him—felt like such a grown-up thing to do, and it caused nerves to spin through Finn's bloodstream.

"Air conditioning," Jerry muttered as he tapped. "Well water, yes. Gas, mm-hm. Water rights." He looked over to them again. "Are we farming? Or raising cattle?"

"Raising cattle." Finn knew how to do that.

Alex had cattle and farmed, as most ranches had to do. Finn had grown up on a large cattle ranch, and he could handle a small one. A hundred head of cattle could yield him enough calves every year to make a good living, depending on the market. Right now, a calving rate of eighty percent would give him eighty cows to sell, and at current market prices, he could expect almost seventy thousand dollars for those in a single year.

"I don't need anything big," he said. "I'm thinking a couple hundred acres. Somewhere I can have a hundred head of cattle." He glanced over to Edith, but he didn't want to talk to her about where he'd get those cattle in front of Jerry Bozeman.

"A couple hundred acres," Jerry said as he typed.

"He also needs room for a decently sized shed," Edith said. "Preferably in the backyard or close to it. Not out by the smelly barns or anything." She smiled prettily, and Finn lifted her hand to his lips to kiss the back of it.

"I do need that," he said. "It's what? Maybe fifteen feet by twenty feet."

"Twelve by twenty-four," Edith said. "With options for electricity and water would be nice."

Jerry looked between the two of them, and Finn's chest filled with pride as he leaned forward. "She writes books for a living, and she has a she-shed-office where she does that." He heard the pride in his own voice, and he looked over to Edith. "So *we* need room for that."

"Room for a she-shed," Jerry said slowly as he typed it in. Several long seconds passed while he studied the tablet, and then he said, "Yeah, we don't have anything like this right now." He looked up with sympathy in his expression.

"I know," Finn said. "I've looked online. I was just thinking if you saw something come through, you could call me first."

"Of course." Jerry smiled at him. "Things change daily, right?"

"Right." Finn got to his feet, feeling sweaty and a little wild. "Thanks, Jerry."

"You bet, man." They shook hands, and Finn let Edith lead the dogs out of the tent. He followed her, and they didn't speak as they moved toward the next booth. They passed monogramed handkerchiefs, which his grandfather would've liked, and a booth full of puzzles.

"I'm thinking of asking my daddy to sell me a hundred head," Finn said. "For a two-hundred-acre ranch. That'll be a decent living every year."

"And you can do that yourself?"

"With some help at major times," he said. "But yeah, I can do it myself, with a good partner."

She nodded and didn't look at him. "Have you asked him?"

"No." Finn sighed and looked at all the people in the park. "It feels a little like a cop-out, you know?"

"Why?" Edith paused and turned toward him. "Lots of people simply take over the ranches their daddies have worked."

"Yeah, I know." For some reason, Finn didn't want to do that. "It's just...."

"You have a problem with your family."

"No, I don't." Finn looked at her when he realized he'd been scanning the park. "Why do you say that?"

"Because it's true," she said. "You love your family, but it's like you have something to prove to them."

Finn opened his mouth to argue and found he couldn't. A soft grunt left his mouth instead, and Edith eased into his arms. "It's okay, Finn. Alex came back here to basically do the same thing."

Finn wrapped her in his arms. "I want something of my own," he whispered. "Something for me, and something for you."

"I know you do, cowboy." She stepped back and beamed up at him. "Now, come on. It's getting hotter by the minute, and I'm done with this Boutique and all these people."

Finn grinned at her. "Thank the stars above. Maybe we can take a nap on your she-shed couch so we can stay up late for the fireworks tonight." He raised his eyebrows in question, and Edith laughed at him.

"All right," she said. "Let me call Alex and see where he is."

"He's right here," Alex said, and Finn turned to find him walking toward them with Link and Mitch.

"We're done," Edith said. "How are you feeling?"

"Hot." Alex glanced over to Link. "Can these guys come to lunch with us?"

"Of course." Edith smiled at Link and then Mitch. "I can't do all the signs. Where do you want to eat?" She did a couple of them, and Mitch grinned, so he didn't seem to mind.

He signed to Link, who said, "Mitch is craving

a good old-fashioned burger," with a smile that seemed abnormally large. Not only that, but they both looked at Alex. "He says he wants to go to Jurassic Burger."

Alex rolled his eyes and said, "Subtle, guys."

"What's subtle?" Edith asked, and Mitch started to laugh. Finn liked his energy, and he'd always found Mitch to be a pretty joyful guy.

"Nicki Johnston works there," Link said as he signed it. "And Alex has a big crush on her." He started walking, and everyone fell into line beside him.

"A big crush, huh?" Finn asked as he linked his hand with Edith's. He looked at her, and she had her eyes narrowed and locked on her brother, who walked on the other side of Link.

"I thought Nicki ran the feed store," she said.

"She does," Alex said without looking at her. "Her cousin owns Jurassic Burger, so she's helping for today, because of the crowds."

"I—" Edith started again.

"Leave him be," Finn whispered as he pulled her closer and let Alex get a little ahead of them. "If you leave that farm, what's he gonna do? Work it alone?"

Edith looked up at him, her eyes widening. "He hasn't dated for a while."

"Then let him flirt with this Nicki Johnston while we get burgers." He kissed her quickly. "And then I'll get you some more ice cream, and we can go take that nap together."

She looked forward again and it took several steps before she said, "Okay, but if he starts flailing, I'm stepping in."

"I don't doubt it," Finn murmured with a smile. He didn't doubt that at all.

He'd have an amazing lunch, hopefully an amazing nap, and then he had to take Edith to Three Rivers Ranch for his family celebration. His pulse skipped, because he could already see his mother's expression when she met Edith as his girlfriend.

And it would look a lot like the squinted glare Edith had for her brother. So Finn restarted the prayer he'd been recycling since he'd invited Edith to the Fourth picnic at the ranch. If anyone could help him enjoy tonight, it would have to be God.

21

Edith laughed with Finn as he pulled up to the farmhouse. "I'll admit," she said. "I've never seen Alex so smiley."

"He did smile a lot." Finn glanced over to her. "And hey, he got her number."

"Yeah." Edith quieted, her own smile pretty permanent today. "He sure did." She leaned her head back against the rest and turned it toward Finn. "Do you really just want to hang out this afternoon? Alex and I can drive out to Three Rivers tonight."

Something crossed Finn's face, but it marched across so fast, Edith couldn't categorize it. Worry, maybe. He even swallowed. "If I go back to the ranch, I'll be put to work."

"Oh, so you're playing hooky." She grinned at him and twisted to get out of the truck. "All right. Let's go get the she-shed cooled down."

"I can do some work around here," Finn offered as they slid out of the vehicle.

"Nah," Edith said. "At least not until we have to leave tonight. We'll feed the horses right before that." She met him at the hood. "You sure it's okay to bring my dogs to the ranch?"

"Yeah, sure," Finn said easily.

Edith sensed something inside him. Something swirling and brewing and somewhat dangerous. "Are you okay?" she asked casually as they went through the shadows on the side of the garage and toward the backyard.

"Yeah," he said, his voice pitched up a bit. "Why?"

"I don't know," Edith said. "I just feel like there's something you want to tell me and haven't."

"I don't know what that would be," he said, his tone settling into normalcy.

"Okay," she said, her voice rising a bit now. "I just—you can tell me stuff, okay? Anything."

"I know that, Edith. I always have."

"Okay," she said as the she-shed approached. "Then let's take our afternoon nap." She grinned as she opened the door and entered ahead of him, the comforting sight of her couch, her book posters, her desk, greeting her.

She paused just inside the door, where she had a small wall unit air conditioner, and pressed the button to get it going.

"How long will that take?" Finn asked. He released her hand and headed the few steps to the couch.

"A half-hour," she said. "We can have some ice cream, so we don't get too hot." Edith set about getting out her sherbet and ice cream, unsurprised when Finn took the ice cream and she settled next to him with a bowl of orange sherbet.

"Okay, with every bite, we have to say something."

"Say something?" Finn took a bite of his ice cream.

"Yeah, you cheater." She grinned at him. "So tell me your favorite food."

He ducked his head, that glorious cowboy hat making him so handsome and the smile making him so dang cute too. "Breakfast burritos."

Edith giggled. "See? Something I didn't know."

"What would you have guessed?"

"I don't know. Steak?"

"Mm, I do love a good steak," he said.

She took a bite and nodded to him as if to say, *Go ahead. Ask me something.*

Finn nodded, his throat working as he swallowed. "All right. You have an hour all to yourself. What do you do?"

"What time of day is it?"

"Evening," he said. "The perfect summer evening, with a little breeze, and the sun setting into darker blues and purples." His bright eyes sparkled, because he did seem to know some of Edith's favorites hadn't changed all that much over the years.

"I'd go for a walk," she said. "Along the river, in town." She sighed and looked up toward the ceiling. "You know, with the big trees overhead, and the wind whispering secrets to me about life, the universe, and God Himself." She smiled and met his eye. The electricity between them flowed easily, and Finn scooped up another bite of ice cream instead of kissing her.

"Your turn to ask me something." He took his bite of ice cream, clearly teasing her.

"Have you ever been in love?"

Finn took the question in stride. "No, ma'am, unless a dog counts, but I don't think it does."

"It does not," Edith said dryly. She put another spoonful of sherbet in her mouth, really enjoying the tangy, tart orange flavor against her tongue.

"Do you think God knows us?" he asked, his voice low. "Like, do you think He cares if I find a ranch here, or about your sinkholes, or...just any of it."

"Yep," Edith said without missing a beat. "I absolutely believe that He does."

Finn's eyes danced around, and Edith reached over and took his face in her hand. "I know He loves us, Finn. Individually. I know He knows you want a ranch, and I know He knows about the sinkholes."

"He could've stopped them."

"Yeah, sure." Edith took another bite of her sherbet, breaking her own rules of the game. "But God doesn't give us challenges we can't handle."

"He gives them to us to grow," Finn said.

"That's what my momma and daddy always say, at least."

"Yeah." Edith glanced out the window that sat beyond her desk. "Mine too."

Finn scraped his spoon along the bottom of his bowl. "Feels like sometimes He gives some people harder challenges than others."

"Well, that's true," Edith said. She took another bite and let her sherbet melt in her mouth while Finn remained silent. They finished their treat, and Edith took the bowls from him. When she turned back, Finn kicked off his second boot and lay down on the couch.

He opened his arms for her to join him, and Edith did exactly that. He stroked her hair off the side of her face and murmured, "Could be a worse afternoon than relaxing with your boyfriend, even if the AC isn't all the way satisfactory."

Edith smiled to herself and twined her fingers in his, their hands almost against her stomach. "Could be better if you'd kiss me." She turned to look over her shoulder, thinking herself clever for inserting kissing into their usually serious game.

"I think I can handle that." Finn touched his lips to hers, and Edith let her eyes drift close as she enjoyed the sensation of falling in love with a good man.

THE TENSION IN THE TRUCK BY THE TIME Finn made the turn to head out to Three Rivers choked in the back of Edith's throat. She'd met his parents before. She'd seen them around town in the past few years, and while his siblings were younger than her, she'd know them on-sight.

"There will be a lot of non-family members there tonight," she said matter-of-factly. "I won't stand out."

Finn said nothing, and Edith had her answer for the storm she'd felt inside him. His nerves screamed from him as the truck moved forward, and soon enough, he rounded the bend and the whole of the ranch, the homestead, the horse training facility, and all of Courage Reins spread before them.

Edith drank in no less than a half-dozen American flags—one on a pole in front of Peter Marshall's house, at the entrance of Bowman Breeds, and at the homestead.

Finn's momma had also draped the stars and

stripes from the deck, and Edith reached to roll down her window. She thought she'd heard music, and sure enough, a good old-fashioned Neil Diamond song piped out of some speakers somewhere.

Edith's mouth tipped up into a smile, because the Ackermans had always been great at throwing a party. "Smells good," she said as her stomach growled.

Three white tents had been set up over the lawn between the homestead and the nearest barn, and as they got closer, Edith saw they definitely weren't the first ones there.

"Is that Henry?" she asked.

"Sure is," Finn grumbled as he followed his oldest cousin's directions for where to park. Henry wore a big white cowboy hat like his father did, and he seemed overjoyed to be waving people down an aisle of already parked vehicles.

"When did he get back?"

"He's just here for the weekend," Finn said as he pulled into the next available spot. "Everyone's here for the weekend."

"You make it sound like they're here to commit crimes." Edith glanced over to him, but Finn gave nothing away as he put the truck in park. He didn't look at her as he got out of the truck, and Edith stayed put so he'd have to open her door and face her.

Instead of letting her drop to the ground, Finn crowded into the doorway. "Fine, I'm nervous about bringing you to this tonight."

"I gathered that."

He kept his head down, and Edith simply let him this time. "There's just so many of them," he muttered. "And they'll say anything."

"Finn," she said.

"We should've just gone downtown to the fireworks there."

"Finn."

He still didn't look up, but at least he didn't say anything more.

"I've met my boyfriend's parents before," she said gently, and Edith realized how much experience she had with such things. "It's going to be fine. They're people. I'm a person." She took his hand gently and said, "Now, take me over there and re-introduce me to your momma and daddy and get me a hamburger."

He did look up then, his eyes finding hers from under the brim of his cowboy hat. "There will be so much food here. It's embarrassing."

"How is having food for a party embarrassing?" Edith meant to tease him, but she genuinely didn't think Finn would appreciate it. She peered at him, seeing the obvious discomfort in his gaze. "Do you just want to go back to Coyote Pass?"

"Part of me wants to say yes," he growled almost under his breath. "But let's just get this over with."

Edith didn't like that statement, but she didn't know what to say or do. She nudged him with her knee, and he backed up. She dropped to the ground and took his hand in hers. "You know, this can be fun too."

"If you have fun tonight, I'll be shocked." Finn led her toward the homestead, the lawn, and the tents.

The music continued to pipe above them, and a group of cowboys in the tent somewhere yelled, "Born in the U-S-A! I was *born!* In the U-S-A!"

The energy here sizzled in the air, and Edith sure did like it. The sun still shone brightly over Texas, but the moment they stepped into the tent, the temperature went down. Finn's dad and uncle stood over by a trio of grills, all of which steamed and smoked as meat cooked on them.

"Howdy, Finn," a cowboy said, and he paused.

"Oh, hey, Cal," he said. "This is Edith Baxter. Did you ever meet her?"

The tall cowboy looked at Edith, his smile filling his face. "No, ma'am, but it's great to meet you."

"You too." Edith shook his hand, and he went on his way. "Am I going to meet everyone by name?" She turned and took in the enormity of the space. Tables and chairs had been set up in the shade, with three of them holding all the food Finn had talked about.

"Finny," a girl said, and he stepped into his sister's half-hug. She kissed his cheek and said, "Introduce me to your girlfriend." Libby grinned at her from her brother's side, and Edith smiled right on back.

"Libs," he said. "Edith. Edith, I'm sure you remember my irritating younger sister, Libby."

"She's not irritating," Edith said. "Howdy, Libby. Finn says you're managing a ranch in Oklahoma."

"I am." Libby stepped into her and gave her the half-hug and cheek-kiss, and Edith did the same to her. It wasn't exactly the most comfortable thing Edith had ever done, because she was still getting used to having more than Alex in her life.

Speaking of....

"Have you seen my brother?" she asked, glancing back toward the parking lot. He'd left only a few minutes behind them, and sure enough, she saw him crossing the lawn toward them. Alone. How he did that, Edith wasn't sure.

"There he is." She went to meet him, and when she and Alex turned back to Finn and Libby, they'd been joined by a few more people. Henry had apparently put in his shift with the parking, and he stood laughing with Libby. His cowboy hat was black while most of the Marshalls wore white, and he cut Edith a look that seemed darker than it should for an Independence Day party.

His older brother, Paul, had joined them, and he looked exactly the way Edith figured a young man on this ranch would. Blue jeans, cowboy boots, red, white, and blue plaid shirt.

She migrated to Finn's side, and the group made room for her and Alex easily. The laughter quieted, and awkwardness descended on them. Edith took a step toward Paul, deciding she didn't want this tension. "Paul," she said. "It's great to see you."

"You too, Edee," he said, because he was the

same age as Alex, and Alex always used her nickname.

"What are you up to these days?"

He threw a look at Finn, who finally seemed to be relaxing, and then looked at her again. "I work here with my daddy and Uncle Squire. Agriculture."

"Oh, sure," Edith said. "I knew that." She looked over to Henry. "What about you, Henry?"

He shifted his feet, and he certainly didn't seem comfortable here. "Finishing up farrier school, actually. Then I'm gonna come back here and work for my daddy."

"You are?" Finn, Libby, and Paul all asked at the same time.

Henry rolled his eyes. "I'm starving. You wanna eat, Alex?"

"Absolutely." They turned to leave the huddle.

"Me too," Edith said, and she took Finn's hand and followed the boys toward the grills. She let Alex and Henry get a bit ahead of them, and then she glanced over to Finn. "No one knew he was coming home?"

"It's not exactly like Henry loved living out here," Finn said quietly. And with the music and the chatter, Edith didn't think anyone else had overhead.

"No?"

"Henry had too many girlfriends," Finn said with a smile. "So he's amazing with horses, but he feels a lot like I do."

"And how's that?" Edith asked as they joined the line to get something meaty from the grills.

"Like I need to make my own way in the world," he said. "Like...I can't take over this place just because I'm the oldest son. It feels like cheating."

"That's how generational ranches work," she said, a thread of confusion pulling through her. "People do it all the time."

"It's just never been for me." Finn picked up a plate and handed it to Edith. "The real problem is, Edith, I don't know what is for me."

"Finn," someone said loudly, and they both turned toward his momma. "Squire, Finn and Edith are here." She yelled that sentence down the line to the grills, and everyone heard her. Edith suddenly felt like a bright, blazing hot spotlight had been placed on her, and she put a smile on her face too late.

Finn's mother had surely seen her nerves, her hesitation, her quick glance over to Finn.

"Momma," Finn said, and he moved easily into his momma's arms though his voice sounded wooden.

Kelly Ackerman grinned as she hugged her son, and as she stepped back, his daddy joined her. "Howdy, son." He looked over to Edith too, and they'd migrated out of line a little bit. Edith wondered if she'd ever get to sample some of the amazing food here at Three Rivers Ranch.

"Howdy, Edith." Squire moved into her easily, swiping a kiss across her cheek effortlessly. "Did I miss the introduction?"

"No, Daddy," Finn said in a tired voice. "I haven't done it yet." He slid his arm around Edith and brought her flush against his side. "You guys obviously know Edith."

"Well, I wouldn't say we *know* her," Kelly said.

"Momma," Finn warned. "This is Edith Baxter. You've met her before."

"As a much younger person."

"Edith, my momma and daddy. Kelly and Squire, needlessly."

Edith grinned at his parents. "It's great to see you both again."

Kelly smiled at her. "Thank you," she said in pure Texan diplomacy. She even dipped her head a little. "I've told Finny not to hide you from us, but he thinks he has to."

"Momma, I never said that."

"You don't need to *say* it, Finn." His mother threw him a sharp look and focused on Edith again. "You two have been dating for what? Seven or eight weeks? And this is the first we've seen of you." She took Edith by both shoulders. "You're so beautiful, Edith. I see why Finn likes you."

"Mom, you are seriously embarrassing me."

Edith grinned at Kelly and then him. "Finn, who doesn't want to be told they're beautiful? She's fine."

"See? I'm fine." Kelly released her, and the four of them stood there and looked at one another.

"I do love this ranch," Edith said as she glanced around. "There's a special feeling here."

"That there is," Squire said. "How's Reagan coming along?"

"Good," Edith said as she moved to rejoin the food line. "What are you grillin' up tonight, Mister

Ackerman?" They left Finn and his mother to talk for a moment, and Edith glanced over to her boyfriend. Kelly didn't look like she was lecturing him, but a ruddy quality still crept up his neck and into his face.

"We've got hamburgers and hot dogs. Typical barbecue fare. But then, we put on some chicken, and Pete's been smoking a brisket all day." He clapped his hand on the shoulder of a cowboy named Jon, who somehow balanced three plates full of just sides. Potato salad. Sweet pea salad. Bright red Jell-O. Cole slaw. Baked beans. Potato chips.

Edith's mouth watered. "I'm so hungry."

"Then you came to the right place." Squire looked at her again, and Edith had the very real feeling he saw more than just what existed on the surface. She wanted to squirm away from him, though his expression stayed pleasant. "It's great to see you, Edith. I know my wife would love it if you weren't a stranger here."

With that, he turned and merged himself into a trio of cowboys who all bore the last name Walker. "Howdy, boys," he said with a laugh, and handshakes and hellos went around.

Edith stood there in line, not sure why Finn

didn't think this ranch was home. She watched him finish up with his momma, and then both of them joined her. "I just saw someone walk by with all the sides I could've hoped for," she said to Kelly. "Finn tells me you have a Jell-O recipe I need to try."

"Do you like to cook, Edith?" Kelly asked.

"Truth be told," she said as Finn picked up his own plate. "Alex does most of the cooking around Coyote Pass. But I'm passable."

"I'll give you the recipe." Kelly picked up a plate too. "Don't worry; I'm not going to eat with you."

"You're welcome to do just that," Edith said easily. "How's your garden doing this summer?"

Surprise filled her expression, and she glanced over to Finn, who had his head down again. Edith hated seeing his light burn so dimly, and she slid her hand into his. He looked up at her, and she wanted to tell him to stop worrying. In that moment, she saw something she hadn't before.

He was truly and legitimately embarrassed of his family. Why, Edith had no idea, but she saw it laid out plain as anything on his face.

"It's going great," Kelly said. "As usual, I'll have way too many zucchini to actually do anything with." She trilled out a light laugh, and Edith joined her.

"Everyone always does," she said.

"Kel," someone said, and she turned to see what Finn's grandmother wanted. "They need more chocolate for the fondue pot."

"Oh, sure." Kelly turned back to Edith and said, "Lovely to see you, Edith. I hope we'll get to spend more time getting to know one another," before she bustled off to get the chocolate.

"Thanks, Grandma," Finn said, and he moved in to hug her too. "Granny, this is Edith Baxter, my girlfriend. Edith, my grandma, Heidi. I mean, everyone knows her, so...." He trailed off, and Edith really didn't like seeing this shell of him.

"Everyone does know you," Edith said pleasantly. She kissed the older woman's cheek and said, "How much of this does Kelly make herself?"

They both surveyed the table with all the sides, and Edith wanted a little bite of every single one. Like a taste test to see which would be the best. The deviled eggs? Or the cornbread? The frog eye salad? Or the grilled street corn?

"Oh, about all of it," Heidi said with a sigh. "She allows some of us to bring things, but she's really a genius in the kitchen."

"So's my grandma," Finn said.

"I brought the apple tarts, dear," she said. "I kept five or six in the house to make sure you'd get one." She beamed at Finn like he was made of stardust, and then she nodded herself away.

They approached the grills now, as his uncle laughed with another cowboy who'd just gotten his cheeseburger. Edith looked at Finn, and he looked back at her. She had a quick internal debate with herself, and then she said, "I will need to know why you're so embarrassed of your family, but it doesn't have to be tonight."

"Fair enough," he murmured, and then it was their turn.

Edith requested a cheeseburger, and then she turned to the long row of tables filled with so many other things she wanted to eat. Cowboy Jon definitely had the best idea, and she decided she'd follow his lead.

She found the table with Alex, Paul, Henry, and Libby, and she put her plate down there. "I'm going to go get a bunch more," she said.

"Get the peach lemonade," Libby said as she lifted her clear plastic cup with the pretty, peachy liquid in it. "It's fantastic."

Edith didn't doubt that, and she couldn't wait to taste the definition of a Texas picnic.

Hours later, she'd met dozens of cowboys as Finn's girlfriend, and darkness was finally falling. Everyone who'd come had brought blankets or lawn chairs, and Edith stood with Henry while Finn had gone to get the blanket he'd brought.

She'd learned that Henry had been engaged once already in his twenty-three-year-old life, and that he'd graduated from college last year with a degree in industrial engineering, then decided it wasn't for him. Thus, the farrier school.

Finn spread their blanket near the back of the crowd, a little further away than others were setting up. "Excuse me," she said to Henry, and she made her way over to Finn. The lawn sloped up slightly here, and she could see the crowd who'd been celebrating with food, music, dancing, and smaller ground fireworks that evening.

"Where do they set off the fireworks from?" she asked.

"Down behind the admin building," he said as he sat down on the blanket.

Edith curled into him, and he puffed up the pillows he'd brought and then laid back on them. She did the same, cuddling into his side as she looked up at the stars. "Finn, I don't think there could've been anything better than tonight." She tilted her head back "With you. Here. On this ranch."

He said nothing as he gazed toward the row of cowboy cabins that stood between where everyone had gathered and the admin building where the fireworks would soon fill the sky.

"You're no fun," she teased as she switched her gaze in the same direction as his.

"I'm not?"

"No." She enjoyed the warmth of his arms around her, and she draped her arm across his stomach. "You're supposed to say, 'I know one thing that could make tonight better, Edee.'"

He chuckled and said, "Well, I don't call you Edee, so I can't say that."

Edith huffed. Around her, the patriotic music stopped, and that seemed to light up the buzz in the crowd again.

"I know one thing that could make tonight better, Edith," Finn murmured, and she smiled as the first strains of *The Star Spangled Banner* started to play.

"Yeah?" She looked up at him again as a loud pop! filled the air. "What's that?"

"A kiss." He matched his mouth to hers as the first firework exploded in the sky, and Edith's eyes got painted with bright white light as the crowd cheered around her. She didn't join them, because she was kissing the man she thought she might be in love with—and that was better than any fireworks show.

22

Jeremiah Walker loved fireworks, though he wasn't a huge fan of late nights. He loved red licorice, though he didn't like the whining of his tweens and teens over how many treats they could have. He loved holding his wife, though it would be a long drive home from Three Rivers Ranch after the show.

All five of his children had come with him, though JJ was a legal adult now. At nineteen, he'd left the ranch and gone into a mechanic training program. He wanted to build and restore cars in his spare time as a cowboy, and Jeremiah hadn't had the heart to tell JJ that cowboys didn't have spare time.

As one with a lot of money, perhaps JJ could have his horses and his ranch and his cars, and Jeremiah would do anything he had to in order to make his son's dreams come true. His three daughters—Clara Jean, Emily, and Hattie—squabbled over the light necklaces, and Whitney reached for the bag of them.

"There's literally fifty of them," she said. "You three don't have to fight over everything." She sounded exasperated as she ripped open the box and her daughters argued back with her a little bit.

"Offer them to everyone." Whit eased back into Jeremiah's arms, and he ducked his head to plant a kiss just above her ear.

Their other son, Jason, a lanky, strong fifteen-year-old, ignored his sisters as the song changed and three fireworks exploded in the sky—one red, one white, and one blue.

Jeremiah smiled up into the sky too, thinking of the enormous American flag painted on the side of his barn at Seven Sons Ranch. He'd had it redone once since he'd come to Three Rivers over twenty years ago.

The light bracelets got snapped and made into necklaces. They got passed to Skyler's kids, and then Micah's, and then Jeremiah lost track of them after that. Rhett had come with his triplet seventeen-year-olds, and Liam and Tripp had both come with their wives and the single child they had left at home.

Wyatt was up in Coral Canyon, and he didn't make the trip back for the Fourth, as that small Wyoming town had a pretty strong Independence Day tradition of their own. Momma and Daddy sat in a pair of lawn chairs somewhere way down by Rory and Ollie, who'd come with their family as well.

The sky filled with pops and lights that seemed to go on and on, and then the music stopped. The crowd gathered on the lawn at the homestead here at Three Rivers Ranch seemed to hold its breath for a moment, and then cheers, whoops, and applause filled the sky next.

"What a great show," Whitney yelled, her smile apparent as the lights on the ranch flooded the darkness. She got up, and Jeremiah joined her to help start gathering up all of the things they'd brought.

Candy, phones, blankets, sweatshirts. "Girls," he said. "Go help Grandma and Grandpa with their chairs. Go on, now." His two younger girls went to do that, but Clara Jean turned to help her aunt Evelyn with her blankets and pillows. *Good enough*, Jeremiah thought.

"Thank you all for coming," Squire said over the loudspeaker. Jeremiah had spent many years here in Three Rivers, helping others on their ranches and attending ranch owner meetings with Squire himself.

"Y'all head to the truck," he said to Whit. "I'm gonna stay and thank Squire." He watched the path between the cowboy cabins and the ranch buildings, because that was where Squire and Pete had disappeared a half-hour ago.

Whitney started to herd the kids away, and Jeremiah moved over to stand next to Skyler. Mal was still trying to get their youngest to find all the pieces of his magnet set. "I don't even know why you brought that," she griped at the eleven-year-old.

"I'd keep my eye on that."

Jeremiah glanced over to Skyler, who nodded his cowboy hat back to the right. Jeremiah turned in that direction and found Clara Jean standing with John Marshall—a man three years older than her.

Three years wasn't that big of a difference, but it was when his daughter still had a year of high school left, and John had been gone to college for two full years. They weren't living the same life at all, but Clara Jean giggled and ducked her head as she tucked her hair behind her ear.

Jeremiah's blood rushed through his veins, but he held very still. John was smiling way too big to be just friendly, and as the activity continued around them, he got whisked away by someone else only a few seconds later.

Clara Jean stood there and watched him, the tide of people who'd managed to get all cleaned up and had started heading for the parking area flowing around her.

"Yeah, I don't like that," Jeremiah said almost under his breath.

"Daddy," Camila said, and she put a blanket in Skyler's arms. "We're ready."

"Yep." Skyler met Jeremiah's eyes, said nothing more, and left with his family.

"Clara Jean," Jeremiah barked, and his daughter startled toward him. "What you doin' here? Momma went to the truck."

She looked in the direction of the truck and then back to Jeremiah. "Yes, sir." She turned on her heel and marched away, and Jeremiah watched her go, her dark hair flowing behind her like a flag rippling in a gentle breeze.

Jeremiah tucked his hands in his pockets, wondering how to handle this. His general rule was not to do things that didn't need doing, and perhaps this was one of those things. Thankfully, Squire and Pete arrived a moment later, and another round of applause lifted into the air.

A smile found its way onto Jeremiah's face, and he moved forward to shake Squire's hand. "Always the best time here," he said cheerfully. "Thanks for having us."

"Of course," Squire said.

"I can bring my family to come help get the tents down in the morning," Jeremiah said.

"Oh, our boys'll have it done before breakfast, I'm sure." Squire shook someone else's hand. "Kelly's feedin' everyone in the morning too."

"It's amazing what food can motivate," Jeremiah said with a laugh. He loved spending time in the kitchen and feeding family and friends, so he understood. "Always a great party. Tell Miss Kelly thanks too."

"Will do." Squire's attention came back to him. "Hey, I still want to hear about how your new machine does."

Jeremiah grinned. "Yeah, of course." He'd bought a new thresher that was supposed to speed harvesting considerably, and he'd shared about it in one of their meetings. "We'll catch up later."

"Good to see you, brother." Squire took his hand again and pulled him into a partial hug. "Drive safe on the way back to Seven Sons."

"I will." He headed to the truck, glad he'd taken a few more minutes before leaving. A lot of the traffic had already cleared out, and he got behind the wheel of the truck, he found Hattie sitting up front between him and Whit, with his older children behind.

For once, they weren't fighting, though Jeremiah caught the glow of Clara Jean's phone on her face as he pulled out—and the whole way home. He said nothing, because he and Whit required the kids to plug their phones in in the kitchen, and they got to check them at will.

So he'd see who she was texting soon enough.

23

Finn waited for Alex to jump down from the backhoe and for the growl of the machine to cut out. "Hey, I'm headed out," he said as he took off his gloves. "I'll stop by From the Ground Up on the way back and get your soil."

"That would be great," Alex said as he came closer. "Then that'll be the last sinkhole." He looked at the ground where they'd been working this week. They'd gotten the big rocks in the bottom. Then the smaller gravel, and then even smaller gravel. The geotextile had gone in after that, and that stuff looked malleable, but it took a very strong arm—and a strong will—to get it in place.

They'd just put the sand in, and Finn had spread it all around. All that remained for this final sinkhole, a wound in the land that spanned about twelve feet across, was the soil. And then the replanting, but Alex could handle that.

"Where's this other place?" Alex asked as he uncapped his water bottle.

Finn's frustration rose though he tried to stamp it down. "It's out on the eastern highway," he said vaguely. He already knew the ranch he was going to look at today—the fourth one in the past month—probably wouldn't work out for him.

The list price was double his budget, but his realtor had said to just come look, that it had been on the market for a while, and that the seller was "motivated."

"You're not taking Edee?"

"She's at lunch with Aggie," Finn said as he shook his head. "I'll tell her about it later." Or he wouldn't. He and Edith had still been seeing plenty of one another, but he still hadn't told her why he was embarrassed of his family. The Fourth had been a couple of weeks ago now, and Finn had not taken Edith out to Three Rivers again.

She went to Courage Reins every single week, but that didn't mean she spent time with his parents. If anyone, she was closest to Uncle Pete, and he'd said nothing about her. What was there to say?

Finn worked here at Coyote Pass. It made no sense to then bring Edith back to the basement at Three Rivers, especially if *he* wanted to spend time with her. Not only that, but Edith wrote after dinner. Finn left sometimes before dinner and sometimes after, but he never infringed on her writing time.

So bringing her out to Three Rivers would do that, and while a tiny pinch existed in his gut that his momma wasn't getting what she wanted—more time to get to know Edith—Finn reasoned that Momma didn't have to marry her.

After he'd gone into the farmhouse and washed his hands, and as he got behind the wheel of his truck, he asked himself, "Do *you* want to marry her?"

Finn had never been in love before. He'd actually never thought too much about getting married and having a family. He didn't have older brothers or sisters who'd gone ahead of him, saying I-do, and having babies.

He didn't have friends who'd done that. He felt isolated as he made the drive through town and then east, past Wilde & Organic to the highway that ran back north. He knew the ranches down here—the Golden Hour Ranch, where the Christmas Extravaganza happened every year, Seven Sons, Shiloh Ridge, and this one he was looking at today: Oak Hollow.

Max Booth owned the ranch and had for as long as Finn could remember. But his only child had passed away several years ago, and his wife had left after that tragic accident. Max was getting up there in years, and he had no family to pass the ranch to. So he'd listed it for sale, and as far as Finn knew, he'd already moved off the property.

Jerry Bozeman waited for him in his truck, his thumbs moving quickly over his phone. But the moment Finn got out and looked up into the blue sky, Jerry was right there, smile hitched in place, and a big laugh ready for Finn.

"So?" He shook Finn's hand. "It's beautiful, right?"

Finn had driven past a pretty white fence on one side of the road, marking a pasture, and wide open fields on the other, on the way to this house among trees. "So far," he said. He'd already told

Jerry he didn't think he could afford this place, so he swallowed the worry again.

"Let's see the house first," Jerry said. He led the way inside, and Finn appreciated that he didn't have to go through things himself. He felt way less pressure to know what to look at, and Jerry knew things about the property the naked eye couldn't see anyway.

"Brand new floors here," he said. "Repainted in February." He held the front door open for Finn, who stepped into a gorgeous home with deep, dark hardwood floors and bright white walls. The house had plenty of windows that let in a lot of light, and the first room to Finn's right was an office.

That would be perfect for Edith, he thought, immediately wishing he hadn't had that thought. He wasn't sure why, other than he felt he shouldn't assume she'd be here with him from the get-go. Or at all.

Yes, he'd been enjoying his summer with her, but he'd had romantic, kissing-filled summers with Edith Baxter before. Life had torn them apart, and such a thing could happen again.

"Beautiful staircase here," Jerry said. "Leads up to three bedrooms and a bathroom. The kitchen is just past this half-bath here." He opened the door as he went by, and Finn paused to look inside. Sink. Toilet. Functional and clean clean clean.

He followed Jerry around the house, asking questions if they occurred to him and staying quiet if he had nothing to say. In the backyard, he found plenty of room for Edith's she-shed, and two twin barns stood tall and proud. Two twin *red* barns, which made his Texas heart happy.

"Enough stable room for a dozen horses," he said. "Big equipment building, and a storage shed too." Jerry pointed them all out from where they stood on the backside of the barns.

Finn could definitely see himself living and working here. "It's four hundred and fifty acres," he said, not really asking.

"That's right." Jerry turned his white-toothed smile on Finn. "One-point-one million—and it comes with two hundred head of cattle." He looked as pleased as a child who'd gotten a cookie before dinner and rocked back on his heels.

"Who's taking care of the cattle right now?" Finn looked into the distance, glad for the shade of his cowboy hat as he looked for the cattle. Like they'd just come lumbering in to see him.

"They opened the gate over to the ranch to the north," Jerry said. "They're wandering the Sunflower Ranch."

"So the fields here are dormant. Fallow."

"That's right." Jerry obviously refused to have his positivity swayed.

"All right." Finn took a big breath. "I gotta be honest, Jerry. It's great. Of course it's great. It's a million-dollar ranch, which is twice what I can afford." He scuffed his boots in the dust along the ground. "I just don't see how I'm gonna pay for it."

"There are options," Jerry said. "We can do a buy-down on interest rates, and apply for loans for people buying ranches for the first time."

Finn nodded, though he didn't really understand the things Jerry said about real estate. So much of it sounded like mumbo jumbo to him. They started back toward the house, and ultimately, their vehicles parked out front.

"Have you talked to your daddy about helping with a down payment?" Jerry asked. "Or co-signing with you?"

Finn shook his head. "I haven't talked to him about it."

"Well, bigger down payments help with the month-to-month payments," Jerry said. "And if he co-signs with that big ranch north of town, I don't think you'd have a problem at all."

"Yeah," Finn said, but he had reasons why he hadn't spoken to his daddy about helping with his ranch. He didn't *want* his father's help.

Everyone needs help sometimes, he thought, and it certainly wasn't in his voice. He thought about how he'd offered to help Alex and Edith and they'd immediately turned him down. Hadn't he quoted to them that for people to be able to serve, there had to be people willing to accept the service?

Yes, yes, he had.

That didn't mean he should ask his parents for a bunch of money, or to put their ranch up as collateral so he could get this place.

As he approached his truck, he said, "Thanks, Jerry. This place is really nice."

"Let me know," Jerry said. "I can pull some numbers for you in the meantime, if you'd like."

"I mean, why not?" Finn asked. "Do that and let me know."

"Will do."

Finn got back in his truck and started it. The AC blew into his face as Jerry drove down the dirt lane, but Finn stayed in front of the big, two-story house at the end of this lane.

"Lord, what am I doin' here?" He looked at the blue sky. The gloriously emerald trees. The pale blue roof tiles on the immaculate house. "What should I be doing? Why do I feel so lost?"

He'd only been home for a little over two months, but he felt like he should be further along than he was. What business did he have buying his own ranch—and possibly starting a family with Edith—when he felt like he was wandering in the wilderness?

Remember your family.

Tears flowed instantly into his eyes, and he pressed them closed. "My family?"

God didn't answer him again, but Finn's memories flowed fast through his mind. When he was deathly ill, his momma never left his side. Grandma Ackerman made soup. Grandma Armstrong took care of his dog for him. Squire spelled Momma when he came in off the ranch.

Every year, Libby had the perfect birthday present for Finn. She planned ahead and sent them every year when he'd been deployed.

When they decorated for Christmas, Momma

brought out a box of old, wooden clothespins that had been painted to represent the members of her family. Her parents, her grandparents, their children.

Grandma Armstrong had inherited them from her mother, and then given them to Momma when Finn was a teenager. She'd added Grandpa, then Momma, Daddy, Finn, and his siblings.

They hung the clothespins on a light string above the windows in the living room, where their ancestors could watch over them.

"I need to trust my family," he said aloud. As he sat there, Finn acknowledged that he was embarrassed of his family. He still wasn't sure why or what he'd tell Edith about that, but guilt gutted him.

His family had never given him anything to be embarrassed about. They loved him. They each wanted the best for him.

"You *have* been hoarding Edith," he whispered. And that was probably really killing his momma. He opened his eyes, the sunshine and blue sky blinding him. "I'll do better," he promised.

And now, he needed to make the long drive back to Three Rivers Ranch—and his family. "Give me the words to say," he prayed as he put the truck in reverse and backed away from the house. For the first time, he was glad for the distance out to the ranch, because he'd have more time to organize his thoughts and his words before he had to face his momma and daddy.

24

Ace Glover led the way into his house, his two boys following him. At least Gun and Ash had stopped begging Ace for a dog. He had no doubt his children would win against him and Holly Ann one day, but that day would not be today.

Shiloh Ridge had plenty of dogs for his fifteen-year-old and his ten-year-old boys to play with.

"Pearly," he called as he entered the kitchen. "The roses sure look nice." He grinned at his thirteen-year-old daughter, who looked up from the peaches she was cutting, her smile bright bright bright.

"Really, Daddy?"

"I love the pale yellow ones," he said as he moved into the kitchen and flipped on the sink to wash his hands. "You boys wash up. Momma and Pearl Jo have breakfast on."

"My sister is four minutes away," Holly Ann said as she leaned into him and kissed his cheek. "And Pearl Jo has shown me no less than sixteen dogs that are up for adoption this morning." She said the last sentence in a whisper, and Ace chuckled as she moved away from him to get the bacon off the stovetop.

"Ash, go wash up," Holly Ann said. "You've been out with the cattle. You can't eat until you wash."

"I didn't touch nothing," Ashton said.

"You touched the dirty air," Holly Ann said.

"You're always telling us to go outside and get *fresh* air," Ashton said. "And now you're telling me it's dirty?"

"Ash," Ace said. "Go."

"The water in the bathroom is always too cold," he complained.

"Then come use this sink," Ace said as he got the last of the soap suds off his hands. He moved out of the way and left the water running warmly as he pulled a towel from the handle of the top oven.

"Pearl Jo, put the syrups on the table," Holly Ann said. "Gun, grab those plates. Aunt Bethy is gonna be here in a minute." She shot a look over to Ace, who took in the rest of the food ready and waiting on the island. He picked up a plate of pancakes and the bacon and followed his daughter over to the table.

"We're here," Bethany Ann called a moment later, and footsteps ran into the house. She and Kevin only had one child—a girl they'd named Mary Ann. She'd turn thirteen this fall, and she and Pearl Jo ran as thick as thieves most of the time.

"Pearl," Mary Ann called now. "You have to come see the new kittens."

Pearl Jo immediately turned to her mother. "Can we go today?"

Holly Ann smiled at her and then Mary Ann. She hugged her niece and pressed a kiss to her blonde hair. "Yes, baby, we're going out to Uncle Kevin's farm today, remember? If you work hard for an hour, you can see the kittens."

"Before you then work hard for another hour," Ace said.

"Right," Holly Ann said.

Bethany Ann and Kevin arrived in the kitchen, and Ace took a long look at his brother-in-law. Kevin had fallen out of a moving tractor during the last harvest, and he'd broken his leg and injured his back. He'd had surgery in March to clear out some cartilage from a couple of his ruptured discs, and he and Bethany Ann had had to face some really hard facts in the past year.

So hard, they were losing their farm. "Losing" wasn't really the right term. But they'd lived on and worked that small ranch for a couple of decades now, and selling it wasn't going to be easy.

Going through their house, their barns, their stable, and their storage sheds wasn't going to be easy for anyone. Thankfully, Ace had recruited Ward, Ranger, and Mister to come help him and Holly Ann and the kids today.

He expected to have to keep after his kids to put things in boxes instead of playing with them. Ward was stopping by From the Ground Up to get one of his wife's big trucks for garbage, and Ace saw a couple of trips to the landfill in their future. And Holly Ann had been prepping lunch and dinner for today—for over a dozen people—

for a few days now, so Ace expected to eat well today too.

He ate well every day, as Holly Ann took such amazing care of him and their family. He shook hands with Kevin after noting the limp, and he pulled Bethany Ann into a hug. "It's going to be great having you guys so close."

"I'm still not sure about living up here," she said. "Don't you guys need that house?"

"No one's lived in it for a fair few years now," Ace said.

"Since Preacher and Charlie built their place," Holly Ann said. "Bethany Ann, stop worrying about it." She threw her sister a sharp look.

Ace turned away from them and found Kevin reaching for the counter as his wife released his arm. "Any idea what the ranch market is like right now?" he asked.

Kevin sighed and said, "It's not great, actually. The realtor said our place needs work—as if I don't know—and that the cleaner we could get it, the easier it would be."

"He said it would probably take three to six months," Bethany Ann said. "But don't worry. We have enough saved up for rent."

"And if you didn't, it would be fine." Holly

Ann threw a look to Ace, but he said nothing. He'd taken the idea of having Kevin and Bethany Ann move into the Top Cottage to Bear and Ranger, and the whole Glover family had to vote on it.

They'd voted unanimously to allow them to live there, and Ace had suggested a modest rent. Not that the ranch needed the money—and that was why Holly Ann kept giving Ace meaningful looks.

He shook his head slightly and moved to sit down. "Come on, boys. Time to pray and eat." He'd talk to Kevin about the issue of rent later, but he didn't believe for a single second that he or Bethany Ann would agree not to pay anything. They had too much pride for that.

As soon as the prayer finished, Ace's phone rang. "It's Ward," he said, swiping it from the table and standing. They had a rule of no phones at the table, because Gun would text twenty-four-seven if they didn't.

And that included him. "Hey, brother," he said as he moved to the fridge. "What's up?"

"Listen, I'm real sorry, but I can't come down to Kevin's place this morning. Judge found a huge section of fence that's down, and we've got to go get the cattle back."

"Sure," Ace said though his heart fell to the soles of his boots. "We'll manage."

"I'm pulling in Mister," Ward said slowly.

"And Ranger?"

"You can keep Ranger."

That still left Ace two men down, and that was four hands he really needed. Defeat paraded through him, but what was he supposed to do? "Okay," Ace said with a sigh. He pulled out the orange juice and set it on the counter. "I'll see if I can recruit a couple of boys from Three Rivers, what with it bordering their land and all. Maybe they can just run over real quick."

In that moment, God shone a light into Ace's memory. He needed to make another phone call right now. "Good luck with the cows, Ward." He ended the call quickly, because Ward might recruit *him* to round up their lost cattle if he stayed on the line too long.

"Ace, baby," Holly Ann said.

"We lost Mister and Ward," he said without looking at her. "I just need a minute." He glanced over to her, caught her nod, and tapped to dial Squire.

"Howdy, Ace," the other cowboy answered.

"Squire," he said. "I'm wondering...well, at the Fourth of July picnic out there, I remember hearing you say Finn was working for other ranches this summer. Could I get his number to talk to him about a job that's come up suddenly?"

"Sure thing," Squire said. "He's done at Coyote Pass now, but I'm not real sure where he is today. He should answer, though." He gave Ace the number, and he quickly opened a drawer to find a pen.

"Say it again."

Squire did, and Ace got it this time. "Thanks so much. We'll be out your way in a couple of hours, and if you have men with nothing to do, I could use their help today." He chuckled and shook his head. "As if we ever just have men standing around."

Squire laughed too. "I can send you some guys. Is Kevin selling his place?"

Ace turned away from the table and kept his voice low. "Yeah. There's just no way he can do what it requires. We're going to be cleaning it up in the next several weeks, so they can list it for sale."

"How big is it?" he asked.

Another idea formed in Ace's head. "You thinkin' Three Rivers might absorb it?"

"Something like that," he said vaguely.

"It's, I don't know." He turned back to the table and took a few steps closer to it. "Hey, Kev, how big is your ranch?"

"One eighty-five," he said.

"It's a hundred and eighty-five acres," Ace said to Squire as he turned again. "Might be great extra grazing or agriculture."

"Might be," Squire said, and Ace recognized a man who wasn't going to say more.

"Okay," Ace said. "Thanks for Finn's number. I'll give him a call."

"Ace," Holly Ann said again. He ended the call and bent his head over his phone to type in Finn's number and then a message, requesting his help at Kevin's ranch that day. *We'll pay whatever you say. I just need more hands, and your daddy says you're the best.*

"Ace."

"I'm coming." He sent the text, tucked his phone in his pocket, and rejoined his family at the breakfast table. "We can't clean this place up ourselves, baby doll. I'm just trying to get help there today."

"What happened to Ward and Mister?"

"Broken fence. Loose cattle." Ace picked up the crustless quiche and took the last two pieces. He'd been gluten-free for years now, and he mostly didn't miss things like crust and other gluten-filled products. Most of that was because of Holly Ann, an extraordinary chef who'd figured out how to make gluten-free things taste delicious.

In his back pocket, his phone vibrated, but Ace ignored it. He could take twenty minutes for breakfast and then text Finn back.

"Daddy, look at this dog," Pearl Jo said, and Ace almost couldn't repress the sigh.

"You guys," he said. "We're not getting a dog, okay? Momma's busy with her catering. Y'all work around the house or ranch all the time, and just because you have more free time in the summer doesn't mean you'll be able to take care of the dog once school starts up again."

"We will," Ash said, his whining in full force again.

"Pearl Jo, you're going out for swim this fall, right?" Ace took a bite of his bacon, already knowing the answer. "And Gun's in high school and doin' all those ROTC classes. He doesn't have time for a dog."

"I can do it, Daddy." Ash wore such an earnest look on his face, but Ace knew his son.

"And someone's been begging Uncle Mister for roping lessons." Ace gave his son a pointed look. "Boys training for junior rodeo don't have time for dogs, and Momma and I aren't going to take care of a dog."

"I could do it," Mary Ann said at the same time Gun said, "Daddy's right." He flicked a look at Ashton and then Pearl Jo. "School starts in a week and a half. We'll be busier than ever. No time for a dog."

Ace waved his fork at his strong, stoic, quiet son. "Gun has spoken." He grinned at the boy, and unlike Bear's sons, none of his boys had nicknames. Gunnison was a pretty unusual name already, and Gun simply fit the boy.

"No time for a dog," Holly Ann reiterated, and she got up with her empty plate. "Now, you kids clear this table and help me get the kitchen clean. Ace, can you get the coolers?"

"Yes, ma'am," he said, though he wasn't finished with breakfast yet. He kept eating while activity happened around him, and since almost everyone had gotten up from the table, he checked his phone.

Finn had indeed responded to his text with, *Absolutely, I'll be there. And Ace? Can I talk to your brother-in-law about his place? See, I've been looking for a small operation to buy, and they're hard to find.*

Once again, it felt like the Lord had trained His heavenly light right onto Ace. Straight into his mind. He grinned at the text and tapped out, *Sure, of course. You might change your mind when you see it.*

Tell me what time to be there, and I'll be there.

Ace did some quick calculations, based on what time it was right now, and then he typed out, *10. We'll be there about 10.*

25

Finn once again had to drive almost all the way to town before he could make a right turn and head west to the small, one-man operation that sat just south of Three Rivers Ranch. To his knowledge, it didn't have a name, and Kevin Bentley had been running it for as long as Finn could remember.

Sure enough, he passed under no sign and saw only a fence with numbers on it to indicate that he'd arrived at the right place. He turned right again, now moving north onto the ranch. He'd taken a few minutes to look it up online, but it wasn't listed for sale, and he hadn't been able to find out much about it.

So he'd taken a few more minutes to text his daddy about it. That was how he'd found out this ranch sat just under two hundred acres. And that it bordered Three Rivers Ranch on the far southwest border. And that it could be perfect for Finn.

"Don't get your hopes up," he told himself as he lumbered along the dirt road. He'd wanted to call Edith, but she and Alex had gone back to their regular schedule of working their own piece of land. He'd been settling for seeing her in the evenings for an hour or so before she started writing, or taking her for a quick dinner, or laughing and chatting with her as they fed the horses in the evenings.

Alex had started dating Nicki Johnston, so he wasn't home as much in the evenings these days, and Finn didn't like throwing wrenches in Edith's schedule. It wasn't her favorite thing, though she could recalibrate pretty quickly if she had to.

Today, though, Finn knew she had lunch plans with Christie, and then she'd be out at Courage Reins this afternoon to work with Reagan. "Besides," he muttered as the road went on and on, planted fields of alfalfa on both sides. "You're not here for a ranch tour. You're here to work."

Ace Glover needed help with this place, and Finn wasn't going to let him down. If he could talk to Kevin about possibly buying it, great. Icing on the cake, with a cherry on top of that.

Finally, trees entered his view, and the way they curved told Finn a river ran through the ranch. He smiled to himself, because there was something cheery about this place. He went through the tree line, and sure enough, he had to go over a bridge to do that.

Immediately, he found a cute little log cabin sitting there among the fields, a red barn, and the emerald green grass. Fine, now that the summer had baked into August, the grass was a little yellower and a little crispier than it would've been in the spring.

"This place is great," he said. He liked how it couldn't be seen from far away. How the trees and river created a private little alcove here. How he could see himself making the drive from Three Rivers to this spot of land when he wanted his momma's cooking, or to see his siblings, or to go horseback riding.

Four trucks had parked in front of the house, which didn't have a garage that he could see, and Finn eased his in next to the black one on the end.

His suddenly felt like a miniature truck next to the big behemoth, and he wasn't surprised to see Holly Ann Glover come jogging out of the house and over to the truck.

Finn dropped out of his and said, "Howdy, Miss Holly Ann."

"Oh, Finn." She jumped back, her hand flying up to her chest. "I didn't see you there."

"Just got here," he said. "Looks like you guys did end up bringing a crew."

She opened the driver's door of the black truck and climbed inside. She grabbed something and slid right back out. "Zona recruited one of her brother-in-laws," she said. "Dawson's here."

"Oh, sure," Finn said, looking up to the cabin. He loved the yellowish-reddish wood of it, and the big wide steps that led up to the porch that spanned the whole width of the house. Edith sure would like that. "I know Dawson. We were in the same grade. Graduated the same year."

Holly Ann smiled at him and held up her phone. "You comin' in? I'll have lunch in a couple of hours, and Kevin's going to go over the things that need the most work."

"Yeah, I'm coming in." Finn followed her up the steps at a slower pace, but she held the front door for him to go in ahead of her. Blonde wood decorated the walls and ceiling, the railing on the staircase that went up and the one that went down.

It wasn't fully a cabin, as carpet covered the floor in the living room and regular tile spread throughout the kitchen. Finn saw it down the hall too, and he caught a glimpse of dark brown leather couches and cheery drapes in blue and yellow before someone said, "Hey, Finn, you made it."

He focused on the people then, all of them standing in the kitchen or along the cusp of it. "Ace." He grinned and shook the older cowboy's hand. "Good to see you again."

"I mean, this ain't no picnic," Ace joked, and they both laughed. "But my wife did bring a lot of food."

"Everyone has to *earn* it," Holly Ann called throughout the house. "With a few hours of good, hard work."

A couple of her kids groaned, with the oldest rolling his eyes. Kevin sat at the table in the eat-in kitchen, his wife next to him. He wore a look of resignation while Bethany Ann looked half hopeful and half scared.

"Dawson," Finn said, and he clapped hands

with the man and shook. "Haven't seen you in a while."

"No kidding," Dawson said with a grin. "You got roped into helping today too?"

"Oh, they asked," Finn said, rocking back onto the heels of his cowboy boots. "I've been roaming this summer, since I got home. I guess word's gotten out that if someone needs help, they can call my daddy, and he'll send me."

"Have you been here before?" Dawson asked.

"Can't say I have," Finn said as he took in the modern kitchen, with clean, state-of-the-art appliances, and smooth, polished countertops that could've been granite or could've been quartz. "Or if I have, I was too young to remember."

"Same," Dawson said. "It's really nice." His voice pitched up on the last word, and that caused Finn to stop taking in the beauty of the house and look at the other cowboy.

"It is," Finn said with much more caution in his voice. He wasn't sure why, but something told him to be careful here. "Are you living at your family's ranch? Working there with your brother?"

He knew Duke Rhinehart had taken over the Rhinehart Ranch south of town several years ago, because he'd been the one organizing his men to help on other ranches after the flood, and Finn had worked on his for a couple of days too.

He lived there with his wife, Arizona—once a Glover—and his four kids. Two girls and two boys. Finn could only hope to have such a perfect life one day.

"Yeah," Dawson said, doing the rocking thing too. "Yep. Live there in a cabin with my brother. I handle a lot of the back-end things."

"Back-end things?" Finn asked as Bethany Ann shuffled papers on the table. No one had started to give out assignments yet, and Finn's skin itched to look into the backyard and see if there'd be room for Edith's she-shed. Surely there would be.

"Making sure we meet zoning laws," he said. "Fill out all the right business forms. The financial accounting on the ranch. All of that."

"Oh, you went to school for some of that, didn't you?" Finn asked.

"Yes, I did." Dawson grinned at him and then around the cabin. "Got a degree and everything." He chuckled and shook his head. "I hear your sister did the same."

"Yeah, she sure did." Finn met his eye again, and all of his defenses fell. If Dawson was so engrained and important at his family ranch, surely he wasn't looking to buy his own.

"All right," Ace said. "Ranger's back, so let's get some assignments out. Bethany Ann?"

"Yes." She cleared her throat. "I need some help in the house to go through closets and pack up anything we don't need. My daddy's coming with a moving truck, and we can put the boxes in that as they fill. We'll have a few pieces of furniture that need moving too...."

She continued to go over the house, but she spoke quickly, with plenty of authority and no minced words. Then she turned to her husband, and said, "All right, Kev. Your turn."

He drew in a deep breath, which seemed to hurt him slightly, and said, "I haven't been able to keep up with the chores outside." He ducked his head as if embarrassed, and Finn's heart went out to the man. "Things are a bit...messy out there. Ace knows most of it, so he'll direct you as a team as you move from building to building out there. Again, anything we don't absolutely have to have here, we're going to put on the moving truck. Our realtor wants the place as clean and as sparse as possible for listing."

"Questions?" Holly Ann asked. "Pearl Jo,

Mary Ann, Fawn, and I are going to stay here and help Bethy in the house. Ace will take all you big, strong cowboys outside with him." She clapped her hands together and added, "And...go! Lunch will be at one o'clock."

"I'm setting an alarm," Ace said as he tapped on his phone. "I'm hungry already."

Holly Ann grinned and shook her head, and Finn moved with Ace and his two boys, Ranger and his teenager, and Dawson as they all went outside. Kevin followed them at a much slower pace, and he said, "Thanks for coming Finn."

"Of course." Finn turned back to the man. "I haven't been here before. It's really nice." His heart pounded as he met Kevin's eyes. How did he say he wanted to buy this place? Did he even want that?

He'd seen only a portion of it, and he wasn't exactly sure how much a place like this would cost. Perhaps with the outbuildings, the cattle, the land, the house, it would be outside of his price range.

"How many head you got?" he asked as the others reached the edge of the deck and went down the steps. The backyard held just as much grandeur as the front, with the river in the distance on the right, and plenty of room for Edith's she-shed on the left.

The chicken coop sat straight ahead, with a paddock with several goats in it beside and behind that. Then the barn he'd seen from the road, as the lane ran right past it.

"I've got a hundred and three cow-calf pairs this year," he said. "We just finished the weaning, which is why things are a bit behind right now."

Finn wasn't a math genius, but he knew a hundred head of cattle could provide a good living. He wasn't going to bring in millions like his father, but he also didn't employ fifteen cowboys and several more to run the administrative side of his cattle operation.

"That's amazing," he said. "My daddy said this place is a hundred and eighty-five acres, so it must produce well to support them."

A flash of a smile crept across Kevin's face. "It does. It has in the past, at least."

Finn tucked his hands into his pockets, feeling a bit guilty as the others reached the end of the gravel walkway that split the grass and went between the coop and the pasture. Ace was obviously speaking, as he pointed to the right, and then gestured to the left.

"How much are you going to list it for?" he asked, his voice anything but casual.

Kevin looked over to him. "I don't know. Whatever the realtor says the market value is."

With a thundering heartbeat, Finn figured he'd already shown his hand. "Well, Mister Bentley, I'm interested in buying it." He swallowed, his throat so, so dry. "I need a place of my own, and I've been looking all summer. This place is perfect for me."

He realized then that he hadn't been able to look straight at Kevin since they'd come outside. He forced himself to do so now, utilizing some of his military training to get the job done. Finn took a slow breath, another tactic he'd learned from his years in the Army. "You work it yourself, don't you?" He nodded back toward the house. "With your wife, of course."

"Yes," Kevin said, the word barely slipping from his lips. He seemed shocked for some reason.

Relief sang through Finn as he looked away and back out to the ranch. "I think I could work it myself too," Finn said. "By some miracle, maybe it won't be too expensive for me."

"Are you—you're serious."

Finn chuckled and removed his hands from

his pockets. "Oh, I'm serious." He smiled at Kevin. "Now, I told Ace I'd come help, so I better get out there and see what he needs me to do." He took a few steps away from Kevin, then turned back. "You'll call me when the realtor tells you a price? Or who are you using? I've got Jerry Bozeman looking for something for me."

"I'm using Jerry," Kevin said, his smile growing. It actually looked genuine now, and Finn felt the same rays of sunshine and heavenly light beaming down on him. Lighting the way through this summer of darkness he'd been treading.

As he went down the steps to the gravel path, he thought, *Finally. Thank you, Lord, for finally putting a ranch out there that I might be able buy.*

As he strode in the direction Ace and the others had gone, Finn definitely saw things that needed work. A leaning gate. Loose chicken wire in the corner of the coop. Barrels that looked wet and rotten, maybe from the flood. The ranch wasn't in complete disrepair, but Kevin had spoken true inside.

It needed a lot of work.

And dang if Finn's step didn't have a bounce in it, because he wanted to be the one to do that work. "I can't wait to tell Edith," he muttered to himself as he rounded a corner and found Ace and the others working on pulling off planks from a cute little building that had obviously been damaged at some time in the past.

A pig pen, and Finn didn't even mind the smell as he approached. He'd always liked pigs, and he wondered if Kevin was going to sell the farm with everything on it. Most likely, and Finn's nerves hummed at him.

Cattle, goats, chickens, pigs, and horses would only add to the cost of the ranch, and Finn was more determined than ever to buy it.

Have faith, he thought. *And rely on your family.*

Since he'd gotten that message a couple of weeks ago, he'd talked to his momma and daddy about what he wanted—a ranch like this. He'd told them everything about Edith, and they'd actually hosted her for lunch one Sunday after church. They had plans for a double date in a couple of weeks, once school started again, and Finn knew Edith and his momma texted back and forth these days.

He worked with the others until lunchtime, and then he took his sandwich, his cold watermelon, and his macaroni salad outside to the shady deck. *You'll never guess what I found today,* he texted to Edith. *The perfect ranch. The one I'm going to buy.*

Don't hold out on me Shortstop, she texted back. *Tell me everything.*

He grinned and chuckled to himself, really enjoying her nicknames, even via text. He could just *hear* her saying it out loud.

Tonight, sweetheart. I'll tell you all about it when I see you tonight.

26

Edith sipped the lemonade Kelly had given her and kept her eyes on the curve in the dirt road where Finn would drive when he finally got home. She'd just finished lunch when he'd texted about "the perfect ranch," and then she'd made the drive to Courage Reins, worked with Reagan, and had her therapy session with Bull.

Her mind still felt a bit mushy, because the counselor kept challenging her to kick down her own barriers. It had been hard enough erecting them. Getting through every layer to break them down sure wasn't easy.

When are you going to believe you can be loved again?

His hardest question from today's session had sunk into Edith's mind and refused to let go. She let her thoughts ebb and flow, move and still and wash away again.

She took another sip of tart lemonade, a slight sweetness right at the end. Kelly had said she could come to the homestead anytime, even if no one was there. Today, though, she had been home, stirring something in a slow cooker and providing Edith with the lemonade before she'd gone back out the door and down the lane to the administration building.

Edith sat in a chair on the deck, and from her elevated position, she could see so much of the ranch. She could see so much of her life a bit more clearly.

"I believe I can be loved," she said, echoing what she'd told Doctor Bull today. And she did. Alex loved her, as did her other younger brother, the one still living in Florida. All four of her younger sisters, the ones that came after Alex and who all still lived at home in Florida, with her parents.

And of course, her parents loved her. The

dachshunds couldn't get enough of her. Reagan adored her, as did Cocoa and every other horse she'd ever worked with here at Courage Reins.

Levi had loved her.

And that right there was the rub. Doctor Bull wanted Edith to admit that someone besides Levi could love her. He wanted her to say she believed she could be loved by someone as handsome, and smart, and hardworking, and kind, and faithful as Finn.

"Never should've told him I felt inadequate." Edith shook her head and switched her attention from the curve in the road—which Finn had not rounded yet—to the glass-front building where she had her counseling sessions.

She'd said as much to Doctor Bull in a moment of weakness. A single moment where she'd been asked to think about the perfect man, and an image of Finn had entered her mind. The way he brought her coffee sometimes, and took her to dinner at her favorite places, and stocked her mini-freezer with ice cream while she was out working on the farm. She'd only discover it when she went to the she-shed to write, and by then, Finn had gone home. She'd been forced to text him her thanks upon the discovery of the ice cream, and kiss him for it the next time she saw him.

"I can admit I'm falling for him," she muttered next. She didn't truly feel inadequate. She and Finn stood on even ground, even if she had broken down in front of him a few times. He had issues with his family he was working on, and she had things in her life that needed fixing too. She wouldn't be human otherwise.

She was just about to call Finn and demand to know where he was when his truck finally came around the corner. She perked up and drained the last of her lemonade, excited to hear about the ranch he'd seen today. She hadn't mentioned it to his mother, just in case Kelly hadn't known about it, and her own curiosity ate at her like a swarm of mosquitoes.

Finn pulled into the driveway, though he stayed off to the side so as to not block the garage. He didn't seem to have seen her, and Edith got to her feet and headed down the steps so he wouldn't enter the house through the garage without seeing her.

She heard the rumbling of the door as it went up, and Edith broke into a jog. "Finn." She rounded the corner and found him carrying a big water bottle and a sack of food. He'd come to a stop, and he grinned at her when he saw her.

"Hey, you." He moved toward her then and leaned in to kiss her cheek. "What are you doin' here? I thought I was meeting you and Alex and Nicki for movie night over at the farmhouse."

She shook her head, her voice trapped behind a ball of nerves she didn't understand. "I told him me and you were just going to do it here." She shrugged one shoulder. "Maybe with Sammy."

"Sure," Finn said. "That's even better. Me and you on the big couch downstairs." He switched the water bottle to the crook of his arm so he could slide his hand around her waist. "It's great to see you." He kissed her right on the mouth then, and Edith felt every eye of the ranch watching them, even if it wasn't true.

"Mm, you taste like lemonade," he murmured. "My momma must be inside."

Edith ducked her head. "She was for a minute," she said. "Long enough to stir dinner and get me a drink."

"You've been waiting long?"

She looked up at him. "Feels like a long time, yeah."

He grinned. "Come on then." He lifted the

bag of food. "I don't know what my momma made for dinner, but Holly Ann sent me home with lots of leftovers. Steak sandwiches. Cornbread muffins. Fruit and cheese and my word, the woman makes the best mac-salad in the whole world. If we're lucky, we can sneak downstairs right now and have a feast together, then start a movie, and we won't even have to see my parents."

Edith smiled at him, but she shook her head. "Right. I'm sure your mother will allow that to happen."

Still, she went inside with him, and they didn't linger upstairs in the main living area for long. It felt a little bit like she was doing something wrong as she followed him down the hall and around the corner to the stairs that led into the basement.

Cooler air reached them, and Finn put the bag of food on the counter in the kitchenette. "I'm just gonna shower and change really fast, okay?" He kissed her again, and Edith didn't mind the sweat and ranch smell of his skin. "I worked hard today, and I'm gross."

"Okay," she said as he slipped out of her arms and around the enormous sectional couch to the bathroom.

"Eat if you want," he called over his shoulder. "I just need ten minutes."

Edith did wander over to the bag, and she pulled out the food and spread it along the counter. Holly Ann Glover ran a catering company in town, and she had loaded Finn up with plenty of food. As a bachelor, it would probably take him all week to eat this much food.

She'd packed macaroni salad and potato salad and cole slaw. He had cornbread muffins and scrambled egg muffins. The steak sandwiches were made on hoagies, not slices of bread, and she laid out four of them that had to be eight inches long each.

A full-size fridge stood in the kitchenette, and Edith put the leftovers in it before she turned to the TV. The shower ran in the bathroom down the hall, and she flopped onto the couch, a sigh pulling through her body.

She pulled out her phone and started to text her mom. *Hey, Mom*, she started. *Deep questions from Edith, Thursday edition. How do you know if you can be loved?*

Her mother was used to her deep questions, as she'd been asking them her whole life. In person, her mom would smile at her and say, "You can ask me anything." Edith had taken her seriously, and they'd talked about anything and everything over the thirty years of Edith's life.

Everyone is lovable, her mom said. *Remember that lesson you had when you were volunteering in the elementary school here?*

Edith knew instantly what her mom meant, and tears touched her eyes.

You thought Benjamin was nothing but trouble, her mom said. *He was so mischievous. Never did what he was supposed to do. Didn't get his homework done. And then you met his mother. And you realized that everyone has a mother that loves them.*

She sniffled and pulled back on her emotions. *Yeah, I know, Mom. But what about a different kind of love?*

Things aren't going well with Finn? I thought they were.

They are, she said. *Really. But my therapist thinks I think I can't be loved. That even if Finn ever does tell me he loves me, I won't believe it.*

Her mother didn't respond instantly, and Edith looked toward the hallway as she heard the bathroom door open. Finn's bedroom sat right across the hall from it, so she didn't see him before she heard another door close.

Why would he think that, Edith?

I don't know, she said. *Probably something I said, but I'm not sure why.*

Do you think you're lovable?

Edith paused again, but she really needed a break from all the heavy thinking. She tried to listen to her inner self. Her spirit. Her soul. She pressed her eyes closed and really felt like she saw herself for who she truly was.

Yes, she typed out just as Finn said, "All right. What do you want to watch tonight?"

She tucked her phone under her leg and watched him come around the back of the couch, pulling a T-shirt over his head as he did. She caught a glimpse of that broad chest and those ripped abs, her mouth going just a bit dry at the sight of them.

"I don't care," she said.

"You put the food away."

"Yeah, I wasn't sure if you wanted to eat right now or later."

"Now, and later," he said with a grin. But he didn't get out the food. He came around the open end of the couch and crawled toward her, his smile bright and wide and full of pure white light. She hadn't seem him like this in ages, and she giggled as he bear hugged her, toppling her back onto the cushy couch.

"Finn," she giggled. He smelled like musky soap and minty toothpaste, and she had no complaints when he kissed her again. She kissed him back, and she definitely felt like she could be in love with him. He kissed her like he could love her too.

"Tell me about the ranch," she said when he moved his mouth to her jaw and then down to her throat.

He pulled back, exhaled, and lay down facing her as she shifted to press her back against the couch. "It's so great, baby." He stroked her hair off her forehead with long, loving strokes, his voice soft and filled with emotion. "It's the Bentley place. Do you know it?"

"Not really," she said. "I know they live kind of across from Alex, right?"

"Right. It actually borders Three Rivers, and if I can get it, that means Daddy and I can share grazing land. I could have more cattle than my ranch could technically support, because I'd be able to use his land." He sighed, and it was a happy, blissful sigh.

"I talked to Kevin a little bit today. He's not sure how much he'll list it for, but he's using Jerry too. I'm gonna call him in the morning just to make sure I have all the bases covered."

"Wow," Edith said. "You're serious about this." She stroked her fingers down the side of his face, his beard soft and still a touch damp.

"If I can't afford it," he said. "I'm going to ask my daddy to help me. Because that ranch...it's just perfect for me. It's not a perfect ranch, but it's a one-man operation, and I can do it, Edith. I just *know* I can do it."

"I'm sure you can." She smiled at him, at the softness his face held while he had his eyes closed, at the tan-ness of his skin that told everyone he worked outside a lot. She touched her mouth to his, glad when he pulled in a breath through his nose and kissed her back.

She maybe carried on a bit too long, and maybe she kissed him deeper than she intended to. But when he broke their kiss this time, and Edith tucked herself against his chest, she absolutely felt like she could be loved.

"It has a log cabin for a house," he whispered.

"And a cute red barn. Chicken coop, pig pen, and a little goat house with a paddock. I think you'd love it, and there's room for your she-shed."

She nodded, a special kind of warmth moving through her as he spoke about this ranch like they'd be living there and running it together. Now, she just had one more thing to weather, and maybe, just maybe she and Finn could truly be together.

"Finny?" she asked, her voice as quiet as his had been.

"Yeah?"

"I have—I go to the cemetery on the anniversary of Levi's death every year," she whispered. "I never let Alex or Aggie or anyone come with me, but this time...would you—I mean—would—could you come with me?"

He didn't immediately blurt out that he would. He held her close and pressed those warm lips to her forehead. "I sure will," he murmured. "When is it?"

She swallowed. "Less than a month now. September second."

"Four years?" Finn asked gently.

"Only three," she whispered, a knife slicing through her heart. Three years felt like such a short timeframe when put in perspective. Only one tenth of her life.

"Yeah," Finn said. "We'll go together."

"Thank you," Edith murmured.

She'd just settled into his touch again, his lips playing with her earlobe when his momma asked, "Finn? Did you make it home?" Her footsteps sounded on the stairs, and Finn rolled away from Edith and stood on his feet before his mother entered the basement living room.

"Yeah, Momma," he said as he moved toward the end of the couch. "I made it home."

"I've got dinner on upstairs," she said. "Did Edith go home? Are you hungry?"

"Edith's right here, Momma," he said. "Holly Ann sent loads of leftovers, and we're gonna have a movie night."

Edith sat up and ran her hands through her hair. "Hey, Kelly."

She blinked and looked over to Finn and back to Edith. Her surprise melted away then. "You sure you guys don't want pulled pork?"

Finn's hesitation said it all, and Kelly nodded. "I'll bring some down for you both. I know you want the hot barbecue sauce, Finny, but Edith, for you? I have sweet, mild, and hot."

Of course she'd have three barbecue sauces for her family of three and their dinner of pulled pork sandwiches. Edith smiled at her and said, "Sweet and mild, please, Kelly. Thank you."

She beamed with all the power of the stars. "You betcha. I'll be right back." She turned and went back up the steps, and Edith twisted to look at Finn.

"You know I'm never going to be able to feed you the way your momma does, right?"

Finn met her gaze, blinked, and then started laughing. At least he thought it was funny, though Edith hadn't lied. She did pray that she and Finn could have a nice, relaxing night together, and as Finn dished up sides to go with their pulled pork sandwiches, her prayers switched to something deeper.

Please, please help me to make it to September third. I just need to make it through the day on the second, and then everything will be okay.

27

Link pulled up to Wilde & Organic, his mother's preferred grocery store in Three Rivers. The town used to only have two such spots, but with the growth in the past fifteen years, more shops and stores had come to Three Rivers. Link liked a popular chain that had come to town, because they had chocolate covered cookies he couldn't get enough of.

He decided as he put his truck in park and pulled out his phone to text the store that he'd arrived for his pick-up that he'd stop by and get himself the cookies. Lord knew he'd earned them this week, what with working double shifts to get the mowing done. He'd watched his daddy and uncles do it his whole life, and this year, Link had taken the overnight shifts so his father could sleep.

After all, Daddy had turned sixty-two years old this year, and Link could see his exhaustion around the edges of his eyes. But not when he got to sleep while Link harvested. So he'd done that this week, and dang it, he wanted his cookies.

He sent the text to the grocery store, and they responded that they'd be out in a minute. Fine. Link leaned his chair back and closed his eyes, because they wouldn't let him get out and help with the groceries anyway.

He had no idea how long he dozed, but the next thing he knew, someone had knocked on the window. Link sat straight up, his heart pounding and his cowboy hat knocked askew. A pretty woman smiled at him from the other side of his driver's side window, and she held up the receipt.

Link hastened to roll down his window, and he said, "Thanks."

"Sammy Glover?" she asked.

"Yes, ma'am."

She handed over the receipt, and Link realized she was Clara Jean Walker. "Oh, hey, Clara Jean."

"Link," she said as she leaned into his truck. "You guys workin' overnight to harvest?"

"Yep." He gave her a weary smile. "Does it show on my face?"

"You're not the first cowboy I've seen napping while he waits for his groceries." She laughed lightly, and added, "See you later, Link," before she bounced away and back toward the grocery store. She was several years younger than Link and still in high school, but Link still liked her bright personality.

He wouldn't ask her out, of course, and his mind flew to Misty Granger. He'd not seen her again this summer, but he hadn't gone down to any more dances. Summer at Shiloh Ridge Ranch could only be described in one way: hectic.

Every day, he woke up with a plan in mind, and every night when he went to bed, he'd done none of those things. Still, he thanked the Lord each morning and each evening for his life in Three Rivers. He didn't want to go back to Amarillo and do more schooling. He didn't want to travel.

Link was a simple man, with a work ethic his momma and daddy praised. He never wanted to disappoint them, so he put his truck in reverse and backed out. He'd get his cookies, and then he'd continue to Meaty Mayhem, where Momma had ordered dinner for the family this Friday night.

He scoffed lightly as he pulled back onto the street. "Friday night," he muttered to himself. "You should be out on a date, like Mitch."

Mitch had only been back in town for a few months, and in that time, he'd been out with five or six different women. He wasn't a player, but he dated a lot, trying to find someone he clicked with. He'd told Link it was harder for him to find someone, because he needed to be able to communicate with them in a different way. He hated typing everything into his phone, and while he could read lips, it was hard for him to speak back to someone who didn't know sign language.

Link had agreed, because Mitch wasn't wrong. But then Link said, "I have the same trouble talking to women," and that so wasn't a lie either. He simply didn't have the charm and charisma that Mitch did, and he'd started to wonder if he should join a dating app or try to meet someone online. That way, he could message them before he had to meet them in person, which was so much harder for Link.

He pulled into the shop that stocked his preferred cookies, noting the line at the coffee truck as he went by. He could use some of that too, and Link suddenly had visions of himself hanging out with other young people in their mid-twenties, dunking his chocolate cookies in his coffee while he laughed and flirted and set up dates with pretty women.

The truck had umbrellas and tables set up, and seeing as it was still pretty early in the evening on a Friday night, they weren't terribly full yet. Not empty either, and Link ran inside to get his cookies.

Then, feeling brave and trying to channel his inner Mitch, he went past his truck and through the parking lot to the coffee truck. The line hadn't dwindled, and Link joined it behind a couple holding hands. In front of them, two girls chatted and laughed, and Link wished he'd arrived just a bit ahead of the couple.

Right, he scoffed inside his head. *Like you'd talk to them.* He'd more likely stare at them until they glanced his way, and then he'd smile, hoping *they'd* talk to *him.*

He gripped his cookies like they could protect him, and he inched forward as he listened to the couple in front of him discuss the menu stuck to the side of the silver Airstream trailer that housed the coffee shop. He watched them touch each other and laugh, and he wondered what it would be like to have a relationship like that with someone.

Link had only kissed one girl in his life, and something inside him felt reckless. Out of control. Wild.

More people joined the line, and Link looked behind him to the group of high school boys. Maybe this wasn't his scene. Maybe he should've driven through somewhere to get his coffee to go with his cookies.

His phone chimed, and he pulled it out of his pocket at the tone of his mother's notification. Daddy had his own too, and Link tried to check his phone when either of them texted him.

Dinner will be ready to pick up in twenty minutes, she said. *Sorry it's taking so long.*

He quickly thumbed out, *It's fine. I stopped to get my cookies and some coffee. I'm good.*

The couple in front of him moved to order their coffee, and a shock of panic ran through Link. It would be his turn next, and then what would he do? Take his coffee and his cookies and go eat them alone in his truck?

Probably.

If he was being honest with himself, most likely.

Laughter rang out from a table to his left, and Link looked that way. His eyes caught on the gorgeous redhead he'd met at the summer dance, more than two months ago.

Misty Granger. She sat with a couple of other people, including the man who'd towed her away from him and Mitch at the dance. The other person at the four-person table was a woman with dark hair and a wide smile full of white teeth.

"Hey, man, what can I get you?"

Link tore his eyes from the woman he had a secret crush on and faced the window. "Yeah, uh, I'd love an Americano, double, with whipped cream."

"You got it, brother." The man tapped out his order on a tablet and flipped it over. "Seven-fifty-four."

Link jostled his cookies to get his wallet out and pay, and he took his receipt with his number on it. He turned and faced the table of three, one of which was Misty, and it felt like God had opened up the heavens and shone a spotlight right on the fourth seat.

He took steps in that direction, and Misty looked up. He saw the moment she recognized him, and then he watched her tuck that pretty hair behind her ear. Link recognized flirting when he saw it, and he smiled at her.

"Hey," he said. "Can I sit with you guys?" He glanced over to the man and then the other woman.

"Link, right?" Misty asked as she moved some trash that sat in front of the fourth chair.

"Yeah." He pulled out the chair and sat down. He turned to the man. "I'm Lincoln Glover."

"Ralf," the man said. "Great to meet you." His eyes shot over to Misty, and they definitely had a conversation without saying anything.

Link ignored them, and with a pounding heart, looked at the brunette. "Everyone calls me Link."

"I'm sure they do," she said as she reached across the table to shake his hand. "I'm Janie."

"Great to meet you," Link said, feeling too big and too broad to be sitting here with them. "Do y'all work together?" He met Misty's eyes again, and Link did not imagine the sparks and flames and fireworks between them. She had to feel that, right?

"Restoration, right? No." He paused, feeling like he had sparklers fizzing in his bloodstream. "Conservationist."

"Yep," Misty said, leaning into her elbows on the table. "Ralf is our project manager, and Janie just got to town to work on the ceiling at City Hall. She's an expert with art restoration."

"Wow," Link said with a smile. "That's great." He looked around at everyone, the moment turning awkward. Thankfully, his number got called and he swiped up his receipt. "I'll be right back."

He didn't dare turn around as he walked away, but he was sure the three of them would be huddled and whispering. He picked up his coffee and moved over to the table by the front of the trailer to get napkins and a spoon.

Turning back to the table, he found Ralf and Janie cleaning up to leave. His chest collapsed in on itself, because he was going to have to sit alone after all. He forced himself back to the table and set down his coffee. "You guys leaving?"

"We've got to go over some plans," Janie said smoothly, her smile hitched in place. "Enjoy your cookies and coffee." With that, she and Ralf turned and left.

Link pulled out the chair again, trying to control the shaking in his hands. He sighed as he sat. "You don't have to go over the plans?"

"No, sir," Misty said. She leaned into the table again. "I asked them to go, so I could talk to you alone."

Link looked at her, her gaze hooking him and holding on. She smiled prettily at him, and he swallowed. "So...I'd love your number. Then we can talk some more, and maybe we can figure out a time to go out."

Misty practically glowed. "I'd like that."

"Would you?"

Her face fell slightly, and Link managed to tear his gaze away and focus on opening his box of cookies. "Have you had these?" he asked. "You can only get them here, and they're my absolute favorite."

He pulled out a handful of cookies and offered her one. "They're crispy and crunchy, and when you dip them in the coffee, the chocolate sort of melts off into it. It's fantastic."

Misty took a cookie, and Link nudged his coffee closer to her, as if they'd share. "You think I don't want to go out with you?"

"You didn't seem super keen at the summer

dance," he said honestly. "Or, I thought you liked Mitch more than me. And then maybe not cowboys at all." He forced himself to stop talking. He dunked a cookie into his coffee and lifted it to his lips.

He realized then what a mistake this was. Now his fingers dripped with coffee and melting chocolate, and he barely got the cookie in his mouth. Something dropped onto his chin and he'd dribbled all over the table too.

Embarrassed, he reached for a napkin, thinking he should've gotten more, and as he wiped his face, he looked at Misty. "They're kind of messy."

"I can see that." She dunked her cookie too, and she lifted the dripping, melting mess to her mouth too. She let everything fall all over, and then she grinned at Link as she chewed.

He laughed, because she was so sweet to show him she didn't care about his awkward eating. He picked up a clean napkin and reached to wipe her face for her. "You've just got a little something...here."

The moment sobered, and Link saw all the lights in the heavens in her eyes. "I'm free tomorrow for dinner." He wasn't actually sure if he was or not, but he'd beg Daddy for the night off if he had to.

"I liked you and Mitch," she said. "At the summer dance. I just...you know what? I'm going to be really honest with you."

"Okay." Link dunked the other half of his cookie and ate it in a more elegant way this time.

"I don't live here," she said. "I mean, I do right now, but this is a short-term project. Well, I mean, it's a long-term project, because it's a couple of years, but I'm not looking to live here. Settle down here. *Be* here for longer than it takes to do this restoration."

Link started nodding about halfway through her little talk. "You don't want anything serious."

Misty simply ate the other half of her cookie, no dunking involved. "I don't normally date at all."

"Really?" Link wasn't sure he believed that, but Misty shook her head soberly, and he detected no dishonesty in her. "That's surprising to me," he said. "You're so pretty and so personable. I'd think you'd have men lined up to take you out."

"Mm, I don't." She smiled at him. "But thank you for saying so."

Link didn't know what to say next, so he dunked another cookie and took another bite.

"If you're willing to be more...casual, I'd go out with you."

He studied the depths of his coffee as the chocolate melted off the cookie and swirled around. "I don't know," he said. "I have this...fizzy feeling about you, and I just don't know how casual I can be."

Misty met his eyes, her eyebrows raised. "Fizzy feeling?"

Link's face heated, and he suddenly wanted to leave. *Maybe Momma will text*, he thought. *Please Lord, let Momma text.*

His phone remained stubbornly silent, almost like God was telling Link he'd gotten himself into this mess, and he could get himself out.

"It's okay," he finally said, looking up. "I get it." He ate his cookie while Misty watched, and when he offered her another one, she shook her head no again.

She studied him for several long moments, and Link didn't know what to say or do. "All right, cowboy. Give me your phone."

Link wasn't sure why, and his first inclination was to deny her. Then he realized she was giving him her number, and he yanked his phone out of his back pocket and put it in her waiting palm.

"I can't tomorrow night," she said as she tapped on his device. "But now you've got my number and we can...." She looked up, those brilliant green eyes sparkling. "Talk."

"Sure." Link swallowed. "We'll talk."

His phone chimed while Misty still held it, and she said, "Oh, your momma just texted. Dinner is ready." She grinned wider and wider. "Cute. Do you eat with your family every night?" She handed his phone back to him, and Link took it with burning blood in his veins.

"I'm picking it up tonight," he said. "And yeah, I'll eat with them tonight, because I'm not turning down a free meal, I'll tell you that. But otherwise, no. I don't live with them, and I don't eat with them every night."

"I didn't mean—"

"It's okay," Link said, sighing after. "I just heard myself say that, and I didn't mean to be so short." He offered her a smile, feeling so out of his element. Maybe he needed more practice dating other women before he took on someone like Misty.

He snapped a to-go lid over his coffee and

stood. "I do have to go, though. If Momma doesn't feed the littles on time, they'll stage a coup."

Misty giggled. "How many kids in your family?" She stood and started cleaning up her trash too.

"Five," Link said. "I'm the oldest, and my youngest sibling is ten."

"Wow, that's a big span." Misty hid all her questions inside that statement.

Link nodded. "Yeah, it's a whole story." He met her eyes. "I'll have to tell you about it when we go out."

"Oh, so you're back to asking me out?"

Link moved closer to her, glad when she didn't move away. "I'll be as casual as you want." He swept his lips along her cheek, that wild streak inside him now controlling his every move. "I'll text you later."

"Sure," she murmured, everything about her very still now. Link wasn't sure what she felt, but every cell in his body burned with desire.

He pulled back, gathered up his cookies and coffee, and nodded his cowboy hat at her. "Great to see you again."

She blinked, and she did seem somewhat surprised. Shocked? Dumbfounded? Link honestly didn't know.

"You too," she said, and Link left her standing at the table when his phone rang and his momma's name sat there.

"I'm on the way," he said almost breathlessly. He looked over his shoulder at Misty, who still stood next to the metal table. "Momma, I'm dying. I got the cookies and went to Latte Love, the coffee trailer-truck-thing. Right?"

"Link," Momma said. "Take a breath. Why are you dying?"

Link started jogging, and that did nothing to help his breathlessness. He just needed to make it back to his truck before he could talk. He did, and he set the coffee in the console and tossed the cookies onto the passenger seat.

"Link," Momma said. "Talk, son."

He vaulted into the truck and pulled the door closed, his pulse beating, hammering, throbbing through his whole body. "Momma, I met this woman at the summer dance months ago, and she was at the coffee truck. I saw her, and I just went right over there and sat down next to her."

Momma said nothing, which wasn't that un-usual for her when it came to Link and women.

Daddy had been handling those things with Link for years.

"I asked her out, Momma." He started to laugh, that wild thing inside him so giddy. "And she said yes. I can't believe it, but she said yes." He started the truck, everything settling. "I'm on the way to get dinner now."

"Okay," she said. "We can talk about this woman when you get here."

"It's okay," Link said. "I just talked about it."

"Well, I want to address the fact that you're surprised she said yes."

Link would let Momma talk about whatever she wanted. "Okay," he said. "Be home soon." He drove away from the grocery store and the coffee truck, still flying high that he had Misty Granger's number in his phone.

28

itchell Glover pulled up to the hospital, reached for the white box with the blue bow that held the raspberry mousse he'd stopped to get. Without hesitation, he let his dog out of the truck and together, they headed into the clinic and went past a couple of other offices before he turned left to go around the corner, and then left into the doctor's office where Lily Tyders had her appointment today.

After he'd found her in the fields, Mitch hadn't been able to simply continue on without knowing how she was. He'd visited her in the hospital a couple of times. He'd found her bicycle and taken it to Aunt Sammy to see if it could be fixed.

When she'd delivered the news that it couldn't, Mitch had gone down to the sporting goods store and gotten Lily another one. He'd been there when she'd gone home from the hospital, and he'd stood in her kitchen with her balanced on her one good leg while she cried over the new bicycle.

They'd been texting a lot recently, and today, Lily had an appointment to go over her latest MRI. Mitch didn't think anyone should go through that alone, so he'd said he'd come. And he and Honor had done just that.

Lily looked up, her face brightening when she saw him, and Mitch grinned at her. He had no idea of the sounds going on around him in this office, so his attention remained on Lily as he crossed the room.

She didn't know sign language, and Mitch communicated with her by typing out what he wanted to say on his phone and either showing it to her or having it read aloud. Once, that hadn't worked, and Lily had fiddled with his phone until she could hear it.

Hey, she said, and Mitch read the word off her lips. *You made it.* She bent over to give Honor a pat, and then Mitch sat beside her, and Honor came to sit in front of him.

He typed quickly, and hit play on his phone. He held it between them, and he'd said, *Your leg looks good. Only a brace now.*

Lily nodded, her dark hair swaying with the movement. *Yeah, my physical therapy is going well.* She reached over and took his hand in hers. *Thanks for coming, Mitch.*

He couldn't type nearly as fast with only one hand, but he didn't want to pull away from her touch. He'd dated quite a lot this summer, if Link was to be believed, but no one made his blood flow like lava. No one made his heart beat faster and then faster and then faster.

So he went out with a woman here and there, once or twice, and nothing had become serious. Mitch definitely felt like something was missing in his life, and something big.

So much hinged on what he could understand. No, that wasn't right. So much hinged on what he could *say* to others. He was very limited in who he could talk to, and that irritated and frustrated him. Sometimes it made him angry, and sometimes he shrugged it off like it was no big deal.

With Lily, it hadn't been too irritating yet, but something seethed inside Mitch, and he knew it came down to his limitation to be able to communicate with her. For now, he sat with her and held her hand, and that brought a measure of peace and comfort to his life he hadn't had this morning.

After a few minutes, Lily stood, and Mitch looked over to her in surprise. He had never come to a doctor's appointment alone, because he couldn't hear them call his name. His dog was trained to alert when she heard his name, but this was Lily's appointment.

She said something, but Mitch didn't catch it, as he wasn't looking at her mouth. Still, he got to his feet as Honor did, and they followed Lily toward the doorway that led further into the office.

Honor wore a vest to indicate she was a hearing dog, and thankfully, no one touched her or tried to pat her. Mitch felt an even more imposing sense of silence in the smaller waiting room, and he steadied Lily as she turned to sit in one of the two chairs there.

Then he settled next to her, his smile back in place. Sometimes Mitch got so tired of smiling, but he sometimes didn't know how else to express what he was thinking. He typed out another message and hit play.

How are you feeling? Do you think this will be good news or not?

She looked right at him, as he'd previously explained he could read her lips if she'd speak a little slower and face him while she did. *I feel pretty good most of the time,* she said. *I'm back at work, though it's just from home. So I can nap whenever I need to.*

She reached up and tucked her dark hair away from her face. *I'm hoping he says there's nothing. I'm getting restless at home by myself.*

I thought you had a cat named Cloudy, he typed out and played. He wished he could give the speaker on his phone a tone, because this one would be teasing. Instead, he had to cock one eyebrow and grin at her to get the message across.

Her face lit up then, and she laughed. Mitch sure would like to hear that, but he felt her joy as it flowed from her.

Yes, me and Cloudy, she said. *Honestly, she's not great company.* She gave Mitch a coy look. *Sleeps too much.*

He laughed then too, and he wondered what his voice sounded like. He felt the big vibrations in his chest and down his throat, and he started typing before he finished. *I'm better than Cloudy is what you're saying. I at least don't fall asleep when we're together.*

He beamed at her, but Lily resisted his charms. *No, but you fall asleep when we're texting sometimes.*

Oh, boy. He laughed again. *You try mowing fields for fifteen hours and then we'll see how long you last after a shower and a good dinner.*

I'd like a good dinner, Lily said. *I'm tired of eating microwavable meals.*

Mitch met her eye, a pause between them now. He'd visited her in the hospital and at home. He'd gone grocery shopping for her in the beginning, and she got a lot of pre-prepared meals from Wilde & Organic, so at least she wasn't eating the TV dinners he'd lived on during his time at the deaf school.

He was here with her now for this. He texted with her every day. But he hadn't asked her out on a date. They had something playful between them, but also something obligatory. Mitch wondered if he would've noticed her in another situation, and he honestly didn't know.

Does it matter? he asked himself.

He started typing again, this time to ask her out for a good dinner, but the door opened and the doctor walked in.

Lily said hello, and she indicated Mitch. *He's deaf*, she said. *But he can read your lips, and he's here to help me get the information I need. Is it okay if he asks questions?*

Of course, the doctor said, and Mitch put his phone away, because a medical conversation between two people who weren't talking directly to him would take a lot of concentration.

We've actually got a girl here who can sign, the doctor said. *Would you like me to get her?*

Mitch started to nod, and he said, "Yes," though he had no idea how the letters sounded as they came out of his mouth. Lily gave him a smile that said he didn't speak well, and Mitch believed her. Some deaf people spoke and tried to learn how to form the words and letters so others could understand them, even if they couldn't hear.

Mitch had never done that, and he'd rather rely on sign language, his dog, and his phone to be able to communicate.

The doctor ducked back out, and it only took another thirty seconds for him to return, this time with another dark-haired woman. She wore a brightness to her person that Mitch liked, and she started signing.

I'm Claire, and this is Doctor Clemens. He's got Lily's results of her MRI.

Mitch noticed the doctor had started talking, and he turned and flipped a switch on a light box attached to the wall. With his back to them, he pointed to something, and Mitch never would've been able to understand anything he said.

But Claire signed everything, her facial expressions going right along with it. She was an excellent signer, with great fluidity and fluency, and he wondered if she was certified to be an interpreter. Sure seemed like it, because she knew a lot of medical terminology.

The scan looks good, she said. *This shows both hemispheres of the brain, and over here on the left side, where we had the swelling and that bruise I was worried about, we see there's no more swelling in the brain, which is great, obviously. No evidence of anomalies. No lesions, masses, or that bruise. You've healed well, and that's going to be due to you following the directions to stay off screens and give yourself time to heal.*

He turned back to the pair of them, a slight smile on his mouth. *I think you're cleared to go back to work in the office.* He pulled up a chair. *How are you feeling? Headaches still? That optical migraine in your vision?*

Lily nodded, and Mitch's eyes flew back to Claire to see her answer. *Only when I'm really tired.*

Well, you've been the perfect patient so far, the doctor said. *So keep that up. When you're tired, slow down. Stop. Go rest. Okay?*

Lily nodded as she said, *Okay*.

Claire's hands stilled as the conversation stopped, and Mitch reached over and took Lily's hand in his. This was great news, and he didn't understand the tears shining in her eyes. Maybe they were happy tears, as his mom and his aunts sometimes cried even when they were happy.

One of Mitch's girlfriends in Virginia had done that too. He honestly didn't know what to do with it, because when he felt strong emotions and needed a release, he yelled. He went out onto the ranch all by himself and just screamed his frustration to the sky.

Sometimes that worked and sometimes it didn't. Momma said crying always helped her reset, and Mitch wondered what that would be like. He pretty much carried everything that troubled him in a metaphorical backpack, and he only shrugged it off and dropped the rocks he carried when he couldn't stand living his life with that load for one more minute.

I don't think you need any medications, the doctor said. *I can write you a note for your job. Limited screen time. Afternoons off. That kind of thing.*

Okay, Lily said. *Do I need to come back, or just play it by ear?*

I don't think you need to come back. Doctor Clemens stood, the appointment clearly almost over. *You're doing great, Lily.* He nodded to Mitch, then turned and did the same to Claire.

Mitch quickly signed, *Thank you, Claire. That was so much easier.*

She grinned and said, *You're welcome*, before she followed the doctor out of the room. Mitch took a long breath and faced Lily.

He didn't want to type out his congratulations. He just wanted to be able to celebrate with her that she'd recovered from the terrible accident that had left her out in the elements overnight, injured, and desperate to be found.

The human body really was so amazing, and

Mitch hated that he couldn't speak to Lily in this moment.

Good news, right? she said, her eyes shining with those unshed tears.

He nodded and then gathered her into his arms. *The best*, he thought just before he lowered his head and kissed her.

29

Edith couldn't let go of Finn's hand as he drove down the dirt lane away from Coyote Pass. "So the price is too high?"

Finn sighed out all of his air it seemed, and he sure wasn't happy today. Edith wasn't either, because Levi had passed away three years ago today. They were currently on their way to the cemetery, and Edith had a bouquet of wildflowers and a couple of figurines of horses. Things Levi loved, so he'd know he was loved.

She'd taken pictures to send to his parents and hers, and Edith really just wanted the next hour to be over with.

"It's really high," he said. "Number one, I'm

trying to buy it in the middle of the harvest. So they have to charge me for that. Otherwise, this whole year is a loss for them."

"And the cattle," she said, all the dots coming together into a complete picture. "They haven't gone to market yet."

"No," he said. "And he's got probably eighty-five thousand dollars worth of cattle on that ranch. It's his entire year's worth of income." He glanced over to Edith. "So Jerry said they have to add that to the price. Or I can wait to buy it after that, but then I can't control what cattle Kevin decides to keep or sell."

He rolled his neck as he came to a stop at the highway. "And interest rates are expected to rise next week, and I'd really just like to get this done before too much longer." He made the turn and glanced over to her. "In fact, Jerry says I have to put in an offer by Tuesday, or Kevin and Bethany Ann are going to list it."

"They can't do that," Edith said. "You've been over there all month, talking to them and working with them. They know you want it."

"Wanting something and being able to get it are two different things," he said, clearly exasperated. "It's okay." He shook his head. "This isn't what you need today. I'm dealing with it, and everything is going to be fine."

Finn looked over to her for longer. "Edith, I'm real sorry. It's going to be fine. I'm not going to say another word about it."

"It's okay," she murmured. "I'd be frustrated too." She was frustrated for him, because she knew how excited he was to get Kevin Bentley's ranch. He'd said on more than one occasion that it felt like God had orchestrated an accident a year ago, so that Finn could somehow have the perfectly sized ranch at a decent price.

But now, it felt like things had just inflated until they were too big for either of them to hold.

Finn continued the drive to town and then over to the little white church where they went each Sabbath Day. The cemetery sat behind it, and today, on a benign Thursday afternoon, the parking lot didn't hold a single vehicle.

He pulled in and put his truck in park. Neither of them moved, and finally Finn looked over to her. "Do you want to go out alone first? I can follow you in a few minutes."

Edith liked that idea, and she nodded. "Yes, thank you." With that, she collected the things she'd brought for Levi and slid from the truck. Her legs operated, but they felt like wet straw, like they might collapse underneath her weight at any moment.

Employing all her muscles, she made it past the church and out of sight of Finn. That caused some of the pressure on her to lessen, and she didn't know what to think about that.

Levi had been buried along the back fence of the cemetery, which made for a long walk there. "I'm here, Levi," she said when she was still several rows away. "It's such a beautiful day today. Hardly any wind."

He used to sit on the back deck with a blanket over his legs, because he was always cold. When she'd come in from the farm, he'd give her the best smile he had inside him and say, "Hardly any wind today, Edee."

Tears filled her eyes, because she'd forgotten about those times on the deck. So much of Levi had faded, and a sudden tug of guilt pulled through her that she'd removed his pictures from the spare bedroom.

She made it to the last row and turned right, with Levi's headstone only a few down. Edith arrived, and she dropped to her knees. "Hey, baby." She set down the flowers and horse figurines next to her and pulled out the utility rag from her back pocket. "Your face is a little dirty."

She sniffled as she brushed the dirt and dust and debris away from his headstone. She rubbed the rag over the letters of his name and the numbers of his birth and death dates. When she finished, she twisted to get the flowers.

"I brought flowers," she said. "Because you said you'd never seen so many until you came to Texas." She leaned them against the granite and smiled. "They look good. You'd like them, especially the orange ones. They're something from the farm. Remember how we planted all those wildflowers? They grow up along the west fence, and they're so amazing."

She sighed and looked past the headstone. "Sky's blue today. It's hot and then hotter. We survived a flood this year." Her throat closed, because one really huge reason she and Alex had done so well after the flood was because of Finn.

How did she talk to Levi about Finn?

Tears flooded her eyes, and she bowed her head. She couldn't speak, so she simply prayed inside her mind. *Lord, I don't know what I'm doing. Tell me what to do.*

She didn't get any answers as she wept. A

slight breeze kicked up, and Edith reached up with both hands and wiped her hair back off her face. "I miss you so much," she said as she exhaled. "I brought you some horses." She collected them and set them up on the base of his grave. "One looks like Cocoa, the horse I've been working with. She graduated, and I got another one. Reagan. So the second one looks like him."

Edith settled into a more comfortable pose and braided her fingers together. "Your momma hasn't texted me yet today." She smiled at the headstone. "I'm sure she will. I always send her pictures, and then we talk. She'll call."

She sat there for another minute, and then the sound of footsteps met her ears. Finn came down the row, his hands tucked into his pockets. "Okay?" he asked.

Edith wanted to tell him to leave, but the words wouldn't come out. She wasn't even sure why she felt like that. So he came closer, and then he settled onto the grass beside her. He said nothing, and Edith didn't hate the presence of him beside her.

At the same time, uncomfortable prickles ran up and down her arms, making her chilled despite the summer September weather. She didn't know what to say now, and it almost felt like Levi was there, eyeing Finn. Like he knew Finn had kissed her, and he didn't like it.

Maybe I'm not ready to move on, Edith thought, and she pulled in a breath.

"You okay?" Finn reached over and took her hand. "Did you get your pictures?"

"Not yet," she managed to whisper. So many other things crowded inside her thoughts and her mouth, but she swallowed everything back.

"Want me to take them?"

Edith took a moment, and then she said, "Yeah, sure." She tugged her phone free and handed it to him. She did her best to smile, and Finn took a picture of her, and then one of her and the headstone.

He handed her phone back, and Edith took in a long breath and then released it slowly. All at once, her thoughts cleared. "Finn?"

"Hm?"

"I—" She took another breath. "I think I need to be alone."

"All right," he said. "I'll just wait in the truck."

She turned toward him. "No, I mean, I'm not sure I'm ready to be...not alone."

He'd started getting to his feet, and he finished

and looked down at her. "I'm not sure I'm following."

She gestured to Levi's headstone. "I just need to take a break." She looked back at him. "A break to just think for a minute."

"You want to break up?"

"No." She shook her head. "I don't want to break up."

"I don't understand," he said.

"I just need to be alone. I need some space." Edith didn't know how else to say it. "I just want to be alone."

"I'll wait in the truck," he said quietly.

Edith wasn't sure he got what she was saying, but she let him go. She wasn't even sure what she was saying. She knew she just wanted to be here by herself, and bringing Finn had been a mistake she hadn't anticipated.

A while later, she got herself to her feet and made her way back to the parking lot. Finn said nothing as he drove her back to Coyote Pass, and when they arrived, Edith looked over to him.

"I'm sorry," she whispered. "I'll call you, okay?" With that, she slipped out of the truck and headed around the house. Her destination loomed ahead of her, and she ran the last few steps to the she-shed.

Inside, she gasped for air, and she locked the door as she slid down it to the floor. She hadn't cried much at the cemetery, but now that she had some privacy and she'd seen Levi, the floodgates opened.

She'd sworn she wasn't going to do this this year. She thought with Finn there, she wouldn't be as emotional. But the pain and anguish of losing Levi overcame her again and again, as if she'd just lost him an hour ago.

Edith had managed to move to the couch with Otto, Frankie, and Gumbo by the time Alex pounded on the door and demanded she unlock it. She looked at it for a full minute before she could move her body, and when she opened the door, she fell into her brother's arms.

"Hey," he said quietly. "Hey, hey, hey, what is happening?"

Edith didn't have to answer him, because he knew what had happened. He'd been here through it all. He'd given up his spare bedroom and his house for Levi. "I can't do this," she gasped. "I can't do this alone."

"Then why did you send Finn away?" Alex

asked, and Edith pulled back.

"I—what?"

Alex peered at her, pure worry in his expression. "I hadn't seen you since you left for the cemetery," he said. "I thought maybe you'd gone to Three Rivers, so I called over there, because you said we were gonna have grilled shrimp in memory of Levi, and no one was here."

Edith searched his face, her memory returning. She didn't have a defense for herself though.

"He said he dropped you off here hours ago and broke up with him."

"No." Edith shook her head. "I didn't break up with him. I said I needed a break."

"From...."

"Just—everything." She blew out her breath. "I specifically told him I didn't want to break up with him."

"Well, Edee, he's confused. Heck, anyone would be confused with what's gone on today." Alex gestured back toward the house, his bright eyes blazing with frustration. "I'm confused. I honestly didn't expect to find you curled up in the dark, the door locked, and a year's worth of dried tears on your face."

Edith's anger fired at her then, and she wiped

her face. "I—you didn't."

Alex glared at her and stepped outside the she-shed. Then he turned back. "I'm almost sure that man is in love with you, and you literally told him you needed a break as you sat in front of your deceased fiancé's grave. He thinks he's never going to measure up. That you'll never love anyone but Levi." Her brother marched away from her. "Honestly, Edee, what would you think if the tables were turned?"

He scoffed out an angry breath and stalked away, muttering.

Edith watched him go, not sure what she was supposed to do now. The scent of the barbecue grill filled the air, and her stomach growled. But Edith retreated back inside her she-shed, this time to her desk. She didn't lock the door, and she pulled up the website for her favorite dog breeder.

She had a lot to work through, but not tonight. She didn't have the mental energy, and she just wanted to look at pictures of puppies.

Edith remembered she'd told Finn she'd call him later, and she'd do exactly that. She'd call him when she could, and right now, she simply couldn't do anything more than look at the cutest dachshund puppies she'd ever seen.

30

Finn suffered through a couple of days before his mother threw a piece of bread at him and said, "Okay, enough moping. It's time to talk to me and Daddy."

Finn looked up from his lunch, then around the table. Sam was gone, and most of the table had been cleared. Daddy pulled out his chair and sat down, a couple of bowls in his hand. He set one in front of Momma and said, "Cherry chocolate, darlin'."

He threw a glance at Finn and dug his spoon into his chocolate ice cream. "Momma's right. You leave on Thursday, telling us it's the day Levi Kingsley died, and then you come home spitting mad, and you haven't said two words to anyone since."

"I have too," Finn argued back. He looked at his full plate of food, not even realizing he hadn't eaten it.

"He wasn't spitting mad," Momma said. "He's heartbroken."

"There were a lot of slammed doors," Daddy said as Finn got to his feet. He took his plate into the kitchen and scraped the food into the trashcan. "And he has to decide about that ranch in two days, and it's time to talk." Daddy took a bite of his ice cream as if they were talking about nothing at all.

"*He* is standing right here," Finn said, seething in air through his nose.

"Then talk," Momma said as she too calmly dug out a bite of her cherry chocolate ice cream.

"Edith said she needs a break," he said. "She said she doesn't know how to be 'not alone,' which is a really weird way for her to say she doesn't want to be with me." He wanted some ice cream too, but not badly enough to go out into the garage and dig some out of the freezer.

He returned to the table, because he was an adult and he could have hard conversations. "Not only that, but the ranch is way more than I can afford. I'm going to lose it." He felt like buckling and crying too as his chest tightened and everything on his face turned numb. "Kevin wants so much more than I thought it would be."

"Why's that?" Daddy asked.

"The harvest and the cattle," Finn said miserably. He ran his hands through his hair and then laid his head down in his arms on the table. He stared close-up at the saltshaker, wondering how his life—which had been going so well—had come to this.

Staring at a glass container, the rest of the world blurry beyond the facets of light glinting on the saltshaker.

"If I buy now, I'm reaping the rewards of the cattle and the harvest, so Jerry's baked those into the price to make it fair."

"Seems fair then," Daddy said.

"But it prices me out." Finn closed his eyes, shutting out the saltshaker and the rest of the world. If only it was that easy. He hadn't slept well either, because even with his eyes closed, the situations around him remained.

"And I know I can sell the cattle and reap the harvest, but that means I have to have more money upfront, and I don't qualify." He opened his eyes and looked at his father helplessly. "I've been over it and over it. I could buy the ranch, sell the cattle, put up the harvest, and pay off the higher loan with the sales. But then, what do I live on for the next year?"

Finn lifted his head and shook it, the thoughts inside his head racing, and he couldn't catch them. "And if I wait, they're going to list it, and someone else could get it. And interest rates are climbing, and it just feels impossible." He hated this defeatist talk, but he really had been over it and over it.

"So Edith's timing is just bad," he whispered. "I don't want to lose her, and I don't want to lose the ranch, and it feels like I'm going to lose both." He exhaled and wiped both hands down his face, his eyes burning too much to be comfortable. He really didn't want to cry in front of his momma, and worse would be Daddy.

"I feel like I'm back at square one, fresh out of the Army, and I should get a cheap apartment in town and hire myself out to anyone who asks." The way he'd been doing this summer as it was. "It's pathetic. I'm thirty-one years old, and I'm pathetic."

"Okay." Momma dropped her spoon into her ice cream bowl, the metal clanging against the dishware loud enough to startle Finn's attention over to her. "That's enough. You are not pathetic, Finley Aaron Ackerman. You have served your country with honor for a decade. You left us all here and you went off and learned, and worked, and served well. That's *not* pathetic."

Finn blinked at her, because Momma could lecture, but it was usually because of something he'd done wrong, not all the things he did right.

"I don't want to hear those self-deprecating things," she said, shooting a look at Daddy. "I'm really sorry about Edith. I know you love her, and I just have to believe that true love will win out."

"Momma," Finn said in the same tone of voice as the exhaustion that ran through his body. "She might be my One True Love, but I'm not hers." He looked away, the truth of his relationship with Edith right there in front of him, in black and white. "Her One True Love was Levi Kingsley, and no matter what she says about having room to love me too, the fact is, she doesn't."

"Yet," Momma said, and she could be relentless about things for sure.

"Kelly," Daddy said softly. He shook his head. "Leave it for now."

Finn gave his dad a small smile. "Daddy, I have tried to be self-sufficient." He swallowed, but his bravery—which had failed him miserably a couple of days ago when Edith had said she needed a break—kicked in.

"I can't lose that ranch." He sat up straight and puffed out his chest as he drew in another lungful of oxygen. "It's perfect for me. For us. It borders Three Rivers, for crying out loud. So." He clasped his hands together to quiet them. "I'm asking you to help me buy it. If you give me a chance, I will show you I can run my own place. I'll pay you back over time. I promise with everything I have."

Daddy watched him say every word, his dark eyes drinking in Finn.

"I can qualify for the loan without the addition of the cattle or the harvest," Finn said. "So I've figured out what I need." He pulled a slip of paper from his pocket, and his mother made a high-pitched yelp.

"You've got a paper?"

Finn looked at her. "Yes," he said. "I've been over this and over this."

"Squire, he's been over this and over this," Momma said.

"I heard 'im," Daddy said. He reached for the paper and took it, then reached for his reading glasses.

Finn's pulse sprinted from his chest down to his fingertips. "Daddy, I'm just asking for a loan. The cattle are being valued at eighty-five thousand. The harvest another twenty. I need a hundred and five thousand. I can get the loan for the rest."

Daddy peered at the paper, and Momma huffed as she got up, collected their ice cream bowls, and went into the kitchen. Finn appreciated her restraint, actually, because she usually said whatever she wanted to say.

"Squire," she barked several long moments later. "You tell him right now that of course we're going to give him that money." She slapped her hands on the kitchen counter, and both Finn and his father looked over to her.

She looked downright angry, and that surprised Finn. He watched her for a moment and then switched his attention back over to Daddy, something she'd said tickling his mind wrong.

"I don't want you to *give* me the money," he said. "I will pay you back."

"No." Daddy shook his head and refolded the paper. He tossed it toward Finn, who flinched slightly. He so hadn't expected his father to say *no*.

"You won't be paying us back," Daddy said. "If you want a loan, the answer is no." He cocked his eyebrows at Finn, whose mouth had gone dry. "Now, if you want to ask me for a gift, then ask me for a gift."

"I...can't," Finn whispered, the words choking as they came up his throat.

"Finn." Momma marched back over to the table and pulled out the chair Libby usually sat in. "Libby is going to come back to Three Rivers within the year, with the intent to take over the ranch. Daddy isn't going to make her pay for that. This is what families do. They pass things along to their children through the generations." She gestured to Daddy down at the end of the table. "Daddy didn't buy this ranch from his father, and we're *not* doing a loan for you."

"I'd buy that whole ranch for you," Daddy said nonchalantly.

Horror washed through Finn. "You will not."

Daddy finally smiled, and something inside

Finn triggered him to relax a little. "No, I won't, because you won't allow it. But I'm saying, Finley, my son, this boy I met when he was only four years old and who's grown up to be the most amazing, beautiful, hardworking, faithful man."

Daddy paused and smiled at him, his own eyes shining with glass. "I'm saying, my boy, that I *would* buy it for you. The whole thing. Free and clear." He shot a look at Momma. "We won't, because we know that would kill you. But if you want that ranch, and you need an extra hundred grand to cover the cattle and the crops, then *that* will be a gift. No loans."

Finn stared at him, then looked over to Momma. She sniffled and wiped her eyes, then nodded at him. Finn heard himself say *All right*, but nothing had come out of his mouth yet.

His head started to nod, and Daddy's smile grew.

"All right," Finn said, really forcing the words out.

"All right, then," Daddy said. "That's settled. Call Jerry and let him know you want that ranch, and that you have a two hundred thousand dollar down payment."

"Okay, I—what?"

"That's the deal," Momma said as she jumped back to her feet. "You want some ice cream, Finny? Now that this is settled, we can talk about Edith."

Finn groaned, and he looked to his father for help. "First, really? She's going to make me drag out everything with Edith?"

Daddy grinned and leaned back in his chair, his arms crossed. "What's second?

"*Two* hundred thousand dollars, Daddy?"

"It's a good down payment," he said. "You won't have mortgage insurance, and your payment will be far lower without that."

Finn studied his father's face while Momma dished him the ice cream he hadn't asked for. "Do you guys have that much money?"

"Yes," Daddy said simply. His expression turned sharp again. "And we're not kidding, Finn. If you refuse this as a gift, you'll lose that ranch."

"He's not going to refuse the gift," Momma said. She put a bowl of butter pecan ice cream in front of him, complete with more caramel topping and additional pecan nibs. "And he's going to tell us everything about Edith, so we can help him get her back."

She pulled out a chair and sat down. She held

out a spoon but pulled it back when he reached for it. "Starting now, Mister."

Finn swiped the spoon from her and said, "Fine. Let me have one bite of ice cream first, would you?" Maybe then he'd be able to articulate all the thoughts in his head, and maybe, by some miracle from heaven, his parents would be able to help him figure out what to do to get Edith back.

31

Edith entered the kitchen to the sight, scent, and sound of Alex scrambling eggs. Then he said, "Yeah, sure, Finn, I'll be there."

She froze, her socked feet growing roots and embedding into the floor where she stood. Alex turned from the stove and saw her, his eyes narrowing slightly. Finn said, "I don't want to talk about Edith, but I just need to know if you think I should text her about it."

Her throat narrowed, and tears burned in her eyes.

"You've been texting her, haven't you?" Alex asked as he flowed into motion again. He set the pan of eggs on the counter and turned back to get his phone.

"Only if she texts me first."

Edith pulled her phone from her pocket and held it up in a silent show for Alex. She quickly swiped and went to her string with Finn. True, they hadn't been talking much in the past couple of weeks, but she had made an effort to do what she'd said she'd do—call him. Talk to him. She really didn't want to break up. She just needed some space to think through a few things.

What those things were, she didn't know. She hadn't written them down or defined them. She simply knew she'd lost herself in this summer romance with Finn, and she needed to make sure she knew who she was before she became part of him.

She thought she'd known that woman, but sitting in front of Levi's grave had shown her she hadn't.

Hey, Finn, she said. *I know you're headed to market day soon, and I'm wondering if you'd like some help with lunch? I'm sure I could convince Alex to host here, or if your momma is handling it, I could coordinate with her.*

Her stomach swooped and trembled, and she

wasn't even sure Alex and Finn were talking about market day. She assumed, because they'd chitchatted about it in the past few days, and she hit send before she thought too hard about it.

Alex had taken the call off speaker, and he said, "Just let me know. I can do whatever, and I'm sure Edee will too." A pause, and he looked her way. "Yeah, she's right here." He turned back to get plates out of the cupboard, and Edith marveled that her younger brother could and had taken such good care of her.

For years now, Alex had been so *good* to her, letting her and Levi come live here, putting up with her extra dogs and the cat who never stopped meowing. Her flippant nicknames. Her mood swings. Her need for more dogs and more horses and more scrambled eggs.

She sniffled and went to help him get out the silverware and orange juice while Alex said, "Mm hm, I'm sure that's true," and then several seconds later, "I'll send you the receipt."

Edith dished herself some eggs and set a couple of pieces of bread in the toaster for Alex. He loved sourdough, and she'd spent hours wandering the grocery store yesterday, her mind stuck in a fog and making it twice as hard and take twice as long to put their necessities in the cart.

Alex ended his call and scooped up his breakfast. "Good morning, Edee," he said.

"Morning," she said. "I've got your toast down." She took a bite of her eggs while she stood in front of the toaster, waiting for the bread to pop up.

"Finn and I are sharing the semis for market day," he said as he sat down at the table.

"That's a good idea," Edith said. The toast popped up, and she reached for it to butter it. With it ready and on a small plate, she took it over to Alex. Her brother looked up at her, and Edith wrapped her arms around him and held on.

It was awkward with her standing and him sitting, but Edith didn't care. "I love you, Alex," she said. "You take such good care of me, and I'm so—I appreciate it."

"We take care of each other," he said gruffly.

Edith nodded, sniffled some more, and then finally released him and returned to the kitchen to get her eggs. She sat in her usual spot kitty-corner from Alex and looking out the back window. "What did Finn want my help with on market day?"

He hadn't answered her text, and she set her phone on the table so Alex could see it. "I texted him."

"It's not about market day," he said.

"Aren't we doing lunch?"

Alex finished his bite of eggs and looked out of the corner of his eye to Edith. "They're hosting at Three Rivers. Kevin and Bethany Ann won't be out of the house yet, so Finn doesn't want to do it there. I didn't think our place was big enough."

He forked up another bite of food. "Plus, with both of us going on the same day, it'll be dinner, and not lunch."

Edith nodded and picked up a piece of egg. She leaned over and fed it to Frankie, who crowded out the other dogs, even those bigger than him. "Okay, so I'm not needed."

"Edee, you're always needed," he said. "You know Kelly Ackerman's phone number, and you can have as big of a role as you'd like."

She nodded, because he was right. She tried on a smile, and it wobbled, but it stayed. "You're right. Okay, I'll call her today."

"It's not for a couple more weeks."

"I'm sure she'll have the menu set and half the food in the freezer by now." Edith sniffled and drew in a breath, the tension in this farmhouse off the charts.

Alex chortled, but he didn't argue back, which meant Edith was right.

She managed a bite of scrambled eggs, and though they'd cooled, she got them down. She fed a bite to Otto, then Gumbo, and then Olive. Bandit sulked behind all the other animals, and Edith picked up a big bite and extended it toward the last border collie.

He came toward her and took the food with a gentle mouth, and Edith asked, "So if you and Finn weren't talking about market day just now, what were you talking about?"

Alex gave her his grumpy cowboy glare, the one that disappeared completely when Nicki walked in the room or when he got to rent big machinery or when his collies did exactly what he'd trained them to do.

"He asked me for the dimensions of the she-shed," he said calmly. "What facilities he needs for it, that kind of thing."

Edith's heartbeat came to a complete stop right there in her chest. "*My* she-shed?"

"Edee, that man is in love with you." Alex picked up a piece of toast and held it without taking a bite. "He is planning on doing whatever necessary to have you in his life, and—"

"He told you that? That he's planning to do whatever necessary to have me in his life?"

"No," Alex said. "Not in those words. He hasn't said he loves you either, but Edee, it's not about what a man *says*. It's what a man *does*." He bit into his toast, the crunch punctuating the truthfulness of his words.

She finished her breakfast, with most of it honestly going to the animals, and then she slid Alex's plate on top of hers and went into the kitchen. In front of the sink, she looked out the window and over the farm while the water ran. It took several long seconds to get hot here, and while she waited, Edith saw her she-shed in the corner of the yard. She saw the barns and stables and the extreme gift God had given her to be here.

Love poured over her in a strong, unrelenting stream of water, the same way it gushed out of the sink and over the dirty dishes. And just like hot water could rinse away crumbs and oils and debris, the love of God could heal all wounds in a person's heart and soul.

His love could cleanse anyone, including her.

His love could heal any rift and any scar and any heartache.

Her insecurities.

Her scars.

Her heartaches.

Edith had always believed in God's love, but it had almost existed somewhere outside of her. It didn't apply to her as fully as it did others. Until now.

"I think it's hot," Alex murmured as he joined her at the sink.

Edith looked over to him, the rugged handsome face of her brother blurred by her tears. "Do you really think he'll forgive me?"

"Without a doubt." Alex pulled Edith into his chest, where she clung to him as she cried. The tears for her fears and worries and insecurities flowed out quickly, and then Edith's tears became those of hope and joy and love.

The sound of the running kitchen sink finally reached her ears and irritated her enough for her to pull back. She reached to flip it off. "Okay." She took the kitchen towel Alex held toward her and pressed the whole thing to her face. Why did crying make her eyes so hot and her lips feel like they'd been blown up with a tire pump?

"Okay," she said again. Gumbo meowed as he ran himself along her ankles. She looked over to Alex, holding onto that hope and love and using it as a barrier against the fears which threatened to seep back in, creep back in, and steal her future from her again.

"What should I do? Call him? Go over there?"

"He's helping Kevin and Bethany Ann pack today," he said. "At least some of their things in the storage sheds. They have a truck coming this weekend to get the outbuildings clear." Alex started the sink again and washed his hands with the kitchen lemon soap Edith insisted they always have on hand.

"Was he asking me to come help with that?" she asked.

"We were talking about him moving in," Alex said. "I said of course I'd be there, and I'm sure he wants you there too."

"But he's not moving in for a couple more weeks." Edith frowned, trying to see her way through this plot point to the happy resolution.

"He doesn't have much, but his momma and daddy are helping with the furnishing, so there's still plenty to move."

Edith nodded. Finn had told her a little bit

about the gift his parents had given him so he could get the ranch, and she knew he had to complete the harvest and sell the cattle though he wasn't in full ownership of the ranch yet.

His texts on the matter had said, *It's just a matter of time so the loan can go through.*

"So you have no ideas of how I can get him back." Edith gave her brother a glare, and he rolled his eyes as he took the kitchen towel back from her.

"Edee, he's a man. Go to where he is and tell him you're sorry and that you love him, and that'll do it." He turned back to the dogs. "Come on, guys. Everyone with me this morning. Edee's got her riding clothes on, and that means she's going to cheat on you with Reagan." Alex grinned at her and indeed took all four dogs and a meowing Gumbo out the back door.

Edith did the dishes and made herself a stack of toast before she pulled on her boots and collected her cowgirl hat and keys to her SUV. She did have an appointment with Reagan this morning, but that didn't bother her. It was the one with Bull afterward that would challenge Edith.

"But you can answer his questions now," she

told herself, and that knowledge got her out the door without hesitation.

Forty minutes later, Edith's heart stopped again when she saw Finn jogging around the homestead and to his truck. He still hadn't answered her text, and Edith simply didn't know what to do. She hated this fragile ground between her and Finn, like she had to start all over with breaking the ice again.

He got behind the wheel, but he didn't pull out immediately. Edith started inching her car toward the homestead instead of pulling into the parking lot at Courage Reins the way she should've.

Finn didn't move his truck, and her phone chimed with a text from him as her front bumper went past his back one. She stopped, grabbed her phone but didn't look at it, and slid from her SUV.

She went around the back of his truck to his window, where she found his head bent, the brim of that sexy cowboy hat concealing a lot of his face as he texted.

Edith loved him so much, and she hadn't even known it until that moment.

Then she reached out and knocked on his window.

Finn dang near jumped out of his skin. He jerked his head up and looked out the window, expecting to see his momma standing there with his forgotten lunch.

Edith Baxter smiled back at him, and in that split second where his mind tried to catch up with his eyes and his heart hammered like a scared jackrabbit on ten pots of coffee, tears started leaking out of her eyes.

Oh, that simply wouldn't do, and Finn hastened to unclip his seatbelt and get out of his truck. "Edith," he said, his adrenaline still racing like it had sixty more laps around the track. "Edith."

He took her into his arms and held her. He had questions for her. So much to say to her. But now that she stood in his arms, nothing came out of his mouth. Momma would be disappointed, but Finn hadn't been able to do any of the things she'd suggested.

Instead, he wanted to make a big gesture. Do something so Edith would know how he felt and that everything he said had merit.

"What are you doing here?" he asked. "Appointment with Reagan and Bull?"

Edith stepped out of his arms and wiped her face. "I hate that I'm crying in front of you again."

Finn smiled at her. "I'm just so happy to see you."

Her eyes flitted around and then met his. "I'm really sorry about this...this...reversion I went through." She reached for him, then suddenly drew her hand back. "I'm—I missed you. I'm sorry, Finn." Her voice grew in intensity, but Finn couldn't stop smiling.

"I'm in love with you," he said, the words just there. They didn't stick in his throat or rust on the way out. He spread his arms wide. "I know you might not be ready for it, and that's fine. I'm *in* this with you, Edith, and I'm not going anywhere. If you need time, you'll have time."

Edith started shaking her head, but she didn't say anything.

"If you want space, you can have all you want. The ranch is big, right? And your she-shed will be there, and you just have to look at me a certain way, and I'll back right off."

"Finn." A tiny smile touched her face, but again, she didn't say more.

He turned back to his truck, where the driver's door still sat open. "I've already called the industrial tow truck, and they have a couple of dates in October they can come." He grabbed the clipboard that he'd been making plans and notes on for the past few weeks since he'd first gone out to the Bentley Ranch.

"I've been making a ton of notes on what we might call the ranch, and then I started panicking that you wouldn't want your she-shed moved until we get married." He flipped a page and then another one, his nerves catching up to his mouth. "And then...things sort of go haywire there, because I don't know when would be a good time for us to get married, because I'm not sure...when you...might...want to get married." He whispered the last few words, realizing just how far ahead of himself he'd gotten.

Edith grinned fully at him now, so Finn figured he hadn't messed up too badly. Still, he tossed the clipboard back inside the truck and closed the door for good measure. When he faced her again, her smile had slipped slightly.

"You're so pretty," he said.

She ducked her head, her hair falling over her shoulder. Finn wanted to wipe it back, but he refrained. *She'd* knocked on his window, cried in his arms, and then said only a few words.

Good words, but still. Only a few of them.

"Say something," he said.

"I'm in love with you, Hopscotch."

Finn blinked at her and watched as her smile spread and her laughter filled the sky.

"I love you, Finn," she said as she sobered. "And I don't need time…or space…or, or for us to have special looks that tell you to back off. I don't want you to back off. I want us to walk into the future side-by-side."

"You're speaking my language now." He took her into his arms again and whispered in her ear, his lips so, so close to her lobe. "So when would your perfect wedding be?"

"April," she murmured.

April felt impossibly far away, but Finn had just finished giving his speech on time and space and patience. "April it is," he whispered.

"Are you ever going to kiss me?"

Finn lifted his head and looked into her eyes. "After your therapy, do you want to come over to the ranch and help us pack?"

"I'd love to," she said.

"Okay," he said. "Then I'm going to kiss you now." He leaned in close, taking his time to really breathe in the essence of this woman. He realized in those few slow moments how difficult it must have been for Edith to approach his truck, and she'd done it anyway.

"I love you, Edith."

"I love you too, Finn. I'm so sorry I—"

He stole her apology with his lips, the kiss between them sweet for the first stroke and then turning passionate as the familiar fire between them blazed to life and she did the only thing Finn ever wanted—she kissed him back.

33

"You're looking good today, Edith," Doctor Bull said.

Edith crossed her legs and looked out the third-story window that overlooked the pastures, paddocks, and fields here at Three Rivers Ranch. "I feel good," she said.

"Something's changed."

She finally turned to face the doctor, though she'd done sessions with her gaze out the window before. "Yeah," she said. "*I've* changed."

Doctor Bull smiled too and tapped the end of his pen against his knee. "Tell me about it."

Edith hadn't even told Finn or Alex about her experiences in the past couple of weeks, but she supposed that was why she came to therapy. To open the doors inside herself that let out the most vulnerable version of Edith Baxter.

"It wasn't even anything earth-shattering," she said.

"Last time, you told me you'd told Finn you needed a break, and he thought that meant you wanted to break-up."

She nodded her agreement. "I didn't want to break up, though. We've been talking. I've been really trying to find myself, and figure out the version of myself I'm supposed to be with Finn. Like, is it the same Edith as who loved Levi?" She shook her head, because a lot of her journaling and inner thoughts didn't make sense, not even to her.

"And is she?" Doctor Bull asked.

Edith shook her head. "I think people are ever-changing," she said. "You can't ever land on a single version of yourself. And one thing I felt deeply just this morning is that God loves me exactly how I am right now, and how I was last night, and how I was this morning, and how I'll be tonight, tomorrow, next week, and month, and forever."

Her voice choked, and Edith glanced back out

to the fields, expecting Doctor Bull to give her a moment.

She should've known better, because this was Doctor Bull. He said, "So you know you're lovable now," and he wasn't asking.

Edith nodded, and when she found the emotional strength to look back at him again, she found him smiling. "I'm really glad, Edith," he said quietly. "How did Reagan take the news?"

She brightened. "He's so patient with me," she said. "He refuses to go right when I want him to, so I let him go left all day today." Edith half-laughed and shook her head. "But he listens to me. He knows Finn and I got back together and we're going to get married in April."

Doctor Bull's eyebrows went up. "Is that right?"

"Yeah." Edith ducked her head then, the same outpouring of love she'd felt that morning in her kitchen, then again in Finn's arms beside his truck, flowing through her again. "And you know what, Doctor Bull? I have to thank you."

"Me?" He chuckled. "I have to say, I was not expecting that. You've not been very...warm to me."

Edith wasn't surprised her coolness toward

him had shown. "I know, but you asked me really hard questions." She swallowed but decided she had to keep going. "I actually blamed you a little bit for what happened with Finn."

"Is that so?"

"Yeah," she said. "You kept pressing me on if I was lovable, and I didn't think I was. Certainly not by someone like Finn, who suddenly felt like a Levi-replacement."

Doctor Bull quirked that right eyebrow that she hated. "Do you still think Finn is a Levi-replacement?"

She shook her head. "No," she murmured. "I know now how unending love is. I know that it has no bounds. I know that I can love Levi the way I did, and I can love Finn the same. More. Better, because he's here, and he loves me too."

Doctor Bull grinned and grinned, and he finally put his pen on his desk. "This is all great to hear, Edith."

She thought so too, and she focused outside on the pastures again. A group therapy session had started, and she watched as Pete walked along with five people and five horses, talking to them as he did.

"I love it here," Edith said as she breathed out.

"Do you love it here, Doctor Bull?" She found him looking out the window too.

"Yeah," he said. "I really do love it here." He took in a long breath and then slowly exhaled it. "And you say Reagan will only go left? That's so fascinating, because for me, he only goes right."

Their eyes met, and Edith blinked before she started to laugh. Doctor Bull joined her, and Edith felt truly free for the first time since Levi's diagnosis so long ago. Truly and utterly free.

"THIS SAYS *KITCHEN* ON IT," EDITH SAID AS SHE entered the farmhouse where Finn would live from here on out. And in six or seven more months, she'd be here with him. "But it looks like bedroom stuff."

She hefted the box onto the countertop anyway, where Finn's momma and grandmother worked to get his dishes, pots, and pans unboxed and put away. Kelly looked into the box. "Oh, this is his nightstand. He just threw it in whatever he had." She looked up and smiled at Edith. "It does go in his bedroom."

Edith smiled and nodded back. "Okay, I'll

take it that way." She left the kitchen, though she did want to have more opportunities to spend time with Kelly and get to know her better. After all, as soon as Finn got through this move and they could get to a jeweler, he planned to propose. Edith would be marrying Kelly's son.

At least she still had that in her plan. No, she wasn't wearing a diamond, but she and Finn talked about their life on this ranch every single day. He had not decided on a name for this place, nor had they chosen a date, and Edith's impatience threaded through her as she walked down the hall to the master's suite that took up the back half of the cabin.

"Finn?" she asked as she neared, because this was his bedroom.

"Yeah," he called, and Edith's stride didn't break as she entered the room.

"Your mom says this stuff goes in here."

She found him holding a cordless drill while Link stood back and eyed the shelf they were clearly hanging. "Hey, baby." He grinned at her and lowered the power tool.

"Looks good," Link said. "Nice and straight, and I don't see how anyone would know it hasn't been here as long as all the other wood in this house." He smiled at Edith and tipped his hat at her. "Edith."

"Hey, Link." She took Finn's hand in hers. "I heard you were seeing someone." She raised her eyebrows and got her answer in the quick flush of his face.

"Yes, ma'am," he said. "I mean, sort of."

"Sort of?" Finn asked, glancing from Link to Edith and back. "Is it new?"

"It's...casual," Link said, his face clearing of his embarrassment. "And yes, it's new too."

"What's her name?" Edith asked.

"Misty," Link said. "She didn't grow up here."

"Dresser incoming," someone yelled, and the three of them had to move.

Finn pulled Edith further into the room, and Link separated from them and moved to the other wall as Squire and Pete brought in a clearly home-made piece of furniture. It stood six drawers tall and had been stained a beautiful golden color to match the rest of the wood in the house.

"Where, Finny?" Squire asked.

"Where Link is," he said.

"I'm movin'." Link ducked out of the room and out of the way, and Finn's daddy and uncle got the dresser in place. They both released their breath simultaneously, and they gazed at the dresser and then looked over to Finn as if they'd rehearsed their movement.

"When y'all get married," Pete said. "I'll make one for you, Edith."

"Really?" she asked.

"Sure, if you want." He grinned at them and then left the bedroom, Squire on his heels.

Edith continued to look at the dresser, and she did like it. When she switched her gaze back to Finn, he still held the drill and looked a little lost. "Okay, give me the power tool." She took it from him and set it on the dresser, hoping that wasn't a punishable offense. "Come talk to me."

She took his hand and led him to his bed. It was a bare mattress that hadn't been made up with sheets and a comforter yet, but Edith didn't think for a moment his momma would leave this cabin without her little boy ready for the night. Or the next week, or month, or year of his life.

"What are we talkin' about?" Finn asked as he sat beside her.

"I want to pick a date," she said. "So my parents can get it on their calendar."

"You mean so Alex won't take all the good

weekends in April." Finn grinned at her and chuckled.

"He's moving really fast with Nicki," Edith said. "It's surprising to me is all."

Finn lifted his phone. "Okay, so let's pick a date so Alex doesn't ruin everything for us."

She really liked that he said "us" and not "you," and she wrapped her arm through his and leaned into his strength as he tapped and swiped to get to a calendar.

"April thirteenth?" he asked.

"Be serious, Ramses."

"Ramses?" He burst out laughing again, and Edith sure did love the sound of it. She loved this tender time between them despite a very busy, tension-filled, and stressful day.

"We can't get married on the thirteenth," she said. "Every few years, our anniversary will be on Friday, the thirteenth." She shook her head, dead serious. "No. Not happening."

"The sixth?" Finn tilted his phone toward her. "Is that too early?"

"Could be windy." Edith worried through a few thoughts. "Or rainy. Later might be better."

"Sunday, the fourteenth?" he asked. "Or Saturday the twentieth. I think those are your best choices, my love."

"Yeah," she said. "I agree." She looked at the little boxes on his phone, a clear answer emerging. "I want to get married on Sunday, Finn. Levi wasn't super religious, and we were going to get married on a Saturday."

"Sunday, April fourteenth," Finn said as he started typing into his phone. "Finn and Edith get married." He spoke slowly so his voice matched his fingers, and then he turned it toward her. Right there, in a blue bar on April fourteenth, Edith read the words

Finn and Edith get married.

Nothing could've made her smile bigger or for more joy to wind through her system.

"I love you, cowboy," she whispered.

"And I love you, Edith."

34

Finn left through the back door of his house and headed across the deck. To his left, the leaves in the pumpkin patch had started to dry and wither, and the orange squashes had started to show their faces.

Something as simple as a pumpkin made him smile, brought him such joy. Of course, it would not be replanted next spring, because Edith's she-shed would go in that spot. He'd been talking to Alex about what he needed to make the transition of the shed from where it currently rested to its new home here, and Edith needed electricity.

She didn't need water or sewer, as she came back into the house to use the bathroom, and if she got too messy eating her ice cream while writing, she'd have to make the trek inside as well. Finn found himself smiling over that image too, and he fought a river of impatience at having her living with her brother for another six months.

Of course, he couldn't expect her to get married immediately, as they'd really only been dating for a few months as it was. "The extra time will be good," he told himself. He'd get through birthing season, and by the time they were ready for branding, Edith would be here to hold the calves.

This morning, he entered the stable, which had been swept and sprayed clean before Finn had moved in two horses—one for him and one for Edith. She didn't know that he'd asked Uncle Pete for Cocoa, but she did know that his daddy had given him a good sturdy working horse from Three Rivers—a bay named Apollo.

And today, Apollo and Cocoa were taking a little ride from this ranch, through the newly installed gate, and onto Three Rivers. Edith would be there, working with Reagan, and Finn wanted to surprise her with a horse...and a diamond ring.

Panicking, he patted his shirt pocket for the ring and thankfully, felt the hardness of the gold band and the round-cut gem. A sigh slipped from his lips, and Finn set about saddling Apollo.

Uncle Pete would have Cocoa's gear ready at Courage Reins, so she just had to walk alongside Apollo until Edith was ready to ride her back. Once he had everything ready, he texted his mother. *Leaving now. Don't let her see you, okay?*

You've told me that five thousand times, Momma sent back.

Edith is observant, Finn said. *If she sees you and Aunt Chelsea hovering around with your phones up, she'll know something's up.*

I won't ruin this for you, Momma promised.

Reassured, Finn tucked his phone away and faced the horizon to the north. "Come on, guys," he said. "This is why we bought this place. So we could be close to home, but not home. So that we could have our *own* home."

He hadn't refused his parents' gift, and he wasn't going to refuse any of the gifts of God either. Finn had had to humble himself that day at the lender, when his father had written out a check for two hundred thousand dollars. Finn didn't have to do anything to earn it besides be important to Squire Ackerman, and that bond had strengthened and cemented because of the monetary gift.

"Ah, look how pretty this place is," he mused out loud to his horses. He hoped to add more equines to his stable, but for now, he'd be just fine with the two he had. He'd done well on market day, and by the sweat of his brow—and the help of a half-dozen cowboys from Three Rivers, he'd gotten his crops in too.

He planned to put in some winter wheat himself, and Finn couldn't believe these were his thoughts. He'd spent so long away from home, doing anything but riding in saddles and planning winter crops. But as he rode, he truly felt like the cowboy part of him reawakened, and the blood that flowed through his body suddenly felt like it had spurs and chaps running through it.

As he approached the gate that would take him from his ranch to his father's, Finn slowed his horses. "This is our ranch, guys," he murmured to himself, to the pure blue sky above. "This is our home."

The meaning of the word *home* had never meant as much to Finn as it did now that he had his own place. Now that he had a house, outbuildings, fields, and animals all his own to care for.

"And soon," he whispered. "A wife. Maybe children."

Finn couldn't believe such blessings could be his. He couldn't believe Edith wanted him to be her husband and the father of her children, but by some miracle, she did.

He prodded Apollo, and the three of them got moving again. It was a long ride from this ranch to Three Rivers, and Finn fully intended to get God to listen to his pleas about what to name this place.

He couldn't just keep calling it "this ranch" after all. Any Texan worth their salt named their ranch, and Finn had been living on his for a couple of weeks now. He'd made quite a list of names on the papers on his clipboard, but none of them had been exactly right.

Edith had gone over his ideas with him, and they'd laughed over silly things like Root Beer Ranch and Nickname Ranch.

Hopscotch, Butterscotch, Cupcake, Flower Pot, he thought, his smile growing. He wasn't going to name the ranch after one of Edith's pet names for him. They were just funny things that came shooting out of her mouth.

They needed something they could say

everyday of their life. A name that could be printed on invoices and checks and on a big wooden sign that hung over the dirt lane that led back to the cabin.

Something to establish a legacy.

Finn sucked in a breath through his nose. "Legacy," he said, trying the word out in his mouth. Three syllables. "Legacy Ranch."

He quickly pulled his phone out of his pocket and called Edith, but the line went *beep-beep-beep* in quick succession, then paused and did it again. He didn't have service here, and while that normally gave Finn a sense of panic, he sometimes craved the freedom of being truly out of touch with the rest of the world.

It provided space for a man to think, to question, to talk to God.

"Lord," Finn started. "First, thank You for all the blessings Thou has seen fit to bestow upon me since I returned to Three Rivers." He chuckled, enjoying the steady clomping of the horses' hooves. "I can't believe it's only been a handful of months. I feel like I've grown a lot in the past half-year, and I know it's because of the challenges and trials You've placed in front of me."

He drew in a breath and let his words fade up

into the heavens. "I also know You would not give me—or Edith—anything we couldn't handle."

Finn let several more paces of the horses pass. "And now, Lord, can we talk about this proposal? I'd sure like it to go perfectly, but I literally have a ring and my momma and aunt ready with their phones to record it."

Beside him, Cocoa snuffled, and Finn looked over to her. "I guess I have Edith's favorite horse too, but I feel like I need more than a horse and a diamond. Those are things, and I need my words to come across as more than *things*."

He continued on toward the epicenter of the ranch, the fields and fences and fierce serenity around him everything Finn needed in his life right then. He'd like some words for the perfect proposal, but God did not provide them on the ride to Courage Reins, and before he knew it, Finn had arrived.

"Dear Lord," he whispered when he saw Momma and Aunt Chelsea sitting on his aunt's back deck, glasses of lemonade on the table and Momma with her phone up already. She must've taken a picture, because she lowered her phone and waved.

As if he couldn't see her.

He tipped his hat at her and started looking for Edith. She'd said she'd be out in these back pastures today with Reagan, as she and Doctor Bull were doing a dual one-two punch with the horse today. Apparently, Edith could get him to go left and Bull right, but he wouldn't go both directions for either of them.

Horses sure could be stubborn, and in some ways, they reminded Finn of people. They reminded him of himself, of Edith, of how stubborn Alex had been about getting those sinkholes fixed and his ranch back in pristine condition.

In the end, Finn spotted Reagan first, as the horse stood tall and proud, with all that dark black hair along his neck. Both Edith and Bull walked alongside him, and Bull had a long stick with a bright orange flag on it. He tapped it on the ground every so often, and that kept Reagan walking in a straight line.

Finn slowed his horses and hovered near the trees along the back of Aunt Chelsea's yard as he watched. He didn't want to interrupt the lesson, but Bull knew he was coming. Everyone knew, except Edith, as he watched Bull turn and Uncle Pete come jogging toward them. Bull said something to Edith, handed her the flag, and turned to go back toward Uncle Pete.

That left Edith alone, and that meant Finn could do his proposal at any time. Now. He could go right now. He sat in the saddle, his pulse ping-ponging around inside his body and nothing worthy to convince Edith Baxter to be his wife.

You're enough, he thought.

Finn sat up straighter in the saddle, as if buoyed up by the thought. He didn't need fancy diamond rings or pretty horses or the words in the right order. He was Finn Ackerman, and that was enough for Edith.

That got him clicking at Apollo to get the horse moving forward, and it didn't take long for Edith to look up and see him coming. Her step slowed, as did Reagan's, but Cocoa had also seen Edith, and she picked up the pace.

Finn hastened to untie the rope from his saddle horn so Cocoa could go ahead, and Edith giggled and murmured to her horse as she arrived. After greeting her, she peered past the light brown horse and asked, "What are you doing here?" She stroked both hands down Cocoa's neck. "With her?"

Finn slid from the saddle, the time here. He

better just say whatever lingered in his heart. "She's yours," he said as he walked toward her.

"She's mine?" Edith stepped all the way to the side of Cocoa now, her eyes wide. "What does that mean?"

"It means I bought her from Uncle Pete and Courage Reins for you. Cocoa lives at my ranch now, and she'll be there any time you want her."

"You're kidding."

"I am not," Finn said with a smile. He slid one hand along the side of Edith's neck and leaned down to kiss her. "And I thought of the perfect name for our ranch."

"Mm, okay." Edith kissed him, and Finn sure hoped the recording hadn't started yet. Cocoa tried to stick her face in there too, so he felt reasonably sheltered. Cocoa snuffled, and Edith broke the kiss as she giggled.

She shoved Cocoa back. "You're too close, my friend."

The horse certainly was, and that would obstruct some sight lines.

"So what's the name of the ranch?" Edith asked as she turned Cocoa in the same direction as Reagan.

Finn did the same with Apollo. "Legacy," he said. "Legacy Ranch."

"Oh, I really like that," Edith said as her whole person lit up. "That's perfect, Finn."

"I thought so too." The air between them turned silent, and suddenly the diamond in Finn's pocket weighed enough to make his shoulders sag forward.

He cleared his throat and glanced over to his aunt's house. The recording had commenced, and he turned to Edith. She looked at him too, her eyebrows raised. "What?"

"What?" he asked back.

"You're nervous," she said simply.

Finn was, and he didn't like that Edith knew it. Or maybe he did, because it meant she knew him well enough to know his energy.

"Edith," he said, and he worked hard not to clear his throat. "We have a date on the calendar for our wedding."

She said nothing, which he'd learned was her way of letting him say everything he wanted to before she interrupted.

"You have the perfect horse to ride for that wedding." He reached into his breast pocket and pulled out the diamond, then took a couple of running steps in front of her. "April fourteenth is about six months from now, and you've said that'll be enough time to plan the perfect spring wedding."

"It will be," she murmured.

Finn dropped to both knees right there in the pasture and held up the ring. "I'm so in love with you. Going home to sleep in my bed alone is terrible. I want you at that ranch—our ranch—our Legacy Ranch—with me. I want to work beside you, and I want to raise a family with you, and I want *us* to be a family."

"I want all of that too, Finn," she said with a sniffle.

"You are what it feels like to come home for me," he said. "We could go anywhere and do anything, but if you're there, it'll be home for me."

Tears ran out of her right eye, and she quickly reached up and wiped them away.

He held up the ring as if she hadn't seen it yet. "Will you marry me?"

She nodded, sniffling and tears flowing freely now. "Yes," she said out loud. "Yes, Finn, I'll marry you." She held out her hand and he clumsily slid the ring onto her finger. "Oh, it's so pretty."

"You're so pretty." Finn got to his feet and took Edith's face in both of his hands. "I'm so glad I came home to Three Rivers, to you."

"I'm glad you did too."

"I love you, Edith."

"And I love you, cowboy."

I love second chance romance with my whole heart. And I love Edith and Finn and all they went through to be together. **I hope you loved this book too!**

And keep reading for the first two chapters of the next book in the series, **THE COWBOY WHO LOOKED AGAIN**, featuring Lincoln Glover and Misty Granger!

There's going to be a months-long gap between Books 1 and 2, plus tons of extra content in small town Three Rivers! If you're interested in deleted scenes from this book, as well as bonus chapters before it and following it - which include Edith and Finn's wedding! - **become a subscriber by scanning the QR code below with your phone.**

Sneak Peek! The Cowboy Who Looked Again Chapter One:

Lincoln Glover straightened his tie, his eyes roaming from his throat to his eyes. A sigh slipped through his lips, and he turned away from his reflection. He'd let his hair grow out since the New Year, and now it hung almost to his collar despite his momma's frowns every time she saw him.

She'd brighten afterward, but the way she tucked his hair behind his ear and let her fingers linger there told him plenty. She still smiled at him, and still loved him, and Link simply needed something different in his life than every other cowboy he saw around him here in Three Rivers.

He left his bedroom and found Mitch decked out in his fancy clothes too. "Ready?" he asked, making the sign for his cousin.

Mitch put another bite of cold cereal in his mouth and nodded, a dribble of milk sliding down his chin. Link grinned at him and tossed him a paper towel. He hadn't eaten, because Alex Baxter and Nicki Johnston were serving a full dinner at their wedding that night.

Link had been out on several double dates with Alex and Nicki, but his plus-one that night was Mitch.

He wished it was Misty Granger, but Link hadn't spoken to the woman who'd dominated his autumn and winter, but it turned out that he didn't know how to do casual dating. His parents had started asking about Misty, and Link wanted to bring her up to the ranch to meet them.

But apparently, that wasn't casual behavior, and Link had decided he wanted more than that. Misty still didn't, and while his heart had been smashed, flattened, and nearly ripped out between two ribs, Link had broken up with her.

If he could even break-up with someone he wasn't really dating.

Link turned away from Mitch and his

thoughts and went to get a drink out of the fridge. After all, another June had arrived, and that meant the summer dances Link refused to attend, as well as the Texas heat.

So the drive from Shiloh Ridge Ranch to the apple orchards on the east side of Three Rivers, where Alex and Nicki were tying the knot, required a Gatorade in Link's favorite flavor. He twisted the lid and guzzled the cherry-flavored liquid before facing Mitch again.

His cousin stood and put his bowl in the sink, then picked up his jacket and shrugged into it. He'd dated Lily Ryders for a while, which for Mitch was three or four months. But they had a pretty big barrier in their communication, and Mitch had finally ended things with her. He hated typing or writing everything out, and if someone didn't know sign language, that was how he had to talk.

Link wouldn't be surprised if this was the last summer Mitch stayed on the ranch, truth be told. He'd been talking more and more about going back to Virginia and working at his deaf school, training hearing dogs, and trying to meet a woman who knew how to talk to him. Who he could talk to more easily.

Link wanted that for him, but he missed his cousin already. If Mitch moved out, another cowboy would move in, and then Link would have to navigate how to live with that person. He'd started thinking about where he should be in a more permanent way, and while he wanted his life to be here at Shiloh Ridge, he didn't want to live in the cowboy cabins forever.

He knew that if he went to Daddy, or Uncle Ward, or Uncle Preacher, or Uncle Bishop, and said, "I want a place of my own," they'd be meeting the next day to go over blueprints and where the house should be.

Link knew that, and he hadn't done it yet, because he wasn't sure he truly deserved it. He wasn't a Glover by birth. He had no Glover blood in his veins, though the lot of them treated him like he did.

Mitch handed Link his truck keys and led the way out of the cabin. Link followed him, ready to breathe in apple-scented air, and smile at the flickering candles, and congratulate his friends on their wedding.

Like his daddy said, he only had to wear the teddy bear skin for a couple of hours, and then he could relax the muscles in his face, come home, and try to figure out what to do this summer that would ward off the boredom.

Since he had to drive, he couldn't swipe on his phone, flirting with the idea of using Two Cents to find his next date. Uncle Ranger had added a Connections Center a few years ago, and now the app not only boasted the best places to eat in Three Rivers, or ranked the favored activities around town, but men and women could connect with each other over their votes and choices.

He scoffed lightly as he thought, *I should tell Uncle Ranger to put in a section for how serious someone wants to be when they're dating.*

He wouldn't. Absolutely would not, because he wouldn't even say anything to Mitch about it. Everyone knew he'd broken up with Misty, but Link had been pretty clammed up as to why.

With the radio on loud, he drove himself and Mitch off the ranch and down out of the gentle hills to the apple orchards. Plenty of other cars and trucks were arriving, as Alex owned a one-man family ranch that he'd been running himself since his sister Edith had married Finn Ackerman only a couple of months ago.

The cowboys on all the ranches—big or small—around Three Rivers pitched in and helped one another when needed, so Alex knew all the ranch owners, all the cowboys, and most people in Three Rivers that had anything to do with ranching.

Link parked and looked over to Mitch. *Maybe we'll meet some pretty women here*, he signed, his smile wide, and he got out of the truck before Link could respond. Link's response was, "Yeah, right," because he knew everyone in Three Rivers too.

He'd been back from his two-year college stint in Amarillo for six years now. Six years. Working the ranch. Running his momma's errands. Eating Sabbath Day lunch with his family. The summer bonfires here at the ranch. The dances. The Christmas traditions.

Link had lived all of it for six years, and the only blip in the monotony of it had been Misty Granger.

"Gotta move past her," he muttered to himself as he got out of the truck. He'd broken up with her five months ago, and he vowed not to let another one go by with him sighing like a lovesick schoolgirl while he flipped through the old photos on his phone. He could choose to act a different way. He could choose to delete those photos. He could choose to have the same attitude as Mitch—maybe he'd meet a pretty woman here tonight, sweep her off her feet, and be married by the holidays.

Link joined his cousin as they went under the welcoming arch and deeper into the orchards. Not really too deep, though, because the Apple Valley Orchards had a reception center specifically designed for big groups, and plenty of people got married here.

So the path was well-kept and lined with railings to keep people away from the apple trees, and Link found himself getting spit out into a tea-light-lit area with a tent roof wafting overhead. Fans blew air here, and misters kept things cool in the shade, and twinkling music filled the air, and Link looked around in wonder.

It almost felt like he'd stepped into another time and place, and he found himself smiling at the thought. Just like his video games with portals to other worlds, where he played as a character he got to design and name.

He could be anyone here, as he often thought about who he'd be in a group of people who didn't know him, didn't know the last name Glover, had never heard of him or his family.

"Howdy, fellas," a young woman said, and Link automatically signed it for Mitch. The woman glittered and grinned and giggled and she added, "Names?"

"Lincoln and Mitch Glover," Link said.

The woman couldn't be older than Link, and in fact, she was probably a few years younger. She looked down at her clipboard, then glanced back up. "You're this way, please." She turned and walked into the crowd, and Mitch once again led the way as he followed her. Link wished he could live his life that fearlessly, because if that woman said anything to Mitch, he wouldn't be able to communicate with her.

She led them to a table that seated eight but only had one couple sitting there, and Link smiled at John and Nina Malone. He owned both hardware stores in town, and he nodded over to Link and Mitch.

"You're here," the woman said. "You can sit anywhere, but the tables are full tonight, so we ask that you don't leave a single seat between couples." She smiled over to Mitch, who stood there with a smile on his face. "My brother and Nicki are so glad you could join them tonight."

Ah, so she was Alex's sister, and definitely one of the younger ones. Alex and Edith had several siblings that Link knew of, but they all lived in

Florida still. Of course they'd make the trip to Three Rivers for their brother's wedding, and Link pulled out a chair across from the Malones and sat down.

Mitch sat beside him, and Link had deliberately put his back to the rest of the party. He didn't want to look around at everyone walking in, holding glasses of champagne, and making small talk. He was just fine, sitting here and talking to Mitch.

Too young for you, Link said with a smile, and Mitch laughed.

You're right, he said. *She's pretty though.*

You think everyone is pretty.

Mitch didn't wipe away his grin, but he did shake his head. *Glass half full, brother.*

Sure, Link said. Then he leaned forward, and with his hands still moving so Mitch could keep up with the conversation, he asked, "How are you, Mister Malone? How are things in the paint shop?" He added a smile to his questions, because Momma would've.

John Malone smiled, his relief not hard to see and feel. "It's going great, Link." He glanced over to Mitch as Link signed what he'd said. "How're you boys up at Shiloh Ridge? Don't suppose you need more of that blue paint for that barn?" His eyes shone like bright lights on a dark night.

Link chuckled and shook his head. "Uncle Bishop just had it redone last year, Mister Malone. I don't reckon he'll do it again anytime soon."

Mitch tugged on his sleeve, and Link turned to look at him. *What about wrapping my truck? Could he do that?*

Link relayed the question to John, who looked right at Mitch as he said, "Not me, Mitchell. If you want to wrap your truck, you've got to take it to Ginny at the sign shop."

The sign shop? Mitch asked.

"Yep," John said with a slow nod. "Now, if you want me to paint your truck, I could get you in touch with Barry, a new mechanic in town who customizes in...." He looked over to his wife. "What did he say?"

They grinned at one another. "Tricking out vehicles," Nana Malone said as she lifted her wine glass to her lips.

"Tricking out vehicles," John said, and Link laughed as he signed it to Mitch. "Does that even make sense to you young cowboys?"

"Sure does," Link said with a grin, glad he'd decided not to sit here silently.

"Glad it does for someone." John chuckled as another couple arrived, and Link looked up at the pair of women. Mitch lurched to his feet, his hands smoothing down his tie and buttoning his jacket.

He clapped his hand on Link's shoulder as Alex's sister gave them the same spiel about where to sit, and they looked at the two chairs between Link and John, and then the two between Mitch and Nina.

"What about over there, Abby?" one said, and they moved to go around Link and Mitch. To Link, it felt like a complete stab in the fleshiest part of his heart, because they'd clearly chosen Mitch over him.

Nothing new, but still. Didn't mean it didn't hurt.

"Hi," Abby said as she sat next to Mitch. She had the dark hair he liked, and he positively beamed from every pore. He touched his chest and signed, and Link leaned forward a bit.

"He's Mitch," he said. "I'm Link." He looked over to the other woman, and they looked like sisters. Cousins. Something. They were probably relations of Alex's too, or maybe Nicki, though the

Johnston's had been living in Three Rivers for years.

But Link knew better than most that people had aunts and uncles and cousins, and these two dark-haired women could be related to Nicki as cousins.

"You two are Abby, and...." He looked at the other woman, and she smiled as his fingers finished spelling out Abby's name.

"Julienne," she said. "Nicki's our aunt."

Aunt? Mitch asked. How old are you?

Link ducked his head, because he didn't want to ask that question out loud. "Mitch," he muttered as Abby tried to explain she didn't know what he'd said.

"He just wants to know how old you are," he said finally, lifting his head to save everyone from further embarrassment. He gave the women a smile. "He's looking for a date."

Mitch swung his attention back to Link in time to catch the last word, and he zipped his attention back to the women, a flush crawling up his neck. His hands moved quickly, but Link caught what he'd said.

Abby and Julienne glowed like the sun, moon,

and stars, and Abby said, "I'm twenty-two, and she's twenty-four."

"How are you nieces for Nicki then?" Link asked, not bothering to sign their ages for Mitch. He could read lips. "Isn't she only about that old?"

"Nicki is thirty-four," Julienne said. "She's the youngest in her family, and our momma is almost fifty, so."

"She's our aunt," Abby finished.

"Thirty-four, wow," Link said. "I didn't realize she was that old."

Julienne unfolded her napkin and placed it in her lap, only looking up through her eyelashes at Link. "Is that old, cowboy?"

"Oh, no," Link said quickly, his own embarrassment rising now. "No, not at all." He shot a look over to Nana Malone, who gave him a smile. "Sorry, that came out too harsh."

"This is your table," a woman said, and Link mercifully looked away from the two women seated on the other side of Mitch. "Seems like these are your seats. My brother and Nicki are so glad you could join them tonight."

Link looked up and found another man standing there, this one not wearing a cowboy hat. And in Three Rivers, at a formal wedding, that said a whole lot. His eyes darted over to his date, and then he was the one lurching to his feet.

His thighs hit the table, and the dishes and silverware clinked together as it all moved. "Oof," he grunted, the yelp of Mrs. Malone filling his ears. His face flamed hot, but he couldn't look away from Ralf's date.

Misty Granger.

"Misty," he bellowed right as the music cut out. Of course.

She looked at him, and she wasn't the only one. Link felt dozens of eyes on him, and he prayed the Lord would suck him down into that portal he often fantasized about.

Sneak Peek! The Cowboy Who Looked Again Chapter Two:

Misty Granger touched Ralf's arm, and then they shifted together. Him to the left and her to the right, so that when they took their seats, she'd be right next to the best-looking cowboy in the state of Texas.

Probably the whole country. No, the continent.

Misty's thoughts sparked and flew up into the air like bits of paper had caught fire and then been picked up by a tornado. She smiled at Link as the feedback from a microphone filled the silent night.

Everyone cringed and groaned, Misty included, and she half-shrank into Link as the shrill screech faded and Alex's daddy chuckled nervously into the mic. "Sorry, everyone," he said. "If you'll take your seats, we're ready to begin."

Misty twitched her hand slightly, as if to pull out her chair, but Link lunged in front of her. "Let me," he said, and Misty ducked her head, her newly colored hair falling down between them.

"It's not as red," Link said, barely giving her room to sit down. "Your hair." The last words came out as a whisper, his breath drifting across her cheek and reminding her of when he'd take her into his arms and kiss her.

Misty's pulse throbbed through the big vein in her neck, making her hearing fuzzy and her throat so narrow. "Yes," she finally managed to say. "I got it done for the wedding."

"It's really blonde."

"She took out some of the red," she admitted. "Could you give me a couple more inches, Lincoln?"

He cleared his throat and backed up all the way, and his cousin grabbed onto his sleeve and practically pulled him back into his own chair. But he was a big, tall, broad-shouldered cowboy, and this table held eight chairs. If she relaxed her knees so they weren't so rigidly pressed together, her leg would touch Link's.

For some reason, that made every cell in her body vibrate. She'd held the cowboy's hand. They'd laughed together. Laid together and watched the stars come out. Hiked together. He'd brought her lunch at City Hall, where she'd been working, and they'd toured these very orchards together near the end of the season last year.

She'd kissed Link Glover plenty of times, and these past five, kissless months had been torture without him.

I don't want to be used.

Some of his last words to her, and Misty had never felt so guilty. She'd also never cried over anyone...until Link. She wasn't sure what that meant, but she also still didn't have plans to stay in this small town in the Texas Panhandle, and she hadn't found the courage to reach out to him and apologize for "using him."

She hadn't thought at the time that she was, but as she'd had some time to reflect in his absence, she'd been able to see their relationship from his side. "Link," she started, but the wedding march started in that moment, and they all got to their feet again.

He'd grown his hair out, and Misty found she couldn't look away from him, though the bride and her father were walking down the aisle on her opposite side.

"Are you gonna stare at me all night?" Link murmured out of the side of his mouth.

"No." Misty linked her arm through his, marveling that he didn't shrug her off instantly, and turned to look at Nicki Johnston in her gorgeous wedding dress. As she moved, her shoes flashed with blue, and that made Misty smile. She did love a good wedding, but until she met Link, she'd never wanted to be the one with the glowing eyes, the painted lips, and the pure joy radiating from her.

She couldn't believe she was even thinking about it right now.

It was Link's cologne, infecting her mind and confusing her, twisting her thoughts and making her wonder if there were indeed good men in the world.

Of course there are, she thought. She and Link had been out on double dates with Alex and Nicki, and she'd seen how Alex treated his almost-wife. He absolutely adored her, and he'd never belittled her or spoken ill of her.

Link had treated Misty the same way, and when she'd started to feel him getting too close, slinking in too close, she'd had to remind him that they weren't serious. Misty couldn't *be* serious with anyone.

Especially not someone from this tiny town Misty had been planning to escape since the moment she'd arrived.

As Nicki reached Alex, he took her into his side and pressed his lips to the side of her face. Nicki's eyes drifted closed in bliss, and Misty found herself sighing. The love permeating the air seemed to scent the orchards with roses instead of blossoms, and baby powder and everything sweet and pure and good.

"Alex and Nicki would like their wedding party to come forward," the pastor said. "To act as witnesses to their union."

Link cleared his throat and moved his arms to button his suit coat before he moved away from her without a word. Mitch went with him, as did the two brunettes they'd been talking to before Misty and Ralf had arrived at the table.

Misty watched him walk away in those matte cowboy boots, every stitch of clothing on his body exactly right. She could admit she found him incredibly attractive, and something inside her absolutely needed to be next to the magnetism inside him.

"So you're not over him," Ralf whispered from over her shoulder, and she ducked her head, finally breaking her stare on Link. She said nothing, because she didn't have a defense and she'd been working to be honest in all things. With herself. With her friends. With her family. With God.

"All right." The pastor beamed out the same love and sunshine that Alex and Nicki possessed as she surveyed the guests. "The very best part of my job is performing ceremonies like this."

Willa Glover carried such a good spirit with her, and Misty could admit she'd attended a few of the woman's sermons simply because she liked the idea of a female pastor. She'd always been glad when she'd attended church with Willa at the pulpit, and she smiled at the woman now.

She said, "There's nothing more amazing than two people in love, willing to commit to each other —and God—that they're going to work together, sacrifice for each other, and build a family."

Misty let her words sink into her ears and really sit there. So much more existed inside the curves and dips of the letters, and Misty had never thought of marriage as something to work toward. Something to want. Something...good.

All the examples she'd had in her life had convinced her from age ten to never, ever trust her happiness to a man. By then, her mom had been married three times, and each husband had brought massive complications to her life, Misty's life, and her younger brother's life.

Danny currently sat in prison for his role in a bar fight, and Misty's heart suddenly felt too big for her chest. Everything hammered and throbbed through her, because neither of them had been protected by a mother or father, and Misty wasn't even sure she understood what a family looked like.

She held an ideal in her mind, and she simply didn't want to be disappointed. It had been when Link had wanted to start introducing her to his family that Misty had panicked and reminded him that they weren't serious.

But with his aunt officiating the ceremony, Alex and Nicki must know the Glovers. With the amount of people here in this massive outdoor ceremony center, surely the Glovers had been invited. That meant his parents could be here.

Misty glanced around, trying to determine

which of the cowboys she saw could bear Link's last name. Before she knew it, cheering and whooping started, and she yanked her attention back to the altar, where Alex had his wide smile pressed to Nicki's.

They laughed and turned toward the crowd, and they stepped down off the stage where they'd been a few feet higher than everyone else. Their wedding party parted, and Misty started clapping along with everyone else as the bride and groom walked back down the aisle together.

"Ladies and gents," someone said into the microphone. "They're just going to mingle for a few minutes, and then we'll settle down to dinner."

Sure enough, Alex and Nicki came back down the aisle to the front tables to hug their friends and family members. Nicki stepped into her mother's arms, both of them emotional, and Misty's stomach clenched and swooped.

She didn't have that relationship with her mom. If Misty were to ever get married, she wasn't even sure her mom would come. She'd left Texas several years ago, and she currently lived in New Orleans, in a tiny apartment that surely had mice and bugs for how unclean it had been the last time Misty had seen it.

As the crowd near the altar started to break up, Misty turned to Ralf and gave him a shaky smile. "That was nice."

"Sure was." He indicated her chair, and Misty sat. Only a few minutes later, salads and bread started arriving, and Misty focused on eating, even when Link and Mitch and the women returned to the table.

They all chatted excitedly with one another, and Misty didn't dare look over to Link. He wanted what Alex had just achieved; Misty knew that. He didn't date casually, and Misty suddenly didn't want to either.

She didn't know if she could just tell him she'd had a change of heart, maybe ask him out, and see if they could try again. Thankfully, it didn't take long to eat, and then the dancing was announced.

Misty looked over to Link before she could stop herself. But Mitch met her eyes, not the gorgeous cowboy she'd spent all of her free time with for a few months.

Wanna dance? he signed and then he pushed back from the table.

Link tilted his head slightly to look at her out of the corner of his eye, no smile in sight.

"Sure." Misty signed as she spoke, and she got

to her feet too. She flashed Mitch a smile that felt fake and forced, but he wore an easy-going grin as he took her hand and led her away from the table. From Link.

They couldn't talk while they danced, and Misty's heart pounded. Too many eyes watched her, and when the song ended, Alex's father said, "We're going to have Alex and Nicki's first dance now."

The music changed dramatically, and surprise shot through Misty as a rambunctious country music song filled the apple orchard. The crowd cheered and parted, and Misty went with the others to the sidelines.

Smiling, she watched Alex and Nicki do a lively country line dance for several counts, their joy practically a being on the floor with them.

Cowboys and ladies clapped along, with an occasionally "Yeehaw!" thrown in, and Misty found herself enjoying this immensely. It felt like a perfect small-town, country-cowboy celebration, and like she *belonged* here.

These were her friends, and she'd rather be here than anywhere else. So she clapped with everyone else, and when a man said, "All right, ladies and gents, join 'em out there," the floor got flooded with those willing to dance, and the man with the mic continued to call the moves.

Misty loved a good country line dance as much as the next Texan, and she laughed as Ralf grabbed her arm and said, "Let's do this."

They joined the other dancers, and Misty finally felt herself relaxing completely. She'd been invited to this wedding. She could dance with everyone. With abandon.

And she did.

When the song ended, Misty's breath came in pants, and she'd lost Ralf somewhere. She found herself retreating to the sidelines again and someone said, "You must be Misty."

She turned toward a blonde woman who wore the prettiest flowered dress Misty had ever seen.

She took a big breath, trying to calm her beating heart and said, "Yes."

"Momma," Link said in the next moment, appearing at her side. He didn't look at her, but kept his eyes trained on his mother. Misty remembered her name to be Sammy—and her husband and Link's daddy, was Bear.

"Do you want to dance?"

The music had gone back to the subdued, flowery wedding music, and several cowboys and their women swayed back and forth on the dance floor.

"Not with you," his momma said with a smile. She tucked her arm into the tall, bearded, glaring cowboy at her side. "Daddy and I are going to take a breather after that line dance."

Link frowned, and he looked over to Misty. She stood there with him and his parents, no one talking, no introductions being made, for two breaths before he drew one and opened his mouth.

Before he could say anything, another blonde woman joined them. Breathlessly, she grabbed onto Link's arm. "Link, I need you."

"I—" he said, but she towed him away.

"Wonder what's got Hailey worked up." Link's daddy glared around, as if his gaze alone would scare off anyone daring to hurt Hailey.

"Her ex is here," Sammy said.

Misty watched as Link took Hailey into his arms and they started dancing. She spoke with him rapidly, and Link simply wore his gruff cowboy face as he nodded a couple of times.

"She's his cousin," his momma said.

Misty turned back to his parents, her heartbeat flailing in her chest. Link hadn't looked over to her at all, and she glanced back to him.

Their eyes locked for a beat of time, and Misty employed every ounce of bravery she had as she tore her gaze from his and looked at his glowing mother and his grumpy-cat father. "I need some help with him," she said. Every cell in her body quivered. "I hurt him. I know that."

She took a breath and pressed her palms together. "I want to fix things with him. Maybe try again. How do I—?" She exhaled heavily, her lungs suddenly holding too much oxygen.

"How do I do that? Any ideas?"

Bear looked at his wife. Sammy looked back at Bear. Then they both looked at Misty, and she stood there in agony, waiting for one of them to give her the key to Link's heart.

Ohhhh, boy. What is Sammy going to say? And Bear?? I'm dying! If you want to keep reading THE COWBOY WHO LOOKED AGAIN, you can **preorder it by scanning the QR code with your phone.**

Second Chance Ranch: A Three Rivers Ranch Romance™ (Book 1): After his deployment, injured and discharged Major Squire Ackerman returns to Three Rivers Ranch, wanting to forgive Kelly for ignoring him a decade ago. He'd like to provide the stable life she needs, but with old wounds opening and a ranch on the brink of financial collapse, it will take patience and faith to make their second chance possible.

Scan this QR code with your phone to see and order this series in eBook, audiobook, large print paperback, or regular paperback:

Third Time's the Charm: A Three Rivers Ranch Romance™ (Book 2): First Lieutenant Peter Marshall has a truckload of debt and no way to provide for a family, but Chelsea helps him see past all the obstacles, all the scars. With so many unknowns, can Pete and Chelsea develop the love, acceptance, and faith needed to find their happily ever after?

Fourth and Long: A Three Rivers Ranch Romance™ (Book 3): Commander Brett Murphy goes to Three Rivers Ranch to find some rest and relaxation with his Army buddies. Having his ex-wife show up with a seven-year-old she claims is his son is anything but the R&R he craves. Kate needs to make amends, and Brett needs to find forgiveness, but are they too late to find their happily ever after?

Fifth Generation Cowboy: A Three Rivers Ranch Romance™ (Book 4): Tom Lovell has watched his friends find their true happiness on Three Rivers Ranch, but everywhere he looks, he only sees friends. Rose Reyes has been bringing her daughter out to the ranch for equine therapy for months, but it doesn't seem to be working. Her challenges with Mari are just as frustrating as ever. Could Tom be exactly what Rose needs? Can he remove his friendship blinders and find love with someone who's been right in front of him all this time?

Sixth Street Love Affair: A Three Rivers Ranch Romance™ (Book 5): After losing his wife a few years back, Garth Ahlstrom thinks he's ready for a second chance at love. But Juliette Thompson has a secret that could destroy their budding relationship. Can they find the strength, patience, and faith to make things work?

The Seventh Sergeant: A Three Rivers Ranch Romance™ (Book 6): Life has finally started to settle down for Sergeant Reese Sanders after his devastating injury overseas. Discharged from the Army and now with a good job at Courage Reins, he's finally found happiness—until a horrific fall puts him right back where he was years ago: Injured and depressed. Carly Watters, Reese's new veteran care coordinator, dislikes small towns almost as much as she loathes cowboys. But she finds herself faced with both when she gets assigned to Reese's case. Do they have the humility and faith to make their relationship more than professional?

Eight Second Ride: A Three Rivers Ranch Romance™ (Book 7): Ethan Greene loves his work at Three Rivers Ranch, but he can't seem to find the right woman to settle down with. When sassy yet vulnerable Brynn Bowman shows up at the ranch to recruit him back to the rodeo circuit, he takes a different approach with the barrel racing champion. His patience and newfound faith pay off when a friendship--and more--starts with Brynn. But she wants out of the rodeo circuit right when Ethan wants to rejoin. Can they find the path God wants them to take and still stay together?

The Ninth Inning: A Three Rivers Ranch Romance™ (Book 8): The Christmas season has never felt like such a burden to boutique owner Andrea Larsen. But with Mama gone and the holidays upon her, Andy finds herself wishing she hadn't been so quick to judge her former boyfriend, cowboy Lawrence Collins. Well, Lawrence hasn't forgotten about Andy either, and he devises a plan to get her out to the ranch so they can reconnect. Do they have the faith and humility to patch things up and start a new relationship?

Ten Days in Town: A Three Rivers Ranch Romance™ (Book 9): Sandy Keller is tired of the dating scene in Three Rivers. Though she owns the pancake house, she's looking for a fresh start, which means an escape from the town where she grew up. When her older brother's best friend, Tad Jorgensen, comes to town for the holidays, it is a balm to his weary soul. A helicopter tour guide who experienced a near-death experience, he's looking to start over too--but in Three Rivers. Can Sandy and Tad navigate their troubles to find the path God wants them to take--and discover true love--in only ten days?

Eleven Year Reunion: A Three Rivers Ranch Romance™ (Book 10): Pastry chef extraordinaire, Grace Lewis has moved to Three Rivers to help Heidi Ackerman open a bakery in Three Rivers. Grace relishes the idea of starting over in a town where no one knows about her failed cupcakery. She doesn't expect to run into her old high school boyfriend, Jonathan Carver. A carpenter working at Three Rivers Ranch, Jon's in town against his will. But with Grace now on the scene, Jon's thinking life in Three Rivers is suddenly looking up. But with her focus on baking and his disdain for small towns, can they make their eleven year reunion stick?

The Twelfth Town: A Three Rivers Ranch Romance™ (Book 11): Newscaster Taryn Tucker has had enough of life on-screen. She's bounced from town to town before arriving in Three Rivers, completely alone and completely anonymous--just the way she now likes it. She takes a job cleaning at Three Rivers Ranch, hoping for a chance to figure out who she is and where God wants her. When she meets happy-go-lucky cowhand Kenny Stockton, she doesn't expect sparks to fly. Kenny's always been "the best friend" for his female friends, but the pull between him and Taryn can't be denied. Will they have the courage and faith necessary to make their opposite worlds mesh?

Lucky Number Thirteen: A Three Rivers Ranch Romance™ (Book 12): Tanner Wolf, a rodeo champion ten times over, is excited to be riding in Three Rivers for the first time since he left his philandering ways and found religion. Seeing his old friends Ethan and Brynn is therapuetic--until a terrible accident lands him in the hospital. With his rodeo career over, Tanner thinks maybe he'll stay in town--and it's not just because his nurse, Summer Hamblin, is the prettiest woman he's ever met. But Summer's the queen of first dates, and as she looks for a way to make a relationship with the transient rodeo star work Summer's not sure she has the fortitude to go on a second date. Can they find love among the tragedy?

The Curse of February Fourteenth: A Three Rivers Ranch Romance™ (Book 13): Cal Hodgkins, cowboy veterinarian at Bowman's Breeds, isn't planning to meet anyone at the masked dance in small-town Three Rivers. He just wants to get his bachelor friends off his back and sit on the sidelines to drink his punch. But when he sees a woman dressed in gorgeous butterfly wings and cowgirl boots with blue stitching, he's smitten. Too bad she runs away from the dance before he can get her name, leaving only her boot behind...

Fifteen Minutes of Fame: A Three Rivers Ranch Romance™ (Book 14): Navy Richards is thirty-five years of tired—tired of dating the same men, working a demanding job, and getting her heart broken over and over again. Her aunt has always spoken highly of the matchmaker in Three Rivers, Texas, so she takes a six-month sabbatical from her high-stress job as a pediatric nurse, hops on a bus, and meets with the matchmaker. Then she meets Gavin Redd. He's handsome, he's hardworking, and he's a cowboy. But is he an Aquarius too? Navy's not making a move until she knows for sure...

Sixteen Steps to Fall in Love: A Three Rivers Ranch Romance™ (Book 15): A chance encounter at a dog park sheds new light on the tall, talented Boone that Nicole can't ignore. As they get to know each other better and start to dig into each other's past, Nicole is the one who wants to run. This time from her growing admiration and attachment to Boone. From her aging parents. From herself.

But Boone feels the attraction between them too, and he decides he's tired of running and ready to make Three Rivers his permanent home. **Can Boone and Nicole use their faith to overcome their differences and find a happily-ever-after together?**

The Sleigh on Seventeenth Street: A Three Rivers Ranch Romance™ (Book 16): A cowboy with skills as an electrician tries a relationship with a down-on-her luck plumber. Can Dylan and Camila make water and electricity play nicely together this Christmas season? Or will they get shocked as they try to make their relationship work?

The First Lady of Three Rivers Ranch: A Three Rivers Ranch Romance™ (Book 17): Heidi Duffin has been dreaming about opening her own bakery since she was thirteen years old. She scrimped and saved for years to afford baking and pastry school in San Francisco. And now she only has one year left before she's a certified pastry chef. Frank Ackerman's father has recently retired, and he's taken over the largest cattle ranch in the Texas Panhandle. A horseman through and through, he's also nearing thirty-one and looking for someone to bring love and joy to a homestead that's been dominated by men for a decade. But when he convinces Heidi to come clean the cowboy cabins, she changes all that. But the siren's call of a bakery is still loud in Heidi's ears, even if she's also seeing a future with Frank. Can she rely on her faith in ways she's never had to before or will their relationship end when summer does?

Seven Sons Ranch in Three Rivers Romance™ Series

Meet the cowboy billionaire brothers at Seven Sons Ranch! Scan the QR code below with your phone to check out this complete series.

1. Rhett's Make-Believe Marriage
2. Tripp's Trivial Tie
3. Liam's Invented I-Do
4. Jeremiah's Bogus Bride
5. Wyatt's Pretend Pledge
6. Skyler's Wanna-Be Wife
7. Micah's Mock Matrimony
8. Gideon's Precious Penny

Shiloh Ridge Ranch in Three Rivers Romance™ Series

Meet the cowboy billionaires in the southern hills outside of Three Rivers! Scan the QR code below with your phone to check out this complete series.

1. The Mechanics of Mistletoe
2. The Horsepower of the Holiday
3. The Construction of Cheer
4. The Secret of Santa
5. The Gift of Gingerbread
6. The Harmony of Holly
7. The Chemistry of Christmas
8. The Delivery of Decor
9. The Blessing of Babies

About Liz

Liz Isaacson writes inspirational romance, usually set in Texas, or Wyoming, or anywhere else horses and cowboys exist. She lives in Utah, where she writes full-time, takes her two dogs to the park everyday, and eats a lot of veggies while writing. Find her on her website at www.feelgoodfiction-books.com.